# THE REMNANTS OF
# AN EXOTIC PLANE,
# THE RUINS OF AN ANCIENT SEA

Something rumbled and cracked from the direction
of the stream, followed by a heavy breathing like
the bellows of a hellish forge. The ground shook again,
and Uthalion stood, breaking his stunned silence.
"Run."
Ghaelya sprinted wide-eyed behind Uthalion.
Brindani kept close behind her, and behind him came
the snapping of trees and the dry scraping of rough skin
over leaves and dirt. Unseen claws pulled at the earth,
ripping trees from their roots.
She didn't dare turn to look, imagining its hot breath
washing over her, her thrashing legs caught in an
unbreakable grip as the thing keened in victory.
Childhood stories flashed through her mind, and she
cursed at the memory, knowing the Mother of Nightmares
had found her and knew her name. The pale serpent
of her old fears, with its long fangs and madly rolling eyes,
would devour her and forget the taste in an instant
as it clacked its cold teeth and whined for more.

## YOUR WORST FEARS THRIVE
## ON THE FRONTIER OF AKANÛL.

**FORGOTTEN REALMS**

# THE WILDS

FORGOTTEN REALMS

# THE
# RESTLESS
# SHORE

### James P. Davis

THE WILDS

Wizards
OF THE COAST®

**The Wilds**
# The Restless Shore

©2009 Wizards of the Coast LLC

Published by Wizards of the Coast LLC

FORGOTTEN REALMS, WIZARDS OF THE COAST, and their respective logos are trademarks of Wizards of the Coast LLC in the U.S.A. and other countries.

Printed in the U.S.A.

Cover art by Erik M. Gist
Map by Robert Lazzaretti

First Printing: May 2009

9 8 7 6 5 4 3 2 1

ISBN: 978-0-7869-5131-4
620-24028740-001-EN

U.S., CANADA,
ASIA, PACIFIC, & LATIN AMERICA
Wizards of the Coast LLC
P.O. Box 707
Renton, WA 98057-0707
+1-800-324-6496

EUROPEAN HEADQUARTERS
Hasbro UK Ltd
Caswell Way
Newport, Gwent NP9 0YH
GREAT BRITAIN
Save this address for your records.

Visit our web site at www.wizards.com

For Mr. Shanks, thank you for all the red ink.

Far from love the Heavenly Father
　　　Leads the chosen child;
Oftener through the realm of briar
　　　Than the meadow mild,

Oftener by the claw of dragon
　　　Than the hand of friend,
Guides the little one predestined
　　　To the native land.

　　　　　—Emily Dickinson,
"Far from Love the Heavenly Father."

# PROLOGUE

*24 Tarsakh, the Year of the Ageless One*
*(1479 DR)*
*Airspur, Upper Districts*

Moonlight shining through a small stained glass window played on Ghaelya's face in a myriad of muted colors as she slept. Tossing and turning, she dreamed. Her arms, etched with bright blue energy lines, contorted above her smooth head as she fought against a deep and limitless darkness.

In her dreams, she swam clumsily in a murky sea, spinning in slow circles, frantically trying to determine up from down. She breathed easily under the water, though the taste of it was stagnant and foul as it flowed down her throat and filled her lungs. Thunderous noises echoed through the depths from unnatural throats. Massive, formless bodies tumbled lazily in the distant shadows, seeking her with unfathomable hungers. She recoiled at the sight. Shafts of light pierced the shadows, and she followed them, grateful for their orange brilliance, but not wanting to see the creatures that swam by or to look too long into the burning gazes of the terrible things that hissed as she escaped their reach.

A whispering song echoed up from the dark. Tendrils of its ethereal melody pursued her kicking legs, tickling the soles of her feet. Panicking, she broke the surface, clawing at the air as if she might climb through it and escape the terrors beneath her. But out of the dark water her fear faded, leaving her adrift on a gentle expanse of waves that rippled gently with the water in her genasi spirit. The waters stretched to the horizon beneath a purpled sky, the waves flashing gold in the soft light of a troubled sunset.

As she marveled, something curled around her ankle, something fleshy with hooked teeth. She fought, breaking the surface briefly before being dragged back into the murk, her screams lost in the depths. . . .

An over-stuffed cushion caught the brunt of Ghaelya's rage before she realized she had woken up. Groaning, she slumped back into the large chair, her head pounding from a long night of drinking, the shadowed common room of her family's house slowly spinning. She rested her head in her hands, closed her eyes, and counted down from the highest number she could think of in such a state—an old sobering up trick that had never really worked, but usually helped her get back to sleep.

Just as the spinning in her head had begun to slow, the sound of breaking glass disturbed her from her counting ritual. She waited for her father to curse or her mother to fret over a broken family heirloom. When nothing followed the sound, she opened her eyes carefully.

A scattered pile of coins she'd dropped on the floor

during the argument with her sister, Tessaeril, caught the last light of the dying fire. She smiled and closed her eyes again, always appreciative of Tessaeril's concern and worries, though too stubborn to admit it very often.

Muffled voices drew her attention to the eastern stairway, and for once she did not curse herself for passing out in her leather half-armor with an uncomfortable broadsword jabbing her leg. She swayed as she stood and caught her balance with outstretched hands. Reckoning she was at least steady enough to handle a simple thief, she crept up the eastern stairs, stumbling on a couple, but quietly enough that she caught a low hum coming from the end of the hallway, near Tessaeril's room.

She made her way down the hallway, her footsteps crunching on shards of a broken vase. The humming stopped, and Ghaelya froze in place.

A single, frightened whimper pierced the silence.

Ghaelya drew her broadsword, took a deep breath and charged the closed door, grinning at the crack of the latch. She burst into the room. A dark-robed figure slipped nimbly out of her reach. Crashing against the far wall, she whirled around, her sword wavering but level, to see her sister hoisted over the shoulder of a second robed figure.

"Tess!" she yelled, catching a flash of sharp teeth from within a deep cowl as the figure ducked out of the room, "No!"

A short sword glinted in the pale hand of the first figure, and he advanced screeching like an animal. She skipped backward, battering the smaller weapon away, but unable to slow her attacker's momentum. The cowled figure leaped at her, throwing her off balance easily. But she had wit enough to control her drunken stumble, and her attacker crashed into the wall behind her, using both hands for support. Ghaelya spun around, her heavy broadsword aimed at his chest. The figure snarled, revealing several rows of sharp teeth in his wide mouth. His hooked claws dug into the wall as he turned a black-eyed gaze upon her.

Ghaelya's blade sliced through robe, skin, and between the bones beneath, burying itself in the wall at an angle as the figure scratched at the wood and plaster in a frenzied fit to escape the blade buried in his back. He slumped down as she yanked her blade free. She caught a glimpse of silver dangling from his throat—a silver seashell.

"Tess!" she said and dashed out of the room, crunching on the shattered vase. She could barely make out a dark figure at the front door and noticed a third, hidden in the corner outside the hallway, too late. Her sword-arm flexed and her right foot planted itself in the floor, her body instinctively ready to block his attack, but she was far too slow, too drink-addled to dodge it.

Something heavy clubbed her in the back of the head, and she fell, sprawling at the top of the stairs, slowly blacking out. The sound of the front door opened too far away, too distant for her to stop it. Stars swam before her eyes and her heavy lids slid closed, shutting out the light. In the dark, spinning and aching, she found herself back in the murky depths of the shadowed sea, dreaming of teeth, burning eyes, and ghostly singing as curling arms and barbed hooks pulled her down.

She screamed, calling for her sister in the dark, and a thousand alien throats screamed back, mocking her struggles as the setting sun gathered in its golden shafts of light.

# CHAPTER ONE

*10 Flamerule, the Year of the
Heretic's Rampage (1473 DR)
Caidris, Akanûl*

The little town of Caidris was quiet long before sunset. The farmers had hidden themselves and their families away, leaving soldiers and sellswords to the kind of harvest that common working folk wished little to do with. Sharpened swords had replaced old plows, and the chatter of a lively market square had quieted to the occasional clink of well-worn armor and booted footsteps on dusty hard-packed streets.

Under a darkening sky, on the front porch of an old farmhouse with boarded windows, Uthalion considered the distant shadows of the southern horizon. Fields of grain waved in the wind, bending toward him as heavy clouds rolled northward, rumbling with thunder and flashing with lightning. He kept his breath slow and even, his eyes narrowed and watchful. He could not banish the coiled tension in his muscles, the aching readiness to react, stand, and perform the duty for which he had been recruited. His stomach twisted at the thought, but his determination never wavered.

Absently he twirled a band of gold around his left ring finger, running his thumb over the tiny scratches in the imperfect bend of a once perfect loop. It had been two weeks since he'd left Airspur with promises to his wife and newborn daughter of a safe return and coin enough to leave the realm of Akanûl for good. He had spun stories of his grandfather's farm in Tethyr, of wide fields and ample work. Yet the only story his wife would recall, the only promise she would hold him to, was that he never take up the sword again.

He sighed and unhooked the long sword on his belt, a new blade placed in his hands by a dying man three days—three endless days of marching—before. He hated the weapon and the broken promise he saw in its finely sharpened edge. Even more than that, he loathed the responsibility his acceptance of the sword signified.

"Captain?"

The word was repeated before Uthalion realized he was being spoken to. He was not yet accustomed to the title and eager to be rid of it as soon as possible. A half-elf stood at the end of the porch, his sword drawn and eyeing the southern approach warily.

"Yes, Brindani?"

"The last of the townsfolk have been secured, doors are boarded up, and livestock have been locked away until . . ." Brindani's voice momentarily trailed off as both men spied the first pitch black clouds reaching the far end of town "Until the storm passes," he finished.

Uthalion studied the half-elf's face for several breaths, seeing through the stoic façade to the spark of fear in the soldier's eyes and the breath he slowly forced from the tightness of his chest. In that moment Uthalion hated the half-elf, but only briefly—a flash of malice that urged him to be cruel, to mock the young warrior who'd signed on for glory and story. Brindani's friends, also brash and eager for the gold a good fight might bring, had fallen three days ago, their bodies broken and left for carrion in the ruins of old Tohrepur.

Growls of thunder drew his attention back to the storm. The black clouds stretched from east to west as if they would swallow the entire world. Uthalion could still imagine the deep well from which they'd burst and flowed into the sky like a geyser of pure shadow. The Keepers of the Cerulean Sign, mystic warriors bound to the destruction of agents of the Abolethic Sovereignty, had stuck their swords in where they weren't wanted and had gotten more than they'd bargained for.

The unnatural storm was the least of their worries now. The Keepers were all dead as far as Uthalion knew, leaving their underpaid mercenaries to clean up the mess. Three days the black clouds had chased them across the Mere-That-Was; three days and counting for the last defenders of Tohrepur to fall.

"Are the men in place?" he asked Brindani who nodded, speechless. "We'll maintain a wide, even circle, closing slowly and converging here."

Soldiers took their positions in the distance, barely visible in the sudden and early night, their blades flashing in the long streaks of lightning. Beyond their evenly spaced line, shambling over the southern rise and backlit by the lightning storm, the last citizens of Tohrepur, thralls to abolethic masters, crested the hill. They walked awkwardly, many struggling to make their twisted limbs obey basic commands, their bones either horribly changed or gone altogether. The thralls' throats stretched and distended, producing only gurgling sounds as the servitors tried to speak, tried to find their lost voices.

Brindani gasped, staring as the horde pushed on into Caidris. His blade dipped, and he took a step backward. Uthalion descended the porch steps and grabbed the half-elf's shoulder firmly.

"Just do the work," he said, shouting to be heard above the thunder and howling wind. "Keep moving, don't think, and do your job."

"They're people," Brindani said, unable to look away from the grisly crowd. "They're just people."

Uthalion released the half-elf's shoulder and drew the dead captain's long sword, stretching his neck and calming nerves that had waited too long for the storm to come, for his work to arrive.

"Yes. And when you order that first round of drinks after all this is said and done," he replied, eyeing the sorcerous storm with a determined stare, "you remember what you just said before you tell the tale. You remember it very well."

The thunder in the storm buzzed through the town, an alien voice whispering dark words that tingled like magic on the air. Uthalion could feel that magic descending from the clouds, caressing his cheek with silky tendrils of suggestion. Nausea spun his stomach, matching the racing course of his thoughts. He advanced, ignoring the brief pangs of anxiety that accompanied the start of any battle. The dark swallowed him, leaving him in a black void with only the dusty road beneath his boots to keep him grounded.

He paused several feet from the farmhouse as the babbling voices of Tohrepur's host grew louder, gurgling screams that chased the thunder and echoed somewhere in his memory. The sudden sense of having done it all before was overwhelming, and he turned, looking back at the farmhouse and the open door banging in the wind. Khault stood on the porch carrying a glowing lantern. Khault, the brave farmer who'd invited Uthalion's men to stay and rest in Caidris, and who had volunteered to help when he'd heard news of the coming disaster.

With measured steps, Khault descended the porch steps as if in a trance, his eyes fixed on the advancing thralls as they clashed with the mercenaries at the end of the road. In his free hand he held an old axe, its blade glowing dully in the orange light of his lantern.

"You should be inside!" Uthalion shouted over the thunder. But Khault did not answer and did not stop. Panic took the captain in an icy grip, and he strode forward, grabbing the farmer's shoulders and shaking him, "Why? Why risk it? Think of your family! Why would you leave them alone in this?"

Khault merely stared, the orange light digging deep shadows in the man's face.

Shouts caught Uthalion's attention as the soldiers' circle formation closed, edging nearer to the farmhouse. He shouted back, instructing his men, though the words were too familiar, like a script playing itself out and using his voice without his consent. He stopped and tried to remember, placing a hand on his head as if he could pluck the memory free through scalp and bone.

"We can't all be heroes, Uthalion!" Khault called out, walking into the dark, toward the flash of distant blades and the shining eyes of Tohrepur's people. "But you should not judge us for trying!"

"Nonsense!" Uthalion yelled back, blinking in the wind and turning in circles, narrowing his eyes as the struggling memory crawled sluggishly to the forefront of his mind, "Follow orders," he muttered. "Just do the job."

"Don't be naïve, Captain," Brindani whispered, though the half-elf was nowhere to be seen. "Wake up!"

Shadows twisted as a figure shuffled toward him from the right. He raised his long sword, abandoning confusion for the simple clarity of combat. Lightning blazed across the sky, sparkling in the drooping eye of a young boy whose twin mouths opened wide to reveal multiple rows of needle-sharp teeth.

"Wake up. . . ."

❖ ❖ ❖ ❖ ❖

*6 Mirtul, the Year of the Ageless One (1479 DR)*
*The Spur Forest, Akanûl, South of Airspur*

Uthalion woke with a gasp to find himself lying on the forest floor, staring up into a thick canopy of trees. Moonlight streamed through the leaves as he blinked in a daze, the nightmare slowly retreating into the murky depths of his thoughts. Sitting up, he saw that his knife and the rabbit he'd snared earlier were gone, but his silver ring, plain and unassuming, lay on the ground where it had slipped from his finger. As he set it back in its place, the cold metal soothing against his skin, he breathed evenly and wiped the sweat from his brow.

The soft crackle and glow of the campfire behind him and the smell of cooking rabbit eased his mind, and he sat for a long moment, the drying blood of the rabbit sticky on his fingers, staring into a middle distance that held only the promise of a quiet darkness. He could only have been asleep for an hour or so. His left hand, bearing the silver ring, clenched into a fist that would not soon release the simple loop.

At length he stood up. A small stream ran along the edge of the grove, and he lowered his hands into the cool waters, careful not to lose the ring on his finger.

"Did you sleep well?" Vaasurri asked, and Uthalion closed his eyes.

"You know better," he said as he focused on removing the blood from his hands.

"I suppose," the killoren replied. "But I always hold out hope."

Uthalion nodded with as much finality as the gesture could convey. Despite the magic of the ring, he was tired. It had been six years since he'd walked away from Caidris and nearly three weeks since he'd last had a night's sleep. The dream was always the same, carrying him back to Khault's little farmhouse and the dark basement where he and his men had ridden out the aboleth's storm. The repetition of the dream, night after night, invading his sleep had given him splitting headaches for months—until he'd found the enchanted ring. Its silver shine was dull compared to the gold band it had replaced.

Uthalion watched as thin clouds of dirt and blood bloomed in the clear water of the stream. Maryna, his wife, would have teased him for the blood on his shirt, her skill at cleaning a kill much better than his own. He would have taken her jibes graciously, complimenting her wonderful cooking in a sneaky attempt to escape the duty himself. But she'd known his tricks quite well. He paused and held his breath, shutting out the memory of her smile, before drying his hands on his tunic. He sighed in exasperation.

Vaasurri entered the light of the campfire, bearing his strange, knowing smile that seemed almost permanent at times. With his light green skin traced with leaf-line veins and deep emerald eyes, the killoren's features were like extensions of the forest itself. Uthalion could only barely recall a few faces that he knew as well as Vaasurri's.

"What did he say this time?" Vaasuri asked.

"Can't a man wash his hands in peace?" he asked.

"Apparently not," Vaasurri answered, an edge of frustration creeping into the fey's voice that Uthalion had not expected.

"Oh, I disagree. I've seen it happen you know," he replied, turning and staring up into the trees in mock wistfulness.

He took a deep cleansing breath. "A simple man washing his hands—not a care in the world and not a soul to disturb him. That's just good living. Quiet moment. Clean water and maybe a bluebird singing nearby."

"Point taken," Vaasurri said with a half-smile, his eyes gleaming in the firelight.

"Apparently not," Uthalion added and approached the fire.

Uthalion sat, his stomach grumbling in anticipation as he stared into the steaming pot over the campfire and put behind him the unexpected sleep—and the dream that came with it.

"Well, you needed the rest. It's been almost—" Vaasurri began.

"Not now, Vaas," Uthalion said, not taking his eyes away from the stew. "Truly. Not now."

"As you wish," the killoren said, and he filled two wooden bowls in silence.

Uthalion's hand shook slightly as he took his portion of the evening's meal. His nerves were still on edge, the dream not yet done with them. That night in Caidris had been only one of several in the Keepers' campaign, though it had been one of the last. Unfortunately, his memory had served him better the farther they'd gotten away from Tohrepur. What little he could recall of that city was fragmented by flashes of sorcerous light and heavy fogs of limitless darkness. He'd seen little of the aboleth itself and was grateful for that. The dying captain's face was a blur, though his sword of rank remained with Uthalion, its details carved deeply into the fabric of his mind. Beyond that only the screams remained. And something else: a haunting, half-heard sound almost like singing.

Uthalion ate slowly and in silence, the sinuous melody hiding somewhere in his thoughts and taunting him behind the dying cries of the Keepers and honest sellswords. Each time he removed the silver ring and allowed himself to succumb to slumber, the nightmare worsened. The ring's magic maintained a sense of being well rested, though it could do little for the rigors of simply being conscious. Vaasurri had told him that dreams were necessary—in Uthalion's case a necessary evil—for the mind to remain balanced and whole. Uthalion had pushed the limits of that balance each time, swearing he'd not remove the ring so soon the next time. The night's rest had been an accident, and the nightmare had proved itself more than able to make up for lost time.

He shook his head and flexed his hand, willing the dream away and breathing in the fresh air of the forest. He'd told little of his tale to Vaasurri, and though his curiosity was boundless, the killoren had never pushed too hard for the details.

The bile of the nightmare crept up in his throat. He set his bowl aside and turned to the grove, the circle that he and Vaasurri had cultivated over the years as a focus for what the killoren called the energy of the Feywild. The Spur Forest had been affected as much as any part of the world by the Spellplague of years past, but it had also been infected by the Sovereignty. The aboleths' minions and magic had descended upon the northern city of Airspur almost fifty years before, their nightmarish power spilling into the Spur before being turned away. Vaasurii claimed the circle could begin a cycle of healing for the forest, restore some of what the aboleths had turned wrong.

The spot they had chosen was greener than it had been before. Flowers bloomed, and Vaasurri's small herb garden had begun to flourish. Uthalion sighed, thankful for such an oasis and the good work it gave him to be proud of. He buried the dream until the next dreaded moment when the ring would slip away along with the world he had carefully cultivated around him. An old notebook lay wrapped in his cloak, containing all the knowledge he'd discovered in the Spur since choosing to live away from the crowds of Akanûl's cities.

Uthalion had once promised Maryna a fine home and a beautiful garden. Having grown up on a farm in Tethyr, he knew quite a lot about chickens and potatoes, but had been lacking in the knowledge to deliver on his promise. He still meant to keep it one day, somehow.

He looked over his shoulder at Vaasuri, also staring into the Spur, and noticed the killoren's curved bone sword leaning against a nearby tree.

"Any reason we're joined by your dragon's tooth, Vaas?" he asked.

The killoren's expression changed, like a shadow crawling across the moon, and he seemed wilder than a moment ago, an animal smelling something on the wind.

"I've just had a feeling, is all," Vaasurri replied, his eyes piercing the dark like a predator.

"A *feeling?*" Uthalion said and sat forward, raising an eyebrow in interest and mentally cataloguing the location of his own weapons. "Sometimes I think your feelings are better than a scout's eyewitness report. Anything specific?"

"Not just yet," the killoren said. He reached for the bone sword, its smooth blade covered in dark images of hunting beasts and cunning prey. "Could be anything, but I do not think it natural in any sense of the word . . . At least, not in any sense that the world recognizes as natural anymore."

Uthalion considered Vaasurri's words, furrowing his brow. "No bears or dragons then."

A piercing howl interrupted his attempt at a jest, and both of them sat bolt upright, their eyes wide. Their ears focused on the trailing edge of the unnatural sound that existed somewhere between the howl of a wolf and the cry of a man. The hair on Uthalion's neck stood on end, and a shudder passed through his shoulders, chilling him to the core.

"That was not a bear," he said, getting to his feet.

"Nor a dragon," the killoren replied and stood as well. His sword was at the ready though the howl had come from some distance away to the north.

"Small favors," Uthalion muttered quietly as he went to uncover his sword and bow. He took up his light leather armor and listened for the howl to return, almost longing for it. Something strangely beautiful—and horrifyingly familiar—existed in the sound. That hint of beauty gave him more cause to be alarmed than any fang or claw he might have imagined a heartbeat ago.

The howl came again, joined by others. The sounds of the forest ceased as the unseen predators called to one another, marking their positions. A dull ache pressed against Uthalion's temples as the howls faded away. Large predators were not entirely uncommon in the Spur, but newcomers warranted investigation.

Uthalion nodded to Vaasurri, who returned the gesture and disappeared into the forest. A well-practiced strategy had begun, and despite the disturbance of the peaceful night, Uthalion was eager to leave behind thoughts of the dream—and his dear Maryna. He ran into the forest, following paths by memory rather than cleared ground or landmark, until the unearthly green of the forest surrounded him.

Between the twisted roots of trees and the reaching thorns of low bushes, Ghaelya flowed through the forest like a mountain stream, graceful and powerful despite being well outside the city streets she called home. Tired of running and annoyed at keeping an eye over her shoulder for pursuit, she kept a steady hand on the broadsword at her belt. Though every instinct told her to turn and fight, she could not let hot emotion threaten what little chance she'd been given to make things right.

Ahead of her, Brindani quietly led the way through the Spur, his boots barely a whisper in the murky depths of the forest. Crouching low in a shallow ravine, he turned and motioned for her to remain still as he listened and scanned the area. Brindani's half-elf eyes pierced the night far better than her own, and he knew the forest paths almost as well as she knew the streets and towers of Airspur. But he'd taken them in one small circle already, and she was beginning to doubt his confidence.

"Are we close?" she asked.

He turned to her and ran a hand through his shoulder-length black hair, his hazel eyes sparkling pinpoints in the dark.

"Hard to say," he answered. "As well as I know the forest, Uthalion knows it far better. He could have concealed the grove where I spoke with him last . . . Or perhaps he's moved on."

"Moved on?" she replied with not a little anger, fighting to keep her voice low.

"It is possible, though I very much doubt it."

Ghaelya sighed and bit back a useless retort. She sat on her haunches and ran a hand over the smooth skin of her scalp, wiping away tiny beads of sweat before they dripped into her eyes. Much as she regretted taking on a companion in her quest, she needed a guide to help speed her journey across the wilds of Akanûl. She had no time to waste. Brindani seemed capable enough, but he claimed his friend Uthalion knew more than he about the lands beyond the Spur.

She used the moment's rest to adjust her armor. In the gaps between the straps and armored protection, her sea foam green skin was cooled by the night air. Faint blue lines of energy traced the surface of her flesh in unique, serpentine patterns.

She traced the blue pattern on the back of her hand absently, proud of the watery element that marked her soul and her skin, though acutely aware as always of being an outsider, even among her own kind. In Airspur, elements of wind and storm took dominance among the majority of the genasi. She smiled slightly. She enjoyed being different—rebellious in her own way—though it had proven a hindrance, the night her sister, Tessaeril, had been taken.

Brindani waved to her, and they continued into the ravine, alert for signs of movement on either side. Strange beasts had been trailing them for days, always one step behind and gaining. Thankfully, they had seen no sign of the hounds' masters, a group of strange monks calling themselves the Choir. Along with her sister, the Choir had disappeared from Airspur a tenday before, but had returned as mysteriously as they'd first appeared.

Howls sounded in the distance, and she tensed, a painful ache erupting in her temples at the sound of the hunting beasts. They were getting nearer, closing their circles and gaining momentum in the Spur rather than losing it. The pain subsided, but she feared its return. The beasts' baying voices burrowed into her thoughts and clawed at memories that seemed both false and familiar all at once, like an old dream or forgotten tune fighting to break free of her deeper mind.

Brindani stopped, frozen in place, and cocked his head to listen. Angry at her own distraction, Ghaelya drew her broadsword and eyed the edges of the ravine. Glancing at the half-elf, she found him staring at her intently, Though he didn't say a word, his quiet nod spoke volumes—after all the miles they'd run and the difficult terrain they'd crossed, the beasts had finally caught up.

# CHAPTER TWO

*6 Mirtul, the Year of the Ageless One*
*(1479 DR)*
*The Spur Forest,*
*South of Airspur, Akanûl*

The creature stalked along the top of the ravine, sniffing loudly and whining as if frustrated. Ghaelya knelt low, careful not to shift and draw the creature's attention. Brindani followed suit and gestured to a curved hollow in the side of the long path, just hidden enough to keep them from sight. Ghaelya cursed the half-elf inwardly. She wanted to face the creature, indeed had hoped to be forced into doing so. She had no desire to hide in a ditch and wait it out.

But she had heard their howls—there were too many for her to dispatch without the half-elf's help. She ran after him.

Before she crossed even half the distance, she heard the whisper of Brindani drawing his blade, and she smiled grimly. No more running.

Up ahead the ravine turned south, and it was there Ghaelya caught her first sight of the strange hound, pushing through the thick bushes and sending clods of dirt rolling into the ravine. Glittering eyes swiveled lidless in their sockets, shining in the dark. The shape of broad shoulders rose above a thickly muscled neck. It turned toward them and raised its head; moonlight trailed across its pale gray fur. It's face, illuminated in the light of Selunê, looked strangely human, as if someone's face had been stretched over the creature's blunt skull.

Ghaelya crouched low, poised to spring as the creature stalked forward, sniffing at the air and emitting a series of soft whimpers.

Brindani's hand rested softly on hers. He was tense and ready to run or fight at a moment's notice. She kept her other hand firmly on the hilt of her sword. Steel had been far more protective of her best interests than half-elves with good intentions.

The creature howled, the oddly melodious sound causing her to gasp in pain. She closed her eyes, fearing the pressure in her head might force them from their sockets before the beast's voice trailed off. It was answered from far away by the rest of its pack. She'd heard the longing and anger that hid behind its black eyes before, but the memory of it was slippery and lost in a haze of pain . . .

Or was it? In between the sharp spikes of agony, she could almost hear a wonderful singing, weaving in and out of her mind like a forgotten rhyme from childhood. It began to slip away, and she tried to grasp at it, to claim the song as her own—an irrational impulse that stunned her with its power.

The beast turned and loped off, disappearing into the woods.

The fading pain on Brindani's face was obvious, as was the horrified wonder in his eyes. He turned to her and sheathed his blade.

"What in the Hells was that?" he whispered.

She shook her head, but the slight movement jarred loose the evasive memory, freeing it and the image of her sister to her conscious mind. Its appearance shocked her with its suddenness, and she spoke quickly, lest it slip away from her again.

"They are called the oenath, the Dreamers . . ."

The words felt alien on her tongue, but she could not deny them. She knew the truth in them as surely as she knew her own name.

Brindani narrowed his eyes in curiosity. "You dreamed this?" he asked solemnly. He knew of her recent nightmares and placed more stock in them then she was yet ready to accept.

Sighing, she nodded, uncomfortable in his gaze and finding the idea of herself as some kind of oracle distasteful. There had been no place in her life for prophetic dreams or voices or even gods, and in the past she'd ridiculed those who claimed to be the sources of such things. Though Brindani had shown her nothing but the utmost respect, she found it hard to accept his assessment of her recent dreams as genuine.

"So we know what to call them! It does us no good now does it?" she said coldly.

"No, I suppose not," he agreed, joining her on the path, "Let's get out of this ravine and onto some higher ground so I can get my bearings."

He took the lead, and she fell into step, grateful not to have his eyes on her back, as if watching her every move and gesture for signs or portents. She would have torn the dreams from her head were it possible, but they had proven honest, placing words and images in her mind of which she had no previous knowledge. Two nights before she'd spoken in her sleep, and Brindani had shaken her awake, agitated and fearful. She had no memory of the dream itself, but knew the word he had recognized. The following morning they had set out to find a guide to a place she'd dreamed but never heard of—a place called Tohrepur.

The Spur grew suddenly quiet as they neared the sloping rise out of the ravine, and moonlight guided them into a small clearing surrounded by tall, twisted trees. Broad leaves, semi-translucent and reflecting light, gave the forest a haunting quality that dazed her eyes momentarily. But the snapping of a single twig set her nerves on edge. Squinting through the half-light of the trees, she raised her blade. At her side, Brindani froze.

The beast, the dreamer, paused as their eyes met, its legs pulled under its barrel chest, ready to pounce. Slivers of moonlight illuminated the beast's thin gray fur and the white skin beneath. Its face was short—angular and expressive, and utterly unlike a wolf's. There was an intelligence there that made her reassess the danger the creature represented. A low humming growl churned and rumbled through its thick neck as Ghaelya slowly circled to the left.

A night wind shook the leaves overhead, dappling the ground with disorienting moonlight. The creature's growl rose and thundered in her head like a living thing, crawling through her thoughts and rooting in her fears. She blinked once, wincing at the pain of the noise, and found the beast already in the air, its teeth bared as it bore down on Brindani.

The half-elf sidestepped and slashed, barely scoring the dreamer's thick skin before the beast landed and pursued its quick-footed prey. Ghaelya charged its back, slicing downward with her broadsword, eager to draw blood after so many days of running. But the dreamer was quicker still. It dodged her attack and caught her leg in a powerful grip, throwing her to the ground like a rag doll. She rolled away, clenching her teeth in anger as the dreamer accepted a close cut from Brindani, only to pounce as the half-elf's blade was drawn back, taking him off guard. His sword bounced from his grip as the pair slammed into the dirt.

Ghaelya charged again as Brindani was taken down under the beast's weight. She slashed at the exposed back of the creature, drawing a thin line of dark fluid. The smell of the beast's blood hit her nose. She drew back to slash again, sidestepping as it swiped at her with its claw. Brindani strained to keep the dreamer's jaws at bay, groaning with the effort and slowly losing. The creature's clawed fingers scraped against the half-elf's old armor as it whined pitiably with a sickening hunger, its jaws gaping wide to reveal tusklike fangs.

Distant howls rose through the Spur, each answering the last. Desperate, Ghaelya stepped in, thrusting at the black, fishlike eyes as they turned to face her. The sudden roar of the beast struck her like a fist, dazing her as a wave of hazy force knocked away her broadsword. Pressure pushed against her chest, turning the forest into a blur of ethereal greens and murky shadows, and the canopy overhead spun wildly through her wide eyes. In the brief moment she hung between land and sky, the unknown song flashed through her mind. A chorus of angelic voices pressed into the space of a heartbeat before reality took her back to falling.

She crashed into the ground, stunned and gasping for breath. All sound felt sucked away, as if cotton had been stuffed into her ears. The trailing edge of the beast's roar still rumbled through her body, the force of it having left her skin numb where it had struck. Her ears popped, relieving the all-encompassing sound of her pulse. Groaning, she pushed herself up, amazed that she'd held on to her weapon. Recovering swiftly, she got to her feet, undeterred. The stench of the creature's blood stung her nostrils as she came at it again, scoring a strike across the back of its thick skull. It whimpered and drew back, more dark fluid dripping down its not-quite-human face. It yelped as Brindani thrust the blade of a dagger into its shoulder.

The half-elf stabbed madly as he fought the injured beast, kicking free and rolling to his dropped sword. Ghaelya kept slashing as the beast backed away, giving Brindani time to regain his footing. The dreamer huffed, an expression of anger spreading across its weirdly mixed features. Before the creature could give voice to its roar again, two arrows sprouted from its throat. It gagged, coughing and spraying blood across the ground. A stench like dead fish filled the air as it drew back and thrashed in the dirt, clawing at the offending shafts. Scrambling to its feet, the beast sprinted into the forest's shadows, wheezing and gnashing its teeth.

Ghaelya turned her sword eastward, squinting into the trees for the source of the arrows. Brindani placed a hand on her shoulder that she quickly shrugged off, but she calmed somewhat as he stepped forward, seeing more in the dark than just more enemies. She did not lower her blade as a human, armed with a longbow, approached cautiously. He was tall and lean, with a hard stare that pierced through the forest's ghostly gloom. An arrow was strung tightly in his bow, and she braced her feet, ready to move at a moment's notice.

To Ghaelya's alarm, Brindani lowered his own blade.

"Uthalion?" he asked quietly.

The human stopped, half raising the bow for a heartbeat as if deciding whether or not to kill the half-elf, but the arrow's point turned away even if the taut string didn't budge.

"Brin—?" the man replied and seemed about to say more when the howls of the approaching pack filled the air. Pain flashed through Ghaelya's skull, nearly driving her to her knees. Both men winced in pain and dropped their guards completely until the sound passed. Uthalion shook his head and eyed Ghaelya and Brindani shrewdly, his lips drawn in a thin line. He turned to the south with a purposeful stride.

"No time," he called over his shoulder. "Follow me unless you're waiting for them."

"Is that him?" Ghaelya asked, sheathing her blade. "The man you spoke of?"

It seemed Brindani looked right through her for a breath before he blinked and nodded at her question. He motioned to the retreating human, seeming out of sorts as he followed the guide they had sought.

"And he knows the way? He will take us to Tohre-pur?" she asked, keeping up. Yet he did not turn to her; he avoided eye contact and appeared lost in some other thread of thought.

"He knows the way." Brindani muttered at length.

Ghaelya paused at his answer, narrowed her eyes at his back, and shook her head for a moment before continuing, cursing herself quietly. Once upon a time she'd known better than to take a promise at face value; but, she reasoned, she'd taken a chance on the half-elf—it fairly followed to allow him his gamble on the human. Whatever occurred, they were moving south again, and that would serve her well for the time being.

She could hear the dreamers giving chase in the distance, their growls and whines echoing hauntingly. Uthalion guided them through the forest as if he'd lived there all his life, turning swift corners and avoiding sudden drops or hidden patches of thick thorns. His knowledge of the Spur kept them safely ahead of the monstrous pack, but with the dreamers' speed Ghaelya doubted their distance would last forever. She followed carefully and quietly, keeping a safe distance from the strange human and a close eye on Brindani.

Her attention was so focused on spying any suspicious action from Uthalion, that she almost drew her blade on him when he stopped suddenly and turned with an upraised hand. Brindani approached Uthalion's position, and both men looked down the edge of a sheer cliff, its bottom lost in darkness.

"After me, count to three," Uthalion said, looking up at the pair. "Then follow."

With that he jumped, falling into the black. Ghaelya held her breath, waiting for the sound of an impact, though none came. Brindani looked to her and nodded as if it were perfectly normal.

"You cannot be serious!" she whispered. He placed a hand on her shoulder even as howls erupted close by. Placing a finger to his lips, he secured his sword and dagger and jumped into the dark.

Ghaelya had never been afraid of heights. Airspur was a city of towering structures, some of them suspended freely in the air. Many a thrill-seeking genasi knew how to leap from one district to the next, arresting one's fall by a window ledge here, a banner-pole there. She had imagined herself as a single drop of rain, flowing and changing, as she had navigated the soaring heights of the city. As graceful and as brave as she might have seemed at home, she always knew where and how to land.

She stepped closer to the cliff's edge, one foot hovering over the bottomless gulf and her neck stretched, finding her center of balance. She closed her eyes and shook her arms out, loosely hanging her fingers like rolling drops of rain collecting on the petal of a flower. The weight of the inevitable fall flooded her senses and rushed chillingly through her arms. Muffled growls drew nearer; claws scratched at bark and dirt.

Somewhere in the dark below her she felt the singing again, though she could not hear it. It tugged at her, pleaded with her, and for a moment she swooned in its power. Bending her knees slightly, she cursed.

"I'm coming for you, Tess," she said.

Brindani hit the dirt hard, rolling over the thick roots of a tree and tucking into a crouch. He turned to stand across from Uthalion, watching for the descending form of Ghaelya. He tried not to look at the human, still dazed by the indistinct memories racing through his mind. He kept his eyes skyward, the moonlit dark little more than thin shadows to the sharp eyes his elf mother had given him. The hands he held at the ready—perhaps, he had often mused, the hands of his unknown human father—bore the scars of too many battles.

Born in the battlefield, Brindani thought. Why bother fighting it? You'll die there too.

Ghaelya appeared falling gracefully through the darkness, her arms outstretched, the pale swirls of energy on her skin burning. He and Uthalion caught her arms. She broke free of Uthalion's grasp and they rolled across the ground in a tangle of limbs and curses. The roots he had missed before were lodged in the small of his back, the genasi's weight on top of him. For the briefest of moments he welcomed the pain, until her eyes flashed in anger, and she stood.

The forestmote they had landed upon floated peacefully between the high cliffs of a deep valley in the Spur, drifting eastward so slowly the movement could barely be seen. Brindani looked to Uthalion, surprised and realizing just how long the human had lived in the forest. The skills Uthalion had gathered would be useful.

"Was that really necessary?" Ghaelya asked, leaning against a tree and rubbing her leg. "I won't be able to run on this now."

Uthalion glanced at her, annoyed, before turning back to his perusal of the cliffs above, watching for signs of pursuit. Brindani held up the gore-splattered blade of his dagger, the smell of the dreamer's blood overpowering.

"Smells like an abandoned fish market at high noon," he said, turning his nose away. "If we'd gone around the cliffs, we might as well have carried torches and sang tavern songs at the top of our lungs. Uthalion just broke the trail."

Ghaelya raised an eyebrow and nodded in understanding, but was unsatisfied by the answer. "How do we know they won't follow?"

"We don't know," Uthalion answered, turning to face them with his arms crossed. "If they show up again, you can tell them I made a mistake and share a joke at my expense. Until then, I don't see them making that jump, and the trail is broken."

"You could have broken my leg," Ghaelya responded hotly.

"Better than breaking mine," the human replied as Brindani stood to get between the two. "Besides, people I don't know break legs every day. Why should I make an exception and care about yours?"

"Uth," Brindani said, holding up his hands and gesturing to the genasi. "This is Ghaelya. We didn't come here for a fight, but the last few days we've just been . . . a little on edge. Thank you for helping us."

"You're welcome," Uthalion replied, eyeing the genasi for a moment before facing the half-elf. "Why are you out here Brin? It's been three years since I told you not to come back."

Brindani sighed and lowered his hands, having dreaded the moment since entering the deep woods.

"Yes, that you did," he answered, trying to think of how to continue, how to put into words the insanity he'd been dealing with for the last tenday—not to mention the last three years. A cold sweat had broken out on his forehead, and he quickly brushed it away as a familiar headache returned with a dull throb behind his eyes. Taking a deep breath he forced his trembling hands to his sides, balling them into fists. "I—no, *we,* came here looking for you. We need your help. There is—"

Howls rang from the forest, increasing in frequency as the dreamers closed the wide circle of their hunt. Uthalion turned back to the edge of the forestmote, and Ghaelya ceased cleaning the blood from her sword to listen. Following the eerie howls was the soft chanting of a powerful voice, its song drifting from sweet and ethereal to the harsh scream of metal scraping on glass. Old pain stabbed at Brindani's stomach, and his headache grew stronger, but he fought to conceal his discomfort.

"Quick," Uthalion said, facing him with a look of urgency. "Long story short."

"We need a guide," Brindani replied, studying Uthalion's eyes and ignoring the dim screams trying to escape the recesses of his mind. "A guide . . . to Tohrepur."

Uthalion blinked, a flash of something like confusion crossing his stern features, though otherwise he appeared unmoved by the statement.

"Oh," he said at length, lowering his head as if in thought, then uncrossing his arms and walking to the southern edge of the forestmote.

"No," Uthalion continued. "Not ever. Let's keep moving."

"Uth, wait. . . " Brindani began. He stopped as Ghaelya stood and flashed him a look of anger.

"Leave it," she said as Uthalion took hold of a low branch and climbed up to reach a second limb bridging a deep gap between the forestmote and the other side of the valley. "We don't need him. We'll rest, reassess, and be on our way."

She followed after the human, climbing in silence up the edge of the cliff towards the forest above. Brindani wanted to agree with her, but he had traveled the length of Akanûl once before, though much of the journey had been a blur. He shook his head at the recollection. Even saying the name of the place had taken effort. At one point in his life, months before, he'd almost forgotten that Tohrepur and the little town of Caidris had existed. But, as he was growing tired of discovering, he could not escape them forever.

He fumbled at his pack as they pressed on into the southern Spur, unable to find the bottle of spirits he'd stowed away or the wine he'd purchased in Airspur. His lips were dry, his throat ached, and the pain in his stomach was escalating with each step.

The forest changed as they pressed deeper into the plague-changed landscape, its leaves turning from a dappled, ethereal green to intermittent waves of dark, glowing orange. Twisting roots came to life as yellow winged beetles crawled out from their lairs to buzz in clouds around the tree trunks, their wings and the light both bright as flames. The brightness of the display hurt Brindani's eyes, and he squinted, nodding to Ghaelya when she turned with a look of concern on her face. He waved her on, concealing his near blind search through the pack.

The bottle of spirits was empty and the wineskin held only a mouthful that Brindani gratefully swallowed. He left other useless sundries in his wake as he rummaged and quietly cursed—no drink meant he had no choice. His frustration grew, until his hand closed around a soft bundle wrapped in rough cloth at the bottom of the pack. He breathed a sigh of relief. The bittersweet aroma of silkroot reached his nose, and instantly his headache seemed a little less. The gripping pain in his stomach subsided.

Brindani paused, gasping quietly as he clenched the bundle and strained to listen, hearing the faintest whisper of singing from somewhere in the night. There were no words or any melody he could describe, but just the feel of the sound made him want to possess it for his own. It was gone in a breath, leaving him dazed on the winding path and clutching the silkroot in his fist.

Uthalion never turned from the path, and Ghaelya seemed lost in her own thoughts. Brindani forced himself to remain patient, a twinge of shame resting like a brick in his gut until he could be alone with his demons. He could make it. No one would have to know. His hand trembled as he released the silkroot bundle back into his pack, patting it securely several times to remind himself that it was still there.

Uthalion kept his eyes forward and his feet moving, focusing on their path and winding it just enough to hopefully throw off any further pursuit. Several times he studied a well-hidden, shadowed trench or an old tree within easy climbing range of the upper canopy, but he passed them by, shaking his head. As much as he might like to, he would not abandon his visitors to the not-so-tender mercies of the Spur. He would see them to safety and look forward to their departure. He had no wish to relive the past—as he'd told Brindani well enough the last time the half-elf had come calling. He desired even less to cross the length of the wilder Akana to go and visit that past.

He'd had enough of old times and unwanted nightmares for one night.

Though he stifled the sharp edge of paranoia that pressed against in the back of his mind, he kept a ready hand on his sword as he navigated the maze of the Spur. He eyed the trees, searching for Vaasurri among the leaves, though he suspected the killoren was still busy drawing the howling beasts away from the grove. Within sight of the glow of his abandoned campfire, he breathed deeply and narrowed his eyes. He kept the genasi in his peripheral vision, eyeing her movements closely. She seemed sure-footed, though she had the heavy step of a city dweller. The half-elf seemed as stealthy and as unassuming as ever, but though Brindani hadn't specifically said they'd been chased, Uthalion knew there was plenty of easier game in the forest than a well-armed genasi and her half-elf escort.

"Trouble," he muttered. "Nothing good can come of this."

The smell of half-eaten stew, still warming on the fire, filled the grove. Though he'd eaten less than his share earlier, he found he was no longer hungry, already dreading any further mention of Tohrepur.

# CHAPTER THREE

*6 Mirtul, the Year of the Ageless One*
*(1479 DR)*
*The Spur Forest,*
*South of Airspur, Akanûl*

Uthalion stalked the borders of the grove, searching for any sign of a disturbance with his tracker's eyes. Finding naught but his own footprints and those of Vaasurri, he calmed a bit, but the nearness of his guests kept his nerves on edge. He wasn't fond of keeping company and had no intention of entertaining the presence of Brindani or Ghaelya longer than necessary. The genasi stood with her arms crossed, studying the grove coolly, but the half-elf shifted nervously from foot to foot, his gaze darting from shadow to shadow.

"There's stew if you're hungry and a safe place to rest by the fire," Uthalion said at length, turning to retreat to the hidden cavern where he kept his oft-ignored bedroll. He added over his shoulder, "I suspect by morning you'll be anxious to be on your way."

"We should talk," Brindani said, and Uthalion stopped, gritting his teeth.

"We already did," he replied coldly. "I'm not going back."

"Lives are at stake," the half-elf pressed.

"I have no doubt," Uthalion said. "You'll have my best wishes and mayhap some cold stew for the road."

Brindani shook his head and threw up his hands, pacing into the shadows on the northern edge of the grove. For half a breath Uthalion felt a pang of regret, still seeing in Brindani the foolish youth that had marched into battle in the Keepers' campaign all those years before. He paused and let down his guard for a moment, looking at the pair again with shrewder eyes. Ghaelya sat by the fire, her eyes half-lidded and tired, her boots dirty and stained by her long journey through the Spur. Flames danced in her blue-green eyes, her thoughts apparently leagues away from the unfamiliar forest she found herself in.

The half-elf, though knowledgeable in the wild, seemed as lost as ever, still trying to find some purpose in the world for the life that had been spared in battle. Uthalion had seen it before: the guilt of the survivor, seeking meaning for their existence when others had died in their stead. When Brindani had come to the grove three years before he'd been much the same, wanting to go back, to Caidris and Tohrepur, somehow sure that the Keepers of the Cerulean Sign had failed, that some battle yet remained in which he might die and claim the gift his fellows-in-arms had received.

Looking again to the genasi, Uthalion shook his head derisively. *She isn't a cause to him,* he mused. *She's just an excuse.*

"Pay him no mind." Ghaelya's voice startled him from the thought. "I'm not anyone's mission or quest or obligation."

Approaching the fire, Uthalion crossed his arms and studied her, admiring the strength in her set features and tone of voice. "No damsel in distress then?" he asked.

She glared at him a moment, her eyes flashing an unspoken threat, then resumed her long stare into the flames without answering. He nodded quietly and felt slightly more at ease—until Brindani approached from the shadows. The half-elf's eyes were clear and focused, his earlier shaking and nervousness gone. The smoothness in his step caused Uthalion to stand slightly at guard, his sword within easy reach. There was a fight in Brindani's stare, and though Uthalion was familiar with the nightmares that stalked in his old friend's past, he would not let empathy slow the stroke of his blade.

"We'll talk now, Uthalion," Brindani said. "I don't care if you listen or just pretend to, but I know deep down you're a good man, and we need your help. The Mere-That-Was and all beyond it is a dangerous place; you've been there and back, twice."

Narrowing his eyes, a hard edge of anger settled in the stiffness of Uthalion's jaw.

"This isn't about this land or that, or what lies between," he said, staring the half-elf down. "It's about one gods-forsaken place."

"Tohrepur," Brindani supplied solemnly.

"And you are bound and determined to go back," Uthalion said.

"It's not like that—"

"It's always been like that!" Uthalion's voice raised, and he stepped forward. "I wanted no part of it then, and nothing has changed in the meantime."

"They took my sister," Ghaelya said.

The genasi's voice startled both men, and Uthalion stared at her in the light of the campfire. Her eyes blazed as she continued.

"Over a month ago, they came into the city, strange monks calling themselves the Choir. Few paid them any mind—cults to unknown gods come and go and are typically harmless. But Tessaeril was drawn to them despite all her good sense." She shook her head, displaying a softness in the memory that caught Uthalion's attention. "One night, the Choir came for her and I—I did what I could. I killed one before being knocked out by another, and in the morning . . . They were gone, along with all of those they had charmed into their fold."

She blinked and tore her eyes from the fire.

"I will find her," she said fiercely, looking at both of them. "Whether you come with me or not."

Uthalion glanced at Brindani once, ignoring the hopeful look in the half-elf's eyes and knelt down to look deeply into Ghaelya's. Having been deceived by field commanders and incompetent officers in the past, he was confident in his ability to detect a lie.

"I'm sorry about your sister, truly," he began. "But, what does any of this have to do with Tohrepur?"

She broke his stare at length, her lips drawn into a tight line as if ashamed of something.

"I—" She broke off, clenching her teeth and looking off into the forest before turning back to face him. "I saw it . . . in a dream."

"A dream," Uthalion repeated the word in disbelief, getting only a reluctant nod from the genasi before he stood and brushed off his hands on his trousers.

"Well, I've heard enough," he said, glaring at Brindani and turning away, eager to be alone and to put the business behind him.

"It's true," Brindani called after him, a desperate tone in his voice. "We need your help . . . You owe me this!"

Uthalion stopped and turned, his fists clenched as he rounded on the half-elf. Brindani raised his hands as if he were about to explain himself, but Uthalion gave him no chance.

"Owe you? Is that what you think?" he yelled and grabbed the half-elf's tunic, shoving him backward.

"I only meant—" Brindani began, but stopped short as Uthalion slammed him against a tree.

"Oh, I know what you meant! You'd like to blame me for the old blood on your hands, is that it?" He shook the half-elf hard, trembling with rage. Brindani's heart pounded beneath Uthalion's fist. "We both took the job, volunteered . . . Don't expect anything from me just because you followed orders you didn't like!"

"*Your* orders!" Brindani yelled back.

Uthalion pulled him from the tree and shoved him to the ground. He resisted the urge to draw his blade, but just barely. He turned away and found Ghaelya, her hand on her sword and a threatening glint in her eye.

"Leave him be," she said.

"Take him and be on your way," he said and pointed south into the woods. "You're not welcome here."

"Fine," she said, shrugging. She pushed past him roughly and added, "Useless bastard."

Her insult struck him like a hammer. He stared after her, stunned, as the pair left the grove and struck into the southern Spur. The same words echoed from his past, chasing him through the old front door of a cottage he'd once shared with Maryna. It was her voice screaming in rage as he'd left her for the second time—the last time he'd heard her voice . . . and his young daughter's cries through the open window.

"You can't let them go," Vaasurri said, approaching stealthily from the dark, his emerald eyes boring into Uthalion's. "You know better."

Not startled by the killoren's appearance, Uthalion nodded in a daze, his former rage drained away by the haze of sudden memory. Shaking free of the past, he stared after Ghaelya and Brindani, realizing what he'd truly done. He sprinted into the forest after them. The land sloped downward in the deep Spur, just beyond the foothills of the Akanapeaks. Though the moon was nearly down, he caught their path quickly and focused on the genasi's louder footfalls to guide him.

She spun around angrily in the dark, seeing the glinting glow of the grove's campfire just beyond their line of sight, but flashing dimly on the leaves. Brindani didn't turn at all, but merely stopped and waited.

"Did you come to hurry us on?" she asked angrily, and he felt shamed in her gaze.

"No, I just—" he began, but was cut short by the sound of a thunderous roar. The ground shook as they all looked southward. Leaves shivered overhead as the roar grew ever louder, a plaintive, hungry sound echoing from deep in the southern forest. A sound like splitting trees reached them, wood cracking like lightning and crashing like the rolling front of a distant storm. Uthalion caught his breath, relieved that it was far away, but still alarmed and eager to get back to the grove. Ghaelya turned to him wide-eyed as the roar slowly faded.

"Morning," he said quickly. He gestured back the way they'd come. "You should wait until morning."

Nodding in shock, they turned back up the slope and into the waiting glow of the grove.

Uthalion stood a moment longer, staring into the dark maw of the Spur and reflecting on what he'd nearly allowed to happen. His heart pounded, and he breathed deeply, listening for the roar again, but it never came.

"Useless bastard," he repeated to himself, suddenly hating the man he'd let himself become—selfish, cowardly . . . alone.

He walked back to the grove, his thoughts heavy and far away from the Spur. Vaasurri, not particularly shy and rarely at a loss for words, had introduced himself to their guests and was already warming stew over the campfire. Their words were lost on Uthalion as he knelt and lifted the makeshift door to his hidden cavern beneath the grove. He had no hunger for stew, nor longing for conversation, polite or—more likely—otherwise.

He lit a candle, its light flickering on the rough ceiling of the small chamber, a sanctuary of rock and dirt within the greater fold of the surrounding forest. It held him close, being barely long enough for him to stretch his arms over his head and touch the opposite wall with his boots, and just tall enough for him to kneel in prayer—back when he had a mind to do so. He leaned back against the wall, his arms resting on his knees, and stared at the silver ring on his finger. He was tired despite its enchantment.

Almost without thinking, he reached down to his side, to his unused bedroll and an old cloak, and produced a tiny pouch. As he slipped the knot on the drawstring, a gold ring fell into his palm. He held it up, contrasting it to the silver one he'd been wearing for over five years. Misshapen, more an oval than a circle, the gold ring had saved him from losing a finger by an orc's axe while he was doing mercenary work. That was when he had laid down his blade, returned home, and promised Maryna he'd never leave again. A year later the Keepers had come, and despite his oath, his family had needed the coin.

Time slipped away from him as he reminisced. The candle had burned a quarter of its length before Vaasurri entered the cave and drew him away from his thoughts of years past. Uthalion met the killoren's deep green eyes for a moment before closing his own, already expecting what was to come.

"I'm going with them," Vaasurri said simply, and Uthalion nodded, sighing.

"I thought as much," he answered. "Do you believe them? About her dreams?"

Vaasurri lowered his head, considering the question before shrugging slightly. "It doesn't really matter what I believe," he replied. "Were I to let them go, aimless across the Akana . . . Well, it wouldn't be right, so long as I'm able to help."

Uthalion sat forward, staring at the dirt floor, clutching the silver ring against one palm and the gold against the other. He clenched his teeth and looked up at the fey, shaking his head and forcing the words from his mouth.

"I would have let them die," he said. "If you hadn't shown up . . ."

"No, you wouldn't have," Vaasurri said, smiling slightly. "You might have let them get a bit farther had I not shown up, but you would have stopped them."

"Should I try to stop them now? Going all that way for just a pile of ruins . . . If they even make it that far." Uthalion stared into the dancing shadows at the end of the cave.

"I've spoken to the woman, and I don't think you could stop her."

Uthalion didn't answer. Vaasurri might have a point, but that didn't mean he had to listen to it. He wasn't responsible for the genasi woman. Or Brindani. He wasn't responsible for anyone any longer.

"The better effort," Vaasurri continued, "Might be in getting yourself out of this hole in the ground, out of this forest."

Uthalion leaned back, shaking his head at the idea. The idea of leaving was not an unfamiliar one—he thought of it every day, always putting it off until the next and the next after that. He'd considered it a thousand times, but wasn't sure how to go about reclaiming a life that felt like a candle burned to nothing at both ends.

"Is that her ring?" Vaasurri asked suddenly. "Your wedding band?"

Uthalion held it up, nodding, and turned it over in the flickering light of the candle. Vaasurri smiled, studying the imperfect band.

"I like it better than the silver. You shouldn't keep it buried down here." The killoren half turned to leave, then added, "Though I suspect the man who used to wear that ring might be buried as well, somewhere south of here. Could be worth the effort to go and dig him up."

The candle blew out as the makeshift door closed behind Vaasurri, leaving Uthalion alone in the dark with the two rings. He turned to his cloak and bedroll, placing the silver-ringed hand upon them gingerly. Absently he turned the gold ring in his free hand over and over.

Uthalion's thoughts on the killoren's words were interrupted by a faint sound, like music, emanating from the rock. He strained to hear, catching brief snippets of a breath-stopping melody that shook him to his core. Crawling to the southern end of the little cave, he pressed against the rock, somehow recognizing the song, but unable to place the tune.

The voice wavered in and out of hearing, the singing echoing hollowly as if somewhere nearby yet deep underground. At its loudest, barely a whisper, it brought tears to his eyes and a quickening to his heart. A soft ringing sound caused him to blink and pull back. He'd dropped the gold ring as he pressed his hands against the rock as though he might push through the wall to reach the singing.

As the voice faded away, he stared into the dark, confused and wondering where the song had come from. Despite his curiosity and sense of paranoia, he found himself less curious about where it had come from and more frightened by the sudden and powerful desire to hear it again.

⊛ ⊛ ⊛ ⊛ ⊛

Ghaelya lay back on the soft ground of the grove, turning away from the dying flames of the campfire. Unable to sleep, she could only focus on the coming dawn, escaping the Spur, and pushing on to the south, closer to Tessaeril and the dreams of her sister's voice. Vaasurri claimed to know some of the southern land he called the Akana, and though he'd never been to Tohrepur, he had agreed to guide them as best he could. Unlike his human friend, the killoren was pleasant—if a bit mysterious—and made her feel welcome.

She stared into the forest and listened as Vaasurri peppered Brindani with questions. The killoren's curiosity seemed unending and insatiable. Brindani's voice grew quiet and distant as he described the western borders of Aglarond, as if he were straining to recall the details of his life there, though by his account he'd left his homeland only months ago.

"We stood, hired swords, upon the Watchwall, shivering at night and staring out into the dark of the Umber Marshes." He paused, and she turned to face him, raising up on one elbow as he squinted and tilted his head. "By ones and twos they came at first, staggering through the marshes, wandering from the highlands of Thay. We could hear them long before they came into view, moaning and crashing through the wetlands: an endless parade of the dead finding only our swords and spears to greet them on the edge of Aglarond."

Ghaelya had never ventured far beyond the walls of Airspur. Much to the dismay of her wealthy parents, she had found adventure enough within the city to keep her occupied and well-stocked in bruises and cheap ale. The places beyond Akanûl were worlds away, spots on old maps, the Spur a smudge of green. Mere parchment had been unable to convey the vast depths of trees and shadows in which she found herself.

"No alarm was raised," Brindani continued. "Nor was there ever any need of one. The undead did not hurry, had no strategy of attack, and had no minds with which to formulate one. They just made their slow way, gathering by the dozens, to be casually cut down, over and over again."

He wrung his white-knuckled hands together and stared at the ground.

Before he could continue, Vaasurri sat up swiftly, pulling his legs gracefully beneath him in an animalistic crouch. In an instant he had become something wild, a predator sensing movement in the dark. He stared northward into the woods and prowled forward quietly. Ghaelya froze, watching him closely. She slowly drew her sword, trying not to break the killoren's fierce concentration. A heartbeat later, her blade barely a handspan from its sheath, she heard a faint, raspy whine. It pressed on her mind painfully, throbbing like the insistent pain of an aching tooth.

Rolling to one knee and facing the shadows, she caught the slightest glint of an dreamer's glassy eye before it leaped into the light, its teeth bared and its claws outstretched. Surprised, she threw herself back, slipping and landing awkwardly on her elbows. Vaasurri tumbled out of its path, drawing his bone sword as the beast landed and loosed a skull-splitting roar. Brindani was thrown backward by the powerful sound, its waves rippling through the air. He crashed a hair's breadth from the smoldering campfire.

Ghaelya managed to hold her blade up, scrambling to collect her legs beneath her as the dreamer turned with a feral snarl. Meeting its dead gaze, her eyes lingered on the teeth that would soon have her in a painful grip. Prepared to repay the coming wound with steel, she gasped as the beast turned away and charged instead at the battle-ready Vaasurri.

"It had me," she muttered as she regained her footing and steadied her sword. "Why did it turn away?"

The killoren sidestepped the dreamer's charge, though the beast's claws raked his leg, drawing jagged lines of red across his upper thigh. Accepting the wound with a grunt, he slashed downward, cutting deep into the beast's shoulder. The stench of its blood filled the grove as Ghaelya stepped in from behind, stabbing into its unprotected side. Howling in pain the dreamer whirled, tearing the sword from her hand and sending Vaasurri rolling to the side.

The beast ignored the blade in its side and leaped at Ghaelya as she fell back, pressing her down and pushing the breath from her lungs with its weight. Its glassy eyes hovered over her, and she struggled as its hot breath brought tears to her own. Straining to reach the weapon still lodged in the dreamer's side, she paused as its mind-rending growls softened to a rhythmic, sing-song quality that stole her will to fight. As she gasped for air beneath the tusklike fangs, she could not find strength to resist the soothing purr that washed over her in waves that were both nightmarish and familiar. Tiny sparks of panic were left unheeded in the back of her mind as the dreamer's claws dug into her arms.

The idea of a scream died swiftly in the back of her throat as her eyelids grew heavy. Sliding into unconsciousness, she did not realize at first what had happened when long-shafted arrows slammed hard into the dreamer's left eye and neck. A rattling gurgle escaped its gaping maw as it released her and fell to the side, thrashing on the ground as Vaasurri and Brindani descended upon it with their blades.

Ghaelya coughed and spat as she rolled to her side and regained her breath. Groaning slightly, as if she'd awoken from a long sleep, she realized where she was and pushed away from the stilled body of the beast, reaching for her missing sword. Finding her bearings again, she turned to find Uthalion standing behind them, his longbow in hand, and a light pack slung over his shoulder.

She stood quickly and angrily retrieved her sword from the dreamer's body, holding her breath to keep from gagging in her close proximity to the creature. Its dead black eyes haunted her as she fell back imagining the beast holding her down and its eerie voice singing in her mind. A strange and unwanted sense of pity filled her at the thought of its death, and she closed her eyes, shaking the thought from her head. She spat again, the smell of the beast's blood pungent and nauseating.

Before she could utter the slightest curse, howls erupted from the forest.

As if answering the roar of their fallen pack mate, the dreamers had picked up the trail and were closing in on the grove.

# CHAPTER FOUR

They'll be here soon," Uthalion muttered as he knelt to inspect the beast. He turned it over with a grunt and fingered the broken shafts of two arrows in the right side of its neck. He stood and turned to Ghaelya. "It's the same one that attacked you earlier. It likely left a blood trail all the way here."

She nodded, barely hearing his words as she stared at the dreamer's remaining eye. Her own death seemed to gleam in the glassy eye, and she wondered why she'd been spared. She cursed herself for being complacent for even a moment in the grove. The beast's strange singing stuck in her mind like a planted seed which she would have to uproot and forget, lest it grow and dominate her will despite the dreamer's death.

Brindani touched her shoulder, and she jumped, thankful that she'd sheathed her sword. He handed her the light pack she'd carried since Airspur, and she suddenly regretted her shortsighted preparedness and the meager weight of her remaining provisions.

"We'll find more food and water on the Akana," Brindani said as if reading her thoughts.

The half-elf kept his own pack close, clutching the full bundle as though it might grow legs and run away if he left it unattended.

"No time to wait until morning I'm afraid," Uthalion said and began kicking dirt over the smoldering remains of the campfire. Ghaelya looked from the human to Vaasurri curiously, but the killoren only raised an eyebrow in response.

"You're coming?" she asked in disbelief.

Uthalion didn't answer, only stamped the dirt until the smoking ashes were completely snuffed out.

"We'll be traveling through the deep Spur, in the dark," Uthalion continued, turning with a grave look in his eyes. "There will be little time to rest and no incentive to do so . . . There are worse things in the dark than those dreamers."

"What things?" Brindani asked. But the human kept moving, checking his pack as Vaasurri prepared a small lantern filled with glowing green moss. The light barely lit the grove but was bright enough to be spotted and, she assumed, followed through the dark. Uthalion approached and handed them short shafts of wood, the tightly bound rags at their ends stinging her nose with an acrid, chemical smell.

"Keep these dry no matter what," Uthalion said, drawing forth his own torch. "Be ready to stop when I stop or run when I—"

"What things?" Ghaelya interrupted, repeating Brindani's question. She respected the human's urgency, but did not like being kept in the dark. He paused a moment, long enough to match her stare.

"One thing actually, the one we heard earlier when you left the grove." He sighed and turned away as Ghaelya recalled the ground-shaking roar, the memory helping to blot out the sound of the dreamer's alien singing. She stared into the darkness as Vaasurri approached the grove's edge, his little lantern swinging in his hand. The heavy blade at her side seemed suddenly very tiny compared to the beast she'd imagined in the aftermath of that roar. Uthalion fell in step behind the killoren and turned sidelong to her, a caution in his voice that would have rooted her feet to the ground if not for the distant howls of the dreamers to the north. "We'll be descending into its territory, passing through as quick as we can, hopefully before it senses our presence. We call it the *kaia*."

They kept a steady pace in the dark. Ghaelya's eyes fixed on the faint glow of Vaasurri's lantern, afraid that if she blinked or turned away for a moment it would disappear and she would be left to fend for herself. The land sloped downward, so steeply at times that the trees were all that kept them from tumbling down into a boundless maw of shadows. The night closed in around them like a shroud, their footsteps echoing off the close trees and the canopy overhead as if the killoren led them underground instead of through a forest. Briefly, in the twinkling light of the stars, Ghaelya caught sight of the Akanapeaks to the west, before the trees obscured their slopes once again.

She fought to rein in her sense of claustrophobia, feeling buried in the vast interior of the Spur, lost and dependent on the dim light in Vaasurri's hand. Focusing on the lantern and keeping her feet moving helped keep her mind from Uthalion's mention of the kaia, but childhood memories came racing through to fill the gaps in her imagination. Once, when she and Tessaeril were young, their mother had told them tales of the legendary kaia, the Mother of Nightmares.

Shivering at the idea, Ghaelya gripped the foul-smelling torch tighter. She hoped that Tessaeril had been taken this way during the day. Her sister had always been afraid of the dark.

Her mind drew shapes upon the darkness where she expected to see things prowling or lying in wait for hapless passersby. The shapes moved and shifted, seemingly of their own accord, and she ignored them as much as she could. But they always returned: silent silhouettes dancing to some mad tune, the bogeymen of frightened children.

Uthalion slowed ahead of her, and she shook her head, watching the lantern as Vaasurri moved on, scouting the path ahead. Brindani stood close, his back to hers, watching the path behind. Catching her breath, Ghaelya leaned against a nearby tree and whispered an old rhyme.

"Little nightmare let me be; leave my name from off your tree."

"What was that?" Uthalion whispered, and she felt foolish for being heard playing at a child's game.

"Nothing, just an old story my mother used to tell us," she replied, smiling nervously at the memory and eager to purge herself of its childish nature. "She said the kaia was an old beast, from the other plane, once a mere serpent, charged by foul gods to devour the children of the genasi. But a clever child, unafraid of the serpent, had fought back, tricking the kaia into the burning light of day. Frightened, it had retreated into the deep forest to hide. But when the Blue Breath of Change came, the hungry kaia followed us. It hid in the dark and gave birth to nightmares that were sent to spy upon the genasi children.

"Those they could not frighten were left alone, safe in their beds. But those that cried out and hid beneath their blankets until dawn . . . those children had their names carved into the trees of the kaia's forest, so that it could read them and know which ones were safe to eat."

Ghaelya thought back, having never cried out when the nightmares had come to test her. But she had scolded Tessaeril many times for being scared. Ghaelya had been the brave one, fond of teasing her sister about the kaia-trees, but in reality she had only been better at hiding her fear. Though she'd grown out of the tales quickly, she never forgot the Mother of Nightmares. Watching intently for Vaasurri's return, she whispered to Uthalion again.

"Have you ever seen it?" she asked.

"Gods no, and I thank whatever gods that have pity on me for that," he answered swiftly. "But I've been chased, had a close call or two. . . ."

Vaasurri rejoined them, holding the swinging lantern close to his face. His return interrupted Ghaelya's thoughts of being pursued by the kaia. The howls of the dreamers had ceased quite some time ago, and she'd nearly forgotten the danger that had driven them into the night in the first place.

"There's a spur up ahead," the killoren reported. "We can rest there a moment and get our bearings, then we'll see if we can slip through the thick of it before morning."

The forest floor sloped up slightly as they made their careful way onward. The rock spurs were the namesake of the forest, massive uprisings of smooth stone, curled into figures like sharp claws that gouged at the sky. Rock, flowing like water, had made the strange formations, twisted from beneath the soil in the foothills of the Akanapeaks and surrounded by floating islands of trees. The spur they approached was small in comparison to the others, standing only twice as high as the tallest trees in the forest.

Climbing the base of the towering rock, Ghaelya kept an eye over her shoulder, expecting the shiny gleam of the dreamers' eyes to come bounding from the forest's edge at any moment. She sat watching the clump of shadows the trees had become, her eyes nigh useless in the deeper dark of the wild, far from the constant lights of the city. She'd taken that light for granted, confident in her ability to take on anything and anyone that threatened her even in the lower districts of Airspur. Blades shining in lamplight were little threat compared to teeth in the dark.

She resisted the urge to light her torch, hungering for light as they waited for Vaasurri in the dark. Uthalion paced behind her, staring south into the smooth blanket of velvety blackness beneath a ceiling of stars. Brindani crouched nearby, his vision only slightly better than her own.

Her readiness to move on competed with the tired ache in her legs and the weary shaking of her hands. She closed her eyes once, drifting off for a heartbeat, just long enough to hear the faint edge of the constant song in her dreams. Her eyes fluttered open, a sharp edge of guilt twisting in her stomach at the sound of the ethereal singing. It swam to her, Tessaeril's voice inexorably sliding through her thoughts as if her sister were lost underwater, far from the surface and drowning.

Brindani touched her shoulder, and she gasped, not realizing she'd held her breath.

"We're ready," he said quietly. "Are you all right?"

"I'm fine," she lied, the ache in her limbs forgotten amid the weariness of her heart. She refused to let the others see her weakness. "Let's go."

Descending from the spur, she glanced again over her shoulder, fresh guilt now joining the dreamers in their pursuit of her.

Ghaelya's eyes fluttered open. Sitting up slowly in the dark, she found herself alone in the *Jinn's Favor,* a favorite tavern in the lower districts of Airspur. Her stomach turned, and the night's drinking made her neck feel boneless, her head unimaginably heavy. A faint singing floated through the air. She pushed herself away from the bar and stumbled through the empty common room to the door. She leaned on the jamb and peered out into the dimly lit streets.

A group of hooded monks passed by, humming and chanting their strange songs. She shook her head in disgust, immediately regretting the movement, then fixed a glaring eye upon the backs of the monks as they continued on their mysterious rounds. They called themselves the Choir, and were servants of some unknown goddess— she'd heard them reference 'the Lady' on occasion during the sermons they'd read in the squares and streets.. She cared little what they did or who they worshipped, but their singing bored into her skull like a knife.

Their presence disturbed the powers high above in lofty towers however, and for that she'd raised at least one glass to the monks' health, even though she tired of the haunting songs and wished they would move on. If not for the peace of fewer headaches, then to loose the Choir's powerful hold over her sister.

Not yet fully trusting her balance, Ghaelya fell to her knees in the alley and crawled toward the glow of the street lamps. Ascending the various layers and levels of the city, she regained—unfortunately—a measure of her sobriety back and found no friend or acquaintance that might allow her an uncomfortable stretch of floor until morning.

Turned out on the street by every so-called friend she had, Ghaelya made her slow way, leaning on walls and high railings, to her family's home. Their small tower in the middle-airs of the city was modest compared to the suspended mansions and estates high above, but their family's status was cemented due to her mother's distant relation to the Steward of Fire. Their coat-of-arms bore the mark of a candle's flame for all to see, on every wall, door, and window.

Ghaelya had relished the look on her mother's face when she'd turned to the guiding element of water to shape her destiny. Though she'd been born into the spirit of fire—she occasionally felt the heat of flames burning in her blood—she resisted the urge to manifest the "family flames" as she called them, leaving that duty to the more complacent Tessaeril. An annoyance to her family, Ghaelya had never been forced into a fine dress or made to attend the boring gatherings of the wealthy and delusional.

Placing her hand on the flat metal panel above the door-handle, tiny runes flared blue in recognition, and the lock clicked open. Falling inside, she slammed the door with a wince and leaned against the wall, waiting for the yelling to start. It never came, and she raised an azure eyebrow in surprise. A slow intake of breath made her peer blurrily to the end of the hall where her sister stood with arms crossed.

"Almost made it," she said under her breath.

Shifting her weight forward, Ghaelya made a clumsy salute with her left hand, a mockery of the city watch.

"No trouble here, my lady," she said, smiling as she wobbled on rubbery legs.

"Drunk again are we?" Tessaeril said, and though her sister stood still, Ghaelya imagined a single foot tapping disapprovingly and stifled a drunken laugh. A flicker of flames danced in Tessaeril's eyes, but Ghaelya was accustomed to her glare of disapproval.

"It's been a long night," Ghaelya said, planting her hands on her hips with a too-sudden motion.. "I'd have to remember when I wasn't drunk before to be drunk *again.*"

Her gestures shook loose one of the pouches she wore, spilling its contents. Coins clattered to the floor. Tessaeril knelt and picked up several coins bearing stamps of different cities and nations. Ghaelya rolled her eyes, cursing herself for not securing her purse more tightly.

"Stealing as well," Tessaeril said. "For fun? Or are you trying to get arrested just to mortify mother?"

"Come now, Tess," Ghaelya began and pushed past her sister. She flopped down in an overstuffed chair of the greeting room. "If I stood still in a boring room and spoke not a single word, I could mortify mother."

Tessaeril dropped the coins and stood over Ghaelya. She pulled a blanket over her drunken sister's shoulders and knelt down to catch her half-lidded gaze. Ghaelya stared back into eyes that mirrored her own; the face, framed by tongues of dancing flame, was her twin, though the person behind the stare was a far away day to her deep night.

At one time they'd shared everything; often it seemed even their thoughts and dreams were mirrored in one another.

"I worry about you," Tessaeril said. "I worry that some night you won't come home, and I'll be left here alone."

"Well, I worry every night that I'll end up back home and become stuck here," Ghaelya replied more angrily than she'd intended. She noticed the thin chain of blue silver around Tessaeril's neck, a present Ghaelya had bought from a Branestrian merchant. But dangling from the end was a small metal seashell, the symbol of the Choir. Ghaelya reached out, tapping the shell clumsily. "And if you had any sense at all you'd worry the same thing. By the gods Tess! Leave me be or sing me to sleep! No, wait, don't sing . . . Please don't sing. . . ."

Her vision faded. The last things she saw were her sister's eyes, filling with tears and turning away. As darkness claimed her, Ghaelya weakly promised that she'd apologize in the morning—a promise broken before the sun rose.

❖ ❖ ❖ ❖ ❖

*7 Mirtul, the Year of the Ageless One (1479 DR)*
*The Spur Forest, South of Airspur, Akanûl*

Ghaelya cursed as they pressed into the thicker trees, feeling like an ogre among her more sure-footed companions. Thorns gripped her leather armor; bushes snapped loudly as she pulled free. Her footfalls were so loud, the whole valley might have heard them. Several times, lit by the glow of Vaasurri's lantern, Uthalion cast an annoyed glance her way. Though he said nothing out loud, he truly didn't have to.

She breathed a sigh of relief when they crossed a swift stream, following its current. The cool water flowed soundlessly around her calves, carrying her along as though she were a part of its course. Soon back in the forest, with long vines brushing her face and spiderwebs glowing in Vaasurri's light, she shivered and watched expectantly for the Spur to end. Trees shivered in a sudden breeze, bringing the forest to brief life. Stars glinted through the leafy canopy and danced in a multitude of sparkling reflections.

Uthalion stopped, holding up a cautious hand as Vaasurri turned in a slow circle and lowered his lantern to the ground. Brindani joined them, kneeling around the edge of a circle of freshly churned soil. Roots jutted from the edges, saplings had been torn from the ground, and pale worms squirmed through the soft earth. The look on the killoren's face was not encouraging when he stood away from the sunken area.

"We need to move faster—" he began, then his emerald gaze shot forward, widening in alarm.

A splash echoed through the night, a deep, heavy splash as if a boulder had been dropped from the sky. Ghaelya whipped around, trying to remember just how far back the stream they had crossed was. Her hand drifted to her sword, and she felt foolish even considering the tiny weapon against whatever had caused the sound.

Something rumbled and cracked from the direction of the stream, growing deeper. Another splash thundered the water, the same vibration shaking the trees. It was followed by a heavy breathing like the bellows of a hellish forge. The ground shook again, and Uthalion stood, breaking his stunned silence.

"Run."

The struggle to tread quietly was forgotten as Ghaelya sprinted wide-eyed behind Uthalion. After several long strides, the massive breathing from the stream became a deafening growl, the sound of it raising gooseflesh on her neck and arms. Her reflexes heightened by fear, she had no trouble keeping up with Vaasurri and the pale light of his lantern. Brindani kept close behind her, and behind him came the snapping of trees and the dry scraping of rough skin over leaves and dirt. Ahead of it all came a labored breathing, filled with a whining wheeze that threatened to drive her mad. Unseen claws pulled at the earth, ripping trees from their roots as some massive bulk lurched through the forest.

She didn't dare turn to look, imagining its hot breath washing over her, her thrashing legs caught in an unbreakable grip as the thing keened in victory. Childhood stories flashed through her mind, and she cursed at the memory, knowing the Mother of Nightmares had found her and knew her name. The pale serpent of her old fears, with its long fangs and madly rolling eyes, would devour her and forget the taste in an instant as it clacked its teeth and whined for more.

Upturned dirt, thrown high by the kaia's thrashing, rained down on her from behind, and she tried to grasp at the pouch on her belt, at the flint and steel she'd carried to light the torch. Her toe caught on a root, and she fell forward, jarring her knee against the ground and rolling onto her back. The end of an exhale shuddered above her, a sickening sound of relief making her want to draw her sword, but her shaking arms froze above her.

Giant jaws creaked as they opened in the dark, blotting out the winking stars as though the gaping maw of night itself would devour her.

*Little nightmare let me be, leave my name from off your tree. Tell your mother I am brave, with many years before my grave.*

As flint and iron clicked, she flinched and a new star birthed before her eyes. More trees cracked and snapped in the distance as the thing thrashed and pulled away from the brilliance. Strong arms pulled her to her feet and drew her away from the retreating beast.

Squinting, she caught sight of pale flesh and clusters of shining eyes pulling back into the shadows. She shuddered as she turned and ran, plunging into the woods alongside Brindani. Uthalion remained in the rear, brandishing the brilliant torch. The circle of light he carried kept the monster at its barest edge, whining and wheezing to be let back in, begging wordlessly to be fed.

At each brief clearing, Ghaelya convinced herself they had cleared the Spur. Yet more trees pressed in upon them from all sides, killing hope at every turn. Uthalion's torchlight glimmered in the leaves, and Ghaelya would glance at the light, begging that glow to be sunrise. But dawn did not come. The ground still shook, and the beast lumbered in the dark, crawling along and waiting for the light to falter.

In one clear stretch of ground, she managed to grasp

the pouch at her belt, found the flint and steel wrapped in cloth within, and gripped it hard enough to hurt. She welcomed the brief pain, and was comforted by its presence. The press of trees broke again, and she skipped down a sudden drop into a wide stream. Slipping into the water, she felt its speed fill her with strength, and she chanced a look over her shoulder, just in time to see Uthalion stumble down the bank.

The torch fell from his hand, spinning lazily through the air. She held her breath and stopped. Water rushed around her ankles, and a knot of cold filled her throat, spreading into her chest. Uthalion rolled cursing to the water's edge as the torch hissed in the stream. It's loss plunged the forest into a growling darkness. A huffing breath and a single clack of teeth preceded the pounding crawl of the beast as it descended on Uthalion.

# CHAPTER FIVE

*7 Mirtul, the Year of the Ageless One*
*(1479 DR)*
*The Spur Forest,*
*South of Airspur, Akanûl*

Pain arced through Uthalion's wrist as it twisted beneath the water of the stream. Rolling his weight to the right, he splashed onto his back, already mourning the last of the guttering light behind him. It flashed once on the mass of the kaia, glittering in dozens of eyes, shining on countless teeth, before leaving him to the long horrible moments before death.

He cursed the moment he had left the grove, the impulse that had carried him away and the ghostly song that had inspired his decision. Though the kaia loomed over him, his mind still picked at the half-heard tune, unable to let it go even in the face of the beast that would devour him. It thrummed softly, a piecemeal melody that ran from him like a well-kept secret, teasing him with unspoken promises.

Dirt rolled against his boots, pushed forward by the kaia's bulk, burying his lower legs. A low gurgling growl washed warmly across his face, bringing the coppery scent of old blood and the unmistakable decay of flesh. Uthalion smelled wet fur, too, like the pelts his grandfather would lay out after a hunt. Bits and glimpses of his life came and went, as if the contents of his soul were being displaced by the descending beast.

Maryna's face—in the better times before he'd left with the Keepers for Tohrepur—came to him smiling in the long dreamlike spaces between one pounding heartbeat and the next. He cursed the man that had left her, the man he'd not seen in a mirror in many long years, the husband and father he might have been.

"I'm sorry," he whispered, willing the words to reach his wife and daughter somehow.

Quiet waves rippled against his back, lapping at his right arm as something moved with terrible swiftness to his side. Trailing a faint glimmer of water, an arm shot forward, producing an audible click and a minute spark that birthed a brilliance of light. He squinted as the scent of burning reached him, and he stared into the face of the thing Ghaelya had called the Mother of Nightmares.

A storm of roaring rage thundered from the kaia's gaping jaws, leaving his ears ringing. The stream's bank exploded into clods of mud and dirt. He felt the size of the beast more than he saw it. A humanlike arm, gangly and pale, shielded a lipless, tooth-filled snout. Long tentacles writhed and whipped as the kaia threw itself back from the hated light. Clear yellow eyes swirling in loose, fleshy sockets ringed the vague shape of its skull. It crashed back into the safety of the forest, away from the blazing torch in Ghaelya's hand until the forked end of its lashing wormlike body disappeared from the edge of the torch's burning glow.

Uthalion exhaled slowly, rising carefully to his feet with Ghaelya's assistance. Her eyes never left the gap in the trees where the kaia had fled, her face a mask of defiance though her hands shook with an unstoppable tremor.

"It's gone," he said. She blinked, her jaw unclenching for a moment as she turned, a fluid quality in the movement that slowly faded as she focused on him.

"It'll be back," she said shortly.

"No," he replied, gesturing to the eastern end of the stream where the dim glow of dawn graced the sky. "It won't."

Hesitantly, she nodded as her breathing slowed, and they turned toward Brindani and Vaasurri on the opposite bank. Before the sun even crested the horizon, they had cleared the edge of the Spur and found a suitable place to rest. Uthalion sat listening to the forest for a long time as the others fell into slumber. The howls of the dreamers left them in peace, the haunting voices of their masters never sought him out. But, like an unreachable itch, he came back to the unknown song in the cave again and again, turning his attention to the south as though he might catch it across the wide expanse of the Mere-That-Was.

Gray fog surrounded Brindani as the slow process of waking up brought him to the forefront of a half-remembered dream. He could feel the cool grass of the Akana on his cheek, but could not open his eyes, still trying to grasp the edges of consciousness that would release him from the border between dreams and reality. The familiar, quiet fog was a comfort, though it had grown thinner, billowing slightly to reveal the silhouetted images of the dream beyond. He recoiled from the figures that shambled through the mist, tried to shut out the barking orders that echoed from the ghostly little town that was usually hidden in the dream.

He found a sword in his hand, and blood covered his dusty armor.

A deep breath filled his lungs as he awoke with a start and cracked his tired eyes open in the bright light of the noonday sun.

He pressed his hands against the grass of the Akana, inhaling its refreshing earthy scent, and sat up to survey the land of the Mere-That-Was. Wide fields stretched as far as he could see, rising and falling in a tide of deep green. Long grasses flowed in the light wind, rolling like the waves that had once lapped these shores. Spiraling whorls of crystal dotted the landscape, the sculptures of a mad god, turning sunlight into blinding rainbows that dappled the fields with color. Small birds flew among the prismatic reflections, with translucent feathers and long trailing tails, almost invisible as they hunted flies and beetles.

Shivering despite the day's warmth, Brindani turned away from sight of the Akana, only half-remembering the last time he'd crossed the Mere-That-Was. He was not particularly ready to recall the other half. A soft moan drew his attention to Ghaelya, turning in her sleep, her eyes twitching beneath their lids. She seemed lost in dreams of her own. He leaned close, wondering if he might somehow hear the things she heard in her dreams, but her lids fluttered open, and her hand immediately slapped to the hilt of her sword.

He leaned back nonchalantly as she sat up, shielding her eyes from the sun and peering out across the Akana. The whirling energy lines on her skin flared until she calmed somewhat and rolled back to her side with a sigh of relief.

"Where are the others?" she asked.

"Scouting the area, I suppose," he replied, squinting east and west for Uthalion and Vaasurri, even though their trail would be hard to pick up. "They'll be back soon."

"Any sign of the dreamers?"

"No, but I heard them howling, just before I drifted off to sleep," he answered, shuddering at the memory. Like wolves howling at a rising moon, the dreamers had heralded the sunrise with their own song from deep within the Spur before falling silent. "I think we're safe from them for now, until nightfall at least."

"Not surprising," she said and stood, stretching in the sunlight. "Their eyes never close. I don't think daylight agrees with them much. What about the Choir?"

"Nothing of them either, though I'm not sure I'd know them if I saw them." Brindani looked back to the edge of the forest, wondering if they were watching from the shadows, waiting for the dark. Looking askance at her, he asked, "Why do you think they chase you?"

She looked back at the distant line of trees and shook her head, shrugging slightly.

"I killed one of them, when they took Tess," she said hesitantly. "Vengeance, perhaps?"

"Why not kill you *then?*" he asked in turn, certain that she was hiding something, that maybe she had dreamed more answers than she was willing to part with. "Why would they leave with your sister and then come back for you?"

"I don't know," she answered shortly, fixing him with a hard stare before striding away, pointing at the Spur. "Go and ask them if you wish."

Letting the matter drop, he collected his pack and held it close to his chest. As he squeezed it, water leaked out, soaking his hands and spilling onto the grass. Reaching in, he found the silkroot pouch and placed his hand on little more than a mushy clump. Squeezing his eyes shut, he let it drop and struggled to collect his racing thoughts.

"Ruined," he muttered. Tremors tried to reclaim his clenched fists.

He had stumbled crossing the wide stream last night, too slow to react when the kaia came. Worse he had dropped his torch in the water. He paused as a cold bead of sweat ran down his brow, chilling him—the first herald of the gut-wrenching pain to come. Carefully he opened his eyes, scanning the grassland and the various flowers that grew nearby.

"Useless," he whispered, seeing nothing that might help him. He closed his eyes again, the familiar ache already beginning to grow behind them. He tried to clear his mind, hoping he might hear the song again, drifting as it did from the south, soothing him with wordless promises. But it was silent, and he cursed it for hiding from him.

Catching sight of movement from the west, he squinted through the sunlight and saw Uthalion speaking with Vaasurri.

"He will get us to Tohrepur . . . He has to," he said under his breath. The first needles of pain pricked at his stomach as his hands shook and absently fidgeted with blades of grass. Ghaelya paced at the edge of the narrow field, the land dropping off steeply beyond her, and he relaxed somewhat. He nodded, knowing the song that had lured him to her outside Airspur would come again, that he would find it wherever she went, and that it would fulfill its promise. Looking back to Uthalion, he whispered, "Of all those we fought at Caidris, of all the graves we left behind . . . There is one grave left to dig . . ."

"Do you trust them?" Vaasurri asked.

Uthalion studied the waking pair that had disturbed his mostly quiet life in the Spur. The half-elf sat silently in the distance as Ghaelya paced the edge of the rise, staring out at the southern lands. Uthalion had tried to ignore the spectacle of the Akana himself, unmoved by its savage beauty.

"Not sure it matters now, but I'd be lying if I said yes,"

he answered at length. "One's got too many secrets, and the other one . . . Well, the other one is due for a reckoning."

Vaasurri tilted his head curiously.

"Which is which?" he asked.

"Take your pick," Uthalion answered and eyed the edge of the Spur, still able to feel the moment of death that had loomed over him before dawn. It had been many years since things had been so clear for him, a clarity it seemed only death was capable of summoning. He shifted the heavy waterskins he carried from one shoulder to the other and looked to the killoren. "I suppose we should help them . . . So far as they deserve our help at least."

Uthalion tasted the lie on his tongue as soon as he'd spoken it. At dawn, while the others slept, he'd stared into the sketchbook of plants and animals he'd kept up for years. He'd knelt down by new specimens he'd never seen bloom before on the Akana, and he had ignored both, his thoughts traveling deep into the shadows of the Mere-That-Was.

He'd considered leaving them all as the sun had crested the horizon, setting out for Tohrepur alone. He'd told himself it was finally time to go back and face the ruins, had convinced himself he needed to see that nothing had survived the Keepers' assault. But in the end he feared it was the memory of the song that had driven him to such an impulse.

"Then we'll need to move soon." Vaasurri's voice stirred Uthalion from his darker thoughts.

"Yes," Uthalion replied. "We should get as close as we can to the Wash before dark."

"I suspect dark will bring those hounds, the dreamers," Vaasurri said and caught Uthalion's eye. "They're after Ghaelya. I don't know why, but there's more prey in the Spur than just one genasi girl . . . Their pursuit has nothing to do with mere hunger."

Uthalion nodded slowly, eyeing the shadows of the Spur casually, but seeing far beyond the trees and the foothills of the mountains, looking instead toward Airspur and Maryna.

"I agree," he said distractedly, adding under his breath, "Beyond mere hunger."

"Perhaps we'll find out more when she's ready," Vaasurri said and headed toward the waiting pair. But Uthalion barely heard his old friend, torn between two directions: north and south.

When he considered south, he saw only the end of the journey: an unremarkable collection of ruins called Tohrepur, once a small city on the edge of vast inland waters. It had been standing six years before and would stand for many more, crumbling slowly to dust until only the memory of a city remained, not enough to disturb a soul.

As he stared north, another ruin caught his mind's eye, though that one had been constructed of love. Unlike Tohrepur, the ruins of his marriage might yet be saved, though he did not know how to repair the rifts opened between the two of them. Unlike Tohrepur, he knew Maryna would not grow old waiting for him—and he knew he couldn't go back yet, couldn't make the same mistakes twice.

Uthalion needed to see Caidris and Tohrepur, to kick the dust, to see the dead, and bury his nightmare once and for all. He turned south and truly looked upon the southern lands of the Akana.

He recalled a particular flower in the Spur that lured flies into a sticky, foul-smelling trap, drowning them in its green gullet. Such was the northern shore of the Akana, sparkling and pretty, lulling the unwary into a world touched by the throes of a dying goddess. The morning sun never shone on the waiting teeth or the hidden poison, never dulled its shine enough for one to see the razor's edge of a graceful crystal. The swift little birds never sang of the terrors beyond the north shores, their tiny beaks too full of a bounty of carrion to bother with warnings. The Akana was a perfect illusion, but, he supposed, no more than many other places in the world.

He thought of Vaasurri and recalled one of the sayings of the killoren as he stared through the shine and the glitter of the Akana.

"It is all a road to death," he whispered and strode toward the others, his mind a bit clearer, his purpose more determined. "And it is all a road to life. It is the blood, and it is the bloom."

Giant crystals rose from the tall grass, twisted and shining. Motes drifted over the grassland like storm clouds made of glass and greenery, filled with noisome birds and dragging shadows beneath them. Ghaelya had heard the crystals called Mystra's Tears, and had dreamed of them most recently, like a landmark she was to search for and that she was afraid to look upon. Afraid because if she confirmed where she stood, the dream would evolve, change, and begin to show her other places. It was not the places she feared so much as the things she could only half remember when awake.

The beast in the Spur, the teeth and the eyes, the twisted tail, and the wheezing hunger rumbling in its hot breath—that had been real, not some figment in a dream. She imagined Tessaeril being taken through the forest, running from the kaia, standing where she stood. A sudden cold dread raised the hairs on the back of her neck as she turned toward the Spur.

The grassland rose higher and higher until it met the edge of the distant forest. Its leaves seemed on fire in full sunlight, and beyond them, towering above the tree tops was the Spur itself. The central stone of the forest was farther west than her journey had taken her, its curling top hazy through the clouds that gathered around it. Dots rose and fell on the wind, birds that had taken up residence on its sides. It was an exact image from her dream, and she had little doubt that Tessaeril had stood in the same spot and looked back before moving on.

She started at the approach of Vaasurri and Uthalion, collected herself and checked her meager pack. Uthalion wordlessly handed her a waterskin as he passed and moved toward the long sloping path into the broken grassland beyond. Seeing him in the light for the first time, she couldn't say he was particularly handsome, but nor was he ugly, for a human. His face was rough and lined, his eyes piercing, confident, and strong. Curiously, despite his previous objections to helping her, he did not seem inclined to wait for anyone else, pressing on in the lead with nary a gesture or even a harsh word.

Before she could take a first step to follow, Brindani passed her as well, his head down and his cloak pulled tight around his shoulders. Neither of the men acknowledged her or each other.

"Worry not," Vaasurri said and stood at her side. "I'm sure in a few days you'll be hard pressed to shut them up for all their chatter."

She smiled briefly despite herself and fell into step beside the killoren.

"Tell me more about this Choir," he said at length as they descended. The land revealed its soaring cliffs and perilous drops, a massive field of shattered green and sparkling crystals.

"Little to tell really," she sighed. "Though I expect they are less the men they present themselves as and more . . . well, something else. They appeared in the city streets one day, only in the lower districts, with bandages around their hands and dirty robes. Their every movement, their smell, and the places they would frequent, made them seem little more than beggars. But their voices . . .

"I was sober the first time I heard them singing, and the sound chilled my soul. It was like messengers from the gods pronouncing some judgment upon all who listened." She shuddered at the memory. "After that, I avoided them at all costs, wishing they would move on as quickly as they'd arrived. But then, as they enthralled groups of those that found some kind of hope in their songs, Tessaeril began to listen as well."

"Did she go with them willingly?" he asked.

"What are you implying?" she returned sharply, but she calmed herself, seeing genuine curiosity in the killoren's eyes, "I'm sorry. No, I don't believe so. Their songs are strange, very . . . persuasive. They escaped the city with a dozen other citizens without alerting even the sharpest-eyed guard."

Vassurri nodded and seemed to consider the tale as they journeyed deeper into the Mere-That-Was. Occasionally she glanced over her shoulder, expecting at any moment to find the dreamers—or even the Choir themselves— bearing down on them, calling her name. She'd expected the killoren to press her on the subject and was relieved that he did not. She was still trying to work out for herself why the Choir would come back for her. As the day wore on, and the sun neared the western horizon, she feared the evening's dream would be stronger. She found herself both dreading and looking forward to the strange nightmare and the bewitching song.

"Perhaps I shall learn more tonight," she whispered, watching the sun slowly turn a deep orange.

"Pardon?" Vaasurri said, overhearing her.

"Nothing, just thinking out loud," she answered quickly, still not entirely comfortable with the idea of sharing her dreams with anyone else. "What about Tohrepur?" she asked. "Has Uthalion ever mentioned . . .?"

"Not much," he said as they looked to the human, still in the lead and forging a winding path through the towering crystals. "He's not usually one for speaking about that part of his past lightly or at length."

"So I gathered last night," she said, recalling his argument with Brindani. "It's something he and the half-elf have in common."

Uthalion stopped at the other end of a natural bridge of land, both sides of which dropped down into the shadows of the lower plains. He paced out an area, on the southern side of a hill, and let his pack fall to the ground. The sun had just dipped into a deep red edge on the western horizon, and the sky was beginning a slow purpling toward twilight.

"We'll rest here," he said, studying the area as Ghaelya surveyed the hill and cast yet another worried glance to the north. "Cold camp only, and we'll break before dawn . . . make as much distance as possible between us and them before hitting the Wash."

The statement reassured Ghaelya as she knelt in the grass and eased her legs, but she kept a nervous hand on her sword all the same. The dreamers had surprised her more than once with their speed, and she wasn't quite ready to trust being out in the open after dark.

"I should start a fool's fire," Vaasurri said and shouldered his pack again. "Draw them off if they get too close, and the smoke could help cover what scent we've left behind."

"Your ears will serve us better here," Uthalion said. "I'll take Brindani with me, and we'll set the fire."

Brindani paced at the edge of the site, staring west and keeping his head low. Vaasurri reluctantly nodded and rejoined Ghaelya. The human took what supplies he needed and turned to leave, though Ghaelya noticed Brindani took his pack, refusing to let it get more than an arm's length from his shoulder.

"We'll be back soon," Uthalion added. "If anything happens light the last of the flash-torches. We'll spot it easily in the dark."

With that, the two set out, quickly disappearing among the hills and the crystals. Ghaelya watched the last of the sunlight slowly drain away as she chewed absently on dried fruit and a strip of salted venison. She tasted neither, her gaze darting at every sound, and her pulse jumping at every imagined movement. Scarcely a night had passed in several days when she hadn't been running or hiding from things in the dark. And when she had managed to sleep, the dreams had left her restless and shaken.

Any rest at all, she reckoned, would come uneasily and be spent fitfully. When Vaasurri mentioned taking first watch, she pretended not to hear him, listening only for the haunting howls of the dreamers and the beguiling voices of the Choir.

# CHAPTER SIX

*7 Mirtul, the Year of the Ageless One*
*(1479 DR)*
*The Akana, North of the Wash, Akanûl*

**M**oonlight stretched dim shadows across the ground as Uthalion eyed the dark edge of the cliff on his left, its sheer drop disappearing into an endless ocean of black. Taking a deep breath, he beat back the imagery of teeth and tentacles swimming through the inky expanse of shadow, tore his eyes away from the limitless fall, and focused on the task at hand. Brindani remained in the lead, his half-elf eyes more suited to the pale light of the rising moon, though his occasional stumbling too close to the cliff made Uthalion more than a little nervous.

The half-elf maintained a strange silence, his heavy lidded gaze wandering lazily from one patch of ground to the next as they searched for bits of deadfall. His skin was pale, and a constant sheen of sweat caused his forehead to glisten, a sure sign of fever. Uthalion said nothing, allowing Brindani his show of strength, a denial of whatever sickness had overcome him. But the farther they journeyed into the dark, the more he wondered if Brindani would make it back under his own power.

Uthalion wondered at the myriad of poisons they might have come in contact with since leaving the grove. None of them matched the symptoms Brindani was displaying. Very few of the Akana's toxins left a man able to even walk, but walk the half-elf did and purposely, as if he were searching for something in the dark. Slowly, Uthalion increased the distance between them, feeling uneasy and keeping Brindani just within sight.

Low stone walls, overgrown with grass and weeds, rose from the ground on their right. They increased in number as the pair passed into a city fallen long before, victim to either the Spellplague or the war with the aboleths who had once laid siege to Airspur.

Though there were no signs of the nightmarish beasts now, Uthalion still gritted his teeth at the thought of them lying in wait, keeping his sword handy and a careful eye on the seemingly oblivious half-elf.

The remains of the town rose on buckled earth. Cresting its top, Uthalion turned north, studying the height and the slow rise of land leading up to the far distant Spur.

"Stop," he called to Brindani and laid down his bundle of wood at the top of the hill. "This place will do."

The half-elf paused, wavering unsteadily on his feet for a moment before turning back to the center of the clearing. He dropped his meager pile of deadfall along with the rest as Uthalion arranged what they'd collected into a suitable stack for burning. Brindani stood watching for a heartbeat, then turned back to his mysterious search of the ground.

"Are you really going back?" Brindani called over his

shoulder as he paced the clearing in slow circles, kneeling in places to inspect something before moving on. "Or is this just a show? Some kind of honor . . . or obligation . . ."

Uthalion sighed angrily, breaking a long stick over his knee and continuing his preparation of the fire. He ignored the half-elf and cursed the desire to speak at all to one another, preferring to journey all the way to Tohrepur and back with nothing but dead air hanging between them. The very idea calmed him, but Brindani either did not share the sentiment or did not care.

"Perhaps Ghaelya and I are just some noble excuse for you, eh?" the half-elf continued, his pacing becoming more erratic, his search slightly more frantic. "Maybe you're using us . . . And not the other way around."

"What do you care?" Uthalion replied, breaking another stick, the sound of the snap swallowed by the night. "I'm here. This is what you wanted, right?"

"What I wanted . . ." Brindani's voice came slurred and weak as he stopped his pacing, stared at the ground, and swayed slightly. "Right . . ."

"Get over it, Brin," Uthalion said as he stood and surveyed the packed pile of deadfall in the moonlight. Turning sidelong to the half-elf he added, "Or get it out of your system."

Brindani was kneeling on the ground and fumbling with his pack, his back to the human. He did not reply directly, but Uthalion heard him mutter distractedly, "Out of my system . . ."

Uthalion produced a tightly packed bundle of burn-moss and two chips of flint to start the blaze. The burn-moss ignited easily, glowing with a nimbus of flame as he placed it within the deadfall. He stood back as flickers of light illuminated the high ground of the clearing. Nodding in satisfaction, he froze as a familiar clicking growl reached his ears from the tall grasses in the northern end of the ruined town.

With his hand on his sword, Uthalion turned slowly, studying the shadows at the edge of the light. Brindani did not rise or give any indication of alarm, and Uthalion cursed the half-elf, sorely needing Brindani's eyes to help identify the threat. He cleared his throat loudly, an old signal from their time together as soldiers. There was no reaction.

Indiscernible shadows shifted through the dark, rustling through the grass. Uthalion strode slowly toward his companion, drawing his blade and staring daggers into Brindani's back as he listened for the unseen predators. The unmistakable sound of tiny claws scratching on stone seemed to surround them, punctuated by the clacking of tiny teeth and more of the little growls.

"That thing we faced in the Spur . . . the kaia," he said, still trying to get Brindani's attention away from the dirt. "It eats its own young or runs them from the forest, or so Vaasurri tells me."

The half-elf's shoulders shook, and his head nodded lazily, but he did not rise or notice the squirming bits of blackness at the edge of the fire's growing light. Tiny teeth gleamed among the tall blades of grass, little mouths emitting the clicks and growls as the beasts circled and prepared to advance on the unsuspecting Brindani.

"They start out small, he says," Uthalion said as he turned his sword in a slow circle. "But they're never pretty."

Slippery tendrils of darkness separated them from the gloom, crawling and hungrily whining for flesh. For half a breath Uthalion considered letting them have Brindani as their easy meal. Cursing, he charged at the first beast entering the light.

Ghaelya gradually eased into the hushed quiet of the Akana, lying back uneasily under a moonlit sky full of stars.

She anchored her attention upon their faint light, still not comfortable with the dark of the open land. Cursing all the expanse of the Akana within her field of vision, she knew if lack of sleep did not kill her, then the awful quiet surely would. Thin clouds drifted across the moon like veils of silk, drawing smoky shadows over the land. The grasses rippled and undulated in soft breezes, a deep green tide that stirred Ghaelya's watery soul and made her long for the flashing waves of the Sea of Fallen Stars.

Vaasurri sat on silent watch like a little tree, his coarse, grasslike brown hair whispering in the wind. He had spared her his questions since Uthalion and Brindani had left, leaving her to rest and make an attempt at sleep for which she had no desire. Restless nerves caused her arms and legs to twitch in frustration; she knew she should be on her way, racing across the wild lands to find Tessaeril. She crossed her legs, and folded her arms tight across her belly.

Though she was no stranger to falling asleep on hard ground, it had usually been her bedroom floor after a long night of drinking and not after several days of running. No howling dreamers or singing Choir came to rouse her from her rest and send her running into dark places to hide. There were no calls of the city watch or bawdy songs sung in seedy taverns, no screaming mother or disapproving father to let her know that all was normal. And above all, no Tessaeril to find her and bring her home when she'd strayed too far or had too much to drink, to wince at the sight of a new bruise or cut earned while being foolish.

Am I foolish? she thought. Am I out here for no reason other than my own guilt? A fool's errand to ease my mind?

As the sky slowly turned before her weary eyes, stars exploded into fragments amid the facets of distant crystals. Night flowers bloomed, unfurling long stems to rise above the grass. It was an alien place to her, as most places were when she ran from the things she should have done. She'd lived so long in the shadows of life, the dark places between responsibility and obligation, that she hadn't known true darkness until running away was all she had. She closed her eyes tightly, holding herself still and tried to pretend that in time sleep would come quickly and easily.

"You should get some rest," Vaasurri said, causing her to exhale a held breath and smile despite herself.

"How do you know I wasn't already asleep?" she asked. "Perhaps you woke me up."

Vaasurri shifted in the moonlight, his fey eyes studying her closely as he leaned forward.

"Most people don't act tough when they're really asleep," he answered. "Also, your breathing is too fast, your pulse too strong, and unless you intend to engage your dreams in mortal combat, that grip on your sword was a giveaway as well."

She released the tension in her hand in surprise, unaware she had been prepared to draw the blade. Sighing, she relaxed somewhat and shook her head.

"I used to have no problem at all falling asleep. No matter what trouble I'd get myself into, I knew it would all go away by the next day or the day after that," she said, picturing her soft bed at home with a twinge of guilt. "Out here though . . ."

"We don't call it trouble," Vaasurri replied, sitting up and returning to his watch. "Trouble is temporary. This is survival, and it is constant, one moment to the next, from rest to hunting to being hunted . . . The blood and the bloom."

She turned to him at the last, wondering where she'd heard the familiar expression before and fearing the answer. Though it slipped away from her wakeful mind, she somehow knew her answer would be forthcoming if sleep did indeed find her. She rose on one elbow to face the killoren.

"How did you meet Uthalion?" she asked.

"Actually, he saved my life." He turned and smiled. "By trying to kill me," he added.

"Ah, that's reassuring," she said, eager to hear the rest of the story. But the sound of distant howls, weak and echoing through the broken land, reached her ears like the first rumbles of thunder in a coming storm. Vaasurri turned to face the sound as Ghaelya swiftly rose to a crouch, her sword drawn.

"But that," she said, "is not."

Two of the infant kaia charged into the firelight, squealing and snapping their jaws, their whiplike tails propelling them forward behind clawed little arms. Uthalion's blade intercepted the first, splashing its ochre blood into the grass and splitting its wriggling body in two. Others, smaller than their dead sibling, pounced on the twitching body and dragged it back into the dark, growling and fighting over its flesh. The second kaia made straight for the kneeling half-elf even as more of the beasts crawled from their hiding places to surround the pair.

Wide jaws revealed gleaming teeth dripping with spittle as Brindani finally looked up and saw the beast advancing on him. Uthalion could not see the surprise in the half-elf's eyes, but dearly wished he could have witnessed that one brief moment of clarity. He hurled his dagger, sending it end over end to sink into the little kaia's body. It squealed, a keening that was a blessing compared to the thunderous voice of the adult beast.

The creature flopped away, bleeding yellow fluid from around the knife embedded in its stumpy neck. Its siblings saw their opportunity and charged in at the half-elf who'd managed to rise on one knee and draw his sword. Uthalion rushed in, cursing the bleary look in Brindani's eyes and split the tail of one kaia before skewering another, throwing it from the end of his blade to smash upon the stone wall.

Backing closer to the firelight, Uthalion tried to form an estimate of how many kaia had surrounded them and found himself losing count by the heartbeat. Brindani had collected himself and sidestepped the charge of another beast, cleaving its skull and kicking his blade free as he nimbly joined the human. Uthalion could only stare in surprise at the half-elf's sudden recovery.

"Why didn't you warn me?" Brindani asked, lucid and seemingly fine as he placed his back to Uthalion's so they could view all points of attack. "I barely had time to draw my sword."

"Of course! Why didn't I think of that?" Uthalion answered dryly, stabbing another kaia and shoving its little body back to the others. He added, "I thought you were worm-food for a moment there."

Brindani laughed as he slashed at the beasts. The sound of his unexpected mirth was almost frightening, bordering on madness, and Uthalion did not like the idea of Brindani's sword swinging so nearby.

"No, Uthalion," the half-elf said at length. "All things in their own good time."

The other kaia, frenzied by the scent of blood, swarmed into the light, their budding eyes glistening like drops of sap. The largest of them, the size of a hunting cat, scrambled through the dirt and hurled themselves at the two warriors. A long tail whipped around Uthalion's ankle, and he cut it free, reversing the slash to widen the kaia's snapping jaws. Tiny hands, the size of a child's, grabbed feebly at his blade as he pulled it free and stabbed at the next.

Brindani defended himself skillfully, cutting precise and strong; his quick blade was well stained with the blood of the beasts. Small fangs clamped down hard on Uthalion's boot, needlelike teeth piercing the leather. It shook its jaws furiously. Snarling in pain, he stabbed down and pinned the kaia to the ground. It opened its jaws long enough for him to escape and stomp the fight out of it. He kicked the beast into the fire where it writhed and screamed as the pair fended off the last of the braver kaia. The larger ones were dragged away by the smaller, ending their hunt without having to test the flashing steel and flames.

Slowly, they lowered their blades, watching as the kaia removed their dead, one generation feeding the next. Uthalion fell back to the fire, wrinkling his nose at the smell of the tiny body in the flames. Brindani remained standing, staring intently at the grisly scene. His hands no longer shook, and a flush of color had returned to his cheeks; his eyes were clear and focused.

"Feeling better?" Uthalion asked.

"Yes," the half-elf replied casually, turning away from the feasting kaia. "Much better . . . Just needed some exercise I suppose."

Uthalion nodded and stood, pacing to the spot where Brindani might have been eaten had he come alone. Fresh dirt had been dug up, leaving dimpled little holes in the ground, but no trace as to what had captured the half-elf's attention. Turning back east Uthalion noticed the pack over Brindani's shoulder. He held it close in a tight grip, its side stained with dirty handprints.

They left the blazing circle of light in silence, careful to avoid the low stone walls where the kaia munched and fought over the flesh of their siblings in the dark. Uthalion kept Brindani in the lead, unwilling to turn his back on the secretive half-elf until he had discovered some answers. His thoughts were cut off by a series of low and distant howls drifting down from the high ground where only the tops of the Akanapeaks were visible to his human eyes.

Even from so far away, the dreamers' voices carried a small amount of power, causing his pulse to quicken and his stomach to squirm uncomfortably.

"Let's get back to the others," he said. "There should be

enough time for some rest before dawn. I'd like to be on our feet long before those things find us again."

They jogged along the edge of the southern darkness. The cliff traced a fine line between solid ground and what looked like the end of the world, Uthalion eyed Brindani's pack. A soldier's instinct set off alarms in his gut, sensing yet another threat looming on an already dangerous journey.

"Little troubles," he muttered under his breath. "They start out small, but they're never pretty."

The dreamers bounded down the hills, whining and howling to one another. Their sparse fur rustled in the breeze, and their heartbeats were synchronous beats of muffled thunder as they hunted in the tall grass. Sefir followed closely behind, his dark robes barely concealing his bandaged feet as he enjoyed the cool and crisp feel of the spring grass beneath his toes. He whispered to the dreamers as they searched, singing softly to them through teeth that ached with quickening change. He could already feel the pinpricks of new growth pushing through his gums where his old teeth had been displaced and discarded.

He felt his flesh ripple in the moonlight, responding to its glow like a tide, waves of change crashing through his limbs. His robes hid the blessed scars of the Lady's touch, the gift she gave to all of those chosen to walk among the Choir.

"She moves quickly, Favored One," he said as his companion joined him. "I fear the dawn may yet find her before we do."

An exasperated sigh rattled from beneath the deep hood and dirty white robes of the figure at his side. Even in frustration, the Favored One's voice held a power that shuddered through the very ground, a beguiling melody that could barely contain its undertones of destruction.

He was Sefir's elder, tall and strong, moving gracefully as a fish in water. Scars crisscrossed his red-stained hands; yellowed robes bore the crimson reminders of his seniority among the Choir.

"She has help now. Guides," the Favored One said as they walked in the wake of the dreaming pack. "These men, shadows of our old selves, use her toward their own ends. The girl must be rescued from their hubris."

"Yet they lead her home, to where the Lady calls her," Sefir replied. "Is this not proper?"

"No!"

The voice lanced through Sefir's body like a bolt of lightning, forcing him to his knees as the pain of pure anger coursed through his flesh. He gasped, catching his breath, and was suddenly ashamed of his foolishness, his presumption of the Lady's desire. A strong hand, cold and crusted with old blood, fell gently upon his shoulder.

"Do not make the mistake of confusing coincidence with destiny," the powerful voice said, flooding his thoughts with calm and wisdom. Sefir rose slowly, the pain subsiding and settling in those places where his body seemed ready to burst and bloom with bestowed power. He bowed his head to the Favored One, who continued, "You are young yet among our number, chosen for the sword you wear at your side."

Sefir's hand rested on the old blade, nicked and stained from battles he could no longer remember, the memories of some other life already washed away by the power of the Lady's song.

"You are to be the Lady's warrior, a blade in her hand . . . A song of war." The words filled Sefir with pride as he lifted his head to the half-hidden face of his mentor. "I bid you go and sing. Bring steel and song to those who would judge us."

Sefir turned, his back arching as he stretched, bones

popping slightly, reconfiguring to support the squirming new muscles beneath his skin. He bent forward, sniffing at the air, tasting it on his tongue, and training his ears to the howls of the dreamers. A brief pain distracted him, bringing with it a dim sense of doubt, some forgotten thought rising to the surface of his mind like a corpse thrown in a river.

"She . . . The genasi," he stammered, trying to make sense of the sudden emotion, though it was small in comparison to his desire to return home, to Tohrepur. "She will become the Prophet?"

"No," the Favored One said, turning south. "She *is* the Prophet. Her sister will awaken her."

"And the men?" Sefir asked, tapping the cool metal of the blade at his side.

"Seek them upon the edge of the lowlands, what they call the Wash," came the reply, a current of anger thundering through his mentor's voice. "Should they escape . . . Well, I shall have words with Uthalion myself."

The name meant nothing to Sefir. Most names, save for the one he'd been given at Tohrepur, seemed unimportant devices, divisive markers of loneliness. His urge to ask yet more questions surprised him, but the feeling did not last long.

The song came whispering across the Akana. Trembling at the sound, at the wordless promises of the power growing within him, his vision blurred, and he winced in pain at the moonlight. The brightness burned his eyes, the light screaming at his senses.

Averting his gaze, he turned to the Favored One, to the tight bandages wrapped over his mentor's face, obscuring the deep gouges and bloody furrows where sight had once been seated. Sefir placed his hands over his own eyes, feeling the toughness of his skin, lightly scraping a fingernail across his brow.

"There is a place at a rise among the lowlands," the Favored One said. "A small village . . . called Caidris. Find me there."

Leaving Sefir alone, he strode into the dark, barefoot and blind, but seeing far greater than most beasts of the Akana. Sefir watched after him for long moments, until the howls of the dreamers stirred his blood and drew him into their hunt.

"Yes," he replied to his mentor's back, "Lord Khault."

He loped into the descending land, following the pack through the crystals and along the steep cliffs. His voice swam through the restless waves of the melody of the Mere-That-Was, searching for the woman who would bear the Lady's song and carry it far beyond the lonely ruins he called home.

# CHAPTER SEVEN

*8 Mirtul, the Year of the Ageless One*
*(1479 DR)*
*The Akana, North of the Wash, Akanûl*

Something fell to the ground, but Uthalion did not hear it, nor did he care to glance. The woman's voice, soft and warm, like the glow of a star and sounding just as distant, trapped him in its ethereal notes of whistling wind and deep, echoing tides. The voice seemed to hang in the air like the pitch that followed the ringing of a bell, humming in each long breath he took, buzzing in his ears. It reminded him of home, of the smell of rose petals scattered on a new bed, of a wedding night so long ago it pained him to think about it.

As the song faded, he gasped, feeling a moment of sudden panic. His hands clenched into fists, as though he could grasp the fragile tune, keep it and hold it to his chest. But it left him alone in the silence of the Akana. The lack was painful and he blinked several times, realizing where he was in alarm.

Dawn had not yet blemished the eastern sky. The soft, steady breathing of Ghaelya and Brindani soothed him. Sleep not being an issue for him, he'd been on watch when the song came and stole his senses. Faintly he could hear the distant howls of the dreamers, still searching, still hunting, and still far enough away that morning would arrive before they did. He sighed and swore under his breath, turning to prepare his pack when a patch of darkness shifted and caught his eye.

Vaasurri crouched nearby, staring at him through eyes as black as the night sky. The killoren's cloak was pulled tight over his shoulders; his once-brown hair, now dark as coal, fluttered in the predawn air. His hands rested on the drawn bone-sword as he tilted his head suspiciously.

"What were you thinking about?" the fey asked, a note of accusation in his voice.

"Nothing," Uthalion answered, the lie coming quickly to his lips.

He was accustomed to the killoren's shifts in mood, and the corresponding shift in his features. Vaasurri's appearance reflected different aspects of nature like a mirror and responded to his preternatural instincts. Uthalion had seen many faces of his old friend, but the one that greeted the dawn with black eyes, like nature's wrath, caused his soul to shudder—the fey sensed great danger in the day to come.

The dark gaze looked over the sleeping forms of Brindani and Ghaelya, narrowing slightly before returning to the human. Uthalion defied the look, possessive of the secret song, while at the same time frightened by his need to keep it hidden, lest someone try to wrench it away from him. Guilt wrenched at his insides as Vaasurri nodded and prowled away into the night, likely to scout out the southwest trails to the Wash.

At his feet Uthalion found his old notebook, the pages splayed open where he had dropped the journal, a thin stick of charcoal lying beside it. He collected these in a daze, the powerful urge to flee coming over him suddenly, casting his thoughts to safer, quieter places. No power had ever haunted him as this song did, not even the sorcerous voices of the aboleth at Tohrepur or the thundering rage of the krakens swimming through the storm clouds over Caidris.

His stare fell upon the sleeping form of Ghaelya, the genasi stirring in her sleep.

Is it her? he thought. Did she bring this?

He pondered the idea for long moments, considering the possibility and what he might do if it somehow proved true. Brindani had been acting strangely as well, and had accompanied the genasi far longer than Uthalion and Vaasurri. He wondered what effects the song might have upon him, given enough time—but his thoughts soon turned to envy, coveting the song's beauty for himself . . .

"No," he whispered, taking hold of his emotions and shaking his head, fighting against the confusion of thoughts at war with one another.

Breathing deeply, he resolved to keep a cautious account of himself and a careful eye on the genasi and the half-elf. He made his pack ready for travel and waited patiently for the return of Vaasurri. It was a long time before he realized he hadn't yet honestly thought about turning back to the Spur. Though the late evening breeze was not overly cool, he shivered anyway.

Ghaelya had lain down, staring up at the stars, dreading sleep and the dream almost as much she looked forward to it. Her eyes had grown heavy several times, but to no effect. The stars still remained before her, wheeling slowly in their endless circles.

Uthalion stood watch nearby, his blank eyes turning slowly from north to south in the moonlight. Turning over, she stared into the tall grass on her right, a newly made campfire warming her back. She wondered for a moment why Uthalion had changed his mind about keeping a cold camp. But the fire's warmth soothed her aching muscles and made the thought of eventual slumber a bit more attainable.

The grass swayed in the evening breeze, disturbing tiny beetles that had gathered upon it. They crawled and massed together in frenzied clumps, the imperative of spring summoning them one to another. The buzz of floundering wings filled her ears, seeping in and gathering behind her tired eyes. Scrambling on the ground, some of the insects rolled onto their backs, frantic struggles weakening as the singular missions of their brief lives were performed. Competition expended the last of what energy reserves they had, and they slowly died, small and unnoticed in the deep grass until morning brought birds to find them and carry them home.

Looking past the beetles, deeper in the fire-born shadows of the grass, Ghaelya watched a glimmer appear and grow closer. Two pinpoints of dancing flame spied upon her from their hiding place as the familiar whisper of a song began to form in the buzz of dying beetles. Alarmed, she tried to sit up, but found herself paralyzed, rooted to the ground. She tried to speak, but her voice was nothing but a dry hiss as the grass shifted and parted for the hidden watcher.

Long slender fingers pushed gently past the beetles, and they scurried away from the contact, climbing higher or flying away to settle elsewhere. The hands were pale and well formed. They parted the grass as the flickering

pinpoints neared, half revealing a face in the firelight. The
scent of her sister—always a soft fragrance of lavender—
found her, and she tried to cry out, to reach for Tessaeril.
But she could only watch.

The flames in Tessaeril's eyes grew, consuming the
familiar, crimson-tinted hazel that had differentiated her
from her twin. The fire reflected in those eyes looked upon
Ghaelya as well, a burning guilt from which she could
not escape.

The pale hands pushed more grass and beetles aside,
revealing the image of a small farmhouse, an illusion formed
of twigs and dead grass, dirt and errant bugs. She could
see inside the tiny windows, past the outstretched wing of
a dying beetle, and saw movement, shadows on the walls in
tiny candlelight. A half-ruined windmill stood nearby, torn
fabric glistening as a patchwork of beetle wings stretched
on sharp little legs.

The hands swiftly withdrew, and the farmhouse fell
apart, dissolving back into the components that had constructed it. The whisper of the song faded, but the face
of her sister pushed forward. The burning eyes turned a
deep, velvety red. Little petals pushed from between the
lids, slowly at first, but then bloomed from her sockets into
blood red flowers. They opened wide as if to embrace the
night sky, their petals pulsing like muscle tissue. Ghaelya stared into their depths, horror drawing her in to the
squirming centers where miniature figures writhed in
thick red nectar—a bloom and its blood.

Tessaeril's mouth opened, and the song came screaming
forth. The wind of it blew across Ghaelya's face, and the
sound of it sent shockwaves through her body. A beautiful
terror sank in her heart, sublime and enveloping, warming her soul in the wailing terror of her sister's dreaming
song. As tears sprang to her eyes and Tessaeril's bloomed
yet more of the flowers on long roping vines, she felt the

ground give way beneath her and heard her own scream as it swallowed her.

Ghaelya awoke, slapping her hands on the ground and digging her fingers in the dirt for purchase.

The song was gone. The stars still turned overhead, and the grass showed no sign of being disturbed, though she could still smell the lavender scent of her sister. The campfire of the dream was gone, and she shivered as the sensation of the false warmth faded from her back. Sitting up and rubbing the smooth skin of her scalp, she fought to contain all that she'd seen, memorizing it before it could escape.

Quickly, she looked to Uthalion, who watched her in the moonlight, his eyes unreadable in the dark.

"Did you hear it?" she asked, finding her voice.

He stared at her for what seemed an eternity, as if he held an answer she was afraid to hear or one that perhaps he was afraid to say out loud for fear of believing it himself. But at length he blinked and turned back to his watch before answering.

"No. Haven't heard a thing," he said, then shouldered his pack. "Wake Brindani as well. We'll be on the move again soon."

Lowering her head into her hands, she sighed in frustration and relief. Though she hoped for validation of what she feared was some kind of madness, she was somehow happy that the truth of it was still her own, a secret thing that she didn't yet have to share with anyone. She turned to Brindani and found a lazy spring-beetle crawling across his leg, its little wings fluttering as it attempted to fly, as though it no longer had the strength.

Picking it up, she cradled it in her hand, committing more of the dream to memory before releasing the insect in the grass. Far away howls interrupted her thoughts, and she shook Brindani, rousing him from sleep before readying herself for the day to come. The image of an old farmhouse was foremost in her mind.

Dawn did little to banish Ghaelya's sense that she was still asleep, lying on the ground, dreaming of Tessaeril. Behind every white cloud and patch of blue sky, she imagined a night full of stars, still wheeling toward sunrise as her sister sang to her from the tall grass.

By mid morning they had reached the steep edge of the Wash, and by noon the broken lowland was all she could see to the south, a stilled ocean of ridges and valleys. Where water had once flowed across the Mere-That-Was, now the waves were stone and rock, a tide of browns and greens moving so slowly that only mountains might still see them crash upon a shore. Bright flowers topped the frozen waves in light blues and whites, their scent heavy on the wind.

The land was cracked and shattered into a labyrinth of forested valleys and towering spires. Its only water fell from large forest-motes. The forked streams gathered into rivers, flowing west into the Lesser Mere—all that remained of the vast inland sea.

Spiked formations of stone stood like mockeries of the towns and villages that had once dotted the shores of the mere. Ghaelya's gaze sought the heart of every shadow among the valleys and the high grasslands between, and she listened for the call of birds, but found none. The silence of such a vibrant place was deafening and unreal, further keeping her mind in the state of dreaming wakefulness which kept her stride slow and uneven.

She fell back from the others though they didn't seem to notice or care, still forging the path onward to the southwest. Uthalion kept the lead with the much-changed

Vaasurri at his side. There was a predatory look in his deep black eyes where once she had seen curiosity and understanding, but at least he was on their side. The human remained a mystery to her, personable one moment and cold the next, though it seemed he was getting colder as time passed.

Brindani, once constantly at her side, had grown distant since Uthalion had joined them, spending more time alone, lost in his own inscrutable thoughts. Ghaelya was curious about what had passed between him and the human and the secret they shared about Tohrepur, but she had not broached the subject with either of them just yet. She had hoped once they were closer to the place, one or the other might speak up, unburden himself of their past together. But the more she observed their silence, the more she suspected their secret would be tightly kept.

Her steps slowed as a deep droning buzz echoed through the shadowed valleys on her right. When the sound came again, starting and stopping quickly, a chill ran down her spine, bringing to mind the spring-beetles from her dream. She imagined them swarming over the rocks, building little houses with the empty shells of their dead among long ropes of pulsing red flowers.

When she finally caught up to the others it seemed the day had passed her by in a blur lengthening shadows and half-heard, furtive noises, leaving her to find yet another evening encroaching on the precious light. The winding path of the cliffs lay at her back and before her descended a long slope that led into what Uthalion called the wash. The sky was darkening, fading from red to purple in the west and casting the ravine below into rusty shadow. In the east, a second sunset seemed to mirror the true one, flashing red and splitting the sky into two identical halves.

"Long twilight," Vaasurri muttered, turning his dark

gaze east and west. "The Glass Mesa in the east reflecting day's end. A bad omen."

Ghaelya had heard tales of the Mesa, a massive plateau of translucent quartz left over from the days of Blue Fire. Though no one knew from where or why it had appeared on the Akana, it was a forbidden place, and those who dared approach it faced execution in Airspur.

"I don't think signs or omens are needed to doom this little journey," Uthalion replied and gestured to the end of the slope. "We can use the extra light though, make some headway across the Wash before—"

"We should cross at dawn," Vaasurri interrupted, his black eyes flashing in the twin sunsets with little red flames that sparked Ghaelya's memory—so much like the fire in Tessaeril's eyes.

"There's no need," Uthalion replied. "The Wash isn't very wide at this point, we just—"

"Listen to me, Uthalion," Vaasurri said, his voice deeper, insistent, and soon drowned out by a thunderous wave of buzzing from the south that silenced all argument. Ghaelya wandered closer to the slope's edge and stared into the shadows at the edge of the ravine below with ominous realization. The buzzing faded, and Vaasurri continued, "We should—"

"Cross at dawn. Fine," Uthalion said quickly, though an edge of anger had crept into his voice. "But we'll need shelter. The dreamers will catch up, likely find us out in the open this time, even if we set a fool's fire."

"It's settled then," Ghaelya said, surprising them both. She strode past them down the slope, the seemingly shapeless shadow at the edge of the ravine coming into focus as she neared. Each step felt like a forced march as the shape of a dilapidated old farmhouse came into view, a hollowed out and overgrown windmill, almost reclaimed by the tenacious grassland, standing at its side. She tried to hide her shaking hands as she stared down the dark, eyelike windows of the upper floor and spoke over her shoulder, "We'll rest here."

"Careful," Uthalion said and drew his sword. "We don't know what might be holed up in there."

Vaasurri prowled closer, sniffing the air and crouching in the grass, his bone-sword half drawn from its sheath. Brindani simply stared, his dark-ringed eyes blearily taking in the house and mill as Ghaelya tentatively took the first step on the creaking porch.

"Nobody's home," she said, not quite knowing how she knew, but trusting to the dream to prove her right. A single spring-beetle beat its wings mercilessly on the front windowsill, righting itself and rolling on its back over and over again as she turned to Uthalion. "Not yet," she added.

She climbed the stairs to the porch and looked into the deep shadows of the house. The front door had been torn from its hinges long ago. Motes of dust swirled in the crimson rays of sunset that illuminated the jagged edges of broken furniture and patches of dirty walls. She set her jaw and lifted her chin almost challengingly, daring the madness of the dream to be real, until a faint scent of wildflowers drew her gaze to a split floorboard, where tall spiky blooms of lavender had broken through.

She crossed the porch with a whispered curse and entered the farmhouse, letting shadows and beetles and sweet lavender take her into the unfolding vision of her dream.

Brindani let night fall upon him like a thin shroud, dark and cold. Only then could he hide the trembling anxiety that crawled beneath his skin. He sat on the floor of the farmhouse's common room and waited for a quiet moment alone, staring out the window as the green grasses dulled to rusty reds and deep purples. Shiny brown beetles crawled over the walls and buzzed through the open door, bouncing in lazy arcs against the ceiling, looking for a way out.

Uthalion had paced the house up and down cautiously, searching for any sign of habitation, but found nothing save insects and the occasional spider. Ghaelya had walked the house as well, but more slowly, her long footsteps measuring the creaking floorboards as though she were touring a gallery of fine art and not the crumbling remains of someone's home. Neither of them had paid much attention to the half-elf, leaving him to sit and stare in silence. But the other one, the fey, had kept close watch upon him since sundown.

The killoren was barely more than a crouched lump, wrapped in his cloak outside the house, refusing to come inside. But the black eyes, ever watchful, never strayed far from the window where the half-elf sat. Brindani avoided the ebony eyes and the humorless, tigerlike grin of Vaasurri, fearing that the fey hunter might somehow prowl into his mind and track down the secrets hidden in that dark, cloudy realm. Brindani scratched his arms absently, comforted by the sensation of flesh growing numb as his stomach slowly tightened into a tight knot of needling pain.

"Can't sleep?" Uthalion said as he strode into the room. His heavy footsteps on the old wood startled the half-elf. "You should get some rest while you can. You're not looking as well as you did last night."

The human spoke casually enough, but Brindani detected the barest edge of accusation in Uthalion's voice, and felt the passive air of suspicion that surrounded his old friend leaning close to the open door. Brindani cursed quietly, feeling two sets of eyes upon him, and thought frantically as to how he could escape their scrutiny. Laying his head back against the wall, he managed a brief grin, and made himself appear as comfortably casual as possible. The pins of pain in his stomach complained as his back straightened, but the ache subsided when he was still again.

"I'm usually not an easy sleeper," he said at length, sighing. "And out here . . ."

Uthalion nodded as if in agreement, but his stare was out the window and lost somewhere else far beyond the Akana. Brindani pulled his pack close and raised his right knee nonchalantly, prepared to make good his escape to a more secluded spot when the time was right. The human seemed not to notice the motion at all.

"It's like she knew this house was here, just waiting for us," Uthalion mused, his eyes narrowing as he turned to the farmhouse's interior. He watched the ceiling and the walls as though they might come to life.

"Maybe she did know," Brindani replied. "But, at this point, does that really matter?"

"Actually, I think it matters more now, the further we get into this," Uthalion said, returning his endless stare to the empty view out the window. "The further it pulls us in . . . " he added in a hushed tone.

Us? Brindani thought, a flash of covetous rage briefly tightening his hands into fists, but he let it go as quickly as it had come. He'd not heard the song the last two nights, not since Uthalion had decided to guide them across the Akana. Though he feared the missing song had been his own fault, Uthalion's words left him wondering.

"She's dead, I imagine . . . Ghaelya's sister," Uthalion continued, his stone cold face split by moonlight and shadow.

"I don't recall you having the best imagination," Brindani replied, easing himself up into a standing position against the wall, still measuring his actions carefully and attempting to seem casual. "But I do remember you as being more of an optimist."

"Well, live and learn," Uthalion shrugged, grinning slightly. "The more you hope, the harder the fall. Better to just keep expectations low."

"You don't think we'll find Tessaeril," Brindani said, more to himself than Uthalion. He was unsure of how the idea sat with him after so many nights traveling with Ghaelya, with little to go on but her mysterious dreams.

"On the contrary, I'm certain we will find her," the human replied. "And I'm sure we'll do our best to deal with her remains respectfully, and then we'll . . . be on our way."

Uthalion's pause caught Brindani's attention. He sounded unsure, as if the human hadn't yet thought of much beyond finding Tohrepur. The half-elf edged closer to the door, his breath coming quick as he ignored the growing pain in his abdomen. Pale moonlight lit the cracked boards beneath his boots as he tasted the night air and let it cool the fine beads of sweat on his brow.

"It's a long way to walk just for a funeral isn't it?"

Ghaelya's voice startled them both, but Uthalion did not turn to look at the genasi standing in the hallway. The energy lines of her skin flared in the dim light, and her arms were crossed. Brindani had known her long enough to judge the slow boil of anger that steamed in her blue-green eyes. Uthalion merely heaved a deep breath and grinned a bitter smile as Brindani quietly excused himself and stepped outside.

His darting eyes could not find the stealthy Vaasurri, and he breathed a sigh of relief, swiftly hopping down off the edge of the porch. Waist-high grass and weeds surrounded him as he studied the weathered and overgrown exterior of the old stone windmill. Despite his pain, he crossed the distance to the darkened mill as silent as a ghost, leaning on the stone and listening for any sign of life within. At the sound of raised voices from inside the farmhouse he ducked inside the narrow tower, pushing through cobwebs and thick ivy, searching for enough dark to shelter his secrets.

# CHAPTER EIGHT

*8 Mirtul, the Year of the Ageless One*
*(1479 DR)*
*The Akana, Edge of the Wash, Akanûl*

M y sister is alive," Ghaelya said.

Uthalion watched Brindani walk across the old porch and noted the swift shadow of Vaasurri following the half-elf, before responding. He casually ran a thumb over the hilt of his long sword, not sure of what to expect from Ghaelya or the half-elf, but prepared for anything.

"I don't know that," he replied coolly. "And more importantly, I don't believe *you* know that."

He heard her sharp intake of breath, felt her eyes pierce his back from across the room, and sensed a strange familiarity in the experience. Though there was dust on the windowsill, and the curtains had rotted away, he half expected to blink and find the green flower print curtains he remembered from his old life, the sill clean and smooth beneath his hands as Maryna's voice sang to him from somewhere else in the house . . . He blinked, and the farmhouse remained as it was, the genasi approaching him from behind.

"I know it," Ghaelya said, her voice rising as she strode into the room. "I've always known it, ever since—"

"How could you possibly?"

"I've seen her!" she yelled.

"It's not enough!" he answered in kind, turning to face her and shaking his head in disbelief. "Dreams? This is what you follow, Hells, what you ask *us* to follow to Tohrepur?"

Even as he posed the question he felt some small part of himself want it to be true. Though he had little faith in or desire for his own dreams, his nightmares, he hoped that somehow Ghaelya's dreams had some meaning or truth to them. Despite that faint hope, he was too familiar with the nature of reality to invest in her faith. And he had his own reasons to suspect the nature of her dreams. As she stood in the center of the room, glaring at him, he could almost hear the distant murmur of singing. But this time he could not determine if it was memory or something else.

"I didn't bring you here," she said through clenched teeth. "Brindani didn't bring you here, and my dreams didn't bring you here . . . So why are you here, Uthalion?"

The question slid into him like a boning knife, the kind his wife wielded so expertly on the fish he would bring home for dinner, fresh from the spring. His wife's voice asked him the question again, echoing across the years, her thin shoulders slumped as she leaned back against the dining room table in the lamplight, their daughter fast asleep in the back bedroom. Uthalion blinked, and she was gone. He turned away from the angry genasi with a scowl as fresh pain erupted from old wounds.

"Save your questions and your breath," he answered gruffly. "I have no apologies or excuses for you . . . or anyone."

His hands balled into fists, Uthalion felt stretched between anger and exhaustion. The silver ring was heavy on his hand, and he feared sleep—true sleep—was not as far away as he had hoped. He relaxed somewhat as Ghaelya fell back a step, leaned against the east wall, and let the sudden weariness settle into his spent body even as old resentments boiled to the surface of his heart.

"You know, I see someone running, it's not where they're going that makes me curious," Ghaelya said, quieter, but he still felt the edge of anger in her words. "I've got to wonder: what are they running from?"

Sighing, Uthalion looked at her over his shoulder with a sly, tired grin.

"I think perhaps, on that point, we seem to understand one another," he replied knowingly. He looked away, the answers still only half-formed in his own thoughts and muddled by memory and beguiling song, obligation and compulsion.

The chirping of crickets and the buzzing of spring-beetles filled the quiet between them, though Uthalion knew she wouldn't let things go. There was a youthful stubbornness in her that he envied; or rather, he envied the memory of feeling the same way when he'd been young, leaving his grandfather's farm in far away Tethyr.

"She is alive," Ghaelya said at length, breaking the silence between them. "In the end, I will prove that to you."

"Keep your hope alive," he said. "And I will consider that feat enough, no matter what happens."

She turned away without another word, her footsteps diminishing down the short hallway and slowing cautiously on the stairs at the back of the house. He glanced out the window looking north and wondering how much farther he would have to run before he could turn back, find his family, and try again to be the husband he'd once been, to be the parent he'd never had.

Returning his attention to the old porch and the maturing evening outside, he let the whistling breeze and the buzzing of insects soothe his darkening mood to a mere frown. Though he still did not fully trust Ghaelya's tale, he felt confident that at least she believed in it. Only one voice in their small group did not yet ring fully true.

He listened carefully for the sound of voices outside, but detected nothing of Brindani or Vaasurri in the dark. Tired as he was, he did not remove the silver ring and kept his sword loose in its sheath, trusting to the killoren's instincts, but ready to respond should trouble erupt in the middle of the night.

Ghaelya stood at the closed door for long moments, shaking and wanting to break something. She squeezed her eyes shut, taking easy, slow breaths, before sitting at the edge of the rotted bed frame against the northern wall. Over and over again she reminded herself that, despite the human's uncanny ability to anger her, she needed a guide across the Akana, to find Tessaeril—but also, that she must watch him closely.

No matter where she ran, no matter where Uthalion led her, the Choir had been quick on their heels, the dreamers' howls as predictable as a rooster's morning crow. Until Tessaeril was in sight, in her arms, and safely away from Tohrepur, Ghaelya would be vigilant and guard her trust well. She refused to imagine her sister as just a body waiting to be found.

Furious at the thought, she kicked out, splintering the leg of a bedside chair. The satisfaction of feeling something snap and fall apart calmed her, and she exhaled softly. She flexed her knuckles as she opened her eyes and scanned the sparse bedroom. Two windows, west and south, their shutters fallen away, lay open to the evening air. The scent of lavender, heady on the cool, damp air, blew in the windows and stirred her to investigate the room. She stood and approached the west, hearing crickets outside as she looked up the long hill. The insects were one of the first night sounds she could recall hearing on the Akana. Turning back to the moonlit chamber, she saw nothing of importance, no sign of why she had been brought here, why the dream—Tessaeril—had shown her this place.

She slumped down beneath the window, running her fingers across the swirling lines of energy, the constant tingle of her element, coursing through her flesh. Her thoughts were dull and muddied, useless for puzzling out answers from dust and rotting wood. Instinct told her only that rain was on the way—maybe in a day, perhaps two— and she wondered if her intuition might be stronger when the storm came.

Rolling her cloak into a pillow, she reluctantly lay upon the dusty floor and stared at the ceiling, alone in the dark for the first time in what seemed like months. Time slipped away as she tried to calm the inevitable restless urge to just get up and leave, to keep moving no matter what. Placing her hands behind her head, her elbow bumped against something that rolled away, bouncing and slowing between the uneven floorboards. Reaching out, she found what felt like an old candle, half-melted, but still bearing just enough wick to light. She sat up, took out her flint and steel, and brought the candle back to life.

Sitting in its glow, she watched shadows play along the floorboards and flicker on the ceiling, and felt her eyelids growing heavy. She looked to the south window and saw something on the wall, just beneath the sill. She crawled forward, her curiosity aroused by what appeared to be letters scrawled on the faded wood in dark rust. Bringing the candle closer, her eyes widened as a familiar script came into focus, its color suddenly less like rust and more like dried blood applied with a fingertip. She shook her head and looked away, not yet ready to read the words. Though she believed with every fiber that the message was there, that the medium truly was blood, confronting the possible source of that blood was a concept that set her hands to trembling and her blue-green eyes to boiling.

With a half-lidded gaze of dread, she looked up and read what had been written.

> *The Song calls us*
> *The Choir brings us*
> *The Lady dreams us*
> *And her blood feeds us*

Bile rose in her throat at the last line, and she pulled away, still staring at the letters unmistakably written by Tessaeril's hand. The crickets had stopped their chirping outside, and the message grew darker, more distinct and wet, until a few letters began to drip down the wall.. Her heart hammered in her chest, and her head swam as the floor pooled with red. The letters were lost in a stream of wet crimson, and in their place a crude note was left, barely more than a smear across the old wood.

*HELP ME*

She recoiled from the wall, her movement slow, as if the air had grown thick and viscous. A sound like a hundred large wings beating in unison buzzed around her. Dark shapes fluttered by the window at speed, shadowy forms swarming through a night sky and flashing with white light as she pushed herself to the bed. She attempted to stand, but the wood frame crumbled in her grasp.

A dry whimper, hollow and echoing, came to her quietly from the southwest corner. She fumbled at her belt, unable to draw her sword or look away from the flickering shadows between the windows. There, just at the edge of the candle-light, a small nude figure sat huddled and shivering. Her pale blue skin trembled with a sheen of sweat; eyes as blue-black as the deepest ocean stared at Ghaelya from beneath long tresses of wet green hair; and gracefully pointed ears emerged from between the vinelike strands.

Deep blue lips, puckered and split at their edges, parted, loosing whispers of song, like steel scraping on steel beneath ocean waves. Small bumps formed along the strange girl's skin, rising and turning a deep red before bursting open into fleshy blooms. The song exploded into a screeching chorus, and Ghaelya tore her eyes away and jumped to her feet, suddenly free of the thick pall that had held her down. She ran from the room.

Nimbly leaping down the stairs, she drew her sword and rushed into the common room to find it empty. Uthalion was nowhere to be found. The door at the top of the stairs she'd rushed down creaked open, and slow footsteps pressed noisily upon the old steps. Ghaelya ran outside, searching for Vaasurri or Brindani, but she found herself quite alone and surrounded by buzzing shadows and discordant, sing-ing voices. Raising her sword, she turned to the figure now in the common room and charged back inside.

She yelled a challenge, but coughed as her voice failed her. Lowering her blade in the darkness of the hallway, she stepped closer to the curiously familiar silhouette. Tentatively she raised her hand, placing her fingertips against the cold surface of a mirror. The screeching song and the buzzing of wings faded away as she stepped back in disbelief, dizzy as her mind struggled to comprehend. She stumbled over a loose board and tripped, falling backward and feeling the boards break beneath her weight.

In a long impossible pit of shadow, a well of blackness that caressed her skin like warm velvet, a sudden calm filled her, and she saw the dream for what it was.

She woke up.

Opening her eyes, she found herself still stretched out on the bedroom floor, her hands laced behind her head. Her fingertips were still cool from touching the mirror as she sat up, gripped her sword, and rolled to her feet only to find the strange girl in the corner gone.

There was no blood on the wall or the floor, and not even a ghost of the candle's smoke gave evidence as to whether it had ever been there. On the verge of a sigh of relief, she caught the trailing edge of a haunting howl echoing from the north.

"The Choir," she whispered breathlessly. "They're coming!"

Pushing weeds and bits of abandoned junk aside, Brindani crawled through a labyrinth of refuse into the shadows of the windmill. Spiders skittered out of his way to escape, abandoning unfinished meals in the webs pulled apart by the half-elf. Sitting in the dark, he breathed easier, leaning back against the stone as the rafters above creaked and groaned in the breeze. He sat and listened, studying the dark to assure himself of being alone before setting his pack on the ground and working at the tight knots that held it shut. His nimble fingers worked the knots faster and faster, paranoid and worried that his brief sanctuary would be ruined at any moment.

Slipping his hand into the leather satchel, he could already feel old names and places trying to slip back to the forefront of his thoughts, each accompanied by a fresh stab of pain in his abdomen. He'd been warned about the pain, had seen the bodies, doubled over and burned at pauper's funerals; but he'd never heeded the advice, just as he'd never found a seller that had turned down hard coin in favor of any moral responsibility. There would be no one to see him to a proper grave, and no one who would care when he was gone—no one he would likely recognize by that time anyway. The silkroot would see to that, would take it all away in time.

He grew frantic, throwing things from the old pack in his search for the soft bundle he kept at the bottom. He whispered a stream of profanity so coarse he could almost feel the gentler portion of his elf blood cringe. He turned the pack on its end, spilling its contents into the dirt, and dug through pouches of dried food, loops of thin rope, tinder-twigs, and empty, thick-glassed bottles. Finding nothing, he swore louder and lifted a bottle to hurl in anger, but the sound of a heavier creaking from above stopped him.

He peered through the dust and webs, squinting to see between roping vines of ivy and weeds. Frozen in place, his heart pounded as he searched for movement and pulled close a long silver dagger that had fallen beside his leg. A low shape darted through the murky shadows, sending a shower of dust falling from the rafters. Sudden pain tore through Brindani's stomach, and he leaned forward in agony, struggling to keep his neck at an upward angle. Tears sprang from his eyes at the effort, and the blurry shadows shifted again, growing closer. As the pain subsided, he brushed the wetness from his eyes, raising his head enough to see the gleam of an ebony gaze watching him from above.

Gods no, he thought, the dark was not deep enough.

"How are you feeling?" Vaasurri asked, crouching predator-like upon a low rafter. "Is there much pain? I imagine so, and more to come, surely . . ."

"Wh-what do you mean?" Brindani stammered, averting his eyes from the black stare and trying to appear casual as he gathered his belongings, stuffing them back into his satchel.

A soft bundle thumped into the dirt near his feet, the scent of it unmistakable. It caused his mouth to water, though his lips had never felt drier. He didn't want to look at it, he didn't have to; but he couldn't stop himself, couldn't hold back the needy fixed stare that the pain in his gut and the ghostly voices from his memory demanded. He faced the silkroot, no longer alone, and saw it for all that it was: guilt, shame, secret, and addiction wrapped up neatly in a small leather knot.

"I smelled it just last night," Vaasurri said, prowling down a thick support beam. His long black hair did not obscure the menacing gleam of his pitch-dark eyes. "You must have nearly used it all by the time Uthalion found you in the Spur, else I would have detected it earlier. But your pack has the odor of silkroot—faint, but it's there."

"What do you know about it?" Brindani growled angrily through his pain.

"Some," Vaasurri replied "Speeds reflexes and induces a temporary sense of euphoria, it's also known as Knight's Veil, Styxroot, Velvet, and most commonly Widow-Pin . . . A name I'm sure you are quite familiar with, correct?"

"None of your business," Brindani answered defensively, though a fresh wave of needlelike pains flowed through his abdomen. "I can manage just fine, no one needs to—"

"Oh, I am afraid it is my business," Vaasurri said ominously, the glossy blade of his curved bone-sword coming into view. "You see, out on the Akana the silkroot is also known as Wolfbloom. The stems mark any passing creature with a scent that can be tracked for miles."

"What are you saying?" Brindani asked as his hand closed over the soft bundle lovingly, easily resisting the almost non-existent urge to crush the small lumps within and hurl them into the dark.

"I'm saying"—the killoren crept closer—"that you have betrayed us all."

"Wh-what?" Brindani stammered again, clutching the silkroot to his chest. The scent alone eased his mind and teased the agony in his stomach. "N-no, I haven't—"

He stopped short, his breath quickening as the sound of eerie howls joined the whistling wind through the windmill. With a flash of the bone-blade and a puff of disturbed dust the killoren was gone, disappearing into the night outside and leaving Brindani alone to stare in horror at the leather bundle in his fist even as the familiar, needling pangs worked their way through his gut.

In the notebook laid limply across Uthalion's lap, a half-drawn bloom of lavender had been neatly sketched out in thin lines of charcoal. Tiny notations on the page detailed the region's conditions, the season and current weather, the consistency of the soil, and the sweet scent of the bloom—a smell that somehow, at some point during the drawing, had become important to him, almost familiar.

The tight handwriting scrawled away into meaningless lines near the bottom of the page, forgotten as he stared out the window, peering into the southern darkness. His eyelids felt heavy, but would not close, fluttering as the whispering trickle of song of the last few nights became a steady stream. The corners of his mouth curved into a smile as the familiar tune was made clearer, and the memory—one of his wedding day—more distinct.

Maryna's oldest niece had sung before the ceremony, an old rhyme that spoke of destiny and promise, of a warrior lost and lonely, a love taken away, and a promise of peace at the end of the road. Paralyzed by the tune, part of his mind squirmed at the memory, like the lucid moment of a dream before waking up, when the terrors of a nightmare are drawn clear and escape is but a gasping breath away.

> *Drawn sword in the morning light,*
> *A shield upon his arm;*
> *The long road into the night,*
> *And still the bride's faint call,*
> *"Come here to me.*
> *Come here to me."*

The girl's voice changed, growing deeper as the lyrics slurred and shifted, digging rhythmic claws into his waking mind, dragging him back from the edge of escape. Though he struggled not to hear, he was powerless as the rhyme overtook his senses in a soothing grip of thundering chant.

> *Sword falls to the endless tide,*
> *A shield lies on the shore.*
> *In the deep shall wait the bride,*
> *For bloom, for blood, she sings,*
> *"Bring her to me.*
> *Bring her to me."*

Uthalion blinked at the last words, flailing his arms as he pushed away from the window. He sat heaving deep breaths as the voice faded away. A damp chill passed through him, and he ran shaking hands through his hair, furious at having been caught unawares again. Calming himself, he lowered his arms and stared hard at the sorcerous silver ring on his right hand, somehow certain that he'd been betrayed by his own lack of sleep. Endlessly awake by his own design, he hesitantly gripped the ring, wondering if he might be able to trade beguiling song for recurring nightmare.

As one held breath led to another, the decision was made for him as the howling voices of the dreamers reached him, close to cresting the top of the long slope into the Wash. A hand fell on his shoulder, and his frayed nerves reacted swiftly, gripping the slender arm in a tight grip as his free hand drew a handspan of blade from its sheath.

Ghaelya looked down at him in surprise, wrenching her arm free as he recognized her and loosed his grip. He made no comment, staring at her, troubled, as the eerie lyrics of the song repeated themselves in his mind.

*Bring her to me, bring her to me . . .*

He shook his head and stood, stretching his legs as he joined her by the window and studied the edge of the tall hill, searching for movement.

"They're here," he whispered solemnly.

"Hmph," Ghaelya replied, glancing at him with a wry smile. "Keep up the good work."

He ignored her derision, though he'd earned it well enough.

"How soon do you think?" she asked quietly.

The trailing edge of the last dreamer's howl echoed once from the southern valleys as Uthalion listened. A shadow prowled silently into sight, slowly rising into the silhouette of Vaasurri, his sword in hand at the foot of the porch-steps.

"Soon enough," Uthalion answered grimly, drawing his own sword and quickly shouldering his pack. "Be ready for a fight."

"Not sure I know how to be otherwise anymore," she replied with a sigh and stepped outside.

# CHAPTER NINE

*9 Mirtul, the Year of the Ageless One*
*(1479 DR)*
*The Akana, Edge of the Wash, Akanûl*

The weight of the heavy blade was comfortable in her hand. The thought of resistance on the honed edge, skin and muscle giving way, perhaps the grating of bone on steel, was easier to contemplate, simpler than the chaos of the dream. Sleek forms, pale shadows in the moonlight, prowled down the slope slowly, cautiously, as if they were waiting for something. Uthalion's boots clomped through the farmhouse as he created a racket, throwing things against the walls, muttering to himself all the while.

"What's he doing?" Vaasurri asked as he joined her on the porch.

"Not sure," she answered as a handful of the dreamers quickened their loping strides. "Doesn't matter, not now."

."Get inside," Uthalion said from the doorway, breathing heavy and brushing dust from his hands. "We'll wait for them in the front room."

As Vaasurri nodded and stepped to the door, Ghaelya caught his arm, scanning the darkness at the side of the house curiously.

"What about Brindani?" she asked.

"He's . . . He'll be fine," Vaasurri said, avoiding her gaze. "He's involved in another fight."

"Another what?" she asked. But Vaasurri slipped into the house without another word.

Though she was worried for the half-elf, the dreamers were getting closer. She could already hear them growling in anticipation. Frowning, she followed the others and found the front room piled with furniture. Every scrap of wood or cloth Uthalion could find had been thrown against the walls. A strong scent of potent spirits hung heavy on the air like the breath of a dwarf drunkard with a story of battle to tell.

Uthalion knelt close to the window, his bow in hand and squinting into the night.

"Going to burn us to the ground, or are we opening a tavern?" she asked, anticipation for the fight to come lightening her mood somewhat.

"Something like that," he replied dryly.

"They only hunt at night," Vaasurri added, "Avoiding the day. They do not seem to like the light too much."

"That seems to be true," Ghaelya said, eyeing the kindling-to-be nervously while at the same time wishing there were a spot of the spirits left over for quick drink. She turned to face the hallway behind them. "But there's no back door here . . ."

"Eyes forward," Uthalion commanded, putting arrow to bowstring as Vaasurri crouched near the north window. "They're coming . . . And they are not alone."

⚘ ⚘ ⚘ ⚘ ⚘

Brindani stepped outside and inhaled, smelling the night air as it filled it lungs. Exhaling, he shook his arms out and stretched his neck. A feral sense of exhilaration carried him through the tall weeds, a ready bounce in his step as he drew his sword. Bounding down the slope came the first of the horrid beasts, Ghaelya's dreamers, its glassy eyes flashing, its fangs bared. With a nimble hop, Brindani was on the porch, swaggering across the steps calmly. A cruel grin played on his lips as the dreamer dug its claws deep in the dirt, leaping at him with a vicious growl.

With a twirling flourish, the half-elf slashed his blade lightning-quick across the dreamer's throat as he side-stepped the beast's deadly charge. It crashed onto the porch, thrashing and gurgling in a foul-smelling sprawl of claws and teeth scraping on the old wood. Brindani stabbed it again, piercing the barrel chest deep and stilling its frantic heartbeat.

Pulling the blade free he studied the stinking blood on the sword, feeling the tightness in his wrist and arm, the speed and power bundled in every muscle and nerve. Some diminished part of his mind was haunted by Vaasurri's words about the properties of silkroot, but the concern was fleeting and distant, nothing next to the three dreamers closing in. He turned to the shocked eyes watching him from within the farmhouse.

"Are we doing this or not?" he asked, smiling broadly even as arrows flew past his shoulder and buried themselves in one of the beasts. It tumbled down the slope, yelping and kicking up dust. Brindani laughed and slapped his sword across his chest in a soldier's salute as he faced the twisted hounds. "Excellent!" he cried.

Rough hands grabbed his shoulders and pulled him

backward, still laughing his challenge at the strange pack as he staggered into the shadows of the farmhouse. Vaasurri spun him sideways, shaking him slightly and placing a thin finger to his lips.

"We have no need for wild heroes," the killoren said, his once fearsome black eyes now lacking the terrifying luster they had held before. Porch slats creaked as heavy paws landed close to the open doorway.

"I beg to differ my green friend," Brindani replied and set his blade to receive the growling guest as Uthalion cursed and dropped his bow in favor of steel.

"Plenty of time for differences later," Vaasurri whispered and rolled to the doorway, his bone-sword slashing at the searching paws on the threshold. The dreamer whined and snapped at the fey, but caught only Ghaelya's blade across its thick skull before it retreated to crouch at the edge of the porch. It howled angrily, a call that was answered again and again from its packmates on the slope and beyond.

As Vaasurri and the others winced, covering their ears at the sound, Brindani felt little but the smallest pressure on his temples, barely enough to give him a headache. Before he could breathe easy however, a mournful wail followed the dreamers' calls. Beautiful and full of sorrow, the new voice burrowed through the fog in his mind, tearing through the veil of the silkroot like the screaming groan of twisting metal.

He fell back, shaking his head and tasting the bitter drug on his lips, feeling the burn of it in his throat as the pining voice rippled through his skull. The walls shook, and dust fell into his eyes as the muffled curses of the others overtook the trailing edge of the singer's thunderous tune.

"What in the hells was that?" Uthalion asked, his question lost as another dreamer charged through the doorway. Blades flashed before Brindani's eyes, and he blinked, struggling to take back whatever the wailing voice had stolen.

Ghaelya hacked at grasping claws through the window as teeth snapped mere inches from her hands. Uthalion fought on the floor, his blade buried in an intruding beast's side as Vaasurri took up his bow and loosed several arrows into the night. Disoriented, Brindani tried to react, to call back the strength and speed he'd reveled in just moments ago. Ghaelya swore as a claw scraped her forearm.

"No," Brindani whispered, wincing as yet another beast reached the old porch and the full extent of his unwitting crime lanced through his gut sickeningly. "I brought them here . . . I led them to us."

He fell to one knee, shaking and catching his breath even as a soothing tingle spread through his limbs, calming his trembling hands and steadying his balance. His eyes burned with unspent tears, the brief shame fading as his senses returned. He spun at the sound of heavy claws on wood, his eyes darting to the hallway. Smiling as the fog of silkroot and bloodlust returned, he rushed to the northern bedroom, pausing as the hulking form of a dreamer crouched at the end of the hall.

Glassy eyes and bared teeth greeted him with a rumbling growl and huffing breath.

"Can you smell me, dog?" he asked, prowling forward, the bitter scent of silkroot strong on his breath. "It was me that you tracked all this way. And you shall have me . . . Not her!"

He charged the dreamer, and it leaped through the air, meeting his quick steel with fang and claw.

Uthalion strained under the weight of the dreamer, shoved back a thick paw, and pulled his blade free of the limp corpse. He slashed at gleaming black eyes in the doorway, forcing the next beast back as he regained his footing, yelling furiously and planting his boots to take the next charge. Snapping bone echoed through the room, heralding the pained whine of Ghaelya's kill at the windowsill as Vaasurri sent two more arrows speeding through the other window.

Growls and curses came from the northern end of the house, the walls shaking as Brindani fought on that unexpected front. Uthalion took all of it in, thrusting his blade at the snapping jaws in the doorway and shoving the dead body at his feet into the opening with a grunt.

"We can't last here," Vaasurri said, and Uthalion nodded, the shrieking voice that had accompanied the dreamers still ringing in his skull.

"No need to," he replied, kicking the corpse with his toe. "Just had to set a proper stage."

"Well, I'd say the stage is set and ready for whatever comes next," Ghaelya said as she wrenched her blade free of a twitching dreamer. "Unless you're just having fun."

"Not in the least," Uthalion answered and turned to the back of the room. "Let's get Brindani and—"

"This can end now," a voice said, booming through the house and shaking the boards beneath their boots. Uthalion gasped and stumbled forward, turning as the words reverberated and distorted into meaningless echoes that burned in his ears. Vaasurri had squeezed his eyes shut, ducking down beneath the open window. Brindani's struggle in the northern hallway fell silent, and the dreamers outside mewled submissively as they backed away from the house, gathering at the edge of the porch.

Crouching and crawling forward, Uthalion caught the knowing look on Ghaelya's face as she turned away from the window, shaken by the thundering sound of the newcomer.

"What was that?" Uthalion whispered.

"The Choir," she answered at length. "Or one of them at least."

Uthalion peered out the window and looked beyond the gathered pairs of gleaming eyes ringed around the porch. He caught a glimpse of a tall figure in dark robes. A palpable unnatural aura surrounded the being, clinging like gossamer webs of shadow as he ambled awkwardly down the slope, his movements quicker than his appearance would suggest.

"What is it?" Uthalion muttered under his breath.

"I am but a man, like you," the voice said, oozing into his ears like molten metal. He ducked away from the window, as if he might hide from the approaching figure and the painful sound of its voice. "Unlike you," the voice continued, "I bear a blessing upon my flesh and carry purpose in my heart. Call me Sefir, and let us have an agreement between us, man to man."

"And what might that be?" Uthalion replied, looking to Vaasurri and gesturing to the back hallway as he spoke to Sefir. "For, truth be told, I can't imagine what we could possibly have in common."

Vaasurri and Ghaelya moved quietly from the room, the genasi looking back only to see Uthalion shoo her away quietly. He sheathed his sword loudly, certain that the sharp-eared Sefir would hear the gesture and hoping it might cover the sound of the others' retreat.

"She is not meant for such as you," Sefir growled, causing the dust to dance upon the floor. "Your band will be undone by the genasi, torn from each other by greed and envy, secrets and lies . . . unless you bring her to me."

The words gave Uthalion pause for thought as the musical quality of Sefir's voice spiralled madly into chaos. Each syllable seemed to fall apart and scurry into the cracks of the walls, vibrating through the floorboards. Somewhere in the voice were familiar notes of song, twisted and of a lesser quality than Uthalion recalled, but the connection was there.

*Bring her to me, bring her to me . . .*

He shook free of the memory and crawled away from the window, easily resisting the discordant charm in Sefir's voice. Scowling, he quietly stood, backing into the shadows of the hallway and taking up a small lantern he'd found in the piles of furniture in the common room.

"Well?" Sefir asked impatiently.

"I'm considering it," Uthalion answered. "Can you give me four or five days to think it over?"

A low tone, humming loudly, slowly rose into a shriek of quaking rage that shook the ground. Uthalion fell to his knees, certain that his ears would bleed at any moment as the walls shook, and dust turned his hair a venerable shade of early gray. He gripped the edge of the doorway for balance, the old wood trembling beneath his fingers and creaking as Sefir's show of anger threatened to shatter the farmhouse into splinters.

"I thought not," he grumbled, kicking out the legs of a carefully placed chair. It brought down a pile of debris, blocking the door as he turned to the back of the hallway.

He kicked and punched the old wood, mostly rot held together by rusted nails and the barest memory of what might have once been paint. Satisfied, he gestured to Ghaelya and presented the new, gaping hole in the back of the house.

"Back door," she muttered and sheathed her sword. "My mistake."

The house shook again as the dreamers joined the dreadful singing of their master, roaring and pouncing onto the porch, fighting one another for the opportunity to lead the attack. Vaasurri gripped Uthalion's arm before rushing out into the ravine behind the house.

"Don't take too long," the fey said.

"No worries," Uthalion replied. He clapped his friend on the shoulder as Vaasurri leaped into the dark, swiftly followed by a grumbling Ghaelya.

Uthalion turned back to the makeshift barrier just as Brindani appeared, crashing into the wall from the north bedroom. His leg was bloodied, but still carrying his weight. Uthalion grabbed his arm and pulled him back to the opening.

"Let's go," he said roughly, feeling time slip away with each scrape of a claw on the floor, each creaking snap of wood to the dreamers' fury. But Brindani resisted, pulling away and shaking his head.

"No," the half-elf said. "I'll stay. Ghaelya needs you more than me. I'll hold those things back for as long as I—"

Uthalion shoved Brindani aside, pushing him toward the back of the hallway.

"Already taken care of," he said and eyed the barrier as it shook and shifted, making a quick estimate of how much time it might buy them.

"You?" Brindani said in disbelief. "No, she needs you to—"

Brindani flinched as a spark of flame erupted between Uthalion's fingers, the glow of a tindertwig illuminating the hallway. He flinched again as Uthalion tossed the small lantern onto the barrier. Broken glass scattered through its gaps, and a glistening pattern of lamp oil splashed through the old wood and cloth. The hallway filled quickly with the smell of fresh smoke and oil.

"I'm no hero," he said to the surprised expression on the half-elf's face. He tossed the tindertwig as he added, "I'm not an idiot either."

Oil and old dwarven spirits burst into flames that licked at Uthalion's heels as he turned to the dark outside. The dry wood popped, and the fire caught easily. He managed half a confident grin before he was roughly tackled from the left and pinned to the wall. Fangs pierced his shoulder. Yelling in pain and shock, he punched at the bloodied dreamer with his free hand as he was dragged to the floor. Smoke stung his eyes as the dull burn of shock and pressure radiated from the bite, the beast's teeth breaking through his armor just enough to reach flesh.

Through the blur of smoke, tears, flame, and shrieking beasts, a flash of steel lanced into the vicious dreamer, digging deep and stilling the thunderous heartbeat that pressed against Uthalion's chest. The wide jaws fell slack, and the thick neck twisted away limply as Uthalion pushed free of the creature, pausing curiously as he caught sight of tiny fishlike scales glistening around the dreamer's jowls and glassy eyes.

"I thought you'd already killed it," he said, gripping his shoulder tightly to slow the bleeding.

"Me too," Brindani replied, coughing in the smoke. "Guess we're both idiots."

Uthalion merely scowled, saving what breath he had as he shoved Brindani outside and followed after. A cloud of swirling black smoke trailed them both as they tumbled and rolled down the steep ravine, the furious cries of Sefir and his twisted hounds echoing through the winding cracks of the Wash.

Ghaelya sat at the bottom of the ravine, coughing and bruised, and slapping dirt from her legs. She stared up at the growing nimbus of flames through the thick brush and small trees along the side of the ravine. She grinned at the discordant, yet musical fury of Sefir, but the pained whines of the dreamers gave her a momentary pang of pity. Something in the creatures' voices, almost childlike, touched her deeply. She shivered despite herself.

Vaasurri approached, keeping low and glancing around nervously, a hunter's gleam in his dark eyes.

"We must hide, and quickly," he said and prowled into the dark, motioning for her to follow.

She stood her ground a moment longer, sick of running and hiding. But trusting to the killoren's instincts, she fell in step behind him, dashing into the shadows beyond the moonlight and the glowing flames. He led her to a curving spiral of rock, like the abandoned shell of something from the sea, and crawled inside cautiously. She waited impatiently at the opening, still looking back to the fire above and searching for Uthalion or Brindani to appear at any moment, but finding neither.

"Where are they?" she whispered. A shower of sparks danced toward the stars as some part of the old farmhouse collapsed. Cursing, she made to follow the killoren when she heard something crashing toward her. Muffled curses seemed to answer her own as the human and the half-elf rolled and slid into view.

Coming to a sprawling stop, they coughed and swore. The edges of Brindani's cloak smoldered with sparks that he quickly beat into the dirt with a free hand. Smirking, Ghaelya ran to them, helping Brindani to his feet as Uthalion groaned and stood, bleeding from his shoulder and choking on swallowed dust.

"Well," she said. "No one will ever accuse you of being graceful."

"Fire . . ." he croaked, unable to say more as a fit of coughing overcame him, managing only a brief sign of "thumbs-up" before pressing an already bloody hand to the wound on his shoulder.

"Perhaps that will get them off our trail for a bit," she said. Brindani limped at her side as she led them to the spiraling cave where Vaasurri waited, the fey's eyes constantly on the sky.

"You do not know the half of it," the killoren said grimly as they crawled inside the smooth-walled cave. Like a seashell, the walls were smooth and almost glassy; the evening breeze passing through the spiral made an excellent imitation of a rolling tide. Ghaelya leaned her head close to the entrance curiously.

"What is the rush?" she asked "The dreamers aren't following. We should—"

"Listen," Vaasurri said, cutting her off and placing a finger to his lips.

Reluctantly, she did as he asked, intending to give the fey a moment before renewing her argument. But the faint sound of beating wings sent chills down her arms. Wide-eyed, she leaned forward, watching as trees and bushes across the ravine shivered. Tiny blue-white lights blinked through the foliage, glowing brightly and launching themselves into the air, drifting up to the roaring flames. Large, pale insects crawled from beneath the bushes as the droning of wings grew louder. Thick mandibles clacked below multi-faceted eyes. Soft wings, their span as long as Ghaelya's forearm, spread wide as the insects took flight, careening madly into the heat and smoke above.

"Bone-moths," Uthalion whispered, grunting slightly as he bandaged his injured shoulder. "They use lightning fires in the spring to lay their eggs. And given half a chance, they'd chew through your arm."

Ghaelya shivered at the thought of it, but could not turn away from the glowing swarms of white light streaking through the air.

"It's beautiful," she whispered, then tore her eyes away, leaning back into the little cavern. "Now what?" she asked.

"Dawn," Vaasurri said before anyone else could answer, shooting a swift glance at Uthalion, who muttered and shook his head. "We sit tight until dawn. There are bigger wings in the dark than just moths."

The dreamers bounded up the hill, whining low in their thick throats as they responded to their master's summons. Their sparse fur rustled in the breeze, and their heartbeats were synchronous beats of muffled thunder as they settled in the cool grass, far from the roaring flames of the farmhouse.

Sefir knelt in the grass, wheezing in pain and attempting to catch his breath. The painful light of the roaring flames was little more than a glow at his back, and he could still feel it screaming across his skin, burrowing through his skull. Bent double, he gagged, spitting up streaks of blood across the green blades of grass. His stomach heaved even as his skin itched with its continuing change. Whimpering softly, the dreamers gathered around him, warily watching as waves of agony flowed through his limbs.

Quiet, wracking sobs left him near helpless as the blessing of the Lady and the song spread through him like an infection, settling upon him in his moment of weakness to make him stronger.

"I failed you," he muttered shamefully, feeling unworthy of the gifts that had been bestowed upon him. Several dreamers growled, baring their teeth and creeping toward him like the wolves they resembled, as if sensing his weakness. Sefir quickly straightened, facing them though he was not yet brave enough to open his aching eyes. "Back!"

The command turned them away whining, a simpering mewling tone that only served to feed the impotent rage burning in his chest. Collecting himself, he stood, wavering on his feet and stretching his changing anatomy. New growths writhed on his back, constrained by his robes, and he shuddered at the acute sensation of touch they delivered. Rubbing his jaw and baring the strong needle-teeth that had pushed through, he caught a faint sound of buzzing from the south.

He smiled grimly, imagining the black wings that made the sound, far larger than the annoying moths immolating themselves in the burning farmhouse. Laying his palms upward in supplication, he spoke to the voice that filled his every waking thought, the music that lived in every part of him.

"To Caidris I shall travel then, my Lady," he said and spread his hands to the assembled pack of dreamers, "We shall greet them beyond the lowlands and embrace those that survive through the valley of black wings. It is her will."

Relief flooded through him, certain that his failure had been part of the Lady's grand design all along and pleased that he could be of service. Khault had known, had told him as much, and Sefir felt blind for not seeing the truth. Attempting to open his eyes again, he winced, his left eye still fresh with a pain that was maddening. He pressed his palm over the closed lid feeling the tight thrum of the pulse behind the darkness in his sight, the veins squirming at his touch as if reaching for release.

Sighing in understanding, even smiling, he reached up and placed a dirty fingernail against the soft flesh beneath his eye.

It gave way to his strength easily, in a ritual he had imagined ever since the first soft touch of his Lady's spirit had graced him. The pain was a price he willingly paid, eager to step closer into the fold of the Choir. Rolled clumps of tissue gathered beneath his nails as he led the dreamers southwest, tearing strips of filthy cloth from his robes and blessing each one with a light kiss before pressing them over each fresh wound.

Despite the falling moon and the long distant flames, the night became brighter than any day he'd ever known.

# CHAPTER TEN

*9 Mirtul, the Year of the Ageless One*
*(1479 DR)*
*The Akana, the Wash, Akanûl*

As the night crawled inexorably toward the faint light of sunrise, the flames above their hidden cave died to a smoldering pile of popping wood and ash. Vaasurri awoke and crawled out into the predawn air. Uthalion said nothing as the fey left to find his place among the stilled tides of rock outside. He was well used to the killoren's morning ritual, though he could never have grasped the depths of the fey's attachment to the wild places of the world.

Climbing high upon a spire of rock, Vaasurri searched the shadows of the rocky ravine, hunting for signs of movement. The pale bodies of the bone moths blanketed the northern hillside; their scattered eggs collected in snowlike drifts atop rocks and among the branches of trees. Already he could see the first of the scavengers crawling from the cracks in the rock to feast upon the annual bounty. They would gorge themselves, and still thousands of larvae would survive into the summer months.

Closing his black eyes, Vaasurri placed his hands upon the rock, listening to the distant sounds of the Akanamere stirring, and searching for his place in the coming day. All thought retreated as the wild caressed his spirit, shaped his instincts, and whispered secrets to his fey soul. His heartbeat slowed to the crawl of a mountain through time, as stilled as the tide that had once filled the Akana.

His eyes flew open, and his heartbeat sprang to a quick beat again. He searched the rock walls high above for dusky lairs, where the threat he sensed might hide from the bright day. A threat despised the season, that feasted on death and hated the hope of spring, a betrayal to all it had once held dear.

His senses sharp, Vaasurri looked upon the world with the same coal black eyes as the previous day. His spirit remained prepared to act as the cold left hand of nature's wrath. As thunder rumbled ominously in the south, the killoren could almost hear the hidden fiends above, clawing anxiously at the rock and whispering dark prayers for a day that would see no sun.

Morning had never been his element.

Brindani rubbed at his eyes encrusted with grime, opening them gingerly. Every joint in his hand felt swollen and creaked as he flexed his fingers, stretching out the exhaustion embedded in his bones. A single stab of pain doubled him over, and he clutched the tender layer of muscle over his stomach. It throbbed, though not for long, and he breathed easy as the pain faded to match the ache in the rest of his weary body.

He crawled out of the small cave, careful not to wake Uthalion or Ghaelya. Vaasurri was nowhere to be seen. He took shallow breaths and crouched out of sight of the others, troubled by the killoren's absence and dreading the blazing light of day to come. He looked up to the land that some called the Silent Tide, to the great walls of rock curving like waves to crash down upon the ravines and valleys of the Wash. A constant breeze traveled the labyrinth of stone, creating a sound not unlike the ocean. The sensation of being trapped in a twisting seashell would have been unavoidable if not for the trees and the sky overhead.

The smell of smoke and char was still heavy on the air, and his eyes inexorably drifted up to the edge of the ravine, seeing nothing of the abandoned farmhouse where he should have died—an honorable death stolen away by flame . . . and Uthalion.

"Feeling better?"

He jumped at the sound of Vaasurri's voice, and bright stars flashed before his eyes for several heartbeats as he calmed, scowling unhappily.

"Not a bit," he answered hoarsely. "And I don't expect today's march to help much."

"Better then," Vaasurri replied and crawled down from his hiding place atop the cave. He crouched several strides away and fixed the half-elf with a dark stare. "You should be dead."

"Thank Uthalion for that," Brindani said. "He pulled me from the house—"

"No," Vaasurri interrupted. "You should have died days ago, longer perhaps."

Brindani shook his head, grinning in disbelief as he pushed back against the rock wall. He closed his eyes and cursed himself for not dying, a more preferable fate to the inevitable lecture he heard in Vaasurri's voice.

"Don't sound so disappointed," he replied. "There's chance yet."

"Undoubtedly," the fey said. "But you got rid of the silk-root, didn't you? Perhaps you'll discover a cleaner death than it would have provided."

"How did you . . .?" Brindani asked in shock.

"Its smell is faded," Vaasurri responded and pulled a pouch from beneath his cloak, tossing it at Brindani's lap. "Leaves from the same plant and odorless. Chew on them as you would the root—they'll help with the pain."

Brindani stared at the pouch for long moments before picking it up in his shaking hands, ashamed for the horrors he'd unwittingly aided in following the group. Though as much as he wished to be free of his addiction, it was a weak will that he could wield against it, and he knew it would break. Just the thought of it churned his stomach anew, and the slight sensation of pins and needles in his gut caused him to gasp quietly for air.

"You won't tell the others?" he asked.

"Not her, if that is your wish," Vaasurri answered solemnly. "But Uthalion already knows."

"How?"

"He doesn't sleep," the killoren said, turning back to his perch upon the rock. "He's been listening to us all along."

Thunder rumbled ever closer from the south, punctuating the growing dread in Brindani's heart as Vaasurri drew his strangely carved bone-blade and studied the approaching clouds. Brindani stared at the weapon, blinking in disbelief and certain he'd just seen the patterns on the sword shift and squirm into new designs. Before he could look closer, the killoren nimbly leaped down to the spiraling cave mouth.

In the spaces between thunder and the growing wind, Brindani briefly caught the sound of fluttering wings echoing through the valley even as his hand absently traced the rounded edge of a small lump at the bottom of his pack. Wrapped tightly and tucked away, it called to him like an old friend—out of sight, but not out of mind.

Ghaelya awoke to rough hands shaking her shoulders, curses, and hushed whispers full of quiet alarm. Rising, she brushed Uthalion aside, glaring at him blearily in the murk of the little cave and squinting over his shoulder at the darkness outside.

"I thought we were waiting until dawn," she said.

"Change of plans," he replied, placing a finger to his lips and crawling outside.

Her heart thumped in her chest as she collected herself and followed the human. She was greeted not by the yellow light of a rising sun, but the flashing white glow of lightning across a dark sky. Vaasurri stood sentinel at the edge of the descending valley, his sword in hand, studying the silent tide of curving walls with Brindani. As she and Uthalion joined them, Vaasurri merely nodded and took off at a quick jog.

"Let's go," Uthalion whispered.

She cursed them for their mystery, but respected the need for silence and fell in step. Though tired and still waking up, she quickened her stride at the sound of small rocks rolling down the sides of the valley, bouncing off trees, and trailing lines of disturbed dust. Thunder obscured much of what she strained to hear, but occasionally she caught the sound of scratchy whispers echoing in the dark behind her and high-pitched birdlike calls that kept her moving. She drew her sword, searching wildly for any sign of approaching danger, seeing naught but the flickering shadows of trees in each flash of lightning. The smell of rain and wildflowers carried easily on the quickening breeze of the rolling storm, a soothing scent that did nothing for the growing anxiety in her white-knuckled grip on the broadsword.

Brindani ran just ahead of her, his slight limp becoming more pronounced as the morning wore on. As her own legs grew tired of running, she caught herself huffing loudly for several breaths, receiving a concerned, yet warning look from Uthalion. Biting her lip, she bit back the angry retort that slipped quickly to the tip of her tongue and breathed evenly, passing the human and sticking close to Vaasurri.

Dark shapes flitted overhead, blurs of shadow darting from one side of the valley to another, and she ducked reflexively, gooseflesh rising on the back of her neck. With her eyes up, she stumbled a few times, cursing and slowing down, unable to divide her attention in the dark lest she break an ankle. The dim disc of a late morning sun teased with enough light to make out vague shapes and shifting shadows, but little else—just enough to keep her warily watching and wondering when their pursuers would grow more bold.

"Eyes forward," the killoren said grimly. "Seeing them won't help."

"What happened to being quiet?" she asked, breathless and feeling what seemed to be the first drops of a cold rain fall on her cheek. Brushing at the moisture, she felt it stick, fibrous and icy, like a cobweb covered in frost. She pulled it away in disgust, thin filaments of shadow sticking to her fingers.

"Not much point whispering anymore," Uthalion answered from behind as Ghaelya ran headlong into a thick mass of clinging shadow.

It stretched, cold and clammy, against her skin, filling her mouth with the bitter taste of stagnant water. The fibers stuck to her teeth and muffled her curses. She pushed and thrashed against the dark wall of shadows, blindly pressing through and shivering in the effort. Droning wings hovered overhead as buzzing whispers reached her through the morass, taunting her in a haunting, harsh tongue that made her struggle all the more to escape.

Breaking through with a gasping breath, she stumbled forward into Uthalion's shoulder, and he wisely gripped her sword-arm until her sight returned. Lightning struck at the far end of the valley, tracing thin arcing spots across her sight, and she could see well enough to spot the approaching figure. Barely more than a short silhouette, it hung in the air on large black dragonfly wings and regarded her with blank white eyes.

She froze in that gaze, even as more of the things streaked overhead, swarming beneath the half-light of the growing storm front. The being emitted a wet, smacking sound as it drew back a thin arm, wielding a short spear of living shadow. Its stomach churned with a strange glistening undulation. Ghaelya's grim fascination quickly became the calm simplicity of battle as the beast hurled its weapon.

She rolled out of its path, fluidly giving herself over to the coiled tempest of water that flowed through her spirit. Rising, she slashed at a darting wing, slicing through the tip like thick parchment. She grinned as the thing shrieked and faltered. She turned, reversing the stroke through its abdomen, unleashing a dark torrent of cold, gushing shadow that drifted away like smoke. She charged others that drew too near, still running blindly south. Her companions were close, but beyond the reach of her unrelenting blade.

Dark javelins of shadow thumped into the ground around them, one cutting across her shoulder before disappearing in a puff of acrid smelling mist. The things buzzed overhead, still trailing webs of shadow that Ghaelya ignored. She cut down another as she forced her way through its chilling net, rising and falling with the tide in her heart. Pulses of energy flowed from foot to fingertip and back again as she lent her will and blade to the drowning force of her spirit.

Lightning and thunder struck the valley again, close enough to knock the breath from her lungs and set her ears to ringing. Staggering back as the fluttering creatures faltered in the wake of the thunderbolt, she caught sight of a featureless face, covered in a thick black carapace. There was an alien intelligence in its pale stare, an expression that held no reasoning; but no desire to which she might relate, only a cold nothing.

Vaasurri was right. Seeing them didn't help.

"Here!" Brindani's strident shout reached her through the ringing thunder and flashing lightning. It cut through the constant drone of wings and drew her to him.

He held onto the edge of a wide crevice in the side of the valley wall and waved his long sword high. The blade reflected the flickering white light of the stormfront. Fibrous streamers of shadow drifted into her path, muffling Brindani's shouts as she dived toward him, once again blind and trusting to her instincts. Claws scraped at her cheeks and back, and pulled at her armor as she fought to reach the dim hope of shelter. As her arm brushed against rock, hands grabbed her and pulled her deeper into the dark.

They held her sword down, and she swore at them, screaming a challenge and struggling to free herself.

"Stop it!" Brindani shouted as he shook her once more. She complied, pulling the sticky shadow from her eyes and trying to adjust her vision. A stone wall pressed against her back, smooth and cold, sending a shiver through her legs. A white flash illuminated the opalescent interior of the crevice, and brief rainbows of color swirled on the wall before the dark returned. Uthalion stood at the opening, slashing at anything that drew near, with Vaasurri close at his shoulder.

"Shaedlings," the killoren said. "Though I've never seen them in such numbers."

"No use counting them," Uthalion muttered, straining as he beat back yet another of the shrieking creatures.

Thunder rumbled through the valley again. Buzzing wings drifted away, claws scratched at rocks high above the crevice as the shaedlings continued their whispering conversations, their language unknown and their intentions only guessed at. Uthalion glanced over his shoulder, keeping his sword forward. "Out of the stew pot and into the fire," he said. "Any suggestions?"

"Bring back the sun," Brindani said, his dark attempt at humor overshadowed by the haggard tone of his voice.

"Unless the gods owe you a favor, I don't think it likely that they'll be delivering another sunny day anytime soon," Uthalion replied, brushing shadows like fine black dust from his blade that never reached the ground.

"How close are we to the southern end of the Wash?" Ghaelya asked, eager to escape the cramped crevice. A rushing sense of bloodlust still pumped through her body.

"Close enough to see it given enough light," Uthalion answered. "But far enough to make getting there a steep gamble against mounting odds."

"We should stack the odds in our favor then," Brindani muttered from the back of the crevice. His gleaming eyes fixed on Uthalion as the man nodded slowly and sheathed his sword, kneeling in the dirt.

"How?" Ghaelya asked eyeing the human. "Prayer?"

"If it makes you feel better, by all means," Uthalion replied, rummaging through his pack.

"We're splitting up," Brindani explained as he squeezed past her and Vaasurri to stand near the entrance by Uthalion. "Two of us south and two west."

"Why? So we can die in different places?" she pressed angrily, taking breath to argue more against what seemed a foolish plan. But Vaasurri laid a hand on her arm.

"It's another fool's fire," he explained calmly as Uthalion and Brindani whispered and pointed. "Only this time we may have to burn a couple of fools."

Uthalion crept across the valley floor, following close behind the surefooted half-elf. He made a show of pausing and looking around every few strides, careful not to glance up too high, lest the shaedlings think his stealthy approach was anything more than an act. Their cruel fey nature demanded the illusion, drew them along like cats inspecting an injured mouse, watching and waiting until their prey was sure of escape. Brindani would stop at each flash of lightning, rush forward in the following thunder, and hold his hand out, palm up to signal a halt as he pretended to scan the path ahead.

Uthalion hid his grin at the half-elf's exaggerated show, musing that any field captain worth his command would have had them both shot down immediately—and would have made the archers aim carefully, so as not to waste more than two arrows on such buffoons.

Despite all, it seemed that Brindani was doing well, not yet showing the more extreme signs of a silkroot addiction. But Uthalion knew it couldn't last long. He wondered when Brindani's other illusion, the one of health, would begin to crack and fall apart. Silkroot was not kind; he'd seen men try to tear out their own innards when the drug became too much for their meager purses to afford. It had seemed to him the worst kind of ignoble death for, what he considered, the least amount of reward.

Passing into the western valley, Brindani paused again, bringing Uthalion up short as he angled their path through the center of the deep brush on either side. Low trees and bushes waved in the wind, likely hiding dozens of bone-moth swarms waiting patiently for one lucky stroke of lightning to start the fires they thrived on each spring.

In one burst of lightning, Uthalion spied a spot of color just ahead, but darkness claimed the valley before he could identify what it had been. He kept a watch for it to appear again as he patted Brindani on the shoulder, signaling that they could abandon their show and appear comfortable, as if they'd slipped by the watch of the predators on their trail. They ignored the telltale scratch of claw on stone and buzzing whispers as they made their way further from the crevice where Ghaelya and Vaasurri waited.

As lightning arced across the sky again, Uthalion searched curiously for what he'd noticed earlier and caught sight of it—just a step away from Brindani's boot. Cursing, he threw his shoulder into Brindani's side, tackling the surprised half-elf to the ground in a cloud of dust. Patting Brindani's shoulder, Uthalion sat up and crouched over a small clump of yellow flowers with wide, thick petals and stout stems. He hovered just out of reach of the blooms and held the half-elf back, shaking his head and breathing a sigh of relief.

"Wyrmwind," he whispered, answering the quiet question in Brindani's eye. "This time of year, it sheds pollen at the slightest contact, a deadly poison to anything that breathes it."

Adding credence to his observation, he gestured to several thin twigs scattered around the base of the plant and the valley floor where they stood. Bleached a yellow white, the bones of dozens of animals littered the ground, an occasional skull here and there grinning in the flickering light of the storm.

"Don't disturb the trees, don't look at the shaedlings, and now," Brindani whispered back, "Don't step on the yellow flowers. Is there anything here that *can't* kill us one way or another?"

"Well," Uthalion sighed as they stood and circled around the wyrmwinds, keeping an eye out for more of the deadly plants, "If you happen to see a chilled flask of fine wine don't take any chances . . . let me deal with it first."

"Don't be a hero," Brindani muttered.

Though Uthalion tried to press farther into the valley, hoping to put as much distance between themselves and the others as possible, he could no longer deny the growing mass of shadowed forms trailing behind them. He'd glanced casually a few times, appearing not to notice the white eyes and long claws in the brief flashes of lightning, prowling closer and ready to pounce. Eyeing the edge of the long valley, he cleared his throat. Brindani caught the signal quickly and kneeled to prepare for the next step.

Uthalion knelt as well, drawing a handful of long sticks from the top of his boot and a bundle of thick, sweet smelling grass from his belt. Large wings fluttered closer, landing lightly atop the curving valley walls. Claws scrabbled nearer over the rocks, scraping at insectlike hides as the dark fey fought for position. As Uthalion quickly wove grass and sticks together, Brindani carefully strung the longbow he'd used as a walking stick and swung a quiver of arrows around from beneath his cloak.

"When this starts, if you see a chance to escape," Brindani said quietly, "Take it. Leave me."

"Now who's being a hero?" Uthalion said as he carefully bent his green wooded sticks together, overlapping them to create a roughly spherical shape.

"I'm serious."

"And I am ignoring you until we both get out of here," Uthalion replied as thunder cracked loudly overhead, causing a chorus of buzzing whispers that drew closer with each step. His fingertips tingled slightly with a burning sensation as sap and damp grass mingled in his hands. "Do you see a good spot?"

After a moment of hesitation, Brindani exhaled in frustration and scanned the area slowly, looking up to the narrowed opening at the valley's edge. He nodded and drew a single arrow. Uthalion had gathered a handful of the small bones along the valley floor, and he placed them carefully inside the crude basket-lantern of grass and sticks. He nodded back to the half-elf with a held breath.

"Ready your bow," he said.

Brindani stood, took aim, and loosed the shaft all in one fluid motion. As the arrow thunked solidly into the low hanging branch of a tree bent over the edge of the valley, Uthalion was briefly grateful for the influence of the silkroot still in Brindani's system, though he knew he'd regret the feeling in a few hours. A long, thin length of twine, soaked in water, hung from the arrow, and he swiftly tied the end to the basket as the shaedlings rose into the air, sensing the end of their game.

Uthalion drew his sword and backed away, his eyes widening at the multitude of shadowy figures rising against the stormy backdrop of the sky. Lightning crashed, and thunder growled through the valleys, shaking the ground as the wind howled and whistled through the Wash. Brindani drew another arrow and sparked his flint to the cloth-wrapped end of its shaft.

Buzzing shadows droned toward them, shrieking what sounded like a feigned dismay at finding their prey unsurprised.

"Don't look," Uthalion warned as Brindani strung the arrow and aimed.

Shaedlings dived from the sky, spears of shadow coalescing into their hands as their white eyes glinted with the thrill of the hunt's end. Brindani's arrow streaked toward the lantern, and Uthalion shielded his eyes, lowering his sword and turning as the fire met the basket and flared into a brilliant, blinding white light. Pained shrieks tore at his ears as the dark fey recoiled from the radiance, their lost spears clattering to the ground and disappearing in smoky puffs.

Uthalion smiled at the pained sound of the blinded shaedlings, and clapped Brindani on the shoulder as they made for the darkness at the valley's edge.

The lantern, a fey weapon that Vaasurri called a sugar-star, would burn for several breaths, and time was short. As Uthalion strode forward, gingerly opening his eyes, he turned toward the southern branch of valley. He stopped short for a heartbeat, his eyes widening as Brindani ran past him. His stride faltered, and he stumbled into the shadow beyond the already dying light of the blazing basket as he surveyed the horror that had lain hidden in the darkness behind them.

The floor of the north end of the valley, illuminated by the lantern, shivered and swayed. A rippling mass of yellow flowers shook ominously in the strengthening wind of the storm.

"Mystra's bones," he swore and turned to run. The first drops of a long-held rain splashed on his cheek and roughly disturbed the deadly yellow petals of the wyrmwinds.

# CHAPTER ELEVEN

*9 Mirtul, the Year of the Ageless One*
*(1479 DR)*
*The Akana, the Wash, Akanûl*

Heavy drops of rain splashed over Ghaelya's skin, each one tingling as they ran along the glowing maze of patterns across her body. They were a soothing balm to her spirit, but only fed the tempest of rage in her heart. She pulled herself over the edge of a wide island of green, and saw the jagged valleys of the Wash, the stilled and silent tide, laid out at her feet. Whiplike trees stood as sentinels to the darkness beyond the Wash, their sharp thorns twisting and swaying at the end of long tentacle branches.

Lightning rippled through the sky, spreading far to the south. It was a storm beyond any she'd ever witnessed in Airspur, dark waters drifting like an airborne ocean through the night. Water and lightning mingled, calling to the element in her spirit and summoning her to join them in the unstoppable flood of nature's wrath.

Vaasurri knelt nearby, stringing his bow as Ghaelya paced along the border of the cliff, staring daggers into the dark depths they'd crawled from in silence.

"I do not enjoy being sheltered like this," she said through clenched teeth.

"You would risk your life needlessly?" the killoren asked.

"It's what I'm best at . . . Well, according to my family at least," she replied.

"And what of your sister?" Vaasurri pressed, standing. A touch of anger in his voice gave her pause. "I was led to believe that she was the reason for this little journey. How will she fare if you are dead, I wonder?"

"I—I didn't . . ." she stammered, taken aback by the killoren's sudden anger.

"You didn't think," he said simply, though his black eyes seemed to say much more as they bored into her. "Yes, I understand lack of thought. It seems to be a common curse of late."

His eyes shifted to the skies over the Wash as he adjusted the quiver on his shoulder, nodding as dark shapes rose against the backdrop of the storm and the buzz of their dragonfly wings drew closer. A flash of brilliant light, a brief and dying sunrise, flared to life in the distance, scattering dozens of the dark fey across the valleys, their shrieks echoing through the wind and the thunder.

"Now perhaps you'll get the fight you desire," Vaasurri said, his words stabbing at her even as her bloodlust returned to a quick boil. "I would say fight for your life, but perhaps you should concentrate more on your sister's life."

"Tess," she whispered, the name escaping her lips on a held breath as the shaedlings drew near. A shaft of pure shadow, long and sharp, streaked toward her, silhouetted against the flash of yellow-white cloud lightning. She loosened her legs, letting the fluid motion roll through her body, bending like grass in the wind as she rolled out of the spear's path But it was not the inexorable crawl of the tide that gave motion to her instincts. Deep waters did not surge to draw the dagger from her boot or take aim on the black figure diving toward her.

Something older took her spirit in its warm embrace.

Her sister's soft red eyes rose to the forefront of her mind's eye, heating her soul with a flickering tongue of flame. Her arm hurled the blade burning through the air to blaze into the shaedling's chest. Its shriek of pain and shock fueled a hot spark within her that she hadn't felt since childhood, bringing a phantom scent of smoke that seemed to steam beneath her skin.

The spark cooled slightly as the rain grew heavy, as the twitching body of the dark fey plummeted back into the Wash, but the familiar flame warmed her hands. It throbbed as a living thing in her heart, her element twin waiting and ready to direct her, an unsheathed sword to cut down the descending black wings and reduce her foes to ash.

"Tess," she whispered again, and she assumed a fighting stance as the shaedlings came for her from the shadows of her singing dreams.

Uthalion's boots skidded as he ran, loose rocks bouncing loudly down the valley slope. Bushes shook as he passed, and small thorns scratched at his leather armor. His heartbeat pounded in his ears. Rain, pattering through the underbrush, streamed into his eyes, blurring the dark form of Brindani, limping quickly ahead of him. He dared not look back, knowing without a doubt the danger that crept up behind them, slow and swirling on the wind.

Shaedlings buzzed overhead. The bolder ones were still in pursuit, swooping low and spinning their shadowy veils in an attempt to separate the pair. Half-blind already, Uthalion easily weathered the cold darkness the creatures spun, unhindered by them. He was focused on reaching higher ground where he could place steel between himself and death—rather than a brief moment of held breath in the drowning wave of the wyrmwinds' deadly pollen.

Shadowy spears cracked into the ground around him, shivering in the dirt only a moment before dissolving, filling the valley with a stagnant, sour smell that burned in his throat. With the edge of the Wash in sight, a stone wave crested with green, he drew his sword and cursed the flicker of hope that sprang forth in his thoughts.

"No time for that just yet," he muttered and dived through a wall of clinging shadow, the smoky black mist enveloping him for a single, chilling heartbeat—enough time for a well-aimed javelin of darkness to cut deeply into his injured shoulder.

He winced in pain and lost his footing, one leg slipping out from beneath him as he tumbled forward into the dirt and rolled onto his back. Blood pulsed from the wound as he raised his blade blindly, struggling to find his bearings and push himself up on one arm. Pain flared through his shoulder, and a thundering buzz filled his ears as a dark figure bore down on him.

Rain crashed into Uthalion's eyes as he swung his sword, its edge catching on something he could not determine. Lightning sizzled through the clouds, and thunder matched the pulse pounding in his ears as he imagined himself, prone and helpless before his enemies. There would be no funeral, no missive sent to his estranged family, only a little death in the mud, a body never found nor cared about save by the flies and flowers.

"Blood and bloom," he muttered.

Shrieks broke through the storm, and a strong arm lifted him from behind. Regaining his footing and favoring his injured shoulder, he stepped back as Brindani loosed two more arrows. A shaedling lay twitching on the ground with an arrow in its chest, its broken wings fluttering madly to a sudden stop. Its companions backed off, seeking refuge from the half-elf's range and shrieking unintelligible curses.

Brindani turned without a word and continued on, the cliff and a dangling rope in sight. The shaedlings gave chase, closing again, but the quick release of a snapping bowstring from above scattered the dark fey back into hiding.

"Go!" Uthalion yelled over the thunder, clapping Brindani on the shoulder and swinging the rope into the half-elf's hands.

"No, I'll stay!"

"You'll do me more good up there!" Uthalion yelled, cutting him off and gesturing to his shoulder.

Brindani nodded reluctantly and pulled himself up, hand over hand toward the others.

Uthalion ignored the hidden shaedlings as he waited, leaning against the rocks and watching. In between arcing crackles of light, the undulating cloud of sickly vapor that flooded the valley rolled inexorably toward him. The misty river of the wyrmwinds crashed in slow motion against the walls, breaking like waves through the silent tide. Uthalion raised an eye to the cloudy heavens, considering all the gods to which he had once prayed.

"If any of you give a damn," he muttered, "Here's your chance to give me a sign."

He took the slack rope and gritted his teeth, pulling the first measure of his weight with his wounded shoulder. He pressed on, the pain numbing only slightly, pushing with his legs when he could and quietly swearing with each gained length of rope. With every breath he expected the shaedlings to attack again, ready for the crude javelins that would pierce his back, wounds full of shadow-stuff one moment, then spilling blood the next. The two bows covering his ascent meant they never came. Near the top he could smell the grass, hear the swift whoosh of arrows leaving Vaasurri's bow, though the beating of shaedling wings was distant.

Then, in a sudden hush, his vision blurred again, and what little he could see turned a sickly shade of yellow, like old bones drying in the sun. The misty river of wyrm-wind broke against the wall, surrounding him. His lungs burned with a last held breath, and his shoulder ached anew as he pulled himself up another length. His eyes watered and felt as if they were on fire; he clenched them shut, focusing on the rough rope and the numbness in his hands. Four times his hands passed one another before the pressure in his chest grew too great, and in a panic, he gasped for air.

Thick, chalky pollen coated his throat, filling his mouth with the bittersweet taste of flowers as burning tears streamed from his eyes. One of his hands slipped on the rope, and somewhere he could hear distant voices calling his name as his vision narrowed to fine points of flashing light surrounded by inky darkness.

Ghaelya pulled at Uthalion's arm, yelling with the effort as the human became a dead weight in her grip. Brindani reached down, securing a hand on the man's bleeding shoulder, and the pair dragged him into the grass and away from the edge of the Wash. Turning him over, Ghaelya paled at the sight of his face covered in pollen, eyes swollen shut and nose running. Vaasurri knelt quickly, letting the rain wash away the poisonous wyrmwind as he raised his waterskin and forced the human to drink. Uthalion coughed and spat most of it up, but remained among the living, and for that at least Ghaelya was grateful.

She decided she would wait and yell at him later for his foolishness.

The shaedlings had scattered when the wyrmwind drew near, but Vaasurri warned that they'd not gone far and would likely follow. Heeding that, she and Brindani hauled the human to his feet and began a slow stumbling through the grass, the killoren wielding Brindani's bow and watching their backs. Brindani's eyes guided her, and Uthalion was able to manage almost one step for their every two as the half-elf pulled them slowly toward the east.

The thin trees they passed seemed fragile, their green-skinned bark twisted like free-standing vines and clinging only to the air for support. They seemed harmless at first glance, but Ghaelya cursed loudly as her shoulder brushed against a low branch, causing it to swiftly whip its sharp thorns into her skin. She crouched as low as she could with the human's weight at her side, though several more of the vine-trees caught her with their stings as she passed.

With each needling pain, with each slowed step away from the Wash, the old spark within her grew hotter and brighter, unaffected by the cooling sensation of the rain across her skin.

A low section of broken wall stood in a clearing among the thin trees, a surviving remnant of some ancient village or town. They hauled Uthalion into the wall's single northern corner and laid him down beneath a glassless window. The human mumbled unintelligibly, raising his voice and gesturing emphatically in a weakened delirium. Ghaelya held him still, even as she tried to get him to drink water again, producing another bout of choking and hacking.

Vaasurri knelt beside him as Brindani took over the watch. The killoren reached for Uthalion's hand, his fingers hovering over the silver ring for long moments. Before Ghae-lya could ask what the ring was for, Vaasurri pulled away and laid the hand down, patting it softly.

"No, that might be all that's keeping him conscious," he said quietly. "Leave it for now."

"Will he live?" she asked, brushing a stuck thorn from her neck.

"Yes," Vaasurri said without hesitation, "I believe so. We'll need to keep giving him water whether he wants it or not, but he'll live. The pollen of the wyrmwind can kill swiftly and painfully, but only with several breaths' worth. More than one breath, and we'd be exchanging our swords for shovels."

"Idiot," she whispered under her breath, though a tenuous relief tempered her anger at Uthalion's foolish heroism.

The rain grew stronger, pouring down in intermittent sheets blown by the wind. Ghaelya joined Brindani by the wall, watching the half-elf and waiting for his eyes to see what she could not. He shivered slightly in the rain, and occasionally his breath would come in a wheezing gasp, but each time he mastered himself and maintained his vigil, his bow at the ready.

"They're out there," he said at length, squinting through the rain. "Not sure how many, but a few at least haven't given up, despite the storm."

"Damn it all," Ghaelya muttered as she peered over the wall, seeking movement in each flash of lightning or the buzzing of wings behind every bolt of thunder. A small glow drew her gaze to Vaasurri, who had produced his small lantern of moss. Its green light revealed the trembling form of Uthalion, muttering and shaking, lost somewhere between dream and hallucination.

The light also shone on the blood blooming through the bandages on Brindani's leg, a hindering wound at best. Turning back to the clearing, she stared into the glinting pairs of eyes appearing at the edge of the vine-trees, pressed low to the ground and creeping forward. Ghaelya crouched, caught between storm and shaedling and wounded companions. She clutched at the growing warmth in her mind, let it expand and spread across her body.

"Tess," she muttered, using the name to focus her spirit and the burning beneath her skin. The tides within her slowly pulled away to expose a smoldering shore of warm flame.

"Ghaelya?" Brindani said in disbelief, though his voice barely registered. A glistening river of molten energy flared with her pulse, feeding her bloodlust, reviving it, changing her flesh into the pyre she felt inside. Her seafoam green skin warmed and reddened to a pale crimson as a scent of smoke filled her nose and mouth. Flickering flames writhed within the energy lines across her body and flowed across her scalp in a long mane of fire.

She gazed over the wall with eyes like glowing coals and waited for the inevitable attack.

When it finally came, no word from Brindani was needed. A shadowy spear cracked against Brindani's bow, throwing his shot off-aim. Beating wings swooped close, and her reflexes took over in an explosive burst of speed. The shaedling's sparkling eyes, blank and full of hate, guided her sudden charge. Snarling savagely, Ghaelya placed one hand and one boot upon the wall and hurled herself into the air like a tongue of curling flame.

Her blade flashed as she twisted backward, dragging the edge hard and deep across the dark fey's abdomen. Shadows poured from the screeching beast, a fountain of darkness that gushed over her as she completed the turn and landed in a crouch. The shaedling fell out of the air as Vaasurri's lantern flew over the wall, lighting the immediate area in a vibrant green glow. Ghaelya rushed to match the creature's descent, slicing its throat before it touched the ground. As a thin smoky mist pooled around her legs, she searched for another opponent.

She sidestepped movement from her right, narrowly dodging a hurled spear of shadow as she charged its owner. Arrows whizzed by her shoulder as Brindani spotted more of the fey rising in the grass. The creature met her charge, a dark sword appearing in its hand, a leering skull-like grin on its dark, armored mask of bone. She rolled into the duel, her sword clashing dully against the thing's shadowy blade.

Spinning around its position, she forced it to keep moving, to keep readjusting its stance as she slashed and turned. Her sword edge caught on the dark fey's wrist, and the wavering blade dissipated as it was dropped. She drove the point through the beast's chest and pinned it to the ground, somersaulting over its body as she withdrew the blade and spun to meet the next attack, forcing another of the shaedlings into the edge of the vine-trees. The whiplike branches reacted instantly at the contact, striking like snakes and leaving the fey writhing on the ground, its wings broken beneath it.

Vaasurri crawled carefully between the trees, crouching low. He struck precisely against any shaedling that came within reach over the twisting grove. Ghaelya smiled and fought closer to the clearing's edge, giving the killoren more targets and making the dark fey flutter dangerously near the defensive trees.

As she closed with yet another of the shaedlings, she underestimated the reach of its shadowy spear and received a long painful gash down her arm. Slapping the fey's weapon aside she jumped and wrapped her arms around its waist, dragging it to the ground as a searing heat built up in the wound it had given her. Slamming into the grass, flames erupted between their bodies, bursting from her broken skin. The beast's cries of agony ended with her sword through its throat, and she stood back to face its companions, the smoky smell of burnt flesh surrounding her.

Lightning flashed deep crimson in the quiet space behind his eyelids, burning little spots of light that faded slowly as he stirred. Uthalion tried to get up and rolled over onto his side, the motion turning his stomach and making him choke on bitter bile. With some effort he opened his eyes, blinking at a blurry dark world lit by flickering lights and thunderous crashes. Rain splashed onto his face, and he coughed painfully; his throat burned and his swollen tongue ached. Spasms of pain pulsed through his chest as he tried to find purchase on the ground, to dig his hands into wet grass and soft mud, a surface that seemed determined to evade his efforts.

He was not asleep, though somewhere in the haze of his thoughts he was aware of a thin veil where wakefulness hid among blurry shadows. Between reality and dream he fought to rise, clinging to the ground, barely, as though it would escape him, leave him hanging as it spun away.

He pushed himself up, staggered by something, some injury he could not recall that caused his body to ache and creak. The crimson flashes came again, indistinct and familiar, arcing down from and through a cloudy sky. Voices cried out accompanied by horrid screams and shrieks.

"No," he muttered in horror, squinting through bleary eyes at the storm overhead, searching for the beasts that had swam so gracefully and horribly through the skies over Caidris. "Not again," he added breathlessly.

Alarmed, he rolled to one knee, slowly drawing his suddenly heavy sword, its tip falling to the ground. His men needed him. He would not let them face the terrible task alone, the work that needed to be done. He caught a glimpse of Brindani in the red lightning, and he followed as the half-elf disappeared beyond a low wall.

"Secure the left flank," he mumbled, his voice hoarse and raspy. "Don't let them get . . . Don't let them get to . . . the farmhouse."

Dark shapes flitted left and right, bright blades reflecting the red lightning and chasing shadows. He stumbled to the battle, a determined anger pushing each step. He tasted blood in the back of his throat and breathed its coppery scent through his nose. A shadow approached, crawling in the grass, hiding from the light. He reeled backward as it came closer, blinking and resisting what he saw, the veil separating him from reality lifting for a heartbeat before folding around him again.

Something was wrong.

"You're already dead," he said to the thing, his voice rising in defiance of the image before him. "Y-you can't be real . . . You're already dead!"

It rose into a crouch, the blank face wavering into the image of a small boy, twin mouths gaping with teeth from either side of its face. Various eyes blinked, but the one that struck the most was the remaining normal eye, peering at him beneath a crumpled brow in pain and confusion. A long black tentacle lashed at him, and he deflected it clumsily at first, but as it came again he swung back with more force.

"You're already dead!" he screamed and bashed at its mass.

It shrieked and came again.

They traded blows, and with each one Uthalion tried to reconcile reality. But the line blurred, and he grew frustrated, though the fear for his men remained strong. He heard Brindani's voice nearby, but the words were lost, a jumble of confusing sound that only served to strengthen his sword-arm. He landed a blow against the shadowy child's chest and struck again as the twisted thing staggered.

"You're already dead . . ." he muttered, wondering at the truth of the words as they echoed over and over again around him. The thing fell, trying to get up from the grass. He noted the tall grass curiously. The streets of Caidris had been hard dirt, trampled by crowds of people who had been broken by foul magic. They had come in hordes, shambling from the south, from Tohrepur. The thing leaped wildly from the ground, and he hacked through its gut, kicking it back to the dirt as a fountain of black erupted from the wound.

"You're already . . ." he said as he stumbled sideways, shaking his head and trying to see clearly. From the wavy edges of his line of sight a figure slowly approached. Translucent and familiar, it wore the clothes of a farmer and held the simple bearing of an aging, hard-working man. Uthalion waved the man away weakly, recalling the face of Khault, the brave farmer who had helped a band of lost soldiers and brought doom to his little town. Khault looked at him pitifully and turned away, fading into the dark as Uthalion called out to him, his throat burning with the exertion, "You . . . You should be inside! Think . . . Think of your family!"

He fell to his knees, coughing again, choking on blood and clutching his chest in pain.

"End it . . ." he said, trying to convey orders to his men. "End it and burn what's left . . . Give them naught but ash to defile . . . And watch . . . Watch the left flank . . ."

Someone called his name, a girl's voice ringing out from the battle, and he wondered how his daughter had found him here. His head swam, and he could not form the words to send her away, to make her run from this place. Echoes of his own voice slipped through his mind, repeating and taunting him as he lost his balance.

*Think of your family!*

The world shifted, the ground rushed toward him and

struck the side of his body with all the power of the wide realms. Weakly he lifted his sword and slapped at the dirt, its edge unable to cleave the world that held him fast and kept him from going on.

# CHAPTER TWELVE

*9 Mirtul, the Year of the Ageless One*
*(1479 DR)*
*The Akana, north of the Wash, Akânûl*

Uthalion!"

Ghaelya ran to the fallen human, diving at the shaedling that crawled through the grass toward him. She stabbed at its back, kicking it down until it stopped moving. Shadows curled through the grass, mingling with blood that soaked into the soil. Uthalion mumbled something, his eyes fluttering, but lay still.

She stood over him and turned in a circle, protecting him.

Brindani slashed madly, fighting two of the fey, his sword a blur as he taunted them through clenched teeth. Unable to leave Uthalion, Ghaelya breathed easier as Vaasurri appeared, pouncing like an animal from the vine-trees. The bone-sword became a glowing beacon as blood filled the blade's runes. The curved light dipped down, disappearing in a mass of flesh, then returned brightly, trailing droplets of the doomed shaedling's life behind it.

Instinct made her turn and duck as a shadowy chain swung over her head. As the weapon swung away, and the dark fey reversed its angle of attack, she jumped forward, rolling and rising to slash at the hand that swung the chain as she threw herself behind the bladed edge of the weapon. The chain fell away, and she drove her shoulder into the fey's stomach, gripping its legs and dragging down its frantically beating wings.

They rolled in the grass, and she was blinded by shadows spewing from the writhing spinnerets in its abdomen. Ignoring the blows from the beast's armored fists, she stabbed at it, its resistance growing weaker with each new wound, until she sat, straddling its stomach, her arms wet with blood and dissipating bits of darkness.

She stood over the corpse and looked back, feeling deaf in the sudden silence that had descended.

Brindani walked slowly back to the wall, collapsing against it and panting as he slid to the ground. Vaasurri watched as the surviving shaedlings retreated to find easier prey or to crawl back into their lairs and lick their wounds.

Uthalion breathed deeply, fluid rattling in his throat as he feebly tried to move. The killoren approached and laid a hand on the human's chest, holding him still as he pried the sword from Uthalion's weak hand. Ghaelya helped to drag the human back into the corner of the wall and laid him down, bundling his cloak for a pillow.

They gave him sips of water, and he drank a little easier, only coughing a little as he settled into his delirium again, his eyes rolling at the stars and the clouds. Brindani crawled around to their side of the wall and sat shivering in his cloak, still catching his breath from the battle.

Ghaelya and Vaasurri did not speak as they made a sparse camp of the little shelter. The wind grew stronger, and thunder rumbled as they made futile attempts to shield themselves from the rain. She chewed on dried fruit, letting the fiery tempest within her cool to a still surface of lapping waves and quiet depths. Her heart ached as the element of fire, the chosen element of her family, faded away. It was as if Tessaeril had been with her again, if only briefly. She felt very much alone.

Choosing the element of water had been mostly instinctual for her as she'd grown older, serving as a passive rebellion against her mother despite the awkward rift it had created between the twins. She'd not turned to the fire for many years, feeling only the anger in the flames, but she'd forgotten the bond it made with her sister.

Troubled, she washed the blood from her arms and found herself admiring the clean seafoam green skin beneath.

Water flowed freely, adapting to whatever it encountered. It could move mountains or sit quietly in a pristine pool. She had kept herself in a glass for so long, living in Airspur, and only recently had she spilled herself into an unknown world, feeling it slowly change who she was. She had never had reason to kill in her city life—desire at times, perhaps, but never anything real to fight for. Outside of the city she had adapted to a different way. Something new and strange rippled in the pools of her spirit, mingled with old flames, as she wiped blood from her sword and heard Uthalion's labored breathing grow slightly calmer.

"Blood and bloom," she said under her breath, finding the name for what she felt in Vaasurri's words and hearing them echo somewhere in the back of her mind, in the dreamsong that would return when she slept. She repeated the phrase quietly and leaned back against the wall, covering herself in her cloak and letting the constant patter of rain lull her to sleep on endless shores and thundering tides.

Ghaelya stirred in her sleep, tossing and turning as the dream returned with more force, insistent and irresistible. Somewhere, red flower-blooming eyes watched her from the bottom of a deep stairwell. Dancing flames within the crimson eyes seemed to whisper, calling her down and down into the dark in a singsong voice.

She resisted at first, but as she fell deeper into sleep, her will was slowly overcome.

"Tess?" she muttered in her sleep, a musty scent, of old wood and faint lavender, surrounding her.

A groan escaped Brindani as he awoke. He rolled onto his side and clutched his stomach for long moments before breathing again and carefully sitting up. His entire body trembled in the rain that had become a thin misting, little more than a damp fog. Dark clouds still hung overhead, occasionally growling with soft thunder, and he sighed in relief. Though he was glad the sun hadn't risen to blind his sensitive eyes, he dreaded the day to come and the day after that.

Dreams of Caidris, still fresh in his waking mind, were more detailed than they had been in some years. He recalled standing in the dusty road of the town square, shaking as the horde from Tohrepur had come shuffling into town from the south. Fellow mercenaries had stood with him, their swords ready and fear on their faces. Their names, forgotten for so long, came back easily enough. There had been Faldrath, a talkative soldier who'd been speechless that night, and Efra, a skilled young woman with old dueling scars. And the farmer, Khault, who'd bravely given them shelter in a deep basement after the first long night of bloodletting.

He shook them away, banishing the old faces and the horrible town along with them. He stretched, rising to one knee. Uthalion still lay nearby, mumbling occasionally, but breathing more evenly. The human's eyes were half-open, not entirely asleep, but seemingly unaware of his surroundings. Ghaelya mumbled incoherently in a fitful sleep, but did not wake, passed out after the night's exertions. And Vaasurri—Brindani looked around curiously—appeared to be gone.

Alarmed at first, wondering what had happened to the killoren, Brindani slowly realized he was alone. Shaking quietly, his hand drifted to the small lump hidden at the bottom of his pack, a single bit of silkroot the pilfering Vaasurri had missed. He sat still for a long time, longer than he might have several days before. The small piece of his will that desired freedom had grown stronger, a little louder in his thoughts, and enough to be heard within the screaming pangs of his need.

In the end though, no matter how much he wanted to listen, that piece of him was powerless. He cursed himself for not throwing the drug away—for not having the strength to get rid of it. It made him weaker rather than stronger in denying it when temptation was so close.

Quietly he stood, leaving the others and winding his way carefully through the vine-trees to hide himself in the twitching forest and the drifting mist. The early morning scents of rain and grass were sharp to his nose, more vivid, though sickening as a sudden nausea gripped him. He stopped, squeezing his eyes shut and choking down the bile that rose in his throat. In that brief darkness behind his eyelids, he imagined the road north out of Caidris, remembered bidding solemn farewells to those soldiers who had chosen to stay in the little town. He and Uthalion had promised to return one day—they never had.

Opening his eyes, he stared at his boots, willing them to remain still, forcing himself to endure the growing pain in his guts as he contemplated turning around. For the first time in years, he feared finding that quiet, lonely place where he could sit and lose himself in the drug's fog of buried memories.

"Are the leaves helping?"

Brindani gasped as Vaasurri shifted slightly, revealing himself amid the mist and greenery several paces ahead. The killoren's eyes had returned to a deep green, their darkness drained away sometime during the night, though they held hidden mysteries that still chilled the half-elf to his core. He exhaled slowly, almost relieved at the interruption.

"Some," he answered hoarsely. "Enough to get by."

The lie slipped out so casually he almost believed it, like a reflex to protect his need. He considered for a moment taking the words back, apologizing and telling the truth— but he didn't, still not yet ready to let go.

"A brave thing that," Vaasurri replied and stood straight, comfortable among the vine-trees. He ignored their stinging thorns, and it seemed they somehow recognized him as one of their own. "Few have the strength to abandon the silkroot so readily."

"Few have good reason," Brindani said. "I couldn't risk leading those things, the dreamers, any closer to Ghaelya than I already did."

As he said the words he felt himself die a little inside, wishing he could be the kind of person to say such things honestly. A sudden flash of pain ripped through his stomach, and he could almost feel the tiny holes in his gut, eroded by use of the drug. He slipped to one knee, accepting the punishment for his lies, as he fumbled at his pack for one of the leaves Vaasurri had given him. Stuffing it into his mouth, he chewed hard, as if the extra force would expedite the soothing effect of the balm.

"The pain will pass in time," Vaasurri said quietly, laying

a hand on his shoulder before moving to join the others.

"Perhaps," Brindani whispered through clenched teeth as stars erupted before his eyes, leaving him dizzy for several moments. He looked to the south and could almost feel the nearness of Caidris. He knew they would pass through the town, knew it was inevitable, a marker on his and Uthalion's journey back to Tohrepur. Standing slowly as the pain faded, he wavered a moment before turning back to the little camp.

He made an effort to keep his hands away from the little lump in his pack, folding his arms and wondering who they might find in Caidris, if anyone. He wondered if he could face them, wondered what he might say, what lies he might invent under the dark of yet another storm in a place that had seen one too many.

Coughing and hacking, drops of blood staining his lips and filling his mouth with a coppery taste, Uthalion rolled onto his side and clutched at his chest until the fit subsided. Rubbing his eyes, he blinked, trying to bring the cool morning into focus as memory of the night returned. A broken stone wall was at his back, wind whistling through a hole that had once been a window. The small camp before him was empty save for a discarded cloak and a couple of travel packs.

Ignoring the pain in his chest, he reached for his long sword and found it gone, taken away at some point during his delirium. Wincing, he sat up, braced his boots, and pushed up on the old wall. His eyes darted wildly around for any sign of his companions or, he dreaded, the shaedlings. A stabbing pain accompanied each breath as he staggered forward, spotting his sword near Vaasurri's pack. Gripping the cold hilt, he recalled a half-remembered dream of black wings and vicious flames, screams mingling with the recurring images of his old nightmare.

The silver ring sat secure upon his finger, though he wondered briefly if its magic had failed him, letting him sleep while the others fought.

At a slight noise he whirled, leveling his sword at the intruder, only to find Vaasurri staring at him curiously down the length of the blade. Breathing a sigh of relief, he lowered the weapon, as Brindani appeared in the killoren's wake, confusion in the dark-ringed eyes of the half-elf. Vaasurri scanned the area swiftly, seeming alarmed before looking to Uthalion with a grim knowing stare.

"Where's Ghaelya?" Brindani asked quietly.

Relief faded, and Uthalion stood with a groan, shouldering his pack and sheathing his sword. His body ached, feeling several seasons older than his modest thirty-six, but he was ready to move as Vaasurri studied the ground just outside the small circle of the makeshift camp.

"Vaas?" he asked as Brindani gathered his cloak, wringing the rain from it. Unsurprisingly, the killoren gestured south through the forest of vine-trees. Uthalion nodded. "Let's go. If we're lucky, I know where we'll find her."

"And if we're not lucky?" Brindani mumbled.

"Same place," Uthalion replied and followed the killoren into the thin, twitching forest of thorny trees. Though he held onto a moment of hope, suspecting they might stumble upon the genasi simply answering the call of nature, he quickly discarded the idea as time passed.

He grew accustomed to the popping and creaking of his aching joints, the growing knot of pain in his back from prowling stooped through the low branches of the vine-trees, but the constant stabbing pain in his chest was much harder to discount. The chalky, bitter taste of the wyrmwind filled each hacking cough, bringing with it memories of the ochre wave washing over and around him. It curled above him, breaking against the rocky wall of the cliff, blinding him, filling his lungs with burning, and somewhere deep inside he wondered if, just for a moment, he'd let it in.

Choking back another surge of bitter bile, he buried the morbid idea and focused on attempting to find Ghaelya's path, though his skill at tracking was nothing compared to Vaasurri's.

Breaking through the edge of the writhing grove, lightning illuminated the pale blue morning, flashing across a scattered collection of old, overgrown buildings. The barest thinning of tall grass outlined what had once been a well-used dirt road, now left to the inexorable crawl of the wild, nature reclaiming the temporary haunts of mortals.

Cautiously following the old road, Uthalion stared in wonder at the changes that all the time that had passed since he was last in Caidris created. The well ordered fields of the farmers were gone, gaping holes marked the roofs of buildings on the edge of collapse. The blood-soaked killing ground he'd left behind had produced at least one harvest, the fouled soil feeding people he'd once sworn to protect against the horde out of Tohrepur. He hadn't acted out of honor or even pity. That the town had been here at all had been his only reason for making a stand, a tactical choice of a defensible position.

Several times after that night, though, he'd imagined himself as the man these people had seen, sword and shield against a horrid host.

"She's here," Vaasurri said, interrupting his thoughts, "But the weather obscures her tracks."

Drawing his sword, Uthalion considered the town proper, where the majority of buildings centered around a common square. Standing in the old road, he looked to Brindani and wondered how much like mere ghosts they appeared, haunting an abandoned town beneath the dark clouds of the storm.

"You two stay together," he said. "But call out if you find her."

"Where are you going?" Brindani asked.

Uthalion strode through the tall grass wordlessly, weeds clinging to him as he passed. He did not answer the half-elf and knew he didn't have to as he veered toward the looming silhouette of a large farmhouse just outside the center of town—Brindani knew the place well enough.

Like the lyrics of the nearly forgotten song from his wedding, he felt there was a poetry in returning to the abandoned home of Khault, a rhythmic melody in his decision that he was hesitant to trust at first. Lightning lit the shadowed porch, the house's dark windows gaping like the sockets of a yellowed skull as Uthalion approached, somehow certain that Ghaelya would be inside, but also unable to turn away from the dark at the bottom of those stairs.

Much like the ethereal song that called to him in the night, he had to know, had to see what summoned him and haunted his nightmares. He twirled the silver ring on his finger nervously and placed a boot on the first, creaking step.

After six long years, he'd finally come back.

Ghaelya felt as if she were floating, the world racing by in a dark blue blur of clouds and lightning. She felt her arms and legs moving, knew she was following something important, but could not focus on the details. Thunder and singing filled her ears, the storm's rhythm matching a soft, enthralling voice that sounded so much like her sister—save for a harsh undertone, an insistent, hidden melody that bent her will to its own. The inner fires that bonded her to Tessaeril grew stronger, hotter as she rushed to an unknown place, searching for what she must see, the sign that would shape her quest to find her twin.

Dark shapes prowled gracefully amid the straight-edged shadows of dark structures rising from the ground. Dim, glassy eyes watched her from afar, lightning dancing in the lidless discs as a second wave of thunder rumbled from thick throats. The beasts darted out of view like figments in a nightmare only to melt into a hazy background that rippled like water.

She drifted on the warm currents of dream and song, surrounded by lithe beasts and misty rain until a sudden darkness wrapped cold dusty folds around her body.

Her stomach lurched as she slowed and fell forward, stumbling as the song faded away. The dreaming sense, the detachment from her surroundings, was still strong and made her dizzy. Her boots skidded on a dusty floor, and she leaned against rough wood, splinters scratching at the backs of her arms as her pounding pulse filled the silence left by the singing. As she shivered, the scents of lavender and dust grew more pungent and overpowered her senses as she turned toward a tall rectangle of limitless black.

An old door stood open, and the first step of a stairway was illuminated by blue flashes of quiet lightning. A faint whispering drew her to the dark descent, and she stared into the shadowy depths, bleary-eyed and trying to focus as two pinpoints of deep red light flared to life at the bottom of the stairs. The crimson glow throbbed in time to her heartbeat; the whispers, though unintelligible, beckoned her down in pleading tones.

She took the steps one at a time, pausing at each to balance herself on damp walls of wood and soil. Trickles of water ran between her fingers, the swirling energy lines on her wrists flaring at the touch of her favored element. Flashes of light from the doorway shined like stars at the base of the step, reflecting on the still surface of a basement flooded by heavy rain.

The red eyes shimmered beneath the water, blossoming into flowery blooms that pulsed and grew as Ghaelya drew closer. Slowly they retreated, deeper into the dark beyond the stairway, a soft wake rising and lapping at the lowest step.

"Tess?" she called, though her voice was slurred, her tongue heavy and unwieldy in her mouth. Panic gripped her as the glowing blooms dimmed to tiny dots of fiery light. She tried to descend faster, reaching for the light as the whispers grew softer. She stumbled, disoriented on weary legs, and fell toward the glistening surface of the pool.

Clinging to the shadows, Sefir's clawed hands dug deep into nearly rotted wooden rafters as he writhed and gritted his teeth in the throes of an exquisite agony. His back twisted beyond the range of his old body; bones popped as they loosened and adapted to his changing form. His jaw ached as blunt, useless teeth were pushed aside by rows of sharp, needlelike teeth. Blood trickled through his lips, dripping onto his dark robes as he accepted the Lady's gifts and gave quiet thanks for her blessings and pain.

Only the palm of his left hand, where he'd touched his mistress's warm, sinuous body remained unchanged and painless—the mark of her lasting favor and a symbol of his place among the Choir, her chosen.

His skin had grown cool to the touch, smooth and translucent, during his swift journey with the pack of dreamers. Khault, he had mused, would look upon him with pride when they were reunited. But Sefir remained alone, waiting in a web of shadows as a rhythmic torrent rushed through his veins, making him stronger with each new exertion, each act that professed his faith in the Lady's song and the ethereal beauty of her voice.

Somewhere in his haze of pain he heard footsteps echoing across old wood, clumping on the floorboards as they drew closer, and he grinned widely, his sharp, new teeth scraping unevenly against one another. He hissed quietly in pleasure, his new appendages curling from beneath his robes to grip the rafters above. Puckered slits opened at the base of his neck, flaring excitedly in anticipation.

He studied the dark, searching curiously with his remaining, lesser, right eye, hearing and feeling far more than any mere reflection of light upon a surface could provide. His skin tingled with the slightest movement of air, and every sound thrummed acutely in his sensitive ears.

"How blind I was," he said to himself, "Fumbling through a dull, lifeless world."

Slowly he drew his heavy, serrated blade, the sound of steel sliding on leather vibrating through his palm, a beautiful shriek of battle that was his alone among the Choir. He lowered his head as ripples circled outward from a strident clap of splashing water, the sound reverberating from every surface, shaping his view of the murky basement in fine detail.

"This servant has been patient Lady," he whispered and let the tips of his dangling toes descend into the water as he recalled the prophecy preached by Khault, the purest among the Choir. "Twin shall embrace twin, and all the world will shudder to hear their voices."

# CHAPTER THIRTEEN

*10 Mirtul, the Year of the Ageless One*
*(1479 DR)*
*Caidris, Akanûl*

Uthalion crept cautiously into the old house of Khault, gently pushing tall weeds out of the way with the tip of his sword, avoiding deep cracks where the plants had burst through the floorboards. Moth-eaten curtains, once clean and brightly colored, hung in pitiful tatters that blew ghostlike in the wind. Thunder shook the house, and dust rained down from the ceiling. Uthalion braced himself, ready to bolt for the door; but the structure held, groaning with settling noises that darkly complemented the grim weather.

He paused at the sight of a dusty chair in the common room, its cushions moldy and sagging with age. Khault had once sat there, leaning forward and insisting he help the strange warriors he'd welcomed into his home. As stubborn as he was brave, he had refused to take no for an answer, and had immediately set about warning the rest of the town to take shelter. His wife had fretted in the kitchen, gathering food for the hungry soldiers in the last of the day's light and forcing them to eat what she could spare.

A part of Uthalion smiled at the memory, but his face would not show it as he passed through the common room and into the kitchen. He imagined the strong woman as she'd been as the black clouds had overtaken Caidris—and not as she'd been in the days after, prepared for her grave by a stoic husband.

The images were clear and haunting, as though time had stopped that day. But Uthalion felt he knew better, knew the malleable and inconstant nature of time. He placed his hand on the kitchen table, dusty and still standing, and did not measure the years that had passed so much as he bore witness to a ravaging sense of the present.

Slowly and with held breath he looked up, turning to face the dark place just east of the kitchen, at the end of a short hallway. The simple door remained, marked by deep gouges, stained by life and old blood. He wondered briefly if it had ever opened again after the day he'd closed it behind him and put Caidris to his back. Lightning lit its surface, much as it had the first time he'd opened it.

It stood waiting for him, like a hope chest buried in the back of a closet, a box full of memories and years of nightmares. The silver ring was heavy on his hand, its magic having shielded him from dreams of Caidris for so long. There was no waking up this time. Shaking free of hesitation, he crossed the kitchen floor and gripped the door handle tightly, daring himself to throw it open and face the dark where he and his men had hid for three days and nights as the sorcerous rage of a dying aboleth had played itself out.

He stared down into the basement, listening and watching for any sign of Ghaelya in the dark below. Placing his sword in front of him he took one step, then another, forcing himself to return and wondering if he'd ever truly left. Dust and shadows enveloped him in the stairway, occasionally lit by flickering lightning, the old handrail shaken by rumbling thunder.

He paused, feeling the wall and finding the short nub of an old candle still in its rusty sconce. Fumbling in the dark he managed to ignite a tindertwig and light the taper's wick before continuing his descent. A heavy scent of rust grew stronger as he neared the bottom, the smell reminding him of his grandfather's basement and his childhood fear of being alone in the place.

The sound of dripping water echoed faintly as rain leaked through the soil, but he stepped down only onto a soft, damp floor of thin mud. The candlelight glittered dully on rusted tools hanging on the back wall and reflected on the brimming surface of a well-placed rain barrel, but he saw no sign of Ghaelya or anything that would have indicated she had been in the basement at all.

Ghaelya awoke with a cold slap of water.

Reality rushed her senses, overwhelming them with the chill of the flooded basement even as water filled her lungs. She gagged as she made the swift transition from breathing air to inhaling the cold water, shivering as it flowed down her throat. A taste of rust filled her mouth, and gritty bits of dirt caught in her teeth. Quickly orienting up from down, the images and sounds of her sleepwalk seeped into her conscious mind as she faced the cloudy darkness of the basement waters. Thrashing away from the murk, she braced herself against the wall and waited for the crimson eyes from her dream to come rushing at her through the shadowy flood.

Her body cooled, adapting as she waited, submerged and fearful of where she'd awoken and even more so of how she'd gotten there. As she drew her sword, careful not to disturb the water's surface any more than she already had, she caught sight of a wavering shadow dancing through pale light from a narrow window. Mud and rust settled, allowing the shape to form in fractured beams of flashing light on the basement floor. Her eyes widening, she drifted forward, following the light to the dirty glass of the window.

There, crudely drawn in rust-colored lines roughly the size of a slender fingertip, lay the familiar mark of a candle's flame—the mark of her family.

"She was here," she muttered, her voice sounding swift and strange. Caught in a sudden storm of joy, fear, and relief, she stood in the waist-high water, her sword and caution forgotten at the sight of her sister's drawing. Struck by her own sense of shock, she whispered, "She's alive."

"Indeed she is, child."

Ghaelya spun to the dark, southeastern corner, her sword at the ready as ripples radiated outward, lapping gently against her thighs as the speaker moved. As her own voice had underwater, the newcomer's bore a chilling, drowned quality that echoed in odd directions from the source. Grimly, she realized the voice was quite familiar.

"She is more alive now than she has ever been," Sefir said with reverence as he moved into the dim blue morning light, little more than a crouched shape in the water that swayed slightly, as if he listened to a slow melody that only he could hear. "And she waits for you to join her."

"Where is she?" Ghaelya demanded, the weight of the broadsword in her hand comforting as she banished all thought of escape from her pursuer. The mere idea of his hands on Tessaeril made staying her blade all the harder.

"I will take you to her," he replied, rising from the water, his silhouette manlike at first, but changing, unfolding as he reached his full height. Twisting limbs curled languidly around him, undulating above the water briefly before dipping under again. "If only you will allow me the honor."

"Wh-why should I trust you?" she asked, taken aback and horrified as Sefir slowly approached, gliding toward her. She backed away, keeping the sword between them and found the bottom step of the stairs with her foot.

"You should not trust me," he answered, his voice changing, growing more sonorous and suggestive, crawling around inside her thoughts. "I am unworthy of trust, merely a humble servant, a tool . . . A sword at the end of a divine arm."

Ghaelya took the first stair behind her, rising slightly from the water and eager to escape. Placing her boot upon the next step, she paused as his voice somehow preceded itself, a chorus of sounds pressing on her mind until words formed within the chaos.

"She calls endlessly for you to join her, Ghaelya," he said, nearing the bottom of the stairs as lightning filled the kitchen, giving her a brief glimpse of his tortured visage. A single eye glared dully from a network of fresh scars above a wide, lipless grin of sharp teeth. Blood-soaked bandages covered part of his face, dripping crimson down his cheeks and staining his rows of teeth, reddened spittle escaping them. "She sings in a glorious pain that even I will never know."

She faltered on the next step, a familiar nerve-rattling growl shaking her from atop the stairs as she imagined the glassy, predatory eyes fixed on her back.

Brindani stumbled slowly through the cold, misty rain, his movements awkward and his legs heavy. His breath came quick and, despite the rain, he could feel the cold sweat breaking out on his brow. Each step seemed a forced effort, painful and frustrating, as the lack of his drug was announced by every muscle in his body. His eyes burned, and a pulsing headache had settled down in the space behind them, pushing outward into his temples and filling his ears with a storm that only increased his pain.

Once, when he was a boy, he'd taken deathly ill and had barely survived. He thought fondly of those days as his stomach churned, as if it were eating itself.

"Quickly," Vaasurri intoned yet again from several strides ahead, an undertone of annoyance in the killoren's voice causing Brindani to grit his teeth in anger. "Keep up. Stay alert."

Cursing quietly, Brindani forced himself to move faster, though his gaze drifted from house to house, corner to corner, the details of a former village coming into sharper focus even as his body seemed to fall apart. His mind placed ghostly figures and candlelight in each dark window, families hurrying to board their doors and hide from the coming storm. Turning a corner, he paused, his attention caught by the remnant of an old smithy sign squeaking in the wind.

He rocked back on his heels, staggering in the intersection of two narrow streets. Agony ripped through his stomach, and he bent double, kneeling as phantom cries and shouts echoed in his thoughts. The memory flared to life as he tried to breathe despite the pain in his gut. He placed his hands in the soft mud and wet grass, gulping for air.

"What is it?" Vaasurri called out, running back to join him, "Have you found something?"

Brindani stared blankly at the old street corner, his pain fading though his throat burned with the faint taste of blood and bile.

"Faldrath . . . He died here," the half-elf muttered, shaking his head and recalling the bloodied face of the once talkative soldier, silenced with no last words to pass on. "He was just a boy."

Vaasurri laid a hand upon his shoulder, at first reassuring then forceful. Shoved hard, Brindani landed on his back in the mud, squinting at the killoren as tiny drops of rain stung his eyes.

"Focus!" Vaasurri said sternly, gesturing with his sword at the empty town. "Otherwise just stay here, out of my way . . . out of everyone's way."

"I'm trying—!" Brindani began angrily.

"Try harder!" Vaasurri shouted, shaking with anger. He turned away, back to his tracking, calling over his shoulder, "Fight it or die! Make a choice! I've no time to coddle you now."

Brindani stood, indignant and furious, drawing his sword before taking hold of himself and calming his wounded pride. He closed his eyes, lest some familiar building or patch of ground remind him of more deaths, more long fights, and the people who had once lived in Caidris.

Torn between self-pity and inexplicable rage, his only focus remained on the silkroot.

"Just once more," he whispered to himself. "Once more and I'll be fine. I can do this."

He laid his hand upon the leather strap of his pack, slowly, as if at any moment a fresh surge of resistance might save him from himself. But the pain kept his hand moving. Vaasurri had stopped and knelt at the end of a short street, as Brindani searched through his pack, briefly hoping he'd lost the last bit of the drug. His hand closed on the soft lump of silkroot just as the strident clash of steel on steel rang through the air.

Vaasurri stood and charged toward an abandoned house on the next corner, but Brindani hesitated. Time felt stretched as he warred with two compulsions, and he recalled yet another memory from the battle in Caidris, Uthalion's voice, as darkness had fallen over the town, echoing in his mind.

"Keep moving, don't think, and do your job," he said under his breath as a low growl rumbled from in between the houses ahead of him.

Prowling into the overgrown road, the dreamer bared its tusklike fangs. Its thin gray coat was soaked with rain, and its claws were covered in mud. Haunting roars and raised voices erupted from the house on the corner, galvanizing Brindani's will to resist the urge that gripped him. He left the silkroot to its hiding place and raised his sword, stifling the pain in his stomach and advancing on the beast between him and his friends.

Uthalion stared at the old basement in a daze, seeing nothing changed since he'd closed the door at the top of the stairs behind him six years ago.

Empty bags of stored food were thrown in a corner, some torn at the seams to serve as blankets. And in the darkened space beneath the stairs, the one real blanket they'd found during that time concealed a pile of discarded weapons, cast aside and, with whispered oaths, never touched again. Uthalion imagined that beneath the smell of dust and time, a scent of blood was still on the air. Surely its crusted stains still adorned the abandoned blades.

He stood at the bottom of the stairs and saw them all, each soldier in their place, trying not to listen to the raging storm that had brought no rain. Their faces and names were burned in his memory, sellswords from all walks of life and parts of the world, gathered together under the banner of the Keepers of the Cerulean Sign. A banner of war against the aboleths he had not seen since Tohrepur, nor ever desired to see again.

"We did what we had to," he whispered, his breath quick and his pulse erratic. A sudden anger clenched his fist as he cursed the road that had brought the soldiers to Caidris. "We cleaned up the mess."

"And left a fair mess behind, I would say."

A swift breeze rushed down the stairs as Uthalion turned toward a voice as much a ghost as the phantoms he'd been speaking to. He backed away from the dark figure standing at the basement door, shaking his head in disbelief.

"Khault?" he said, trying to reconcile his memory of the man with the hunched silhouette at the top of the stairs.

"I am surprised you remember my name, Captain," Khault replied smoothly, a humming edge in his words that cut like a saw through Uthalion's skull. "Though I am not surprised to find you here, moping in a dusty basement, speaking only to ghosts."

"Not just ghosts it seems," Uthalion muttered, unable to tear his eyes away from the old farmer. Thunder rumbled as lightning flashed through the upstairs windows, giving him a glimpse of dirty white robes and a ruined, scarlaced visage that bore only a faint resemblance to the man he'd known.

"I was here once, like you, talking to the past, trying to sort out what had gone wrong first," Khault said. The basement door creaked ominously on its hinges; a sound like nails being dragged through the old wood echoed down the stairs. "But I found myself alone. Within months my sons had left me, along with everyone else; but I stayed, unable to leave my wife's side."

Uthalion pictured the simple gravesite and recalled lowering Khault's wife into the soil, burying her in silence as plumes of oily smoke rose from the fields outside town. Hers was the only body not burned that day, the only grave that bore a marker instead of soil darkened by ash.

"I spoke to you a hundred times down here, pleaded with you to leave, thinking I could change the past somehow, make it right," Khault continued. His shoulders shook as he spoke, and his voice rose with a growl that clawed painfully through Uthalion's thoughts. "I killed you a hundred times over as well, Captain."

Casually drawing the first handspan of blade from its sheath, Uthalion stepped forward, bracing his boot on the bottom step. Pity drew him toward the brave man he had once known, the farmer that had sacrificed so much to do what was right, but Uthalion let anger grip the sword at his side, to wield against the thing Khault had become.

"I am no captain," he said sternly, slowly taking the first step. "A dying man handed me a sword and ordered me to lead a retreat. Nothing more."

"I found your Tohrepur, *Captain*," Khault spat. The single thrumming word slammed into Uthalion's chest like a thrown brick, briefly stealing his breath. He fell back, coughing as Khault continued, "I had sought only another answer, some reason for the battle that had come to my doorstep. Instead I found bones . . . and singing . . . and in the ruins of your foolish battle, I found what you left behind."

"No," Uthalion whispered, breathless as his mind raced. He wondered where the Keepers had gone wrong, fearing the horrors they'd left alive in Tohrepur. As the powerful vibrations of Khault's voice shivered across his skin, he looked upon the old farmer with new eyes, seeing the trapped man beneath the tortured flesh, and the work that he had left unfinished.

"You were my only reason for coming back here," Khault said, sliding away from the open doorway. Its rusted hinges groaned as the door swung to close. "I wondered at your reasons at first, but now I see . . . the trembling man, his heart racing, speaking to the long dead . . . He never really left this place, did he?"

Lightning flared, a brief, narrowing band of light.

"Do you remember what you said to me before I left?"

Uthalion said, forcing the words out swiftly. The closing door paused. "You said to save pity for myself, that you didn't want it."

"Yes," Khault growled. Again came the sound of long claws scratching deep into wood.

"Truth be told, I didn't pity you," Uthalion continued, standing straighter and staring hard at the dark silhouette of the old farmer. "Until now."

A long moment of quiet passed between them, and Uthalion suspected he might have goaded Khault into the fight he desired. But the door slammed shut, the sound followed by that of wooden bars being slid into place—then silence. In the dark, Uthalion felt his nerve waver for a heartbeat, a breath of panic that he quickly stifled.

Faraway, through the wood of the old house, he caught the faint sound of roaring monsters. Even through the mud beneath his boots, he could feel the thunderous howling erupting from outside. Banishing the urge to crawl away and wait out the storm as he once had, he considered his options and set a course of escape.

Relighting the nub of the candle, he set it down upon the bottom step. He pulled his hand away and froze at the sight of twin, gleaming flames behind the stairway. The glassy eyes swiveled in the candlelight as the rumbling growl of the hidden dreamer stole his brief hope away.

Ghaelya leaped beyond Sefir's reach as the walls shook with the painful roaring of the dreamers. She gasped, bracing herself until the sound passed, the pressure in her temples threatening to burst outward. Sefir winced slightly, but was otherwise undeterred by the chorus of howling beasts. His bandaged, clawed hand stretched out, offered to her with a smile that reached her most primal fears.

She slashed at the hand, taking another step back, all too aware of the dreamer at the top of the stairs and unsure of which threat she should deal with first. Clouds of dust fell from the ceiling, falling dryly on her arms as tingles of warmth rose like gooseflesh across her body. She gritted her teeth, the elements of water and smoldering flame warring through her spirit, each calling for dominance and promising blood.

"Peace, child!" Sefir called, his hands spread wide, but held beyond the reach of her blade. "We mean no harm to you! Pain is a blessing only our Lady shall bestow."

As she recoiled at the serenity in his voice, her elemental spirit chose. Crashing waves rushed through her body, and she rolled into a swift flow of liquid motion. Her skin erupted with swirling blue flares of light as she charged the mutilated man, her body bending through his faltering grasp, her sword rising to cut at the throat of his maddening voice.

Her blade rang loudly as it caught the rusted, serrated blade that appeared between them, a length of steel that bore her solid blow without bending. Hot, strangely sweet breath washed over her face, an overpowering scent of flowers and blood stealing her breath away.

"I bring to you promises of song and suffering," Sefir whispered over their crossed blades, the power in his words caressing her cheeks lovingly as they tried to soothe the tempest that stormed within her. "Why do you deny what your twin accepted so willingly?"

Shaking free of his voice, she pushed on his blade, bracing one foot on the wall as she jumped and spun. Steel scraped on steel as she turned in the air, dragging her blade up and across Sefir's face. She caught a glimpse of his bandages falling away, of the ruined, empty socket beneath them, before kicking off the opposite wall and charging the dreamer above. A shrill scream of pain chased her up the stairs, the sound rippling across her skin.

With its fangs bared, the dreamer crouched low, snarling and shaking its head as if in pain. White hot needles of agony stabbed through Ghaelya's skull as Sefir thrashed against the walls of the stairway, but she ignored the sensation. She thought of Tessaeril with each step taken, she heard Sefir's promise of suffering with each quick breath, and felt a glimmer of the dream-song pacify the pain of the twisted man's scream. Like a near-forgotten childhood memory, it whispered in the back of her mind and steadied the edge of her blade.

Her sword struck the dreamer just below its gnashing teeth, splitting the flesh of its jowls wide as she rolled in the opposite direction to her gruesome slash. The beast clawed at her nimble legs clumsily as it yelped; its stinking blood splashed on the floor of the narrow kitchen. She huffed like an animal, feeling as though the walls were closing in on her, trapping her and teasing her with scents of fresh air wafting through the window.

She sidestepped as the dreamer pounced, pulling her offered blade deeply through its throat. She turned to leave it writhing and gurgling on the kitchen floor. An unnerving sliding sound arose from the dark basement stairway, accompanied by light footsteps and creaking wood. A massive roar from the front room shook the floorboards, and she flattened herself against the wall as a large object was hurled into the kitchen.

It slammed beneath the window, groaning and untangling leather-armored limbs, a glowing blade of bone rising defensively as the killoren regained his footing.

"Vaasurri!" she cried in surprise and relief.

He faced her, his eyes widening in horror.

Instinctively she turned, her arms feeling sluggish as a dark mass rushed inside the angle of her strike. Sefir pressed himself against her, and cold, wet lengths of flesh grasped her legs and arms in an iron grip. She struggled and screamed in rage, fighting to free her blade. Bloody hands grasped the sides of her head, though she remained trapped in an unceasing grip. Long fingers squeezed across her smooth scalp, their clawed tips meeting at the back of her head, ceasing her struggles.

Forcefully Sefir turned her face close to his as rivers of bitter-sweet scented crimson poured from the vertical gash through his face.

"Be still, child," he said, flecks of blood spattering on her lips as he smiled and shook his head disapprovingly. "Your sister squirmed less."

# CHAPTER FOURTEEN

*10 Mirtul, the Year of the Ageless One
(1479 DR)
Caidris, Akanûl*

Uthalion rolled as the dreamer's weight bore down on him, tumbling and crashing into a row of empty barrels against the wall. Wood slats cracked and split beneath them, digging into his back as he struggled to keep the beast's jaws from his throat. Long claws scored his armor, digging deep and drawing long marks in his skin at the end of each slash. He roared in pain, using the rush of anger to kick one leg free, slamming his knee into the dreamer's ribs.

The beast merely grunted and ignored the attack, pushing down with its fangs. But the effort gave Uthalion the space to gather his legs beneath its stomach. He kicked out, sending the dreamer rolling into the far wall. In a moment of bitter humor, Uthalion spotted his sword just out of reach, and scrambled to his feet. He made for the blade, half running and half crawling, but a thunderous roar intercepted his bid to become better armed.

Waves of sound pummeled his side and threw him, sliding in the thin layer of damp mud. Pain spread through his chest, and he feared a possibly cracked rib, along with the lingering ache of the wyrmwind pollen, might slow him down more than he already had been. Fighting to catch his breath, he caught a glimpse of the onrushing beast's gnashing teeth in the dancing candlelight and instinctively reached for the wall to steady himself. His hand brushed against an object, and he grasped it, pulling it from the wall to defend himself.

He barely noticed the weight of the old hammer as he swung it blindly at the charging dreamer. It connected solidly with the thing's jaw, jarring his arm and breaking the old wooden handle, but it did its job well. Bits of tooth spattered into the mud, and foul blood sprayed his chest and face.

The dreamer loosed a piercing whine as it shuddered and fell sideways, wavering on its front claws. Uthalion cried out in pain, clutching his ears. His pulse pounded in his ears, and he was sure they would bleed, leaving him in an endless silence. As he used the wall to stand, teeth clamped down on his leg and pulled, hurling him across the room.

The quiet in his head shifted like molasses, and he felt as if he were underwater. He crashed against the bottom of the basement stairs, and the small candle fell, rolling in the mud, its wick just above the surface. Pain flared in his left leg, and he gathered his right one beneath him to dive for his sword. His knee buckled, but he caught himself on the banister and turned to face the beast as it rounded on him. Its jaws yawned wide, and he felt a swift wind brush his cheeks before the force of the unheard roar crushed into his chest.

His boots left the ground, and he sprawled onto the stairs, their old wood breaking as he crashed through them.

Splinters bit into his skin, and dust blinded him as he fell. He managed a single breath before finding the ground, gagging on a mouthful of dust even as he clattered to the floor. The fall shoved the air from his lungs. His arms fell out to his sides, brushing against cold metal and cobwebs. Even in his daze of pain he wondered if blood still stained the abandoned sword he pulled free. Opening his eyes, he squinted through the dust at the flashing, glassy eyes overhead, the outstretched claws, and descending fangs of the dreamer.

Metal and rust scraped as he weakly raised the old blade, braced the pommel, and cursed as the dreamer fell on him. The impact twisted his arm, but the sword held strong, driven through the dreamer's chest under the beast's weight. Uthalion gasped for air and lay still as the thing trembled and coughed, its breath strangely sweet, like flowers, in contrast to its stinking blood. Though its long, mewling whine barely registered in his ears, it tore painfully through his skull, a melodic dirge of death in a single, suffering note. A limp claw scratched feebly at his armor a moment before falling still, its pitiful cry of death finished.

Groaning, Uthalion rolled out from under the beast and heaved for breath. The handle of the old sword fell from his hand, its blade broken off at the hilt. He tapped a fingernail on the metal, resting while he listened for the sound and hoping his hearing might return to something approaching normal. When the tiny click of the sound became a more recognizable ping, he sat up slowly and surveyed his would-be tomb before turning his dazed attention to the fallen dreamer.

In the pale light of the dying candle its face almost appeared human—or perhaps even elven—save for the glassy, fishlike eyes and massive fangs. He shivered at the sight of it and tried to stand, gingerly placing weight on his injured leg and grunting in pained relief. It wasn't broken and could wait for more thorough inspection until he could free himself of the basement. Taking up his sword and fishing a short-handled axe from beneath the dreamer, he considered the climb to the door and, for the second time in six years, focused on escaping the basement.

After the last time he'd made a promise to return.

He had no intention of doing so again.

Ghaelya's lungs burned for air as Sefir held her tight in smooth, blue-tinged tentacles. Her vision had blurred, reducing the chaos of the fight around her to dim, quick shapes that crashed throughout the house amid the occasional flare of lightning and ensuing thunder. All she could deduce was that Vaasurri was still alive, though he had no way of reaching her or Sefir. In one flickering moment of helplessness she screamed in anger, flexing every muscle, straining every thought to drown out the constant soothing whisper of Sefir's powerful voice.

"You are stronger than your sister," he said as her strength waned. "Though I think perhaps she is the wiser twin. I can see why the pair of you have been chosen."

His warm, sickly-sweet breath blew hot on the nape of her neck, the heat spreading across her shoulders like a rash, itching and boiling her blood. She felt her skin quickly drying, moisture from her swim in the basement evaporating, little curls of sudden steam rising in the cool spring air. A light aroma of lavender wafted through the window as flames gathered in her spirit, her sister's scent stoking the fires that began to burn in her eyes.

The room wavered briefly, a smoldering mirage that steeled her against the beguiling power in Sefir's voice. Weakly, she raised her sword, just high enough to grasp the blade in her opposite hand. She squeezed tight, wincing slightly as the weapon cut her flesh, but grinning as flames burst from the wound, searing the tentacles wrapped around her.

The endless barrage of whispers became a chorus of pained screams pounding on the back of her skull. The grip around her tightened for a moment, then the room seemed to grow small. Her stomach flipped as she hurtled through the room, only the opposite corner waiting to roughly catch her. The wall cracked when she hit, leaving splinters in her back and side as she fell. Sliding to the floor she coughed, tasting blood in her mouth, and floundered to gather her legs beneath her.

Sefir trembled and fell to one knee, the thin tentacles writhing around him. Several of them had been neatly burned by her fiery blood. The element had filled her again, its flames tinting her skin red and focusing her every thought on her sister. She edged closer to the common room doorway, intent on helping Vaasurri and escaping the abandoned town, but the bloody singer's screams slowly died to pained whimpers, and he rose again, a fang-filled snarl on his face.

"Your flames will die, little one," he said, standing to his full height, his scarred head a hands-breadth from the ceiling. His tentacles spread wide, and the toothy round suckers lining them opened and closed hungrily like a thousand tiny eyes. "The fire in your sister died as well."

"No," she muttered, raising her sword and forgetting the conflict in the next room, shaking her head in denial of the singer's words.

Before she could contemplate plunging the blade over and over into Sefir's body until she found some vital bit of flesh, inflicted some injury he could not recover from, she saw a swift blur in the corner of her eye. A whisper of shadow hurtled toward the singer with flashing steel and murderous intent. Briefly she saw the pale face of Brindani as he collided with Sefir in a tangle of limbs, fleshy tentacles, and clashing swords. The pair strained on the edge of the basement steps in a duel of wills, before they plummeted into the darkness and splashing water.

Ghaelya hesitated, her blade still trained on the spot where Sefir had stood, her eyes fixed on the darkened basement door. Sparks still smoldered where she had cut her hand, and she considered Tessaeril and a purpose greater than simple revenge. She turned toward the common room, catching the glittering eye of an embattled dreamer, and rushed into the room, a gusting flame rippling through her body toward the pyre of battle and escape from Caidris.

Brindani tumbled end over end, a seeming infinity of stairs pounding into his back. Tentacles writhed around him, wrapped around his arms, and slapped wetly against his face, all amid the horrid roaring of a fiendish voice that echoed in his ears like a smithy's hammer. Flashes of blue light illuminated the nightmarish fall, creating monstrous shadows all around that he knew, without a doubt, were all too real. Though patches of numbed flesh announced the imminent arrival of painful bruises, he was somehow assured by a faint and singing melody that gave him strength and the will to keep fighting.

At the end of the long fall, the pair splashed into the dark waters of the flooded basement, wrestling for dominance. Sefir's efforts doubled as the shock of cold water further numbed Brindani's muscles, leaving the half-elf slow against the fluid form of the mutilated man.

The once demonic voice of Sefir was transformed as they plunged beneath the water's surface. A wordless, calming melody issued from the open jaws and rows of sharklike teeth, the hellish image belying the sublime beauty of the singing in Brindani's ears. Long, crooning notes reached out like living things, like the curling tentacles, to wrap around his anger and regret, crushing them both in a soft grip that drew painful knots in his throat and pulled tears from his eyes. The sword fell from his weakened hand, and his struggles faded to feeble motions. The small part of him that realized what was happening was unable to gather the strength needed to continue the fight.

The painful grip on his arms and legs softened as he was lifted from the water, coughing and gasping for air, held tight, though cradled in Sefir's terrible grasp. He could still distantly feel the knot of constant pain in his stomach, could still recall his body's many cries for the silkroot drug, the need that had been his trap for so long, but it too was weaker. Only for that could he be grateful.

"You have been so brave, half-elf," Sefir crooned in his ear, his sweet breath complementing the honeyed power of his voice. "All this time, it was you who led the dreamers. Though you remained unaware, we knew of you and thanked the Lady for leading you to the girl."

"No," Brindani managed to whisper. "I didn't mean to—"

"I know, I know," Sefir replied, tilting his scarred features in a strange expression that seemed a mockery of true empathy. "We are like brothers, you and I. Two souls drifting in an ocean of fate . . . and song."

The very notion that he had anything in common with the hideous man created a fresh surge of resistance in the half-elf, though it was still far too weak to break Sefir's strength. His limbs felt paralyzed, and he shivered, drenched and trembling in the cool air.

"I shall give to you a gift . . . A gift that she bade me give to you," Sefir continued. Thin tentacles curled from beneath his dark and dirty robes, drawing forth a red and pulsing bloom of horrible beauty. Supple petals of crimson flesh hung before Brindani's eyes, tiny veins racing through the flower, bloodlike nectar gathering in little drops like morning dew as it descended toward his lips. "I shall bring back to you our Lady's song, a blessing for those who know her will."

The petals rested against the half-elf's lips, a sweet, crimson kiss that tasted faintly of blood as the nectar flowed into his mouth, across his tongue, and sang down his throat. Briefly, he gagged, trying to spit out the flower, but within a heartbeat the pain in his stomach had lessened, as had his ever-present need for the silkroot. He cursed inwardly as he bit into the bloom hungrily, as Sefir whispered songs in his ear.

> *"The Song calls us*
> *The Choir brings us*
> *The Lady dreams us*
> *And her blood feeds us"*

Ghaelya roared with the flames in her blood, as she slashed and dodged the remaining dreamers. An expression of trailing fire curled from her scalp like a mane, and the world before her seemed naught but kindling. The beasts were smart, keeping them from the door, destroying the old steps leading upstairs with deafening blasts of thunder from their thick throats.

The walls shook as she fought back to back with Vaa-surri, holding a turning circle of sharp edges one moment, then flying apart to divide the four beasts. She kept her strikes precise and painful, careful to take no unnecessary chances, every thought focused on escaping Caidris and finding Tohrepur, finding Tessaeril. Though she held back from more dangerous maneuvers, her patience was wearing thin, and she looked constantly toward the dark doorway to the kitchen, wondering when Sefir would return. She tried to ignore the thought that she had seen the last of Brindani, brave fool that he was.

Flashing eyes and gaping jaws leaped for her, and she sidestepped, spinning and flaying the jowls of a second dreamer as the first found Vaasurri's bone-sword waiting to end its bounding assault. Long claws raked her leg, and she winced slightly, accepting the minor wound in order to gain position for a deeper cut. Her sword fell like a bolt of steel-blue lightning, slicing the thing's throat. Its long, gurgling whine tingled down her back as she abandoned it to its death throes and made for the door once again.

The remaining three howled in unison as if reacting to the death of their packmate. The mournful cry tore at her nerves, aching deep in her bones, and slowed her stride. The cry was followed by yet another deafening roar, and she flinched as a large object blurred through her field of vision. Vaasurri, limp and silent, flew through the doorway and slid in the mud, motionless in the light rain outside. Before she could run to his side, the third dreamer leaped through the open window and prowled over to the groaning killoren.

The other two quickly cut her off, and she backed warily away. Their blank stares chilled the fire in her blood and made all too evident the sound of wet flesh sliding across old wood behind her. The sound rekindled her burning blood-lust, and she charged the beasts. Grasping claws reached for her legs as she jumped. She turned in the air to blind one of the dreamers and, landing in a crouch, hacked at the hamstring of the other.

As she backed toward the door, the beasts' piercing howls of pain were outmatched only by the ominous growl that thrummed warmly on the back of her legs. Instinctively she kicked, spinning and slipping on a patch of wet floor, her boot connecting awkwardly with the third dreamer's jaw. Trapped again, she began to backpedal, but flinched as a warm spray of foul blood splashed across her legs. A thrown axe was buried in the third dreamer's side, and it whimpered pitifully, snapping at the weapon as Uthalion sprang into view, hacking swiftly and finishing the wounded creature.

Rolling past the human and his opponent, she felt the first drop of rain on her skin, a cool water singing through her spirit, cooling her fire. She stood protectively over Vaasurri as he gathered his wits and searched in the mud for his dropped weapon.

Uthalion backed away from the dead dreamer as the other two limped into view from the house. The human looked from her to the killoren, nodding once before raising his sword to the beasts.

"Where's Brindani?" he asked over his shoulder, though the end of his question was cut off by a shrill, discordant scream of agony.

The entire house shook, a section of roof collapsing in a cloud of dust as the dreamers made a hasty escape, limping and whining through the tall grass. Uthalion fell to his knees, covering his ears as painful echoes reverberated through the air, a rippling tide of thick sound.

Ghaelya withstood the assault, forcing herself to remain standing as a tall figure appeared in the doorway. His silhouette writhed with movement as squirming tentacles grasped the edges of the entrance. Dark robes dripped with water and blood as Sefir sighed, his wide mouth smiling as rain streamed across his twisted features, dark rivers pouring through the long wound she'd given him from chin to forehead.

"Brindani is in there," she answered under her breath and tried not to imagine the half-elf's horrible end as Sefir fixed his remaining eye upon her.

❧ ❧ ❧ ❧ ❧

Pale blue light illuminated the rafters slowly spinning above Brindani as he opened his eyes. It was as if he awoke from a deep sleep full of dimly recalled nightmares. With his arms outstretched and his boots resting lightly on the floor, he floated in the chill waters of the flooded basement and tried to sort through the mixture of sensations that flowed through his body and mind.

The various pains of his injuries seemed distant and unimportant, minor details compared to the icy ache in his stomach, the bitter-sweet taste that filled his mouth, and the strange sense of calm in his arms and legs. His hands did not tremble as he raised them to rub at his eyes and splash water across his face. His legs did not falter as he slid his weight forward and slowly stood upright, studying the walls of the basement as if seeing them for the first time. Though his half-elf eyesight had always served him well in dim light, he had never before seen such intricate detail, even in the deep shadows of the chamber's far corners. Amazed, he caught a glimpse of his own sword beneath the water's surface and picked it up, marveling at the flash of wet steel before returning it to its sheath.

As if in a trance or a dream, he placed his hands over his stomach, and though a strange need still tugged at the back of his mind, it seemed to have little to do with the silkroot and his addiction. A pang of nausea gripped him as he recalled the bloody flower and his own unbidden hunger as he had devoured each fleshy petal, but it passed quickly as a soft gust of air hummed across his delicately pointed ears.

The faint strains of a familiar melody filled his mind, long chiming notes accompanied by a female voice. The song had indeed returned to him as Sefir had said, a pleasant summoning that he could not deny, though it did not command. He followed it to the bottom of the stairs, curious as to the strange will that urged him onward. The singing intensified at the top of the stairs, and he remembered his previous sense of urgency, the anger, pain, and bloodlust that had driven him to attack a member of the mysterious Choir.

A part of him recoiled at the blasphemous thought, but he forced it away, confused by his sudden disgust.

Sounds of battle drew him through the kitchen, and he peered into the gloom outside. Ghaelya and Uthalion battled against Sefir, though their struggles seemed awkward and stilted as the singer batted away their clumsy blades with an inhuman quickness, assaulting them with his powerful voice. His nearly boneless body twisted unnaturally, long whiplike tentacles sprouting from his pale-blue flesh—a monster seemingly more suited to water than land.

Brindani instinctively assumed a stealthy crouch and crept slowly toward the singer's back, pausing briefly to squeeze his eyes shut and shake his head, conflicted by a sudden sense of fear. Sefir's voice rang like a hammer against his skull, like the voice of a god warning him to stay his traitorous blade. But the beguiling song on the air grew stronger at the sight of Ghaelya, banishing his doubt.

The genasi spun and dodged, almost dancing to the rhythm of the song in his mind. He swayed to the sound of it, studying the writhing form of Sefir, somehow knowing when and where to strike, what he should wait for, but not understanding why. Gooseflesh rose painfully on his arms and neck in the singer's presence, though he paid it no mind; the sweet scent of the red bloom cleared his mind of all but the task at hand.

He followed Ghaelya's feints and lunges. The music built toward a crescendo, a swift momentum that could not last, ringing like a thousand arcs of lightning through his brain until a flash of steel called his sword to strike. Their swords scraped against one another as they pierced Sefir's chest, one from the front and the other from the back, buried in the singer's left lung.

Sefir spun around in shock as they withdrew their swords, hissing through his fang-filled maw. His rising voice, ruined by a gurgling cough of sweet blood, was no more powerful than a babbling brook. The singer fell to one knee, spitting blood as Ghaelya and Uthalion fell upon him, viciously bashing him down as Brindani stepped back, shaking his head in horror despite the sense of victory that stole over him.

He shivered as the song faded, leaving him alone and frightened by his conflicting emotions. Terrified, he spat the sweet taste of the red flower from his mouth, and he wondered what it had done to him even as he absently scratched an itching patch of skin on the back of his neck.

# CHAPTER FIFTEEN

*10 Mirtul, The Year of the Ageless One*
*(1479 DR)*
*Caidris, Akanûl*

Rain dripped into Ghaelya's eyes as whistling wind cooled her skin to a color of watery seafoam. Thunder pounded in time to her bloody fists as she hammered the twitching body of Sefir. His pale skin was tough and rubbery, covered in a network of long arcing veins that pulsed weakly as she bruised her knuckles and took grim satisfaction in the monster's gasping breaths. His roping tentacles, once so strong and constricting, wrapped feebly around her wrists and flopped against her legs as she knelt in the mud at his side.

"Where is she? What have you done to her?" she yelled fiercely, each question accompanied by another blow to his stomach or his bleeding face. The constant beat of her fury numbed her aching knuckles.

His only answer was a bubbling stream of bloody bile, a pink froth that squeezed through his fangs and ran down his cheeks. Life was yet within him, and she was determined to extract every moment of it from him.

Uthalion paced nervously nearby, his sword still drawn as his eyes darted in all directions, watching for something. Brindani had wandered some distance away, cleaning his sword and averting his gaze as Ghaelya violently interrogated the singer.

"Leave him," Vaasurri said and laid a hand upon her shoulder. She roughly shrugged it away, not bothering to spare the killoren the withering stare that crossed her face as she landed another punch in Sefir's gut.

"He's as good as dead," Uthalion shouted above the thunder. "And he isn't alone! We need to—"

"No!" she shouted back. "He knows! He told me!"

"I'm not disputing that!" Uthalion replied, kneeling down and catching her fist in an iron grip. "But we need to leave this place! Now!"

She narrowed her blue-green stare and matched his stone gaze until he released her hand and stood with an exasperated sigh. He sheathed his sword and limped away, motioning for Vaasurri to join him as he turned to the southern road out of town. Gritting her teeth and rising to one knee, Ghaelya spared the singer one last glance and caught his wide pale eye staring back at her.

"Not dead yet . . . child," Sefir rasped, the effort of speaking leaving him gasping for air and coughing. The others turned, alarmed as a weak hand clawed lightly at Ghaelya's boot. "I was chosen . . . to bring you home . . . to Tohrepur."

Ghaelya knelt again, suffering his touch if only to keep him speaking, to glean what she could from him before leaving him to die.

"What have you done to her?" she asked, forcing herself to remain calm and clear.

Sefir arched his head back, a scratchy sound like laughter escaping his tortured throat, a haunting noise that grated painfully in her ears.

"I do naught but that which my Lady bids," he answered at length, pausing as a fit of choking coughs left him unable to speak for several breaths. "No one lays hand upon your sister. Only you may have . . . that glorious honor . . ."

"You said—" Ghaelya began angrily, then caught herself, clenching her fists. "You said she was in pain."

Sefir's twisted smile faded, his morbid mirth draining as he regarded her. His remaining pale orb turned in its scarred socket to look upon her with a solemn seriousness.

"Oh yes . . ." he replied, sighing and sounding as though he might weep in a sudden ecstasy. "Her pain shames all who gaze upon her . . . Her blessings outnumber even those of the Choir . . . as will yours . . . when you are delivered . . . upon her restless shore . . ."

Ghaelya's breath came quickly as she stood. She could not tear her gaze from the dying thing before her or banish his words from her mind. Yet she wanted nothing more than to take back her question, to erase the sight of his twisted body from her mind so that she could still doubt her quiet fears.

"You failed," she said simply. "And you will die here, a failure."

Again came the wheezing, horrifying laugh as Sefir writhed in the mud, craning his head as though looking for someone.

"No child," he said, a gurgling chuckle still in his throat. "I have delivered you . . . as sure as I die . . . our Lady's will and song . . . shall walk at your side . . . "

She puzzled over his words and slowly backed away. The others stood by, listening to her strange conversation with furrowed, thoughtful expressions.

"Kill it," Brindani said suddenly and turned away. Lightning ripped through the clouds, the rain growing heavier in a resounding peal of thunder as the half-elf wrapped his cloak tight and headed south.

Uthalion and Vaasurri waited a moment then turned away as well, leaving her to quietly contemplate the mutilated man's mysterious claims. His broken body's twitching movements slowed, and his jaw went slack, though a thin, raspy breath still rattled from between his rows of sharklike teeth. She left him, dying in the mud, and stared at the dark, sweet-scented blood on her sword as she followed the others out of Caidris.

Uthalion felt strange as they made their cautious way out of the abandoned town. His body felt light, his step too soft in the mud. His arms and legs were unprotected by chain mail or greaves; no shield hung upon his arm. The foul blood so real in his nightmares of the town did not mar his skin, did not grow sticky in between links of chain armor, or gum his eyes shut when he closed them for too long. The storm overhead bore dark shades of blue and gray, coloring everything in azure tones instead of the pall of unending black he had once fought within.

With each breath he realized he had not been dreaming, that this time Caidris had been real—and that horrors still haunted the places in his nightmares.

He could not release the tight grip on his sword, and stood ready to draw the blade at the slightest threat. He flinched as Vaasurri or Brindani splashed through a deepening puddle. His heart pounded as he searched the hollowed homes and shadowed stables they passed, knowing with a grim assuredness that they contained more than nesting birds and rats.

Nothing hurtled from the dark, baring needle teeth and twisted limbs, but he imagined them there all the same.

He searched obsessively for Khault, or rather the thing Khault had somehow become, but the old farmer was nowhere to be seen. Instinct kept Uthalion on guard, a paranoia that had served him well in years past. With Sefir fallen, Khault might come slithering back to finish the job. A shiver passed through him. Though both of them had been truly hideous, the mutilations of Sefir's visage seemed almost trivial in comparison to those of the brave, kind farmer who had given strangers shelter and had sacrificed so much.

The shallow wounds in his leg burned with sweat and exertion, forcing him to measure his long stride. But the pain cleared his mind some and kept him focused on staying alive until Caidris was far at his back.

The last farm faded to a dim silhouette, and the rain lessened again, rumbling thunder growing softer as the storm traveled north. But Uthalion did not let go of his blade and continually scanned for threats in the tall grass. He paused occasionally, sensing something and holding out his hand to halt the others, lowering it only when he was reassured that danger, if there had been any at all, had passed. He caught a questioning, concerned look in Vaasurri's eyes, but he ignored it, wordlessly gesturing instead to the path.

His jaw ached, and he unclenched his teeth, trying to calm his shattered nerves. He had the sense that the world would fall away at any moment, that the nightmare would end, and he would awaken in the Spur, back in the Grove, and Vaasurri would question him about the nightmare. He would jest, avoiding the subject, and try to forget the dream.

But he hadn't slept in four days, and the silver ring had not left his finger.

"We need to stop," Vaasurri said at his side, and Uthalion flinched at the break in the long awkward silence in which they marched. "We need to rest, and you are bleeding."

"Shallow wounds," he replied numbly. "There's still some light, such as it is, and we shouldn't waste it."

He glanced at the others, searching for dissent. But Ghaelya and Brindani only trudged along, watching the faint outline of the overgrown path and little else. Quietly he cursed their inattentiveness, shaking his head and ignoring Vaasurri's solemn stare.

"You're not the only one who's wounded," Vaasurri pressed, an edge of anger and concern in his voice. "And not all of us can stay awake for tendays on end."

"We're not stopping," Uthalion said a little louder. "Too far to go, not enough distance behind us."

"Distance from Caidris you mean," the killoren replied.

"Not now, Vaas. Let it go," Uthalion grumbled. His eyes remained firmly on the southern horizon as if glued there, drawn like the needle of a compass. He found, after several tries, that he could not look away from it for long. He couldn't hear the mysterious song, but its constant pull was unmistakable.

"Fine, keep your secrets," Vaasurri said and turned off the path, gesturing for Brindani and Ghaelya to follow. "We are stopping. Should you happen to work things out and stop for a moment, perhaps we'll catch up."

Uthalion did stop and turned on the killoren angrily, his sword half drawn and a swift rebuke on his tongue, but he caught himself. He let the unspoken words go and sheathed his sword, staring at the leather bracers on his arms, the tired half-elf and the genasi. The storm was passing, and he was no longer the Captain he'd once been. These were not his soldiers.

Vaasurri led them to a growth of rock that curled from the ground like the tail of a burrowing dragon. Uthalion cooled his anger somewhat, though he could not quell the sense of eyes spying upon his back, of beasts crawling through the grass waiting for him to let down his guard. It felt as though they were everywhere, and naught could banish them save reaching Tohrepur and dealing with Khault.

The Choir had been to Airspur at least once, he thought and suppressed a shudder. Might they take my family next?

He shivered and made his slow way to the little camp, not sparing a glance for the killoren as he climbed the curl of rock, seeking higher ground from which to observe the surrounding area.

"I'll take first watch," he muttered.

From above he noticed the haunted look on Ghaelya's face as she cleared an area to lie down, though Brindani, he noted, looked nothing less than a ghost. He pondered this briefly, then looked again to the south, slowly turning the silver ring upon his finger as the muted sun crawled to the western horizon.

Vaasurri sat quietly by the small fire, rubbing the chill from his arms and keeping a worried eye upon Uthalion until well after sunset. The human seemed as though he'd been hollowed out and filled with something else, bearing little resemblance to the man Vaasurri had known in the Spur. Though Uthalion did eventually tend to the wounds on his leg, it was the wounds of an older conflict that the killoren spied in the blank stare of his friend's face, in the anxious paranoia that started at every sound.

Brindani appeared to have fared little better since leaving Caidris. He was pale and wrapping himself tightly in a wet cloak, trembling with something beyond just the cold. At first Vaasurri had suspected the silkroot, but he had witnessed the addictions of mortals in the Feywild—silkroot having been a popular method of easing the fears and inhibitions of those caught in the fey realms—and the half-elf suffered far differently than he recalled.

The encounter in Caidris had marked both the man and the half-elf in a way that Vaasurri could not fathom, though he suspected both had seen something in Sefir that had been wholly unnatural and yet familiar at the same time. In all his life, even in the fantastic beings of the Feywild, he had never seen anything like the mutilated singer. He had no word for such a thing as Sefir, though he had witnessed sorcerous infections—diseases that affected not only the flesh, but the will and spirit of the infected. Some had worked according to nefarious design; others, occasionally, had spread like wildfire, epidemics attributed to the Spellplague and beasts caught in the terrible blue waves of its chaos.

He shivered, considering their destination, the strange wolflike dreamers, and the thing called Sefir, only one representative of a group Ghaelya had called the Choir. Muttering a curse under his breath, he let the first glimmer of doubt cross his mind. Though he'd been well intentioned when he agreed to help, he doubted one city dweller's ability to survive for so long, surrounded by such nightmares.

As the idea settled in, darkening his already somber mood, he looked to Uthalion and Brindani. Casually shielding his eyes, he glanced at Ghaelya, dreading what he knew he must attempt. He felt very much alone in that moment, but as the seemingly sole voice of surviving reason, he could not remain silent. Certain that only madness and death would greet them in the ruins of Torehpur, he said what none of them wanted to hear.

"We should turn back," he said, forcing the words out and shattering the awkward quiet that enveloped them as surely as the darkness of the chill night air.

In truth, he spoke only to Ghaelya, his green eyes watching her reaction closely. She said nothing at first, her expression unreadable as he waited. But it was not her voice that first protested.

"No," Brindani said, stirring lethargically beneath his cloak, his shadowed eyes reduced to two flickering glints of light in the campfire. "We will not turn back."

Vaasurri ignored the half-elf, waiting only for Ghaelya to respond. It was her quest he had agreed to, and he would abandon it only by her word. She blinked and looked down, her hands balled into fists as a mix of emotions crossed her troubled features.

"We've come too far," Uthalion said from above, glancing down only for a moment before returning his gaze to the south. "Best to just see it through now, stop these . . . things . . . If we're able."

Vaasurri glared at the human, wondering what mysterious force had Uthalion in its grip and fearing where it might lead them when all was said and done. He held his tongue for the moment and turned back to the genasi.

"Ghaelya?" he said, and she flinched as if startled from her thoughts. "You heard what Sefir said and saw what he was—or rather, what he had become. I hate to suggest the worst, but your sister—"

"I don't know," she said suddenly, fixing him with a hard stare that she quickly broke. She fidgeted with her sword as she prepared to clean the still bloodied blade. "I just . . . need to think. I need to rest."

Vaasurri merely nodded, feeling ashamed for broaching the subject. But he knew he would have regretted turning away from what he felt what right, even if it was painful to hear. He sat back, troubled, but willing to wait for the morning light and Ghaelya's decision. It was some time before he noticed the dark, withering stare of Brindani from across the low flames of the campfire, and he wondered if his suggestion of turning back had already come too late.

In the abandoned, overgrown streets of Caidris, distant lightning flickered in empty windows and flashed in stilled puddles. A soft breeze whispered through the grass and tall weeds, like secrets being shared among conspiratorial ghosts. Water dripped languidly from the rotted rooftops, splashing like soiled tears on the wet ground, as Khault slid sinuously between the empty homes and shops of his former friends and neighbors. With quiet, unnatural grace he approached the battered, broken body of Sefir, and he lifted one of the singer's lifeless hands, caressing the pale flesh and sharp claws as if comforting an injured child.

"How they have savaged my dear friend," he said, the sound of his voice pouring over the body in ripples, echoing and reporting Sefir's injuries in greater detail as Khault blindly studied each cut and swollen limb. "Beaten. Impaled. They even stole your voice in the end, but it was always meant to be, I suppose."

A thin, roping tentacle unfurled from beneath his voluminous, dirty white robes and lifted the serrated blade of his fallen brother from the mud. He turned it over curiously as other growths reached out, stroking and studying the weapon, even tasting the rust-marked steel.

"The warrior that presents the sword to his enemies must always find its twin presented back upon him. They could not have known your mercy, dear Sefir," Khault intoned somberly as he stood back from the body. He cast the blade into the mud angrily, overcome with a primal urge that caused him to gnash his many rows of teeth. He calmed himself after a moment, a sliver of reason still strong in his mind. "But you have succeeded, though you sacrifice your flesh to do so. They shall come to us, ushered to Tohrepur by one of our blood as our dreams foretold. The Lady shall have her twins, and their song shall be carried far and wide, a glorious crusade of Voice and Prophet."

With a wide, fang-filled smile of sharklike, uneven teeth beneath his scarred, eyeless visage, he turned to the south, imagining the simple mortals escorting the girl to her destiny. The idea of the brutish, blood-thirsty men gawping at her and protecting her as if she were as low as they, turned his stomach, and his smile faded to a jagged scowl.

"I should like to sacrifice them myself," he growled, envisioning the deed and the ease with which he might steal their pitiful wills and wits, forcing them to slay one another for his Lady's glory. "But I shall not disobey the Lady's will."

He stretched, his changed body writhing, defying the physical limits he had once known and filling with a power far beyond the farmer that had known Uthalion. Sensitive tentacles lashed the mud, cooling themselves and tasting the soil even as Khault shifted his weight forward, half walking, half slithering away from Sefir's body.

"I must be swift and greet them upon our Lady's shore," he said, then added over his knotted shoulder, "I shall report your service and make your name well known to your . . . successor."

With a swift, rolling gait he made his way through the shadows of Caidris, sparing little attention to once familiar places. He paused as he turned curiously to a small tree and the rounded stone placed by the trunk. A glimmer of memory flashed among his thoughts, as quick as the storm's lightning and gone in a blink, bringing with it a strange sensation of sorrow. He hissed warily and pressed on to the outskirts of town, some part of him vaguely aware of the once oft-visited grave—that of his wife, a place where he'd spread the ashes of his two youngest sons.

Brindani had turned away from the fire and stared out across the highland in troubled wonder. The thick veil of night retreated, drifting away from him to reveal gently swaying grasses and insects taking wing. As he traced the wandering path of a large moth, he shuddered and closed his eyes. He rubbed them fiercely, afraid to open them again lest they show him even more of what should be hidden by the dark. Even with his eyes shut he could hear the moth, rapidly beating its wings, swooping closer, and fluttering over his left shoulder as it was drawn to the fire.

He imagined that if he'd needed to, he could have deftly plucked it from the air without looking. Gingerly he opened his eyes, stared at his hands, and wondered what would become of him—and what he was becoming.

The image of Sefir, writhing in the mud like a landed fish, gasping for air and gurgling as the wound in his lung denied him breath, was burned in Brindani's mind. He recalled peculiar details the more he thought of it—the set of the singer's jaw, the remaining pale eye and its dimmed blue iris, the smooth curve of an earlobe, and the tendons of Sefir's throat, stretching taut above the hollow of a malformed collar bone. Despite the teeth and scars and squirming tentacles, Brindani could see the man within the beast.

A part of him wanted to dash out into the Akana, lose himself in the broken landscape, and just wither away, to find some end to the waking nightmare in which he found himself. It was the part of him that feared for the others more than he feared for himself, the nobler voice which he had always heard, but rarely acted upon.

The stronger part of him, however, kept him still, hugging his chest and clenching his cloak tight across his shoulders. Even as he clung to the hope that his addiction had led to delusion, that it lied to him, cajoled him into a fear that would lead him back to the silkroot, he knew the truth was nothing to do with a simple drug—his need had been surpassed by more dominant and mysterious desires.

He could feel a gentle tug on his spirit, pulling him south and poisoning his reason. It itched across his skin like ants, though he refused to scratch for fear it would grow worse. It pained him like an aching tooth, swelled beneath his flesh like a cancer, and promised to end his misery if only he would follow its sweet song. The unbidden want to keep going, to find Tohrepur at all costs, needled at his every thought and overrode his better instincts.

He glanced at Ghaelya and thought of warning her away, the words rushing to the tip of his tongue though his throat refused to give them voice. They fell apart, overtaken by a maddening, irrational panic.

Clasping his hands together, he laced his fingers over one another tightly, as if he could hold onto himself, keep his flesh from betraying him and melting away into something else. He might have prayed, but he had never given much thought to the gods—they'd never seemed to take any interest in him or his fortunes, unfortunate as they were. He considered his own sword and the release he might find upon its blade, but lacked the conviction and courage to take his own life.

Overcome by exhaustion, he leaned over and lay on his side. He hoped the morning light might spare him, awaken him to baseless fears and the long road ahead, nothing more. He closed his eyes, covered his ears against the thunderous crackling of the campfire, and quietly gasped as the whispering song came to him, keening softly as it slowly carried him to sleep.

He resisted for a moment, raising his suddenly heavy arm to grasp at a bending blade of grass as if it might anchor him, but the enchanting song was far stronger than his ability to defy its call.

It rolled through his body in ceaseless waves, soothing the itch upon his skin and the pulsing pressure in his muscles. He was drawn into a dark well of sweet oblivion, of haunting dreams where pain was a blessing and flesh was as malleable as clay, shaped to the will of an alien mind to which he was nothing more than a figment. Though he drowned in a thick blackness full of singing and shifting half-formed beasts, he breathed evenly and did not resist sinking further.

As he slept and gave himself over to the dreaming song, that nobler part of himself, a small and tinny echo in the endless black, wished that he would not wake up at all.

# CHAPTER SIXTEEN

*10 Mirtul, the Year of the Ageless One*
*(1479 DR)*
*South of Caidris, Akanûl*

Uthalion blinked.

He sat cross-legged on the curl of rock, his hands at his sides. A deep ringing filled his ears as he narrowed his eyes and tried to recall what he'd been doing. He had no measure of how much time had passed, though the campfire had burned itself down to a glowing pile of orange embers, casting the campsite below in an eerie light. Alarmed, he felt for the silver ring upon his finger, fearful that he'd lost it and fallen asleep while on watch. Though it remained, he was not reassured that all was well.

The night seemed frozen. The wind had stilled, and the whisper of waving grasses was gone, making the ringing that pounded in his skull all the more profound. Panicked, he rolled to his feet and drew his sword, searching for any sign of threat. Vaasurri was curled asleep near the dying fire as still as if he were dead. Brindani rolled and stirred just beyond the glowing embers, sleeping fitfully, but unharmed.

As Uthalion's eyes turned to where he'd last seen Ghaelya, he caught the faint sound of a boot crunching down through long, crisp blades of grass. The genasi's slender leg stepped beyond the circle of the dimmed fire, disappearing into the tall grass with a dreamlike grace.

Uthalion hesitated and ran a hand through his dark hair nervously. He tried frantically to recall the lost time, only remembering the bright flash of sun before it had disappeared in the west. Brindani moaned and mumbled incoherently in his sleep, breaking Uthalion's line of thought and bringing him back to the present.

Leaping down from his perch, he glanced at Vaasurri and the half-elf, unsure if he should leave them alone, but already Ghaelya's footsteps were retreating to the edge of his ability to hear. Quietly cursing, he rushed into the dark after the genasi, though the constant dull ring in his head seemed to grow louder the farther he progressed in Ghaelya's wake.

Deep red lights drifted through the sky, islands of rock floating south out of the northbound storm, called storm-motes by the few who lived on the Akana. Their bulk was scored by strokes of lightning, and they trailed long plumes of white steam streaked with glowing bands of reflected crimson. He could make out the distant silhouette of Ghaelya, walking languidly through the grass, her fingertips brushing the stilled green tide that spread out around her. He almost called out to her, but stopped himself in midbreath, struck by the dreamlike view and wondering again if he truly had somehow fallen asleep on watch.

Instead he remained quiet, keeping her in view as he stealthily followed in the thin trough she had made through the grass. The ringing he heard changed in pitch and tone several times, but never left him, always rising when he thought it might fall, drawing him along despite the ache of pain it caused him. He wondered if it was the powerful song, reaching out to him in some new form the closer he traveled to Tohrepur.

"Is this how Ghaelya was drawn to Caidris?" he whispered, wondering if the genasi were even awake. She had left her sword behind and made no effort to hide herself, walking carelessly out in the open with an almost preternatural awareness of her surroundings.

The land rose slightly just ahead of her, and though there was no wind to speak of, the long, dark mass she approached writhed and twitched. Uthalion quickened his step, lengthening his stride through the grass, but Ghaelya disappeared, engulfed in a forest of animated foliage.

Uthalion stood at the edge of the thick grove, the whiplike vine-trees growing tight against one another. The sudden, swishing movement of one spread to all those around it, causing waves through the squirming trees like ripples that hissed for long breaths, then would grow suddenly silent before starting anew. Dark thorns dangled at the ends of roping branches, glowing with a thin crimson light from above. Uthalion knelt low and made his careful way into the grove.

The ringing in his ears was joined by the constant whispering of the vine-trees, and he found it hard to breathe, imagining himself underwater, with the way the trees swayed. He flinched as their narrow roots moved beneath his hands as he crawled, the soft soil parting easily for his weight. A thick carpet of dried insects crunched against his skin, churned through the dirt, and was joined every so often by a fluttering newcomer, struck from the sky by an accurately aimed thorn.

He could no longer hear Ghaelya moving ahead of him, though her footprints were somewhat easy to track through the soft, heaving dirt. Crawling faster, he felt as though the ground might swallow him if he stayed too long in one spot. Breaking through the shifting press of thin stalks, he stood cautiously in a wide clearing. A glowing rock-mote drifted slowly overhead, illuminating the rising and falling sea of dulled green and flashing red thorns.

Hundreds of small, buzzing insects flitted through the clearing and over the tops of the living ocean, many swarming around a circle of large stones. As he approached the stone ring, he could make out worn, handmade lines amid the cracks and soft moss, bits of ancient architecture gathered together around the edge of a yawning pit of deep black. Thick branches snapped beneath his boots, but as he knelt to inspect the pit, wondering if Ghaelya had fallen in, he realized that he stood on a pile of bones.

As he looked down into the leering face of a dry skull, picked clean of flesh long ago, the ringing in his ears, the whispering vine-trees, and the buzzing wings of insects came together in a strange harmony. He wavered, leaning on the stone circle for support as the soft, beguiling tones of the song reached out through the myriad of sounds and left him gasping for breath on the edge of the deep pit.

Ghaelya descended slowly, her hands carefully finding holds on damp rock or making them in dense mud. Her body seemed to move of its own accord, and she felt more an observer than a part of her surroundings, watching herself drift, drowsy and calm, into flickering shadows and ghostly light. Dripping water echoed in a deep chamber somewhere below, the sound drawing her back to her senses for a breath. She wondered why it alarmed her so, but the feeling passed swiftly. She breathed in tune to the soft singing that led her down, her heart beating in time with the peaceful melody, only vaguely aware of her last descent into a basement in Caidris. Like then, it did not occur to her to be afraid.

Dragonflies buzzed around her, hovering and studying her with their large, flashing eyes before flitting away. A long, spiraling column of drifting motes stretched from the dark below to the open sky above, tiny graceful wings belying the hunger of hundreds of mosquitoes that did not stop to inspect her or feed upon her blood. The walls of the pit fairly hummed with the sound of so much tiny life in the air. As her boots found the soft, gritty floor of the pit, she pulled her hands away from the rock, her fingertips tingling from the exertion of climbing. Trancelike, she turned to continue her dreaming journey.

A thin layer of seashells, bones, and fallen insects coated the sandy floor of a wide cavern lit by some unseen source of flickering illumination. A bowl depression in the center of the chamber bore a still pool of somewhat clear water. A sour smell of stagnancy hung on the air along with other scents that touched lightly upon memories of death and possibly burning, but they did not remain long as she stepped forward. There were more bones set into the walls, most of them old and yellowed, but some still bore the rusty blush of blood upon them. They were set deliberately, forming intricately detailed designs and patterns. She saw a mosaic of fantastic sea monsters amid stylized waves, and symbols of an unknown language that nevertheless spoke to the water in her spirit somehow, like an alphabet to describe the tides.

The largest of the seashells fanned outward from the edge of the still pool, their well-polished, opalescent edges swirling with eerie light.

As she knelt down, little ripples on the pool's surface caught her attention. Dark shapes darted and crawled in the muddy silt of the bottom. The smallest, with large heads and legless bodies twisting back and forth to swim up and down from the bottom, she recognized as the larvae of mosquitoes. When she was little, she and Tessaeril had found some of the larvae in an old water bucket and had taken them home as pets. Their mother had screamed in disgust, emptying the bucket and punishing them for bringing the creatures home. Ghaelya knew better now, but she still smiled at the sight of the larvae.

The others, larger ones crawling slowly along in the mud, she did not recognize until one snapped up an infant mosquitoes. Tiny legs propelled it, hunting for more larvae, a long armlike jaw hinged beneath its upper body. Dragonfly larvae, or water-dragons she'd called them as a young girl.

"They brought me here to die," said the unmistakable voice of Tessaeril. It filled the chamber, wafting gently over Ghaelya's skin. and she did not look away from the water. She somehow expected her sister and accepted her presence as a matter of course, one more part of the dream. A reflection of faintly glowing crimson eyes danced on the water, as did the dark silhouette of their bearer who sat in shadow on the opposite shore of the pool. "The Choir brought us here, one by one, and asked us if we could hear it . . ."

"The song?" Ghaelya muttered, her tongue feeling thick and sluggish as the crimson eyes nodded solemnly.

"Those that could not hear it were slain . . . mercifully," Tessaeril answered, her voice breaking slightly, causing a brief disturbance in the humming melody that held tight to Ghaelya's will. "Those that could hear it . . . were not so fortunate."

Ghaelya swooned, dizzy as the chamber suddenly shifted, the ghostly light flashed, and ripples coated every surface, spreading out from the stagnant pool. She stumbled backward, blinking and shaking her head, trying to focus as Tessaeril's eyes grew and split at their centers, blossoming into brilliant, deep red petals. Ghaelya slowly withdrew into the shadows.

"Is this real?" she mumbled hoarsely. "Am I dreaming?"

"We are, all of us, dreaming," Tessaeril replied from the dark, her voice growing louder, echoing and rippling through the bone mosaic on the walls.

"Wait!" Ghaelya cried, reaching out and advancing only to splash into the pool, far deeper than it had appeared. She sank swiftly as the light faded, kicking as she fought to keep her head high, to keep Tessaeril in sight.

"Only, some of us are trapped," Tessaeril continued, her eyes dripping streams of crimson nectar. "Some of us are not dreaming, but rather, are dreamed . . ."

"I don't understand!" Ghaelya replied, trying to swim forward, but held back by a swiftly growing current. The edges of the pool spread outward, and the walls faded to a hazy black. A sense of unfathomable depth overtook her, and the distant crests of sloshing waves flashed far beyond the meager perimeter of the chamber as she called out to her sister, "Don't leave me!"

"You will understand, when you come to me . . . " Tessaeril said, the last echoing from far away, buzzing and repeating on the air. ". . .Come to me . . . to the blood . . . and to the bloom . . ."

A wave surged over Ghaelya's head, blinding her for a moment and filling her mouth with a taste of seawater. She trod water, bewildered, flinching as thunder rumbled overhead and lightning tore through a cloudy sky, illuminating an expanse of choppy water that stretched in all directions.

"I don't understand," she whispered, once again able to feel fear as a line of brilliant blue flared on the horizon. Gulls wheeled in circles, complaining loudly as they fled a swift wall of sparkling blue fire that roared across the surface of the water. Ghaelya tried to swim away, diving beneath the surface, but even the darkest depths glowed as the blue flames neared. She surfaced again, gasping as the seagulls, unable to escape, were engulfed.

Some simply disappeared, others were incinerated into little puffs of ash, but a handful were horribly changed, twisting into distorted masses of flesh that had little resemblance to the gulls they had been. Plummeting into the water, the lifeless lumps left behind a single bird flapping clumsily, little more than a collection of giant wings and squawking beaks, a monster that hung heavily on the air.

"The Spellplague," she muttered in horror, recognizing and somehow bearing witness to events she only knew of through century-old stories and legends. The Blue Breath of Change had been born in the death of a goddess and ravaged all that it touched as the fabric of magic fell apart at the seams.

Stunned and helpless, Ghaelya froze as the blue fire washed over her, shaking her violently and drawing massive waves behind it. As it passed, she felt no different, and drifted momentarily in a void of utter silence, waiting. The silence was broken by a drowned scream, a melodious shriek that rose from the depths beneath her and touched her soul with pain and terrible sorrow even as it ripped through her body like a thousand spinning blades.

She screamed as well, her vision fading to darkness; and her body lifted, floating in a weightless void for several breaths before everything suddenly stopped.

Opening her eyes, she found herself lying on the floor of the chamber, bones and dead bugs pressed against her cheek. The light was gone, and in the dark she shuddered, inhaling deeply, relieved even by the scent of stagnant water and death. Her skin tingled uncomfortably as she sat up and brushed the filth from her face, a dim memory instinctively guiding her back to the present and the bottom of the pit, though the strange dream sat heavily in her thoughts.

"Something . . . Something in the water," she whispered.

"Ghaelya?"

Uthalion's tired voice called down to her through the

cloud of buzzing insects, and she hesitated, saying nothing and shivering in the dark. She gripped the sides of her head, assuring herself of the solid reality around her, trying to sort through the course of the dream.

Through it all, she felt a grim certainty.

Through finding her voice and calling back to the human, through climbing out of the pit and breathing fresh air, through each new moment that passed, she was certain that Tessaeril was alive and waiting for her. She dreaded the idea with a quiet shame, however, for she was as yet unsure if simply being alive was for the best.

Uthalion stumbled free of the vine-trees, wiped the mud from his hands, and glanced back across the sea of waving plants before putting a safe distance between them and himself. He collapsed to his knees in the tall grass, wild eyed and breathing heavily. He pressed his hands hard into the ground, pushing dirt between his fingers purely for the sensation, to feel the solidity and find control over his own faculties.

The song had taken him, drowned him in the darkness of the pit, and he had been unable to turn away, longing to stay forever in its embrace. He spat, repulsed by the idea, violated by a will that was not his own and yet one that could not be ignored. He could still imagine the surging tune digging into his mind before abruptly ending, leaving an empty space that seemed to shatter his ability to reason the difference between reality and dream.

He closed his eyes as a spinning vertigo threatened to make him sick, but he held on, willing his heart to slow its rapid beating. Only when he had regained some manner of control, a better awareness of his surroundings, did he look to Ghaelya.

She sat just beyond the wide grove, shivering as she whispered to herself, shaking her head and gesturing as though she argued with someone.

"Madness," he muttered and looked away, leaving the genasi to herself until he could compose his own thoughts into a coherent order. Night still ruled the Akana, and he suspected little time had passed since he had fallen by the edge of the pit though it had seemed an eternity. He dug his fingernails deep into the palm of his hand as he stood and tested his balance, reassured by the dull pain.

"Tess was down there," Ghaelya said suddenly, looking at him wide-eyed and wringing her hands. The energy lines flowed over her skin, flaring with a soft light, rolling from one pattern to another like a restless tide.

Uthalion felt an urge to take her by the shoulders and shake her, to slap the faint glint of mania from her eyes. He wanted to say she was lying and that she would find nothing of her sister save bones like those they had just crawled through. But he stepped back, his hands at his side to keep them from betraying his better sense.

"She showed me things," the genasi continued as she rose to her feet. "Horrible things."

Uthalion backed away again, as if her touch might infect him, flood his mind with insanity and nonsense, though he suspected it was already too late. He found he could not keep his eyes on her for too long, drawn as they were again and again to the dark southern horizon. The song had left him, but the summons remained, a powerful force that took some effort to delay, much less ignore.

"We should keep moving," he said and turned back to the camp and the others.

"I—I don't know," she replied, her gaze locked on the south as well. "I'm not sure we should. Not anymore."

"You *do* know," Uthalion said, pausing and ignoring the unnatural instinct to look again, the irrational hope that a shining light and unimaginable music might flood across the Akana and set him free of all worry. "Things like these . . . nightmares, doubt, fear . . . They do not just go away because you are afraid to face them." Absently he made a fist, feeling the cool surface of the silver ring on his finger with a twinge of shame. "In the end it all just depends on what you're willing to live with . . . or without."

He cursed the truth that spilled past his lips, sighing quietly and unable to avoid his own hypocrisy. A solemn clarity had settled back into his thoughts, and though it gave him enough to contemplate and wonder what was occurring, it was not enough to cure him of the song's memory and the familiar tune of his wedding hidden within its strains.

Ghaelya stood still, intently studying the shadowed distances between them and Tohrepur. Uthalion felt as though they stood upon a mystical border, an invisible point of no return. Once they crossed into the land beyond, an elemental plain of storm and frost known as the Lash, there could be no second-guessing, no turning back.

"Tell me," Ghaelya said. "Have you lived with or without Tohrepur?"

Uthalion stiffened at the unexpected question, a shock of alarm running down his spine as if even the mention of his dealings in Tohrepur might awaken the beasts of his past. When nothing came but a soft breeze hissing through the grass, he lowered his eyes to the ground and considered his answer honestly.

"With, I suppose," he said and started back to the camp, hearing her fall into step behind him. He dreaded her next question almost as much as he willed her to speak it while the brief calm in his spirit lasted.

"What happened there?"

A breath caught in his throat before he could think of how to answer. He imagined how he might answer the question if it were posed by his wife. He could almost hear Maryna's voice asking it and wondered if, at some point during the time he tried to be her husband again, she actually had. He pictured the narrow, cobble-stoned streets of Tohrepur, the scent of salt-stained stones from a time when water lapped at a small fishing harbor on the north end of town, and the seemingly kind guards that had met them at the gate.

"I . . . We—Brindani and I—were soldiers once, sell-swords marching to the ruins under the gold-promising banner of a greater cause," he started in a rush, forcing the words out before he could change his mind. "We were to help them battle an aboleth, ancient and far older than those nightmares freed by the Spellplague." A phantom smell of smoke burned in his nose as he recalled the trailing plumes across the city, the screams, and the chaos, "Even in death its unsuspecting thralls . . . just people, twisted and corrupted . . . The entire city came for us. I called a retreat and never looked back . . . until Caidris. We met them in Caidris."

The last he spoke in a hoarse whisper. The memory of that last day was vivid but lifeless, like the mechanical working of a windmill grinding grain. He had done his job and little else—his heart had not fought with him, but remained injured nonetheless.

"You killed them," Ghaelya said flatly.

Uthalion did not respond, focusing instead on placing one foot in front of the other, as mechanical as once he'd been. He rarely missed the heartless mind-set of the sell-sword, his wife having cured him of his ways for a time, but it had served him well when work needed to be done. He stopped when the faint glow of dying embers came into view.

"It was a mercy," he said by way of answer. The truth of the statement was only superficial, only the long considered idea of a clear-minded hindsight searching for an answer to ease his mind. He wanted it to have been mercy, but there had been none of that in his actions—only fear. He glanced at Ghaelya, unsure if he expected judgment or understanding, but she merely nodded and continued on to the camp, her step a little stronger, and her chin a little higher.

"We'll go on," she said in passing, and Uthalion felt a weight lifted from his shoulders only to be replaced by yet another. Despite telling her the truth, he sensed the slow crawl of guilt sliding over his soul like mold. Even his truth had served the echoing will of the song.

Wearily he joined the others and climbed back to the rocky perch he'd held before. At first he was intent on resuming his careful watch until sunrise, but his attention turned to the silver ring, the magic that held sleep and nightmare at bay. It was the one treasure he'd rescued from Tohrepur, and had meant to sell it at Airspur, to make up for the gold he had never received from the Keepers of the Cerulean Sign.

Ghaelya sat wide awake and scanning the grassland, her watery eyes catching the light of a reborn campfire as if flames could not escape her gaze, no matter the direction she turned.

Resigned, Uthalion laid back and secured his sword, stared up at the crimson streaked darkness, and whispered a prayer to whatever benevolent power might be listening. With a slow, torturous pull, the silver ring slipped free of his finger, and many days of lost sleep descended upon him, hungrily dragging him down into a quiet slumber.

# CHAPTER SEVENTEEN

Weak morning light filtered through a gray sky, heralding the edge of the Lash.

Rocky storm-motes floated lazily back to the south, still trailing long ribbons of steam like misty roads across the sky. Bright flowers edged their way through the tall grass, their wide petals straining to glean what sunlight they might find peeking through the clouds. Brindani found himself eerily captivated by the brilliant blues and deep reds, as the wind blowing through the grass rasped dryly, murmuring in his ears like a nest of snakes.

He eyed the flat expanse of bleak sky ahead with a contented stare as he strode toward the chill plains of the Lash with a strength and fluid grace he hadn't felt in days, even years. The pain of silkroot withdrawal remained in his gut, though it was quite overshadowed by a growing army of other sensations. Thin strips of skin had begun to peel away from the raw patch on his neck, his hands were dry and colder than normal, and his teeth had begun to ache with a bitter-sweet throb that seemed to heighten his other senses all the more.

Uthalion and Ghaelya, though they had spoken little since that morning, were closer and more comfortable in each other's company than Brindani would have liked. He studied the narrow distance between them, their confident step, and the way they scanned the path ahead for danger as if in sync with one another. He forced himself to look away, attempting to banish the unbidden jealousy that clenched his fists and pounded in his heart.

*As sure as I die . . . Our Lady's will and song . . . shall walk at your side . . .*

Sefir's words to Ghaelya echoed in his mind unceasingly, almost like a prophecy he was bound to fulfill. He placed a hand on his forehead and squeezed tightly, as though he might extract whatever influence the dead singer had infected him with. From the corner of his eye he caught Vaasurri watching him carefully. Cursing, Brindani low-ered his hand and folded his arms lest the killoren notice the arcing blue veins that had begun to worm their way through his wrists.

Much as he sought to hide and to resist the thing he felt himself becoming, he could not pull his gaze from Ghaelya for long. He was constantly making sure she stayed the path and did not waver. He told himself that all would be fine, that he could make it to Tohrepur, see his obligations through before losing any more of himself to Sefir's flowery curse. He reasoned that the source of the song, the singer full of wordless promise, might have pity on him, cure his imbalanced mind, and set him free of the ruins once and for all—but only should he bring the genasi, the twin.

He did not know why, and he loathed the irrational logic that consoled his nobler instincts, realizing the lies even as he constructed them, but clinging fiercely to them all the same. Ghaelya would be fine, and all would be well and forgiven.

As they crossed over into the long, sloping plains of the Lash, Brindani felt the slightest measure of relief, as if redemption had brushed his cheek to let him know he had done well. The dry grass crunched beneath their boots, and a spiraling mass of clouds rolled high overhead. The wind picked up, the cold biting deep through his cloak and leather armor. He sensed eyes watching him, though none could be seen save those of the tenacious killoren.

In the wind, beyond the creaking of sparse, bare trees or the grating scrape of grass bending upon grass, he could hear a whisper of the song. Not in his mind, no longer a ghostly melody barely louder than a thought, but true sound, hidden in the strengthening gale. Repulsed by his own sickening joy at the sound, his stride slowed slightly, and he felt nauseous, torn between what he wished and the thing clawing at his flesh and identity.

Uthalion squinted through the palette of grays that dominated the Lash. Even the grass was a sickly green bordering on white. The highland had dipped low by mid-morning, descending on a long slope to the lowland Wash and the wide basin of the Lash. Long, flowing fields of jade gave way to a short, stubbly carpet of muted green that crunched beneath his boots, though the sound was felt rather than heard. The winds of the Lash howled, ripping across the landscape in an ever-strong gale of impending rainstorms that never came. Cloaks were pulled tight, and hoods set low against the wind and the fine particles of dust that accompanied it.

Stark white trees were scattered across the landscape like statues, their bare limbs creaking in the wind. Each bore the same oaklike shape, but their sizes varied. Short, thin saplings shared the ground with massive-limbed behemoths that towered over the skeleton forests. The bone-trees shivered in the wind, their branches clicking and scraping as Uthalion led the way, ever faster, through the land of storms.

Uthalion kept his boots moving, his hand firmly on the hilt of his sword, the cold breath in his aching lungs, and maintained a steady southern course. But he could not escape the chilling horror of one night of sleep.

There had been no dream, no nightmare to which he'd become accustomed. He had been almost ready to welcome the unforgiving dark of the recurring dream, to search the storm for Khault the farmer, ready to confront the memory after having confronted the man, or what had been left of the man. The nightmare would have changed, he felt it in his bones, had he chosen to act differently, to accept that old night for what it was and somehow change the nature of his secret fear that it all could happen again. But the dream that had come to him had not been of Caidris.

In the dark where once had sat the town of Caidris he'd found only a single, familiar cottage. Inside, the cottage—his old home—had been abandoned. The table was set for dinner, a lantern was lit in the common room, and the small bed of his daughter, Cienna, was empty. He'd called for them over and over, as strange red flowers had begun to grow out of the walls. The only answer he'd received, through an open front door which faced a hazy southern horizon, was singing.

"Slow down," Ghaelya said at his side, struggling to keep

up with his long stride and freeing him, briefly, of the terrifying dream.

"No time. Keep moving," he replied, unable to shake the thought of his wife and child being dragged across the Lash, of Khault's vengeful, twisted hands on his family. "Almost there," he added under his breath.

"Can't you feel it?" she asked, glancing over her shoulder. "Something is watching us."

Distractedly, Uthalion studied the flat landscape closer, noting nothing out of the ordinary besides blooming clumps of bright blue flowers—they were hardy blooms for such a cruel environment, but spring on the Akana was typically a study in the unusual. He saw no movement save for the waving trees, the continuous swirl of the racing clouds, and the slow inexorable crawl of storm-motes drifting like smoking mountains just beneath the cloud cover.

"I see nothing. Woman's intuition perhaps?" he muttered just loud enough for her to hear. He earned a stern glare from the genasi.

Almost ready to dismiss her concern, he did slow by half a step, noticing a small group of darting birds with flashy, metallic feathers. They settled on the ground, hopping and searching the short grass for food, though he noted he had seen none of the birds near the trees. The more he watched them, the more it seemed they avoided the bone-trees altogether. Uncertain as to whether that was call for an alarm, he sensed a sudden hush.

The familiar quiet crawled up his spine, awakening his battle-hardened instincts such that they fairly screamed at him to watch for some kind of ambush. He flinched at the loud screech of a nearby bird, drawing a handspan of blade from his sheath as the flock took to the air, their sparkling wings carrying them farther away from the intruders to their land.

It dawned on him as he waited for the Lash's surprise

to appear that he had been so focused on the nearness of Tohrepur, he hadn't considered the consequences of such a proximity.

"What is it?" Ghaelya whispered. "What do you see?"

His gaze darted from the ground to the sky to the ominous trees, searching for the source of his paranoia.

"So close to reaching Tohrepur," he answered thoughtfully. "We haven't considered that Tohrepur might reach out for *us*."

Vaasurri kept an eye on Brindani even as the killoren edged closer to Uthalion. The half-elf's strange fidgeting had subsided suddenly, and Vaasurri wasn't sure if that made him relieved or even more alarmed. He'd witnessed the stages of silkroot withdrawal before and had expected Brindani to be in some pain to be sure, but his mind should have been clear, and his eyes should have lost the distant glaze of a drug-induced state.

Brindani exhibited none of this and seemed on the edge of becoming an even greater liability than he might have been while on the drug.

"No time for that now," he mumbled, sighing angrily and turning his attention to their surroundings.

The Lash was a study in contrasts, or so it seemed by the howling winds and static, unyielding trees. But Vaasurri noticed growing changes that would have been easier to catch had he been standing still. He stared intently at the bone-trees. Their bare limbs, crooked and branching, bore no buds upon which leaves could grow, nor did the ground show evidence of the past autumn which might have left at least a handful of such growth. Many of the trees' roots seemed superficial, clawed into the ground by their narrow ends, but held above the pale grass—an apparent weakness that the forceful wind should have long since exploited, yet barely a handful seemed bowed or bore any deadfall at all.

"The trees," he said, startling Uthalion. "I don't believe they are standing as still as they should be."

"I suppose any movement beyond rooted-to-the-spot is likely bad news," the human replied coldly. "If there's some kind of an ambush here we should keep moving, lure it out, and use the surprise against it."

Vaasurri cast a cursory glance across the flat plain, shaking his head.

"We cannot defend this," he muttered just above the wind.

"All the more reason to take what advantage we can," Uthalion said. His voice had taken on a commanding, edgy tone, more like the cold soldier he'd been when Vaasurri had found him wandering the Spur. "Any estimate on numbers?"

"Perhaps two, at least," Vaasurri said as he squinted, trying to make out the trees that didn't quite fit the natural order of the others. "Though I don't suspect the numbers mean much until we know what we're up against."

Uthalion increased his speed again, forcing Vaasurri and Ghaelya to catch up. Brindani had fallen behind several strides, seemingly oblivious to their conversation. The wind picked up, its howl becoming a rising and falling moan as the Lash's constant storm whirled faster.

"You don't remember any of this your first time through here?" Ghaelya fairly yelled as she leaned into the wind, her cloak whipping around her shoulders.

"It was dark," Uthalion answered, barely loud enough to be heard. "I lost a few men, and didn't have time to stop and investigate."

Vaasurri noticed a few trees seemed to have changed their positions, though he couldn't be as sure as he wanted to be. The wind obscured his line of sight, and the smallest blink was confusing as he readjusted and tried to focus.

"How close are we to the ruins?" he asked.

Uthalion's reply was cut off as a strange clicking sound joined the moaning wind. Random at first, it quickly grew rhythmic and strong, something more than mere chance. Vaasurri had an image of bugs on the march, tiny voices chanting a cadence in a singsong melody.

"Too close," Uthalion answered at length and tapped the blade of his sword, a reflexive, if unnecessary, signal to be ready as they searched for the direction of the new sound. "Is Brin with us?"

Vaasurri glanced back swiftly, his hood fluttering across his face as he eyed the trudging stride of the half-elf and shook his head. Something about Brindani made him nervous, and he wondered if the half-elf's stride was actually moving in time to the clicking tempo on the wind.

"He'll catch up," he said, uncertain if his words should be construed as hopeful or a looming threat.

The insectlike clicks became a buzz, whirring with the gale and forming new sounds. They organized themselves yet again into more intelligent, sentient patterns that drew Vaasurri's attention away from Brindani and back to the path ahead. As he strained to listen, to make sense of the murmuring wind, he heard the slow coalescing of syllables gathering to form a word.

*Ghaelya . . .*

"What?" she blurted out, stopping and drawing her sword.

Her heart hammered in her chest as she turned in a circle, listening carefully and hoping it had been merely a trick of the wind. The buzzing devolved into rapid clicking and back again, each little sound floating around her like puzzle pieces falling inexorably into place. They sounded like the myriad ravings of a mad mind, making sense only occasionally, and then only to minds just as mad.

Uthalion and Vaasurri had stopped as well, listening and watching, before turning to her questioningly.

"You heard that?" she asked, flooded with a relief almost as powerful as the anxiety that had kept her sword raised, waiting for an inevitable attack.

Uthalion raised an eyebrow, tilted his head, and appeared about to speak, but Vaasurri answered first with words that turned her blood to ice.

"There," he said simply, nodding as he gestured to the path behind them.

Ghaelya turned swiftly, staring in shock as she froze into a guarded position. She caught the hiss of drawn blades as Vaasurri and Uthalion turned alongside her.

Brindani stood perfectly still, his hood thrown back and his head lowered, but his eyes fixed on her, glinting with a strange and alien light. Ghaelya had seen men affected by sorcery in Airspur, their wills taken away either willingly for amusing street-shows or forcefully by wizards hired to collect unpaid debts from clients of the Lower District's more unscrupulous business owners. Brindani had the look of a man who had taken leave of himself, one who had been mastered by something beyond his control.

In a rough half circle close behind him stood three bone-trees that effectively blocked the path, rooted loosely in ground they had walked upon just moments before. Over twice as tall as the seemingly enthralled half-elf, the trees and their bare branches shivered unnaturally in the wind, like puppets on taut invisible strings, playacting for the benefit of an audience. Their bark was smooth and shiny, showing no grain or knots, no natural trait of any kind.

Ghaelya barely repressed a shudder, sensing in the trees an ominous, hungry presence that was far more aware of her than she was comfortable with.

"Brin," Uthalion said, taking a cautious step forward. He raised a steadying hand as he stared down the half-elf. "Very slowly Brin, just come toward—"

"Hush," Brindani said in a whisper that rushed over Ghaelya like rolling thunder, a sibilant hiss drawn out until it merged with the wind and the buzzing clicks. "Can't you hear them?"

Ghaelya took a step back, glancing nervously at Uthalion as the human took yet another step forward. Uthalion remained cool and stern, his stony gaze unwavering.

"Hear what Brin?" Uthalion asked, drawing closer. "What do you hear?"

Several crooked branches twitched in opposite directions to the driving wind, their sharp tips dipping like the flexing claws of a predator about to pounce on its prey.

"They sing, Uthalion," Brindani answered and swayed slightly, his eyelids fluttering wistfully as the buzzing undulated in languid waves of sound. He shook his head, wincing as if in pain, and added in a strained voice, "They ask me why I am still here, why I have not yet delivered the twin . . ."

*Ghaelya . . .*

Brindani cried out in sudden pain, clutching the side of his head as he reached for his sword. Ghaelya's breath caught in her throat at the sound of her name again, the word rising out of the dark rhythm with a longing that seemed to reach for her with grasping hands. White branches creaked, snapping as they bent to the ground in awkward segments.

"Step away from the trees, Brin," Uthalion said, a little louder now, more commanding. He repeated the half-elf's name each time he spoke as if to draw Brindani out of his strange trance, to remind him of who he was. "Don't listen to them!"

Bright blue flashes caught Ghaelya's eye, popping in the distance and dotting the ground in small clumps. The blue flowers, barely buds when they'd begun crossing the Lash, were blossoming with ghostly blue light, tiny arcs of energy darting through their thick petals as thunder rumbled overhead.

"They are calling for her," Brindani said suddenly through clenched teeth, drawing his sword and eyeing Ghaelya threateningly. "Singing for her . . ."

"He's gone," Vaasurri yelled over the wind and edged closer to Uthalion. "Leave him!"

"No!" Uthalion replied angrily and stepped closer still, refusing to give up on the half-elf.

"Not one of you!" Brindani growled as the trees shifted, shaking from their roots to the tips of their branches. Their white, unnatural bark wavered, rippling like a mirage as deep cracks appeared in their trunks, growing and splitting as thunder roared through the sky. Brindani's voice joined the cacophony, "I am not one of you!"

The deep cracks spread through the trees in long curving lines. The rippling bark smoothed out, revealing large, bulbous knots that squirmed against one another. Long branches fell into well-ordered groups, gathering beneath the bulges and falling away from one another in a scampering tangle of limbs and skittering bodies. Shining blue eyes sprouted like gems above screeching sets of long mandibles and circular mouths set with rows of triangular teeth. Tiny, handlike claws pawed at the ground beneath the large, white spiders as they separated into groups, abandoning their treelike illusions.

For a moment, Ghaelya hesitated, feeling the slow buildup of an inevitable inertia pushing her to the edge of a long drop. She raised her blade to defend herself, heightened her senses, and bent her knees into a fighting stance. The white spiders rose on their back legs, waving their forelegs in a threatening display as they edged forward in quick, scurrying steps. Remnants and distortions of her name emanated from the beasts, a constant hum of clicking chanting from their horrid maws. Brindani turned, his sword drawn high over his shoulder. Uthalion started forward, waving his free hand and yelling, but Brindani's blade fell and struck true, cleaving the small head of a spider in a spray of viscous yellow fluid.

Ghaelya felt her stomach turn as the brief moment of impending threat descended sharply into the chaos of battle. She rolled and slashed as a pouncing spider hurtled over her, slicking her blade with yellow blood. Her loosed cloak flew out with the wind, blinding the seeking eyes of one beast as she sliced at the legs of another. Tiny segmented claws reached for her from all directions as she bent her will to the water in her spirit.

Twisting and turning in a crowd of clamoring spiders, she danced wildly out of their reach, leaping cautiously over the blue flowers which continued to brighten and crackle. Thunder and wind hid the voices of her companions; white claws and bobbing abdomens dominated her field of vision. A popping shower of sparks exploded from the ground, sending one spider rolling and thrashing, several of its legs charred by a patch of glowing flowers. Another creature quickly took its place, careful to avoid the blooms as it joined the droning chant of the others.

*Ghaelya . . . Ghaelya . . .*

She leaped at the newcomer, dodging its nimble forelegs to vault over its back. As she turned through the air, she glanced outward, catching sight of the flashing plains and the growing number of white trees. Her stomach turned again, and she hit the ground in a panic.

"Too many," she whispered, swinging her broad sword in a wide arc for breathing room. "Nowhere to run."

Uthalion and Vaasurri held their ground, fighting back to back as Brindani tore through the spiders like a man possessed, his blade no more than a steely blue blur. She managed a single step toward them before feeling a strong tug on her arm. Spun by the force, she struggled against a long strand of sticky gray filaments roping around her wrist. She hacked at the webbing even as the tiny arms of a spider pulled her closer. The heavy broadsword managed to sever the line, but another web snapped out from her right, snatching the weapon away.

Lightning struck nearby, close enough to leave bright forked lines through everything she saw. The resulting thunder deafened her as her legs were pulled out from under her. The world spun, and she struggled to hold on, lashing out at anything that came near. The spiders surrounded her, cooing softly in their alien voices, their legs reverently grasping her ankles. She screamed and kicked furiously, the energy lines on her skin burning where the creatures touched, sending shocks of heat through her body and threatening to ignite the flames of her family's heritage.

Clouds flew overhead, swirling faster and faster across the gray plains. Tiny arcs of lightning, so high they were barely more than threads of jagged light, lit the highest parts of the spinning storm. A mandible crunched beneath her heel, and she tore out a set of blue eyes. Yet still the spiders held her, singing her name as she was slowly dragged across the ground. Thick webbing muffled her angry cries, and in the midst of it all she briefly imagined being strung up among the white trees. She recalled Uthalion's words, coming back to replace one fear with another.

"Tohrepur reaching out for us," she whispered to herself.

As another strand of webbing covered her eyes she heard the shivering crack of more trees falling apart, the scamper of eager legs across the dry grass. In the dark she imagined Tessaeril's fiery eyes waiting for her, blooming and weeping red nectar, and she renewed her struggle against the webs and groping claws.

Suddenly the spiders stopped and pulled away. A faint high-pitched whistle carried through the wind and thunder and buzzing song of her captors. The constant chant quickly changed, becoming painful shrieks and screeching. Heavy bodies fell to the ground, rolling over and around her. Sharp claws scratched her exposed skin as the spiders writhed, screaming in unison, and she felt as though her ears might bleed from the noise.

She screamed along with them, barely able to make out the familiar whoosh of missiles darting solidly into tough, white carapaces. The loss of several voices did little for the cacophonous chorus pressing against the sides of her skull, though with each silenced scream she could better hear the swift retreat of skittering legs through the grass.

Dazed and in pain, splashed by the spiders' warm fluids, she struggled to free herself of the tight webbing.

# CHAPTER EIGHTEEN

*11 Mirtul, the Year of the Ageless One
(1479 DR)
The Lash, Akanûl*

Uthalion winced as he ducked low and pulled his sword free of a twitching spider. An arrow grazed his ear, the fletching sending a shock down his spine as it passed. He cursed at the near miss, flinching and holding up the edge of his cloak as a makeshift shield. Though it couldn't have stopped the speeding missiles, it gave him a little peace of mind. The white spiders scampered awkwardly away as fast as they could. The lightning strikes intensified, reaching down from the clouds to make contact with the patches of glowing blue flowers and vibrating the air with thunderous crashes. Distant trees fell apart into more of the beasts, also fleeing the high-pitched whine that reminded him of an animal trainer's whistle.

Grateful for the reprieve from what would have

been certain defeat, Uthalion kept up his guard, fearful of having traded one dangerous threat for another. Vaasurri crouched nearby in the cover of a dead spider's abdomen; Uthalion could just see the killoren's drawn bone-blade held out straight and low over the short grass.

"Can you see them?" Uthalion called out, adjusting his cloak so that he could see the killoren.

Vaasurri shook his head slowly, not bothering to look up as he inspected an arrow from the spider's body. The head was finely worked bone, and the shaft seemed cut from the bone-trees of the Lash. The fletching shined and sparkled as the killoren turned the arrow over, the feathers bearing a silver, metallic sheen like the birds they had seen earlier.

"Local," Vaasurri said at length, shrugging. He turned to peer over the spider's body as the flight of arrows ceased and the eerie whistling faded. Squinting over his arm, Uthalion saw a line of figures in mouse-brown robes with tall longbows at their sides. Deep cowls hid their features, and there seemed to be an awkwardness in their stance, something less than comfortable yet more than inhuman. Cautiously, Vaasurri stood, gesturing behind him as he prowled closer to the bound figure of Ghaelya. "Perhaps they can do something for Brindani," the killoren said.

Uthalion glanced at the prone half-elf, taking in the many wounds scattered across Brindani's body, a few of which were certainly bites and undoubtedly poisoned. He stirred and moaned softly, the sound little more than a whisper in the increasingly howling winds. Uthalion shivered in the icy chill and limped over to the half-elf, careful to mind his own wounds until they could manage some kind of shelter.

Brindani did not resist or complain as he was hoisted up to hang on Uthalion's shoulder. He was just strong enough to push against the ground and maintain some footing. They turned together as Vaasurri freed Ghaelya, and Uthalion stared down at the genasi curiously.

"The spiders wanted her, sang her name," he muttered quietly. His racing mind was caught between wondering why she was so important and struggling to not care, to keep moving closer to the ruins, to see to his own family. "This is madness."

"Not . . . madness . . ." Brindani said, hissing the last syllable weakly, his reason having returned somewhat despite his many wounds or, Uthalion thought, perhaps because of them "Not madness . . . a dream . . . It's all a dream, Uth . . . Just an illusion . . ."

Uthalion drew his attention away from the babbling half-elf as one of the robed figures approached, its longbow used as a white-wooded walking staff in a pale, long-fingered hand.

"Just keep quiet and save your breath," he whispered in Brindani's ear as they limped closer to Vaasurri and Ghaelya. "You're not making any sense."

"Exactly," Brindani replied and laughed, a wheezing coughing affair that wracked his body and made movement difficult. The sound sent uncomfortable chills down Uthalion's spine. An unusual, ominous timbre affected the half-elf's voice as he calmed and added, "Not making sense."

Ghaelya sat cross-legged on the ground, holding her bare head in a white-knuckled grip before inhaling sharply and opening her eyes. Vaasurri pulled away the last of the webbing from her shoulders and gestured at Brindani.

"Will he live?" he asked.

"I suppose," Uthalion answered uncertainly and nodded at the robed newcomer just strides away. He eyed the powerful bow at the figure's side and the low-slung quiver just visible beneath the whipping cloak. "But for how long?"

"We can arrest the speed of the poison," the figure said in a mostly masculine voice, though it could have belonged to either gender. He raised his thin hand, palm up in a seemingly peaceful gesture. "If you will accept our aid."

Uthalion looked from the newcomer to Vaasurri and to Ghaelya, his sword firmly in his grip as he narrowed his eyes and considered their options. Some innate sense of wrongness emanated from the robed figure despite its assistance with the spiders and offer of hospitality. Before he could put together a diplomatically cautious reply, Ghaelya rolled to her feet and retrieved her sword.

"We will," she answered, sheathing her weapon and glancing at Uthalion. "We don't have much choice."

Oh, we do have a choice, Uthalion thought. And we may come to regret this one.

"We must be swift," the figure said, nodding. He turned abruptly south, offering no further assistance as he swiftly strode to join his companions, calling over his shoulder, "The Tide commences soon."

"Tide?" Vaasurri asked.

The figure paused, cocking his head curiously for a moment before turning and pointing north hesitantly, as if he gestured to the simple setting of the sun or a heavy rain cloud.

Uthalion glanced back as they limped slowly along to the line of figures. He squinted as the lightning's brightness increased, as bolts ripped across the sky and ground in quick succession. No rain fell, nor could he smell any on the air, but the unending peals of thunder sounded like nothing less than the crashing surf of a turbulent sea against a rocky shore.

The strange figures disappeared, one by one, into a circular hole in the ground protected by a lid of what appeared to be earth and grass. Upon closer inspection, after their unlikely saviors had all descended, Uthalion noted the door was lined with and held together by long strands of webbing. Vaasurri lifted the edge curiously, studying its construction and peering down into the dark with a troubled expression.

"What do you think?" Uthalion asked.

Vaasurri tilted his head, listening as he turned to face the north. His green eyes were lit by a blue-white light as a sound like ripping paper echoed in the distance.

"I think we don't have a choice," he said breathlessly, moving aside as Ghaelya entered the pit first.

Uthalion followed the killoren's gaze, wincing as the ripping noise grew louder and looked upon a white sheet of wavering flame. Stretching from ground to cloud, west to east across the Lash, an endless wall of lightning lit the gray plains in blue-white fire. It burned his eyes as it rolled across the Lash, igniting azure sparks on the ground as the flowers accepted the monstrous spring storm.

"Mystra's bloody bones . . ." he whispered, lowering Brindani down after Vaasurri. With one last look at the Lightning Tide, he closed the trapdoor over his head and crawled down into the dark and the unknown.

Ghaelya found the bottom of the shaft carefully, feeling her way through the dark, and slumped against a curved wall. Little bits of web stuck to her fingers, and she wiped them away on her cloak in disgust, stretching her hands and flexing them into fists. The spiders had almost taken her, and she wondered if she'd have ended up in just another tunnel in the ground, one perhaps that led to Tohrepur. She shivered, much preferring to reach the ruins by her own means and with a sword in her hand.

The others crawled down and joined her in the dark. The chamber's size and shape was defined only by the sound of their breathing echoing softly against the earthen walls. Their strange hosts seemed to have moved on, leaving them alone as the lightning drew near. Thunder rumbled closer, shaking the walls like an army of mountains marching to war. Ghaelya's heart pounded as it neared, though she was relieved to hear and feel anything besides the singing of spiders and the clinging grip of webbing across her body.

"Spiders . . ." Brindani muttered sibilantly from his place against the wall. "Spiders . . . in the dark."

Before anyone could respond or quiet the half-elf, the chamber shook violently, an explosion of lightning strikes pummeling the plains as the Tide passed over. Though deafened by the tempest, Ghaelya started to make out details of the chamber as a knotted system of roots overhead glowed with blue energy. The intricate designs reminded her of her own skin patterns as they raced with a burning light.

As she marveled at the brilliant glow, her eyes caught a faint glint of pale green against the far wall, and she slowly made out a figure, sitting quietly in mouse brown robes. She tensed and reached for her blade, but the man never moved—he merely observed her curiously with eyes the color of milky jade. Dust and clumps of soil rained from the ceiling as the lightning passed over, and soon the figure removed his hood to reveal angular, almost elven features. They were touched with a slight, predatory smile that suggested a familiarity with killing and cruelty despite his calm disposition.

"You were brave to face the Lightning Tide," he said as the thunder faded and the lights dimmed. "Spring is not kind to travelers on the Lash."

"Who are you?" she asked, her fingers clenching on her sword as she noted the webbing laced across the walls around them. Uthalion was guarded as well, his own blade at the ready as Vaasurri saw to Brindani's wounds as best he could.

"I am Chevat'teht ti-Skhalles'teht, but you may call me Chevat," he said, angling his head in a slight bow.

"Fine. Chevat," Uthalion growled, leaning forward. "Are we trapped here, or is there a safe passage south?"

"There is a passage south," Chevat replied and leaned forward as well, a delicate finger tapping his chin as he regarded the human. "But I have not yet decided whether or not you are trapped . . . you see?"

"What do you want?" Ghaelya asked, and Chevat turned, flashing her a sly grin of white, sharp teeth.

"I suspect I only want what you want," he replied and sat back against the wall, lacing his long fingers across his lap. "I have been very curious to meet 'the twin.' "

With a sharp intake of breath her blade cleared its scabbard in an instant and leveled on the seemingly amused Chevat as Uthalion followed suit with his own sword. Ghaelya had heard enough of twins from Sefir; she had no intention of letting another monster spout prophecies and blessings without first twisting a sword in its gut.

"The twin . . . the Prophet . . ." Brindani's voice was barely more than a raspy whisper, but it carried through the chamber like the breath of a dragon. Ghaelya pulled away from the half-elf's side, looking at him in shock and horror as he turned darkened, sorrowful eyes upon her. "She who would sing the world into ruin . . ."

"I see you are not entirely ignorant of the danger you face," Chevat said, breaking the awful silence that fell in the wake of Brindani's words. The half-elf looked around blearily, as if he'd forgotten where he was or what he'd been doing, and was overtaken by a coughing fit that wracked his body.

"What do you know of Tohrepur?" Uthalion asked, pressing the point of his sword closer to Chevat's face. "Are you in league with—?"

"The Choir?" Chevat interjected. His mysterious smile was unending and overly wide for his sharp features as he stared casually down the human's blade. "No, though I suggest you mind your weapons and your manners carefully, for my people do not, by tradition, hunt during the Lightning Tide. However, should they feel threatened . . ."

Chevat let the statement hang on the air as he glanced from Uthalion to Ghaelya, his eyebrow raised as he considered their drawn blades. Ghaelya shared a swift glance and a frustrated sigh with the human before withdrawing her sword, though she did not yet sheathe it. Uthalion took a moment longer, but did the same.

"Your people?" Ghaelya asked.

"Aranea," Vaasurri answered. "Shapechangers."

"Spiders . . ." Brindani added in a sibilant rasp.

Chevat bowed his head once and smiled as if enjoying the sudden discomfort of his guests. Lightning flashed again through the tight edges of the trapdoor, and the glowing roots flickered, allowing Ghaelya's imagination to shape the shadows on Chevat's face into a myriad of chilling, insectile features.

"What do you want?" Uthalion grumbled angrily as the thunder faded.

With precise, graceful movements Chevat rose till he stood tall over them.

"I shall tell you on the way, but we must be quick," he said, turning to a southern tunnel. As he placed his hand upon the wall, he added, "Not all of my people are aware of, or would even agree with, your presence here in our warrens. We've had much trouble of late with those that come seeking twins from out of Tohrepur."

"On the way to where?" Ghaelya asked, her voice angry and frustrated as she stood. "And what about Brindani? You said you would help him!"

"Ah, indeed I did," Chevat replied, producing a small flask from beneath his robes and tossing it to Vaasurri. "That should counteract the poison, though I doubt he shall ever recover as once you knew him."

"What do you—?" Ghaelya began, but the aranea had already slipped into the shadows of the southern passage, ignoring her questions and her confusion. She fumed and turned away from the tunnel, her attention inevitably returning to the trapdoor above as she considered their chances on the surface. She caught Uthalion doing the same, but before either of them could speak, Vaasurri helped Brindani to his feet and made for the southern passage.

"No use in dithering now," the killoren said sharply. "In case neither of you have noticed, we are out of choices. You had your chance."

Ghaelya stared after Vaasurri as he and Brindani entered the dark behind Chevat. She had not expected such vehemence from the killoren. Uthalion sighed and followed, stopping to catch her eye before moving on.

"He wanted to turn back last night," the human said thoughtfully. "Was he right?"

"No," Ghaelya answered without hesitation and forged ahead into the flickering shadows. She ignored her own disgust as she felt along the walls, collecting tiny threads of web on her fingertips. Ahead, beyond the silhouettes of Vaasurri and Brindani, she caught the watchful jade eyes of Chevat glittering in the dark and suppressed a shudder, still imagining the spider hiding behind his face. She matched his stare coldly and descended bravely into the warrens of the aranea, a kingdom of spiders.

Uthalion felt the walls closing in as they progressed deeper and deeper into the caverns. The ghostly light of the knotted roots above flickered and flashed with energy as the walls shook, the stormy Tide rolling overhead with deafening rumbles. Down long side-passages and deep, yawning pits, he spied gleaming stares watching them from the dark. Occasionally, the pale green eyes were in somewhat comfortable pairs. But those were rare cases, and the clicking-squish of sharp unseen mandibles, salivating with poison, was unmistakable.

"Just keep going," he muttered. "Almost there."

He focused on an image of his wife and child, steeled his nerves for whatever could come hungrily crawling out of the shadows, and kept one foot moving in front of the other. Webbing clung to his boots stubbornly. Smaller spiders skittered among the webs and roots, feasting on gnats that seemed to thrive in the warrens. Though his notebook was stowed in his pack, he kept his thoughts busy, identifying the spiders he knew and giving names to those he didn't.

Leading them all was the quiet, whispering voice of Chevat, echoing back eerily as the aranea spoke of what he knew concerning Tohrepur.

"Once the song was an accepted part of these warrens, like the wind or the storm," he said wistfully. "Strong yet soft at night, weak and subtle during the day. We never questioned its presence; the eldest of us barely heard it unless they listened. But, just over a tenday ago, it changed."

The caverns widened and narrowed as they passed, climbing close to the surface before plunging steeply again. The webbing on the walls became more deliberate, more patterned and decorative. Bones littered the silken designs, arranged in pictures and grisly mosaics that made Uthalion think of the men he'd lost upon his crossing of the Lash six years ago. He wondered if the empty sockets of cast aside skulls watched him accusingly, imagined them whispering his name and asking if he recalled theirs.

"Arasteht was the first," Chevat continued. "He disappeared one night, following some powerful call, a summoning that no one could dissuade him from obeying. He wept when restrained and fought fiercely to escape. Several others followed him in the days after, fleeing in groups to the south.

Not all of us could hear the singing, and a few that could were able to resist. Before we could learn much else, Arasteht returned and he . . . well . . ."

The aranea paused before an ornate passage that glowed with a dancing orange light. His strange, elflike features were troubled as he turned and eyed them all suspiciously. Finally, he gestured them into the passage. "In here," he said simply.

The ceiling of the cavern rose dramatically, and a scent of damp earth and rotting flowers hung thickly. Warm, humid air made a welcome change to the colder tunnels they'd come from. The light came from torches set in makeshift sconces along the walls, adding a light smell of smoke to the chamber. Large rocks obscured their view of the eastern end of the cavern, and swirling clouds of gnats filled the damp spaces between. Fat spiders crawled lazily over their webs, their abdomens glistening in the torchlight as they gorged themselves on the plentiful bounty.

The quiet was broken by a soft moan, a hollow sound that carried loudly in the chamber. It rose to a horrible, groaning cry that set Uthalion's teeth on edge. The sound scratched at his ears painfully, seeming to crawl through his hair and down the back of his neck as he pressed his hands to the side of his head. It faded as quickly as it had come, leaving his skin itching and tingling uncomfortably.

"What is it?" Ghaelya asked breathlessly, her wide eyes fixed on the glowing cleft between two large rocks.

"Arasteht," Chevat answered solemnly as he strode forward. "One of the Choir."

Cautiously they followed the aranea through the rocks into a rounded area that glistened with smooth, wet bones and polished seashells. They formed intricate and beautiful patterns around a shallow pool of dark water, designs rising along the walls and meeting across the ceiling. Ghaelya gasped as she observed the walls, shaking her head slightly at images of sea monsters and strange, watery letters that swirled into one another. Uthalion watched her curiously for a moment, but something else soon caught his attention.

On the far wall, the bone and shell patterns were obscured by a blanket of thick webbing that rose and fell as if with a soft breeze, except that there was no wind in the chamber. Something in the web twitched as they approached, a long-fingered hand bearing hooked claws and pale, mottled skin. Uthalion made out a manlike form, though any similarity to any man he'd ever seen ended at the general shape of the thing. Segmented legs protruded from the web at odd angles; the flesh was covered in dark bumps and spines like a crustacean. Thin, ropelike tentacles were tangled in silk, curling endlessly, weakly, in a futile attempt to escape.

At its head a pair of flexible mandibles pulled at the web while a sharp-angled jaw opened and closed behind them, gasping like a landed fish and hissing through protruding, spiny teeth. Where the creature's eyes might have been was a ridged, chitinous coating streaked with blue markings.

"When they return, those that do, they usually come here first," Chevat said. "This place has been here longer than any of my kind can remember. We call it the Temple; they call it—"

"The Deep . . ." Arasteht's hoarse voice boomed through the chamber, echoing like the weak breath of a dying god yet resonating with a lilting undertone as gentle as a child's song.

"Calm yourself!" Chevat cried, advancing closer to the hanging thing, reaching for something around his neck. "Or you shall be punished."

Arasteht shuddered and twisted his head away, gnashing his teeth and flexing fingers that bent backward as well as forward. He remained silent.

"Why do you let him live?" Brindani asked, his eyes and voice a bit clearer after consuming Chevat's potion. "Why do you not kill him, and be done with it?"

"For information, or at least whatever we can glean from his mutterings," Chevat replied, crossing his arms and turning to glare at Ghaelya menacingly. "He warns us when the Choir, or their servants, are near . . . He told us that you were coming last night."

"H-how could—?" Ghaelya stammered.

"*How* is not a factor that concerns me," the aranea interrupted loudly. "I should think the *why* of it would be of far more importance."

Uthalion stiffened, hearing the scratching approach of spidery legs from all sides. Jade eyes appeared in holes along the ceiling in groups, and others approached from behind the rocks they'd passed just moments ago. He cursed quietly, his hand edging to his sword as he realized Chevat's intent. Though with all that had occurred, he could not blame the aranea.

"The twin . . ." Arasteht muttered, suddenly focused on the genasi. "The Prophet . . ."

"Quiet!" Chevat yelled.

"She who would sing—" Brindani uttered and took a step backward, shaking his head and wiping his lips as if they'd betrayed him. He looked wide-eyed at the ceiling and walls, turning in a circle. "They're coming!" he added in a rushed whisper.

"Who?" Uthalion asked, narrowing his eyes at the trembling half-elf. "Who's coming?"

Distant buzzing shrieks echoed through the tunnels, followed by growl-like clicking and sounds of combat. Chevat snarled at the sound, his face twisting briefly to reveal his dual nature, his pointed chin splitting at the base like mandibles.

"More of those you fought on the surface," Chevat answered angrily. "The servants of the Choir."

"The Flock," Arasteht grumbled with a low chuckle like rocks rolling in a tin bucket. He faced Ghaelya, his mandibles rising as he spoke. "They see you little one . . . They love you . . ."

"Enough!" Uthalion yelled, drawing his sword and advancing on Chevat. "Get us out of here!"

Chevat bared his white teeth, double-sets of eyes protruding from his cheeks as he fumed and flinched as the sounds of fighting drew closer. Piercing screams rippled through the warrens, bounding off the walls like living things as Arasteht sighed loudly, licking his thin, drawn lips with a long tongue.

"If you want us dead, do it yourself, or give the order," Vaasurri said. He drew his bone-blade though he did not level the weapon at Chevat. "But letting those things take Ghaelya will not solve the problems you have here!"

"And letting you go will?" Chevat replied incredulously.

The sound of dozens of sharp, scampering legs joined the shrieks and screams from the tunnels.

"It's a better chance than sending your own into Tohrepur," Uthalion answered, sensing a kindred warrior in the aranea, a leader pushed to the boundaries of strategy, and understanding the occasional necessity of such sacrifices. "If you kill us the Choir will only get stronger, push harder, take more of your people . . ."

"And if I let you go to them?"

"Then there is a chance!" Uthalion shouted and lowered his sword. "More than you'll have with us dead."

"Go to her . . . to the Lady!" Arasteht cooed, his voice growing stronger despite his apparent weakness, his tentacles reaching through the webbing for the genasi. The power in his words stole everyone's attention, cajoling blades to be set aside, calming rising tempers, and obscuring the frantic struggles of spiders in the tunnels. Uthalion tried to fight back, paralyzed in the effort as Arasteht tore through a section of web. "Go to the song . . . to the shore . . . to the bloom and the—"

A roar of rage overtook the malformed aranea's powerful voice as a blur of movement charged past Uthalion. A flash of steel freed the man's limbs, left him staggering, his heart pounding as he looked up to see Brindani's sword buried in the throat of the monstrous singer.

# CHAPTER NINETEEN

*11 Mirtul, the Year of the Ageless One*
*(1479 DR)*
*The Lash, Akanûl*

Keening voices clashed with metallic clangs, drawing ever closer as Brindani twisted his blade through Arasteht's flesh, growling savagely as tentacles wrapped around his arms and legs in a tightening embrace of death. The singer's gurgling death rattle incited its battling servants, the Flock, to greater ferocity; their shrieks increased as they frantically fought to reach the bone-patterned chamber. Uthalion caught the shocked gaze of Chevat, his lips set in a thin line. He waited for the aranea's decision, though Ghaelya spoke first.

"They *can* die," the genasi said coldly to Chevat as Brindani fell away from Arasteht's body, sweet-smelling blood dripping from his blade. "That's two we've slain in as many days, and they have my sister, my twin. I do not intend to stop killing them, or anything else that gets in my way, until I have her back."

Chevat hesitated for only a moment, sparing one last glance at the dead body of Arasteht before turning to the back of the chamber, a fleetness in his step as he called over his shoulder.

"Come!"

Uthalion waved the others on, keeping a careful watch on the dark tunnels of the northern wall, convincing himself for a moment that he would stand strong if the white spiders broke through, that he would make the necessary sacrifice for his companions. There was some truth in the lie, enough that he knew it was what he should do, but not enough to make him abandon fear for his own family—not enough to banish that part of him that still longed for the beguiling song out of the south.

He turned and ran just as the others disappeared into the shimmering shadows of a southern tunnel, the shrieks and scratching claws sounding dangerously close on their heels. Chevat's voice echoed loudly from the lead, the language unknown to Uthalion, though the tone was as familiar as his own battle-tested sword. The aranea barked orders as they twisted and turned through narrow tunnels and crawl spaces, creating a shadowy flurry of activity in their wake.

Uthalion spied dark cloaks and jade eyes. Heavy-bodied spiders scrambled along the walls and crouched among the glowing roots overhead. Humanoid forms dived out of side passages, their bodies shifting with alarming speed. They landed more gracefully on eight legs than Uthalion mused he might have managed on two. They hissed as he passed, glaring before moving on, clearly not pleased with the newcomers' presence, but loyally gathering to defend their warrens.

The light flashed and flickered constantly as the sounds of battle faded farther and farther behind them. The tunnels slowly widened into ones less ornate than the web-lined artworks of the araneas entrance tunnels and more easily traversed by those unused to such shifting terrain. At length they came to a massive chamber scattered with thin shafts of glimmering light. An incline at the far end led to a loosely circular line of illumination, much like the trapdoor Chevat had led them through. It was a welcome sight for Uthalion's impatience to be free of the spiders' kingdom.

They rested at the base of a narrow tunnel leading out, listening to the passing of the Lightning Tide and waiting for Chevat's word that it was safe to leave. Uthalion kept a sharp eye on the aranea, half-expecting any moment for the spiders' leader to change his mind and seek to slay Ghaelya—it was, after all, a decision Uthalion would have considered had he been in the same position.

"What used to live there, in the Temple?" Ghaelya asked Chevat, breaking the silence. "Did your people ever discover?"

The aranea shook his head thoughtfully.

"Whatever it was, men died trying to possess it," he said after a time. "The walls were decorated with their bones, their drowned bodies used for trifles, the abandoned art-work of a fickle creature that thought little of mortal lives or desires."

Chevat's words turned over and over in Uthalion's mind, stirring an old memory that he couldn't quite grasp. When he was young, his grandfather would tell him stories of fantastic beasts, of dragons and evil elves. Though no one story came to mind, he recalled having a long-standing fear of water before learning to swim years later. He looked to Ghaelya, remembering her voice echoing up to him from the bottom of the vine-tree lined pit.

*Something in the water.*

Uthalion blinked, turning away from the genasi and the flickering ring of light just beyond her at the tunnel's edge, suddenly unsure of which he had been truly focused on. With some effort he calmed his racing, muddled thoughts, though he was anxious to keep moving rather than sit and wait in the dark.

"Almost there," he said under his breath, repeating the phrase for the strange sense of calm it brought him.

"I must admit," Chevat said sternly, "I do not know if I have chosen wisely in this."

"Not all sacrifices involve blood," Vaasurri replied.

"It's always blood," Brindani muttered as he cleaned his sword, not bothering to look up. "One way or another, always."

The chamber's dim light grew darker, and the thin ring at the tunnel's end disappeared as if shadowed from the outside. Chevat crawled closer, listening and raising his head to sniff the air, nodding and gesturing for Ghaelya to approach.

"You must run to the southern foothills. They are not far," he said quickly, his eyes darting to them all. "Climb until you are well beyond the lower level of blackened rocks, and the Tide shall not catch you. Tohrepur lies half a day's journey from the top—just follow the cliffs."

"Thank you, Chevat," Ghaelya said.

"No," the aranea replied. "I might have killed you myself. And by helping you, I daresay I may have done just that."

The genasi merely nodded and crawled toward the trapdoor, followed by Vaasurri and Brindani. As Uthalion took the first handhold, Chevat placed a long-fingered hand on his arm.

"Those affected by the song do not return from Tohrepur as they once were," the aranea said solemnly. "Do you hear the song, human?"

"No," he answered, the lie slipping out before he could stop it, denying that his motives were anything but honorable, though he wondered if they were truly his motives at all. Chevat slipped a leather pouch into his hand and closed his fingers around it tightly before letting go.

"Be swift," the aranea said. "And if I happen to find you no longer yourself in the days to come, I shall slay you quickly."

Before Uthalion could think of how to reply to such a statement, the aranea had dashed into the shadows, his legs lengthening and splitting behind him into the long, sharp-footed legs of a spider. Wind caressed Uthalion's face, and he turned to the pale light outside, scrambling up the tunnel and out onto the stiff, warm grass of the Lash.

Brindani staggered out into the light, wild-eyed and running through the gray. The foothills were just ahead, and he quickened his stride at the sight of them, desperate to reach them, to climb them, and to find the place of the song and dreams. He felt as though he were falling with each step, tumbling toward an end he knew deep down he should fear, and yet he could not resist the summons in his blood. Cool wind blew across his fevered skin like a breath of winter. The sweat on his brow felt like ice, and he ran faster.

He was dimly aware of the poisonous ache in his limbs. Though Chevat's potion had done much to ease the pain, it left him drained and nauseous. He stumbled against the incline of the foothills, falling to his hands and knees in blackened soil that smelled of char. He craned his neck to the top of the rocky foothills above, grinning weakly as he stood, so close to the promise of the song, a promise of peace. His eyes widened as he panicked for a moment, looking around until he saw Ghaelya climbing the hill behind him. He watched her pass with a dazed expression, letting relief calm his anxiety.

"All will be well," he muttered, his eyes fixed on the genasi. "All will be well."

He tried to stand and felt a twisting pang in his stomach. He faltered, confused and trying to catch his breath when the pang returned more forcefully, stabbing his insides with pure agony. A dry scream scratched its way through his throat as he doubled over, rolling in the ash. He felt rough hands grab his arms and haul him up, and tried to keep his feet moving as he was dragged up the hill backward. Rolling thunder deafened him and hid his feeble cries in crashing waves that shook the air. Though his eyes were closed, he could see the Lightning Tide return in bright flashes of red as it scoured the Lash.

His body curled in on itself as pain needled hungrily through his gut. It was not the gentle pain of the song; it did not bring him dreams or enhanced senses and it did not sink through his skin or bear the sweet scent of the red flower that Sefir had fed him. The pain was more familiar, almost forgotten, and it seemed it had returned with a vengeance. As the thunder died, following the Tide on its route around the Lash, he heard the tired grunts and cursing of Vaasurri and Uthalion, heard Vaasurri muttering as they pulled him to safety.

"Silkroot," the killoren said derisively.

"No . . ." Brindani whispered, gasping for air and fighting against the hands that held him. He'd left the silkroot behind him, not having needed or wanted the drug since finding the song and tasting the red flower. But his body was betraying his wishes, filling him with a base hunger that he loathed. He fought harder and found his voice, roaring in defiance of his own addiction, "No!"

He kicked against the ground hard, and he was released in a volley of shocked curses. Hitting the ground he turned and leaped forward, climbing as fast as he could manage, scraping his hands on the rocks, feverishly pulling himself higher and higher. All the while he felt the memory of the summoning song fade a little from his mind, felt his blood grow cold, and wanted to weep. The taste of blood filled his mouth; he huffed it from between his lips to spatter little red droplets on the gray stone as he climbed and scrambled for the top of the foothills.

He blocked out all but the top of the tall slope, enduring the pulsing pain through his abdomen. He listened for the song, but it did not come to him. He wanted to scream, to demand that it return and banish the agonizing remnant of the pathetic man that had wandered Aglarond in a drug-filled haze. Briefly, he considered how high he had climbed, contemplated the long fall over rocks, bits of half-buried walls, and the rotted out hulls of ancient fishing vessels.

"Just one slip," he whispered, the thought coming through his pain in a rare moment of clarity. The song was missing, the grips of the silkroot were fading, and his more substantial wounds had begun to ache, leaving him for several breaths in between desire and necessity, his own man. "One slip . . ."

His head began to swim, and he felt faint. Grasping at another handhold, he tried to lift his suddenly wavering legs. His field of vision narrowed, overtaken by a tunnel of smoky black as his eyelids fluttered. His breath came quick and shallow. The scent of blood surrounded him, his wounds seeping through bandages that felt too tight, itching his skin abrasively. One hand slipped on the rough wood of an old fencepost, and he lurched backward, his eyes rolling in his head.

"Brindani!"

He heard his name but could not place the voice. The ground fell away, and a sickening freefall took him in an airy embrace. In the time between falling, bouncing off a smooth rock, and feeling sets of hands grasp his arms and legs, he heard shocked voices cry out in startling detail.

He felt the rough pattern of swirling fingerprints scrape across his skin. His nose was overcome by powerful scents of blood and sweat as he was lowered to the ground. Though a throbbing, needling pain remained in his gut, another, smaller pain began to spread over his skin and sink into his flesh. Again, he wanted to weep.

"It didn't leave me . . ." he rasped quietly, grabbing at an arm that supported his head. Though the touch of the song was little more than a flicker, unable to totally banish the grips of his old addiction, it was enough to give him a warped sense of hope. The two painful compulsions warred over his spirit and threatened his sanity. "It didn't leave me . . . All will be well . . . tomorrow . . ."

"All will be well," a voice like Uthalion's answered, though a coldness in the human's tone was somewhat alarming as Brindani slipped into the velvety black of slithering dreams and distant singing.

On a wide ledge just over halfway up the long, rocky incline, a small campfire burned with a pale brightness next to the flashing plains of the Lash. Uthalion kept his back to the Lightning Tide, his eyes still burning from his last glance at the gray plains. The sun would set soon, and at length they had decided to rest before pressing on, preferring to enter Tohrepur by day instead of night. And, Uthalion had reasoned reluctantly, they shouldn't leave Brindani behind unprotected.

Vaasurri had been the only one to agree out loud, though Uthalion suspected the killoren's reasons had less to do with the unconscious half-elf and more with the mysterious ruins. Vaasurri hadn't said as much, but their proximity to Tohrepur seemed to be having an effect on him as well. His hair had darkened, and his eyes wavered between emerald green and shadowy gray, a sign of something unnatural, beyond even the experience of the sensitive fey.

Uthalion stared up the slope, tracing the edge with his eyes and pointedly ignoring the urge to keep climbing. He questioned his own motives and desires as he suppressed the impulses that sought to overcome his good sense. Absently, he twirled the silver ring on his finger, pulling it on and off with his thumb, an old habit of his that Maryna used to tease him over, saying that if he lost her ring she'd find another man who could hold on to it better. His breath caught in his throat at the memory, and he waited as the sudden emotion rose and fell in his chest, exhaling slowly as it passed. He wondered if his family truly had been taken to the ruins, not as sure as he'd been that morning, the strong certainty of his dream no longer as strong. But still, the possibility weighed on his mind.

"Almost there," he said under his breath and recalled why the words seemed so familiar. "Leave a light in the window. I'm almost there."

Over and over, through the Lash, the Wash, and the rising lands of the Spur, he had uttered the phrase as he'd led his men out of Tohrepur six years before, all the while focused on his family. Maryna had been waiting for him with Cienna in her arms, just as he'd imagined, ever since their argument over soldiering and gold. But his experiences had been there too, like a hulking shadow in the corner of their little cottage, casting a pall over their lives. He'd come home a different man, a different husband and father than when he'd left, and Maryna hadn't known how to deal with him.

She smiled less and less in the days following. He had slept on the floor when exhaustion had taken him and had spent his days and nights by the window, waiting for something to happen, waiting for the world to tumble away into chaos so that the fear he felt might be justified. He wanted to keep fighting, to keep surviving so that Maryna could have seen what he had seen and know what he then knew— that with the slightest push in the right spot, everything could fall apart.

Nothing ever came. They argued more and more each day until she told him to leave. Eventually he did, promising that he would return, a promise he still intended to keep. With a gentle tug he pulled the silver ring away, reached into a secured pouch, and replaced the band with his wife's scratched and slightly bent ring, suddenly needing a greater magic than the silver could provide to keep going.

"We've been on the road longer than I thought," Vaasurri said, gesturing at the ring as he joined Uthalion by the fire.

"Too long," Uthalion replied with a deep sigh. "How's Brindani?"

"He'll live," the killoren answered. "Though his withdrawal has only gotten worse. He's barely touched the leaves I gave him for the pain days ago. I think he wants to die."

"He'll have his chance soon enough," Uthalion said, glancing again to the edge of the slope worriedly. "I should have listened to you, outside of Caidris," he said as he turned his gaze to his old friend. "I'm sorry for that."

Vaasurri nodded slowly, his gray-green eyes gleaming in the firelight.

"No regrets now," he said quietly. "Almost there."

"Almost there," Uthalion whispered, fearing what the next day might bring.

Ghaelya sat in the dark beyond the fire's light, gazing up to the long divide between the swirling, dark clouds over the Lash and the clear, darkening skies over the south. The setting sun's light was split between the two lands: deep blue and muted to the north, purpled and clear to the south. She rubbed her hands gently, tracing the rough edges of scratches, testing the tenderness of new bruises along her arms. All the while she knew that somewhere, just to the west of where she sat, her sister waited for her, as did the monstrous beings of the Choir and likely the creature that had somehow made them into things of nightmare.

It had proven difficult admitting to the others that she needed rest and stopping herself long enough to consider sitting—even longer to contemplate eating, which she had done sparingly, nibbling at bits of dried fruit and venison. Those were luxuries she felt she neither could afford nor really deserved, though without them she would be useless to her sister. So she sat and waited impatiently for sleep to claim her.

She had thought briefly of speaking with Uthalion, thanking for him for bringing her so far on little more than faith. But at the sight of his haunted eyes, she turned away, feeling foolish. Vaasurri had watched her with a guarded expression, saying little more than was necessary. She could sense a tension with the killoren that she regretted.

Brindani moaned in his sleep nearby, muttering unintelligibly as he tossed and turned. His tortured voice, rasping quietly and rattling deep in his chest, made her wince; the half-elf looked much the worse for their long journey. She pitied him, though she hated herself for doing so, knowing full well that without him she wouldn't have made it here. Given the chance to do things over again, she still would have accepted his help, despite the consequences.

She had used the last of her water cleaning his wounds, leaving only a small sip to slake her thirst before replacing his bandages. His wrists were covered in spidering blue veins, the skin of his forearms almost transparent. A patch of raw skin on the back of his neck had spread to his shoulder, taking on a familiar pale texture that caused her to shudder and turn away.

Biting her tongue, she saved her rage, storing it away for Tohrepur. She was angry at herself for caring what happened to the half-elf, but more angry for not wanting to care. She had no room for regret, not yet, not until she found Tessaeril and fixed the rift between herself and the better person her twin had always pushed her to be.

She rested her head upon her knees, staring into the middle-distance until her eyelids grew heavy. Darkness and light flickered before her eyes, and she caught the sound of her own breathing, deep and throaty, bordering on a light snoring. Gasping softly she sat up straight, realizing what she was doing. She was suddenly aware of the profound silence that had fallen around her.

"The dream," she whispered, lucid and aware. For a moment she doubted that she dreamed at all until the gentle lapping of heavy waves drew her attention to the north and the vast inland sea spreading out across where the Lash had been. The rolling surf of the blue-black mirror of water nearly reached her feet, and a soft, white sand beach stretched from east to west. An eerie singing echoed faintly from the sea, the song sounding like a rusty nail pulled skillfully down the length of a harp string. In the sand, tiny pale figures writhed, sliding over one another and moving in a strange sinuous rhythm to the tune of the song.

She pulled away from the living shore, turning to see Brindani lying on his back, his black glassy eyes reflecting the light of the stars as he quietly gasped for air, surrounded by pulsing red flowers. He was trying to speak. Uthalion and Vaasurri were gone, and the campfire burned with a green light that rolled and wavered slowly, as if underwater.

Beside the fire she saw her sword, its heavy blade shining dully in the light. A dripping coat of blood covered it and pooled around the point. Crawling closer, Ghaelya reached out for the hilt and paused, her hands covered in blood as well. She tried to wipe it away to no avail; her fingertips dripped crimson on the ground and each drop sprouted small red blooms. The little flowers spread, leading her eyes in a long string to the shoreline, where she found the familiar bright eyes, bursting with fleshy red flowers watching her. A blue-black silhouette lounged half on the sand, half in the water.

"Tess?" she asked, leaning forward and squinting in the green light of the fire. "I'm coming, Tess. I'll find you!"

The silhouette slowly withdrew into the tide until only its crimson eyes were visible among the waves. The tiny, writhing figures in the sand bent their bodies toward the figure in the water, their red mouths open wide and their whispering voices joining the haunting song.

"Can you hear the song, sister?" Tessaeril asked from the water.

"I can! I can hear the song!" Ghaelya answered, shouting as the song grew louder. "Is it you? Are you singing?"

"Did you bring your sword?" Tessaeril asked.

"I did," Ghaelya replied and glanced at the weapon as if in a trance. The blood on its blade began to spread into the green fire, hissing as a sweet scent rose in thin tendrils of smoke, "But it's covered in blood."

"It's always blood," Tessaeril answered, her eyes disappearing in the depths of the Mere. "One way or another, always."

Ghaelya turned to Brindani. Hearing his words repeated by her sister sent chills down her arms, and she shuddered. But the half-elf was gone, replaced by a growing mound of pulsing flowers whose crimson nectar ran freely into the sand and mingled with the surf.

# CHAPTER TWENTY

*12 Mirtul, the Year of the Ageless One*
*(1479 DR)*
*Ruins of Tohrepur, Akanûl*

Uthalion stood on the edge of the highland, the sun rising behind him as he stared thoughtfully to the glittering west. On that horizon stood a forest of crystalline spires, and in the shadow of that forest lay Tohrepur. A void had settled uncomfortably in his thoughts; the time between falling asleep and waking up was like an empty space, as if he'd been plucked from sunset and placed at the following sunrise with no regard for the normal course of time. He felt out of place, and as Ghaelya crested the edge of the hill, her eyes and boots fixed on the west, his place seemed taken away.

He was no longer a guide, though there was still work to do.

Brindani crawled into the highland grass as if he were a dead man crawling from his own grave.

Indeed, he had begun to very much look the part. Though he appeared stronger and calmer after last night's attack, he was too pale, almost bloodless as he shied away from the sun. He pulled his cloak tight and trudged along in Ghaelya's wake. He said nothing, sparing Uthalion a slight glance from his over-large and heavy-lidded eyes that were nearly swallowed by blackness.

Uthalion had considered Chevat's last words to him and wondered if the burden of such a mercy now rested on his blade. It was obvious that silkroot was the least of Brindani's afflictions, and though it pained him to see the deterioration of the half-elf, the simple fact remained that Brindani could prove useful. They knew nothing of the Choir save that it seemed to be some kind of infection, likely sorcerous, and Brindani's condition could provide them with answers. He felt ashamed, looking upon his old friend as mere fodder, but the shame of a meaningless death seemed a far worse fate.

Vaasurri stayed close behind the half-elf with a wary eye and a ready blade. Should the killoren sense any sudden change or betrayal, he would finish Brindani's suffering quickly. Uthalion adjusted his sword belt, whispered a curse to any god that would allow such a killing to become necessary, and took up the rear.

The short journey was uneventful and eerily quiet, save for the distant rumbling of thunder across the Lash. No birds disturbed the sparse trees, and the wildflowers competed for the few pollinating insects that drifted near. It seemed as though nature held its breath as Uthalion passed, wondering if the returning human would somehow unleash another dark storm of chaos.

By midday the ruins came into view.

The silhouette of the city was long and sprawling, a collection of packed buildings, high walls, and narrow streets perched on the steep edge of the former shoreline. Its ancient seas, once teeming with fish and livelihood, were just a dry rocky slope. The swirling storms of the Lash rolled and crashed teasingly, like an ocean turned upside down, a tide across the sky.

A thick, deep green carpet of silky grass rippled around their boots like water, the tip of each blade disappearing in a tendril of smoky mist. Uthalion recalled a soup made from the grass, bowls of the stuff having been offered by the disconcertingly kind citizens of Tohrepur as he'd marched behind the banner of the Keepers of the Cerulean Sign. They'd made use of the people's unusual hospitality, and within moments Uthalion had found himself standing guard outside a small shop. Inside, the Keepers had interrogated a young boy, painful and terrifying roars that should have come from a far more monstrous creature shaking the windows and walls as the suddenly quiet and blank-faced population dropped whatever they were doing to gather around the interlopers.

A sudden chill tore Uthalion from the memory, and he looked upon the ruins the city had become. Rusted gates of worked iron hung loose and tangled with vines that roped and snaked across every surface. Deep cracks marked the crumbling walls, filled with more of the encroaching green vines. The mist-grass lapped at the city walls, giving it the impression of an island trapped in an emerald sea. Multi-colored flashes of light glittered from the tall forest of spires that pressed down against the southern end of the ruins.

Ghaelya stood at the gates, fearlessly tugging at the protesting hinges. Uthalion and the others rushed to keep up with the genasi lest they lose her in the labyrinthine streets. The image of her fighting to get in struck him as horrific given that she had fought so hard to escape the grasp of those who might have brought her to the same gates. He had a sudden urge to pull her away and shake the mad gleam from her eyes, but knew the effort would be wasted—she might have cut him down just as quickly as anything else that stood in her way.

He let her slip through the gates without a word, his heart pounding in his chest as he stared into the familiar cobblestone streets beyond. As Brindani entered behind her, he laid a hand upon the gate. A thin web of nearly transparent skin stretched between the half-elf's long fingers. Uthalion shared a horrified glance with Vaasurri and placed a hand on his sword as an ominous wind howled down the narrow avenue.

Cursing quietly and catching his breath, Uthalion pulled the rusted gate wider and entered the ruins.

Ghaelya stepped cautiously over vines and broken stones, turning as if she expected monsters to come pouring from every shadow and crevice. Though nothing appeared, she drew her sword anyway, descending down the empty lane of hollowed buildings, wide-eyed and tense with every careful step. Twisting vine-trees grew through cracks in the street, swaying hypnotically alongside the seaweedlike greenery that choked the walls and slowly squeezed them into dust. Old stone was weathered and discolored, and shafts of shimmering light played upon every surface and shone into every open doorway. Dragonflies hovered in flashing swarms of silver, darting one way, then the next, disappearing into windows curtained in green.

"Where are you?" she whispered angrily through clenched teeth. "I'm here!"

She fought the urge to cry out, to hear something besides the endless murmuring of the wind and the creaking of twisting vine-trees. Her footsteps echoed loudly, her breath seemed to rumble like thunder, and her heart raced in her chest like a charging army. She moved faster, nimbly prowling through the narrow streets and searching for any sign, any clue that might lead her to Tessaeril. Becoming frantic, she worked her way from building to building, peering into doorways and finding naught but vines and dragonflies.

She stumbled into an intersection, cursing and catching herself on her hands amid a braided web of vines. Halfway to standing she paused; a flash of red on the ground caught her eye. Parting the vines she saw a streak of crimson splattered across the stones accompanied by the shape of a red, long-fingered handprint. She looked up, studying the surrounding buildings for anything similar or any trail she could follow.

"Too red to be blood," Uthalion said over her shoulder, and she nodded thoughtfully, though she glanced at Brindani who had leaned against a nearby wall, shivering in his cloak.

"It's always blood," she said quietly. She chose the steepest avenue out of the intersection, following the direction indicated by the handprint and trying to trust to her instincts as she called over her shoulder, "We should go south."

"You know this?" Vaasurri asked.

"Would the direction matter if I didn't know?" she said.

She didn't stop for an answer, driven to accept even the slightest clue. She was tired of wandering aimlessly. With a direction, even if it were arbitrary, she felt somewhat in control, though briefly she shamefully wondered where she would find her sister's body. The sudden idea spawned a hundred others, a myriad of possibilities assaulting her as she pressed on, unable to stop the course of her thoughts.

Overgrown buildings fell into a darker shade near the center of the city. Leaning dwellings, held up only by the wild nature that had broken them in the first place, leered at her like the empty skulls of fallen giants, titans that had laid down to rest and had never woken up. Yawning doorways moaned as the breeze picked up, funnelling like a cold river through the tight streets.

Despite the wind, an ominous silence seemed to vibrate in every part of the city, resting it on an edge between peaceful sleep and all-consuming nightmare. The vines grew thicker, bridging between the buildings and creating a thick canopy pierced by tiny shafts of orange light. The glow played along her arms and shoulders, a harbinger of a sunset that grew closer and closer. Dried vegetation and loose rocks crunched under her boots as she raised her sword, and the shadows squirmed with a hundred different shapes as her eyes tried to adjust.

Uthalion crept closer, his sword drawn as the narrow street opened into a circular intersection of old shops and shattered architecture. The air grew warmer and humid, clinging thickly to Ghaelya's skin as a heavy scent wafted through the intersection. It smelled of unwashed bodies, death, and other things she did not want to contemplate. Her stomach turned, and bile burned in the back of her throat as she struggled to keep her composure.

At the center of the intersection they stopped, the sudden silence of their footsteps lasting only briefly as Ghaelya heard something else filling the spaces between one heartbeat and the next. A swift and rhythmic huffing sound like a thousand miniature forge bellows emanated from every shadowed doorway, every darkened window. Once heard, Ghaelya swore she could feel it, blowing hot on her cheek like the wind at a summer funeral.

"What is it?" Uthalion whispered. "Just wind through the leaves?"

"Not just leaves," Vaasurri answered from Ghaelya's right. The killoren was kneeling, inspecting something on the ground, turning a small object over in the palm of his hand. He held it up in a shaft of red-orange light. "Teeth."

The shadows deepened, and the huffing grew louder, little breaths in unison all around them. Ghaelya blinked in the the dim light, squinting at what appeared to be pale fingers clasped over windowsills and feet lying close to open doors. They were just far enough away from the entrances to make her doubt her own eyes. As she stepped closer to the other end of the intersection, dreading the reddened light beyond the canopy of vines, she winced at the crunching sound beneath her boot.

Shadows moved along the tops of the buildings, blocking the shafts of light and prowling just out of sight. Occasionally a soft, raspy whimper would echo through an open window, sending chills down her spine.

"I hear it," Brindani whispered, the words carrying loudly in the enclosed space. The half-elf grew more animated, dropping the edges of his cloak and walking toward the southern edge of the intersection. Silhouetted in red light, he placed his hands on his head as if in pain. "Can you hear it?" he asked in a strained voice.

He stood still a moment before following the street with an easy stride, shielding his eyes when a shaft of light fell on him from an empty alley. Ghaelya watched him go, hesitating for half a breath as the occasional whimpers increased and the ghostly breathing intensified, becoming faster and faster.

"Let's go," Uthalion said, his voice breaking through the fear that threatened to leave her frozen in place. Despite the cacophony of crushed teeth and leaves that seemed to thunder beneath them, Ghaelya made out the muffled sound of heavy forms thudding against old wood, of fingernails scratching at stone, and tortured throats groaning as some unseen host was awoken by the dying light of day.

Her step quickened as they climbed higher into the city, keeping Brindani one block ahead. He led them inexorably closer to the glittering forest of crystal spires. Faintly, as the shadows lengthened and the eastern sky turned a bright shade of purple, she could hear the slightest whisper of a distant singing.

For the last block, deep in the thick shadows of the dark, crystal spires, she ran as fast as she could. Tessaeril was calling for her.

Uthalion followed as quickly as he could, though the half-healed wounds on his leg had begun to ache with the steady climb of the street. He'd been relieved at first when Ghaelya chose to move south—the lair the Keepers had sought six years ago had been hidden beneath the northern edge of the city. But as they drew closer to the spires, and he heard the first murmuring strains of beguiling song, his relief quickly faded.

At the end of the street he stopped short behind Ghaelya. They stood in a large clearing between several buildings. It might have once been an open air marketplace, or perhaps a stable, but it seemed a gateway only to the encroaching bulk of the spire forest. The towering spears of rock and crystal had crumbled the city's southern wall and pushed forward mounds of dirt and weeds. A passage sloped into the darkness between the spires.

Brindani sat at the center of the clearing, on his knees amid the vines and clutching the sides of his head tightly. He trembled violently, locked in a struggle that Uthalion could not imagine. Ghaelya stepped toward the half-elf, and Uthalion stopped her, shaking his head and placing a finger to his lips. He raised his sword, uncertain if Brindani could fight the song or the infectious influence it had over him, and ready to cut down his old friend if necessary.

Bathed in the crimson light of the dying day, the clearing seemed stained in blood beneath the jagged spires. Veins of onyx ran through the massive crystals, reflecting a thousand setting suns at once like a bizarre timepiece winding down. As the city grew darker, it grew more and more alive with the distant and unnerving huffing, like a thousand breaths merged as one beast, awakening in the dark of a thousand different windows and doors.

The wind picked up as the breaths increased. It whistled through the spires then changed into a whispering melody that rushed through the city streets like an army of keening ghosts. The thousand mirrored suns were halved by the dark silhouettes of their horizons, and Uthalion found himself breathing as hard and as fast as the unseen host in the city below.

"What in all the hells?" he whispered, slowing his breathing, though unable to calm the pounding of his heart. The song slid around him like an old friend, blowing softly in his ear as if it greeted him alone. Bits and pieces of the melody took on the form of the old wedding song it had sung to him in the Spur and in his dreams at the old farmhouse on the edge of the Wash. Alarmed, he looked to Ghaelya and cursed himself, recalling the song's last words.

*Bring her to me.*

*Bring her to me.*

Brindani cried out suddenly, pounding his fists into the ground and inhaling sharply. Control of his faculties seemed to return as he sat still. As he stood, his trembling muscles slowed and his bloody knuckles dripped thick crimson on the dirt and vines. His tortured features calmed, though he stood against the shining columns as if he challenged them, drawing his sword and stretching his neck. He looked sidelong at Uthalion, his eyes reddened and ringed with dark circles.

"It's coming," he said. The words chilled Uthalion to the bone.

The reflections of the thousand suns were mere slivers now, thinly sliced by their horizons and broken in places by the city's mirrored skyline. The haunting song grew stronger, flowing around Uthalion and then wailing past him into the city's depths. Yet despite the eeriness of the singing, he mourned losing its attention, if only for the moment.

Low growls echoed from among the spires, and Uthalion turned, his sword leveled, as wolflike forms prowled through the crystals, their glassy eyes gleaming red and purple. The muscular dreamers appeared, pawing at the dirt threateningly and baring their tusklike fangs. They formed a wall of pale fur and flexing claws at the edge of the forest. Several snapped at the air, gnashing their teeth menacingly, but beyond their threatening postures, Uthalion could see several staring at him almost curiously. They crowded and nosed through the snarling pack, never leaving the edge of the stone forest, but trying to get a look at the newcomers. Those beasts sprawled on the ground, holding their noses low as they sniffed the air and regarded him with quizzical expressions.

He and Ghaelya backed away, forming a semicircle with Vaasurri. Brindani never moved, staring down the growling beasts from only a few strides away.

"What's he doing?" Ghaelya asked quietly. Uthalion could only shake his head. He felt confused, as though he were caught up in someone else's nightmare, a dream he might only escape by waking an unknown dreamer.

He flinched as the ground shifted and buckled, adjusting his footing as the network of vines writhed between his legs. They tightened like deep green muscles, and the broken wall at the clearing's edge cracked a little more, spilling dirt onto the cobblestones. The tremors spread through the ruins, the stone splitting and crumbling as the vines pulled and twisted like a single living thing. An ear-splitting rumble shook the ground as some distant building gave way, crashing into the streets and sending clouds of rolling dust through the long avenues in waves of choking debris.

Amid the destruction Uthalion could make out tiny screams and wailing cries. But they were cut off swiftly, dying away as the dust settled and the vines relaxed. A hush fell over the city like a held breath, and Uthalion tensed. The dreamers had ceased their posturing and sat stoically at the spires' edge as the last thin measure of sunlight dipped below the horizon.

"There," Vaasurri whispered and pointed with his sword. "A path between the spires."

Uthalion squinted in the deepening shadows, just able to make out, between the lithe bodies of the dreamers, a rough-stoned walkway through the crystals. Ghaelya started forward anxiously, and Uthalion grabbed her shoulder.

"Are you mad?" he asked as she wrenched away from him. "There's too many of them!"

"Tess," she whispered, fixing him with a determined gaze. "I can hear her."

As if in answer to her, the tall crystals shook, hairline cracks forming in a few as the ghostly song thundered through the forest again. Wordless and haunting, it sang all around him, unleashed in a flood of tumultuous, screaming melody. At the core of the song was an unmistakable femininity that rippled with unseen fingertips over Uthalion's skin, pushing and pulling him as he fought to remain standing. With soft, resounding whispers it clawed a deep pit in his mind, like a watery grave that promised peace if he would only lie down and submit.

He cried out and fell to one knee, swearing loudly, his voice swallowed in the maddening torrent of song. Vaasurri and Ghaelya remained standing, covering their ears as best they could and turning away from the crystals as the roaring melody shook the city anew. Brindani weathered the song, seemingly unmoved. His black hair was blown in a powerful breeze as he turned; his eyes as dark as a cold forge.

"Can you hear it?" he asked casually.

Vines writhed and twisted around them, erupting small nodules that grew and burst with flashes of crimson. The buds cracked open at their centers like sickly flowers, and the fleshy, red petals they bloomed throbbed and puckered like living tissue. They pulsed rhythmically like little heartbeats, tiny veins pushing to the petals' surface as sweet scents filled the air. The flowers spread throughout the city, almost glowing in the deep twilight. As the blooms appeared, the dreamers growled and whimpered, their long mournful whines blending seamlessly with the song's tempest.

Uthalion fell backward, catching himself with his free hand. He cursed as he looked across the nightmarish ruins, at the shadows of Tohrepur erupting with renewed life. The dark gaping maws of windows discharged sluggish, pale bodies that flopped into the night air. Doorways were crowded with white, slack-jawed faces that peered out into the bruised light of the day's end. Twisted and hairless figures crawled languidly from their hiding places, huffing loudly as they awoke from strange slumbers to gather in the streets. They bared needlelike teeth and dark eyes to the sky, crawling over one another in a sickly mass.

Uthalion picked out several races among the throng, noting the bloated abdomens of large white spiders amid the groaning crowds.

"The Flock," he muttered, horrified as they knelt and tore at the crimson blossoms. Red juices ran through their fingers as they stuffed the petals into their mouths and fed hungrily, the sticky red nectar dribbling down their chins and staining their thin lips.

"The Choir brings us," Brindani said, a bizarre quality in his voice buzzing through Uthalion's skull. "The Song calls us . . . The Lady dreams us . . . And her blood feeds us."

"Blood," Uthalion whispered, staring at the enthralled Flock. The bodies grew slick with bloody nectar, blending together as they slid and pulled themselves deeper into the restless press, the streets disappearing beneath them. Long fingernails caked with dark pulp scratched at the sky, as the bodies swayed with the terrible song.

Reluctantly, Uthalion studied those he could see clearly, moving from one to the next. He dreaded the sight of a bared breast or a curving, feminine hip, afraid of finding Maryna. But he did not see her—did not want to see her—and slowly convinced himself, for the sake of his own sanity, that she was not among the Flock. She couldn't be.

He turned away, unable to look at the pitiful faces or contemplate such a horrid existence. The song had lessened somewhat, and he stood on shaky legs, his sword in a grip so tight he feared his fingers might break.

"Not here," he whispered under his breath, willing the words to be true. "She's not here."

Vaasurri stood close by, his eyes darting between the wailing Flock and the strangely quiet dreamers. The beasts had lowered their heads, sorrowful expressions on their faces as they pawed at the dirt and paced back and forth at the clearing's edge. Ghaelya edged closer to the crystal forest cautiously, earning threatening growls and toothy snarls from the dreamers, though they did not leave the glittering perimeter of the spires.

Brindani had lowered his sword. His dark eyes still gleamed with some alien presence, a gaze that seemed to switch continuously between the half-elf Uthalion knew and something else that raised the hairs on the back of his neck.

"Uthalion," Brindani said, his voice wavering discordantly with strains of the beguiling song as he looked out across the ruins and the reveling Flock. A flash of fear crossed the half-elf's features, and behind him the dreamers flinched, whining low in their thick throats. "The Choir is coming."

A distant, monstrous roar echoed through the streets, answered by others from different parts of the city as Uthalion turned, glaring and searching for the monsters amid the bloody, wailing figures—searching for Khault.

# CHAPTER TWENTY-ONE

*12 Mirtul, the Year of the Ageless One*
*(1479 DR)*
*Ruins of Tohrepur, Akanûl*

Muscles rippled and undulated in waves as the gathered masses of the Flock shifted and wailed at the coming of the Choir. Booming voices trumpeted in eerie whale-song echoes. Misshapen limbs grasped and clawed for purchase on the streets, their flesh in flux even as they answered the call of the song. The ground shook at the Choir's approach, and their sonorous bellows seemed to shake the very air, as if the fabric of reality shuddered to expel such abominations from its firmament.

Brindani staggered, at last released briefly from the will of the song to fall and gasp for air. The singing remained a constant force in his body however, pain and pleasure ripping through him in fine threads of bittersweet melody. Resting on one knee, he endured the scent of the crimson blooms that summoned his unnatural hunger, but as his stomach twisted in agony, he tempered his addiction with the thick taste of blood that flavored each breath in salt and copper. Somewhere between song and addiction he found a balance, a precarious perch upon which to hang his sense of self.

A feminine screech tore through the air, parting the red and white sea of the Flock with thrumming, destructive tones. Almost visible at the end of a steep avenue, a beautiful, angular face rested like a mask upon stretched and pockmarked flesh. Red lips, pierced with barbed, hooklike teeth parted in a deep sigh that rushed through the clearing like an autumn breeze. The Flock swarmed at the thing's feet, fawning over and caressing the Choir, their singing angels in a temple of ruins.

Brindani gripped his stomach tightly, his heart pounding as he drew back his sword. He was prepared to defend himself to the last even as the powerful song lessened his pain. Sweetly, it whispered wordless charms to him, the tendrils of enchanting melody so strong that he imagined he could even see them, wrapped around him in an inescapable embrace. He trembled as the song touched upon his mind, fearful of again losing his will and giving in to his temptations. But deep in the song's core, a strangely familiar voice reached him. Gently it pulsed outward, the tendrils sweeping through the ruins, its touch connecting him to those it found.

He gasped in horror as the minds of the Choir brushed against his thoughts, assaulting him with madness. Wants and needs and unimaginable lusts left his skin crawling, though their singular attention was focused just to his left. He glanced to Ghaelya, an unhallowed image flashing through his mind with a stab of fear for the genasi. The song softened in her presence, becoming a low hum of sorrow, unconditional love, and primal terror.

"Khault," Uthalion muttered as a figure in tattered, dirty robes distinguished itself among the nightmarish horde.

Brindani barely recognized the old farmer, hidden as he was in a twisted body of rippling limbs and warped bones, but the half-elf knew him nonetheless. The song fairly screamed at the sight of the man, filling him with a boundless rage that he fed upon, using it against the pain in his body and holding it tight in the hilt of his sword.

"Captain," Khault replied in a thunderous voice, shaking the ground as the dreamers whined, pawing at the ground. "You bring to us the twin."

The grisly host responded savagely, their voices and hands raised to the sky, each note feeding into Brindani's body through the song. Their exquisite pain ran through him, though it was nothing compared to what he'd done to himself over the years. He endured, but in their chanting exultation, he was shown their shared secret, the source of their reasonless fanaticism and the infection that ruled their bodies. He glimpsed a deep chamber in their minds, adorned with bones, filled with a soft blue glow that glistened like water. A massive blue eye turned sightlessly in the murk as he was torn away from the image and left panting, on his knees before the nightmarish things *she* had dreamed.

"She," he whispered.

The creature of the depths, the whisperer of songs and the seductress of drowned sailors. A collector of polished bone, torn from the ocean by the death of a goddess, changed by the blue fire of the Spellplague into a living scourge of dreams. Unbidden tears sprang to Brindani's eyes as he looked upon the fools that drowned in madness for her now.

It had been a sirine's song that had called them to Tohrepur, and he'd been as much the fool as any of them.

Uthalion stood strong as the Choir approached. None were so bold as Khault; the rest hid among their Flock, excitedly gibbering to themselves and twitching in the shadows. The singing had faded somewhat, though Uthalion could still sense it as if it were intentionally eddying around him, leaving his mind clear and his old sword at the ready. The captain's blade gleamed sharply, returned to the place where its first wielder had fallen. It again threatened the flesh of abominations, though there were no proud banners to hang over its singular purpose.

Khault stood at the head of the misshapen congregation, his arms bent at odd angles, and his legs lost in a mass of fleshy tentacles that writhed beneath his robes. Deeply stained bandages covered the scarred place where his eyes had sat, though he seemed no blinder than those who looked upon him with disgust and pity. The others, beyond simple descriptions of race or gender, shambled on limbs that only played at being legs. Eyeless faces rose and fell among them, peering over Khault's shoulders. They murmured, licking torn lips with doubled tongues and absently picking at deep gouges in their flesh.

Uthalion did not flinch at their appearance or waver beneath their eyeless, horrible gazes. He'd had a thousand nightmares far and beyond more terrible than those of the Choir; he had fought such pathetic beasts before. It was what he'd waited for, what he'd foreseen coming all those nights sitting at the window while Maryna slept alone.

This is my place, he thought sadly, I've always been here.

"Where is she?" Ghaelya demanded of Khault. "What have you done?"

The Flock growled and hissed at Khault's feet, baring sharklike fangs at the genasi. Gasps and sighs filled the tortured throats of the Choir as they pointed and craned their necks to hear the genasi's voice, tasting the air with their long tongues.

"Hush," Khault intoned. The quiet word buzzed like a swarm of spring-beetles yet crackled like flame with a force that pushed on Uthalion's chest challengingly. "Save your steel, child," Khault said and raised a clawed finger to the spires with a growl that parted the assembled dreamers. They revealed a cobblestone path through the crystals. "Go, embrace your twin. It is all that we have ever wanted for you."

"No!" Brindani spoke up, straining to speak and sweating with the effort. His nose began to bleed, running over his lips and clenched teeth. "Not all that you wanted—"

"Quiet," Khault boomed, and Brindani fell back, gasping and clutching his stomach in pain. Khault turned to Ghaelya. "She calls for you . . . Can you hear her?"

She hesitated for just a moment, looking between Brindani and the spires. The half-elf shook his head wordlessly, reaching out for her, but even Uthalion could hear the oddly familiar voice whispering through the crystal forest. He saw a woman who'd crossed half the wild frontier of her homeland to find a sister taken. The brief stare between the genasi and the half-elf was heartbreaking, but Uthalion knew her expression, had worn it himself once—she wasn't coming back, not until things were sorted out elsewhere.

She dashed into the spires without a word, lost in the dark within a heartbeat.

"You will be the first, Captain," Khault said, stretching his misshapen body sinuously. He grew taller, and more hideous, puckered scars opened and closed, some bearing sharp spines. Uthalion stepped back, turning sidelong to the old farmer and presenting his sword. "When she returns from our Lady's chamber," Khault continued, "She will be the Walking Prophet, her sister the Dreaming Voice. Twins blessed by the song. And you will be the first to hear their singing and to live at their whims."

"Madness," Uthalion muttered. But as he looked out across the ruins, the Choir, the mindless Flock, and recalled the power of the song he'd heard for several nights, a song that had drawn him here as surely as many of the things before him, he felt a twinge of fear.

His heart quickened into an even cadence of battle as he turned his wrist in a circle and set his stance solidly. He eyed the gathered host of nightmares, feeling himself once again the madman at the stormfront, the butcher before witless horrors. He glanced at Brindani who had risen, though dark-eyed and ghost-skinned, to stand with sword ready. And when Uthalion looked for Vaasurri, the killoren was gone, having slipped away quieter than a specter's breath.

"Keep watch over her," he whispered, and Khault's head cocked like a bird's, his blind senses reacting to the slightest noise. Uthalion narrowed his eyes shrewdly and swung his blade in a whistling flourish as his left hand reached back stealthily, hidden from Khault.

"You should have died in that basement, Captain," Khault thundered, arching his back like a snake preparing to strike. "Leaving you there was the last of my tender mercies."

The beasts in the streets moaned and growled as they drew away hesitantly, gnashing their teeth and beating the ground with their fists. Uthalion saw past their fangs and claws, their tentacles and stinging spines—he saw the simple people they'd been and, more importantly, the warriors they had not been.

"You should have died with your wife, Khault," he replied. "I buried the last of my mercy alongside her."

Khault's features twisted in rage. His mouth gaped wide, showing the grips of a very human emotion on an anatomy more suited to the dark depths of a gods-forsaken sea than land. Uthalion smiled cruelly, seeing the man Khault had been still hiding in the beast he'd become. As Khault rose higher, several appendages rose like broken wings from his back, flat growths with tiny barbed mouths at their tips swiftly descending.

Uthalion skipped backward, batting one of the whipping tentacles away as his left hand rose to his lips, a wooden whistle between his fingertips. The tiny instrument, given to him by Chevat of the aranea, blew a single piercing note, barely more than a slight keening in Uthalion's ears. But its effect on the hordes of Tohrepur was immediate.

Shocked screams spread through the infected assemblage, and thunderous frightened roars shook the ground as the slippery bodies slid back from the piercing whistle. Ears, heightened by exposure to the beguiling song and suddenly cut off from its soothing melody, ran with tiny crimson streams. Chaos reigned as the Flock abandoned their Choir, clawing their way past the pained beasts to seek refuge from the terrible shriek. Khault flinched in pain, stumbling backward, his head turning blindly in confusion for a moment. Then he lurched forward, ignoring the whistle with a rumbling growl.

The air grew thick as Ghaelya ran through the glittering spires, early stars shining in countless reflections all around her. Shapeless fingers breezed over her skin, dug into her flesh with tendrils of ice, and a voice sang to her of fear. A powerful scent of lavender washed over her coldly, and she paused wide-eyed as the vines that led her on twisted and changed. Their deep, rough green became a smooth pale blue that squirmed with life, pulsing with veins and gently writhing in the dirt. The roping stalks slowly converged toward a single point as she followed the broken stone path. Ghostly beams of early moonlight stabbed brightly through the spires, illuminating a large clearing ahead.

The vines knotted and entwined themselves together, disappearing beyond the edge of a wide cavern in the center of the clearing. The constant song took on a hollow, echoing quality, rising from the ground in waves. She stopped at the perimeter of the crystal forest, trembling, unable to look away from the mouth of the cavern and the web of vines spidering out from its depths.

Approaching slowly, she managed her racing heart, suddenly uncertain of herself. She glanced back the way she'd come, seeing more than just the darkness or the long journey behind her, or even her companions facing the Choir without her. She imagined Airspur and her mother sitting alone in their dark family room, weeping and worrying over the disappearance of her daughters. She pictured her father busying himself with work and unable to accept the disintegration of his family, acting among his friends as though all were normal.

She thought of these things and caught herself avoiding the idea of what she could find in the cavern that issued a music so sweet she'd heard it in her dreams and followed it beyond all reason for the brief hope of finding her sister again. She feared the blood her last dream had prophesied. Swallowing her fear, she took a step into the clearing.

"I'm coming, Tess," she whispered.

*I know.*

Her sister's voice stunned her; gliding along inside the singing, it filled her mind. She took another step, her boot disappearing in the smoky mist-grass that filled the clearing. The sudden sense that she was walking on air twisted her stomach with vertigo, but she continued, ripples radiating out from her boots and lapping at the edges of the spires.

"Tess?" she said hoarsely.

*I can hear you.*

Screams split the night air. The ground shook, and she crouched defensively, her sword turning in a circle and shining in the moonlight. It reflected in the eyes of a figure sitting on the opposite side of the cavern. Rising hope quickly faded as she made out the crouching form of Vaasurri, his black-green gaze fixed with a solemn sorrow.

"It was her song that called us here, a song of the Feywild. I should have known," he said, staring down into the shadows of the cavern and shaking his head. "The song of a sirine, transformed by the Spellplague into a song of ruin, of nightmares made flesh."

"No," Ghaelya blurted out, disbelieving. "It was Tess . . . I know it was her."

"An accident, perhaps fate," the killoren said, his dark eyes rising, "Your sister, she must have run away from the Choir, tried to make her way through the crystals and . . . Well, I will not stand in your way."

*Just a bit farther.*

Tessaeril's voice pulled at her, drew her closer to the cavern with a gentle tug that threatened on the edge of near desperation. Hesitantly she continued, looking between the dark and the killoren, realizing that the worst of her imagination over the past tenday could become horrid reality in the next few heartbeats. She took a deep, calming breath as the fear in the song passed, giving way to an almost undetectable sorrow.

She gripped the edge of the cavern, and looked down to a rocky path leading into an ethereal, glowing pit of shadows and reflected light. The wet rock walls glistened and smelled of brine, and flowers bloomed inside. She lowered herself over the side, hanging by the fleshy vines as Vaasurri appeared over her.

"Do not touch her, no matter what," he warned. "I suspect that's what the Choir wants."

Mystified and unnerved by the emotion on the killoren's features, she merely nodded and continued her descent. The song was focused within the cavern, almost visible as a wavering haze that eddied around her and gushed outward into the sky. She slipped on the vines a few times, her nerves causing her to make simple mistakes as she felt for the cavern floor with the toe of her boot. Setting down on the rocks, she crouched and crawled forward into the ephemeral, glittering light.

Vines squished wetly beneath her hands and led her to a viscous mass that dominated the large cavern. About to search the waters for the source of the song, she noticed a network of branching veins that spread and pulsed rhythmically through the mass. Sluggish waves roiled through the giant, watery body that was curled up before her, rippling like an underground pool. The vague shape of limbs, creases and folds suggestive of a lost anatomy, gave an impression of femininity, of soft curves and once delicate features.

The air hummed, distorted and dreamlike around the slumbering form, a constant song. Or perhaps it was the memory of a song once sung, still repeating itself over and over until fixed in place, a force flooding from the soft blue flesh. Vines fanned outward from the back of the cavern, a network of tangles and knots that crawled the walls in thick, ropey strands. They lay across the surface of the being, framing a large face that stared sightlessly toward the ceiling, occasionally shifting left or right in languid movements that shook the entire mass. Watery eyes, deep blue-black pools in the blue, rolled and turned, lost in a dream.

Ghaelya was frozen, trying to take in the sight of the creature—the sirine she decided, for Vaasurri's word for it was as close as she might imagine could fit. She realized she had stopped breathing and gasped a long breath, the sound echoing in the chamber. The sirine took no notice, the radical changes in her form too extreme, the changes too great to support consciousness. The buzzing air vibrated across Ghaelya's skin in a quick tempo of sound. She was reminded of the cavern outside Caidris, and the deep temple in the warrens of the aranea—places of bones and savage beauty.

The memory struck her with such force that she stumbled backward and leaned against a rock as she realized what she had truly seen. Few bones decorated the walls that she could see, but the handful or more that were visible made familiar patterns. They adorned the walls of a sirine's home, once deep beneath the waves of the Akanamere, waters stolen by the land-shaping earthquakes of the Spellplague.

"She was trapped," Ghaelya whispered, wide-eyed as the long years of the sirine's imprisonment became apparent. She shivered, feeling eyes upon her even as she turned to the rising shadow on her right.

The glittering blue-black eyes caught her and held her still as Tessaeril's face appeared in the ethereal light of the cavern. The bright orange energy lines of her sister's fire were gone, replaced with jagged designs of pulsing green. Fleshy vines wove in and out of her pale blue flesh as she pulled herself along the rocks at the sirine's edge. Her blue lips trembled, mouthing silently, the song an unstoppable torrent flowing from between them. A knot formed in Ghaelya's throat, both relieved and repulsed by the sight of her sister, but she leaned forward, shaking her head slowly in disbelief.

Tessaeril's torso, unclothed and bound by dark tentacles of vine, was cut off at the waist. Beneath the almost translucent flesh of the sirine, Ghaelya could make out a faint silhouette of bone, perhaps the shape of lost legs. Shock kept her from crying, left her eyes dry of tears as she fought to understand what she was seeing. Tessaeril supported herself with a wet hand upon the rock, her long, webbed fingers straining with the effort as she tried to speak. Her teary eyes were unbound by the shock that held Ghaelya in thrall.

She spoke softly at first, her voice an undertone to the song as she found the will to form words in its haunting tune. The song lessened for several heartbeats, as if being drained by Tessaeril's use of its spellplague amplified power, but it bore no compulsion, no demands beyond the ability of her will to resist. The sounds gathered, fighting their way through melody until the words formed and stole quiet shock from Ghaelya's mind, hurling her headlong into nightmare.

*Kill me.*

Before Uthalion could react to Khault's sudden rage, Brindani charged forward. His sword flashed through Khault's reaching arms, stabbed at tentacled growths, and drove the broken farmer back to the edge of the clearing with a vengeance. Uthalion circled the blur of writhing limbs and quick steel, the whistle between his teeth, keeping Khault effectively blind. But Brindani was too close, too easy a target for the singer's fury.

Khault roared, the force of his voice slamming into Uthalion's chest like an anvil and throwing him back to the edge of the crystal forest. He fought to regain his breath, and was scrambling to get back on his feet when Brindani landed nearby, slammed into the low wall of the clearing. Khault, bleeding and growling, slithered back into the shadows of the city, crouching low as he shook his scarred head and spat sweet-scented blood on the ground.

Brindani's black eyes rolled as he sat up, leaning forward on his arms like an animal waiting for a challenger to reappear. His skin had grown paler, and arcing blue veins raced in thick knots through his wrists, creeping up along his arms. The half-elf's muscles bunched and twitched uncontrollably as he raised his sword; blood ran across his fist from new and old wounds alike.

"Brin?" Uthalion asked, sitting up and cautiously pulling away from the infected half-elf.

"I'm fine," Brindani answered. "Now go find Ghaelya and finish this."

"I won't leave you here," Uthalion replied, cursing as he realized he'd dropped the aranea's whistle. "Not while those things are—"

"You will leave me here!" Brindani growled, his voice rumbling dangerously as he flashed Uthalion a black-eyed stare. "I've run from this place a thousand times. This is where I should be, and while I still have the ability to choose, I choose to fight!"

"Brin—"

"Go!" the half-elf snarled, his eyes softening for a breath. "She'll need you more than me. Get her out of here."

Uthalion hesitated, but he could see the toll of infection racing through Brindani's body and the way he clutched at his stomach, wincing with pain.

"I'll tell them you're on your way," Uthalion muttered and backed toward the spires.

"Just do the work," Brindani replied. "Keep moving, don't think, and do your job."

Uthalion met the half-elf's gaze for a heartbeat and nodded once before running into the crystal forest, following the vines and hating his own practical honesty. He pondered their luck and brushes with death across the wilds of the Akana and lied to himself, convincing himself that all would be well. As he neared the wide clearing in the forest, he slowed, watched by a ring of glassy eyes along the edges of the spires.

The dreamers sat, quietly watching gentle ripples flow through the mist-grass as the powerful song poured from the depths of the deep pit. At the edge of the pit, his bone-sword laid across his lap, Vaasurri regarded him with a hard, solemn expression. The dreamers did not react as Uthalion entered the clearing, but merely sat with strange looks on their humanlike faces, sniffing the air before settling down calmly on their haunches.

Despite the song, Uthalion was struck by the eerie silence. Vaasurri said nothing, merely shook his head as he looked down into the pit. As frightening roars echoed from the north, Uthalion took a deep breath, and knew that all would not be well.

# CHAPTER TWENTY-TWO

*12 Mirtul, the Year of the Ageless One*
*(1479 DR)*
*Ruins of Tohrepur, Akanûl*

Uthalion stood over the flickering shadows of the cavern as Vaasurri told him of what lay slumbering inside, of the fate he suspected the Choir had intended for Ghaelya. Uthalion swayed slightly, caught in the endless current of song that ran hungry tendrils of searching melody over his skin and through his flesh. It demanded everything of him, crooning for him to abandon all else and end his days amid blooms and blood. Forcefully he pulled himself away, gasping for breath and shaking away the instinct to dive into the cavern and dash himself on the rocks below for just one glimpse of the beauty that called to him.

He tightly gripped the gold ring upon his finger, determined to not become another of the sirine's pathetic fools, her crimson-stained Flock.

"Has she been down there long?" he asked.

"No," Vaasurri answered. "Not long for what she faces. And Brindani?"

Roars of boundless rage and sibilant screams rang shrilly through the crystals, vibrating in the ground and sending choppy shivers along the wavy tips of the mist-grass. Uthalion gripped his sword, expecting monsters to come pouring through the forest at any moment, knowing that even if Brindani could fell Khault, he could not face the whole of Tohrepur alone.

"He's . . . on his way," he replied, turning, careful to keep his distance from the pit. "We've got to get her out of there. If she touches that thing—"

"Then we know what to do," Vaasurri said. And though the killoren seemed not to move a muscle, his gleaming bone-sword shined briefly in the moonlight as if the weapon itself knew its own purpose. "One way or another, we know what to do."

Uthalion knelt, staring into the dark thoughtfully, sobered by the idea of striking down the girl he'd led to this place. But he could not let the sirine's song—her infection—spread. He imagined Ghaelya striding among the warrens of the aranea, an army of beguiled spiders in her wake, drawn to the sirine's flowers and terrible caress. He saw her at the opening gates of Airspur and thought of the throngs she might enchant, a silver-tongued conqueror succeeding where the armies of the Abolethic Sovereignty had failed.

Twirling the gold band round and round his finger, it was evident what had to be done should things go badly. But like any decision that rested on the edge of a sword and a man's determination to do the right thing, he didn't like the taste of it.

"It's always blood," he muttered, stony eyed.

Something shambled through the crystal spires. Wet, fleshy sounds slapped against the spires as rough skin was dragged across the broken stones of the pathway. There came a low growl rumbling with power, a voice Uthalion recognized as little more than a dim reflection of the sirine's. Standing, he leveled his sword, waiting stoically for the thing to appear, knowing that no matter what, it was not Brindani. "One way or another," he repeated.

"No," Ghaelya said, feeling the word cross her lips again but barely hearing it as she pulled herself away from the monstrous image of Tessaeril. She didn't want to be so close, afraid that even proximity to her sister might make Tessaeril's words happen, let time slip away until little remained but tears and death. Her throat burned, and she felt sick, but she kept her stomach and whispered hoarsely, "I can't."

Tessaeril did not interrupt, but held on to the wet rocks of the sirine's shore and shivered as Ghaelya crossed her arms, binding her hands close to her chest where she could keep them still. She breathed deeply, staving off the effects of shock, and tried to think clearly, finding that all but impossible. Tessaeril shuddered as the song poured through her and pulsed in deep waves from between her blue lips. The walls hummed with its power, sending out an endless call to a trap where men no longer drowned, where their bones no longer decorated the wet cavern walls.

The fate that men found with the sirine had become much worse and the presence of Ghaelya's sister seemed to only amplify the song's power. With each slow and labored breath, the azure vines of the sirine's flesh dug deeper into Tessaeril's body, anchoring her to the malformed fey so that escape alone would surely have meant certain death.

Hope had fabricated within Ghaelya illusions of finding Tessaeril hurt, but alive. She had imagined that they would escape the Choir and return to Airspur. Their mother would receive them with open arms, scolding Ghaelya for leaving without a word or message, but happy to have her daughters safe and sound. There would be a family meal. Their father would complain about coin or politics and perhaps grudgingly acknowledge Ghaelya's courage in setting out to rescue her twin. They would sleep peacefully and wake the next morning to a new day.

*You must do this.*

Tessaeril's voice was unavoidable. Ghaelya could not cover her ears or run away, for it would find her, either in the long restless nights or in her dreams when she could no longer avoid the exhaustion that would run her down. When she looked on her sister, she wished she could mask the chaos of emotion that twisted her features, somehow convey a sense of hope. But in Tessaeril's eyes there was no hope, only a pained and suffering resignation.

*I ran from them when they brought me to the ruins . . . I tried to escape, but the song drew me here . . . and I fell . . . The sirine uses me and the song . . . grows more powerful . . .*

Ghaelya tried to speak, but a knot caught her words, entangled them in her throat, and tried to replace them with the wracking sobs which she refused to give in to. It hurt to do so, and she squeezed her eyes shut, clenching her teeth and digging her fingernails into her sides. She inhaled sharply, the sound rippling through the sirine's mass, wavering the subtle undertones of the dreaming-song of the plaguechanged fey.

"I came so far," she managed, "To save you."

Tessaeril nodded slowly, pulling herself closer, able to move within the perimeter of the sirine's waterlike body, but not beyond it. Shaking, she held out her right arm, exposing the gruesome network of vines, the sirine's hair, that had flowed through her body. Thick veins from Tessaeril's legless torso mingled with those of the slumbering fey, fed by the sirine's lifeforce. Her dark eyes pleaded, her webbed fingers spread wide as she gestured at her disfigurements, changes that no known magic could overcome.

*To save me . . . you must go a little farther.*

Ghaelya's hope had also turned to darker thoughts beyond Tessaeril's unlikely rescue. She'd imagined any number of horrors that might have befallen her sister, that might have left Tessaeril's lifeless body upon an altar of sacrifice or cast aside amid Tohrepur's ruins. Dried blood, jagged wounds, even the predations of scavengers had filled her imagination when she indulged the hopelessness of her optimism. But she would have been prepared on some level. She would have been ready to collect the broken form of her sister and carry it away. Shamefully, she'd thought of what she might have said, prayers she might have sung to ensure her sister rested in some kind of peace, all the things mortals could do to ease the hurt of losing someone they loved. An image of a gravesite flashed through her mind, herself standing nearby; she tried to imagine what it must be like, as if it were someone else.

"We can find a way," she blurted out, grasping hold of the fleeting, ragged edges of hope that threatened to leave her altogether. Denial crept selfishly into her thoughts, and she welcomed it for the brief respite, the faint thought that everything could be made better if only she had more time. "There must be something . . . The Choir—"

*Is too powerful . . . Should you fail they will force your hand . . . They will use the bond we share . . . I will sing forever, and you will walk, singing ruin with the sirine's voice . . . and we will both become their slaves . . . You must finish this.*

Sounds of battle echoed distantly from above. Ghaelya turned to the open mouth of the cavern, and the stars glittered in the soft blanket of night, winking at her as if from another world. Khault's words could not reach her, but the effect of his voice on the song was unmistakable, breaking the melody slightly and causing the steady stream to waver. Tessaeril winced, flinching at the sound and straining to keep it at bay. It was then that Ghaelya felt hope slip beyond her reach and sensed the heavy presence of the sword at her side.

Her sister's pleading eyes glanced at the blade.

The dreamers paced nervously along the edge of the crystal spires, growling as they gathered east and west of the sirine's cavern, their glassy eyes fixed on the shambling thing that approached. Uthalion watched the beasts warily, though they made no move to enter the clearing and simply acted as curious witnesses to what was to come. Vaasurri crouched in the mist-grass, shaking his dark, grasslike mane and stretching his lithe body. The fine edge of his bone-sword still glinted dangerously in the moonlight.

Sweat and blood beaded like pink jewels and dripped in streams across the puckered edges of a scarred visage that leered at them from among the spires, prowling into the edges of the mist-grass. Uthalion fought the brief sense of relief he felt as Khault approached, knowing that Brindani must have fallen and using that knowledge to hone the cool fury within him that patiently awaited the first cut into Khault's flesh. The old farmer's shoulders were hunched and misplaced, bent at strange angles that exposed knobs of spiny bone. Gill-slits along his throat hissed with bubbles of crimson foam. Uthalion shook his head, pitying the nightmare a good man had become.

"Look well, Captain," Khault uttered hideously. "I was remade in her dreams, blessed by her singing . . . A far cry from my nightmares in Caidris."

"You defended your home; gave food, water, and shelter to strangers," Uthalion replied angrily. "You took a stand and lost your wife. The nightmares of Caidris were earned—honorable scars that many men might envy, that I envied. What I do now honors that memory."

Khault chuckled, a disquieting rumble edged with high-pitched echoes. He stood taller, growths writhing behind his back as he slid forward, his ruined face arching low on a distended neck. His tattered robes writhed with movement, as if he were unfolding, remaking himself into new shapes. Uthalion noted the fresh blood dripping from the torn, bone white robes and felt his pulse quicken.

"Did you know that I prayed for death, Captain? An honorable man weeping and begging to die?" Khault said. His features twisted in a snarl of contempt, exposing rows of sharp, triangular teeth. "Is this the answer to an honorable prayer? Is this what you envy?"

"No," Uthalion growled, his lip quivering in anger. "You're just a body. Just the remains of the man I knew."

"Shall you bury me, Captain?" Khault said, crawling closer, his thin legs followed by a mane of tentacles growing from his back. Uthalion could see where scabrous, toughened skin grew in patches on his arms and neck. Long spines, nearly translucent and needle-sharp, protruded in rows from his jawline, giving him the look of something dredged from the darkest depths of a forgotten ocean where there was no need for the eyes he had scratched from his skull. "Would you drag me to Caidris and lay me down beside my wife?"

"You don't understand," Uthalion said, taking a step forward and motioning for Vaasurri to flank. "I don't care what happens to you now . . . as long as it hurts."

Uthalion charged, slashing at Khault's arms. The twisted man rolled backward, rearing high as whiplike tentacles grabbed at Uthalion's legs. They laced around his boots, tugging him off balance and laying him flat on his back. He hit the ground with a grunt as Khault bent low, his claws reaching for Uthalion's face. But he kept his sword moving, slicing into the hands that sought to smother him. Khault howled in pain and skittered backward, releasing Uthalion's legs as Vaasurri joined the struggle.

The killoren was quick, but his blade cut only ragged wounds that seemed to have no effect. Uthalion rolled to his feet just as Vaasurri was batted away, sliding through the mist-grass. Khault towered over him, hissing through his teeth and spreading his arms wide as if welcoming the steel that sought to pierce him. Uthalion took the opening and thrust at Khault's stomach, too angry to worry about himself or draw the fight on any longer. The tip of the blade slid on the tough, slick skin, scraping a gouge that bled a thick, clear fluid.

Tentacles shot forward beneath Uthalion's blade, punching him in the gut and staggering him backward as Khault knelt low and unleashed his terrible voice. Pure sound slammed into Uthalion like an invisible wall, hurling him to the edge of the sirine's cavern. The back of his head pounded with pain, and stars filled his eyes as he gasped for breath.

"You pained my Choir, Captain, and have spurned our blessings," Khault purred at the end of his thunderous attack. He slid sinuously through the mist-grass. "Again you bring suffering to those I cherish."

"You left me little choice," Uthalion spat, tasting blood from his lip as his hand fumbled through the mist-grass, searching for his dropped sword and trying to stall for time. "Besides, you still don't seem to understand . . . I don't care."

Vaasurri's curving bone-blade bit deep into Khault's shoulder, producing yet another howl of pain. The killoren grasped at the lashing tentacles, and the pair fell away in a blur, tumbling through the mist-grass as Uthalion rolled to his knees. Darkness clouded his vision for a moment. His hand closed on the cool metal of his sword, and he tried not to let relief and dizziness lay him back down.

Twin voices whispered from the pit before him, echoing through the rock, one nearly indistinguishable from the other. The words were lost, and he tried not to hear, leaving Ghaelya to her task, her decision. He hoped she would make the right one. And if not, he hoped he would live long enough to make the decision for her.

He stumbled on his feet, finding his balance and feeling a warm, steady drip of wetness on the back of his neck. Lost for a moment and staring at the ground in confusion, he fought the urge to shake his head. Breathing deeply, he faced the blurred forms of Khault and Vaasurri, just as the killoren's body was hurled past him. Uthalion slashed into the first tentacle that reached for him, but could not move fast enough to stop the next.

Tiny teeth bit into his armor as the tentacles bore him down, holding him in a vicelike grip that brought stars to his eyes. The crystal spires reached for the moon overhead as he groaned and tried to sit up, to fight the pressure that held him down. Khault crawled closer, leaning over him and staring at the cavern mouth.

"You struggle in vain, Captain," Khault said. Long streams of wildflower-smelling spittle and blood dribbled between his teeth. "The twins embrace even now."

Uthalion fought the nauseating dark that trembled at the edges of his sight. His arms felt like leaden weights, his sword just an immovable length of steel. He kicked and pushed against the ground to no avail. And as he turned his face away from Khault's hot breath, he caught sight of irregular ripples flowing through the mist-grass, and beyond, the dreamers' glassy eyes had turned to the north.

"The flesh is weak, Captain," Khault muttered. "It bends to the will of the Song and cannot stand when the Lady calls."

A droning growl emanated from the spires, and Khault turned, hissing as the dreamers prowled to the south, their flashing stares fixed upon him. The immense weight of Khault lifted from Uthalion's chest, and he coughed, fighting for air as the tentacles slid away. He staggered to his feet as Khault snarled at the seemingly defiant beasts among the spires. Behind him, lurching quietly from the north, a shadow fell upon the mist-grass.

"I'm still standing," Uthalion grumbled hoarsely, spitting up blood and wavering on his feet. His sword dragged weakly through the grass, the smoky tendrils lapping at the blade. "I suppose you've forgotten just how strong flesh can be."

Khault stalked forward, his clawed hands twitching and the tentacles sliding through the mist-grass like a low tide. The dreamers stilled their growling and anxious pacing, lowering their heads as a piercing note keened loudly through the clearing. Khault's body tensed, his back arched in pain, and blood streamed from what remained of his ears. A sword ripped through his chest and tore at his pale skin like a knife through paper.

Uthalion stumbled, his sword falling from his hand as he spied the bloodied face of Brindani at Khault's back. Deafening roars shook the clearing, rippling outward in waves from the struggling pair as they fell back in a tangle of blood, steel, and thrashing flesh. Khault screamed in denial of the blade that worked its way through him. Uthalion tried not to see the details of the half-elf's injuries—the limp broken arm, the hideous wound across his stomach, or the exposed section of scalp over his right eye—but his eye was quicker than his good judgment.

Uthalion fell to his knees, his hands clasped to the sides of his head as the ground quaked and the air hummed. The endless song embraced him through it all, caressing his tired limbs with a soothing melody, a silken thread of beguiling voices amid the chaos and blood. He glanced down into the cavern, and the flickering shadows of nightmare clawed at his ability to resist as he fell forward and crawled to its edge.

Howls carried softly down through the cavern, an uncanny compliment to the song as the dreamers raised their voices in either sorrow or exultation, Ghaelya wasn't sure. Tessaeril shivered on the rocks, weak and almost frantic with barely hidden impatience, her blue-black eyes fixed on the sword at Ghaelya's side.

*The dreamers were here first . . . They despise the Choir . . . and rejoice that one of them has fallen . . .*

The words were quiet and muttering, absent thoughts drifting through the song as Tessaeril reached out tentatively, her fingertips crawling toward the sheathed blade then drawing back. She shuddered and twisted her bound torso, her eyes pleading for release.

"Does it hurt?" Ghaelya asked as she let her hand slip to the sword at her belt, feeling the rough surface of its leather-wrapped handle and pulling clear the fastening loop of the sheath.

*No . . . not anymore . . . There is no sleep here . . . not for me . . . Her dreams are all I have, all I see . . . endlessly . . . The sword . . .*

Ghaelya's body was numb, moving slowly and almost of its own accord, distant and mechanical. A handspan of blade cleared the sheath, and Tessaeril looked upon its edge almost hungrily, her lip quivering at the sight of a promised freedom from the sirine.

"I love you, Tess," Ghaeyla said. The words slowed the steady pull on the gleaming blade. The steel reflected the ethereal glow of the sirine's body like a beacon. Her sister did not answer, straining as the song rose and fell, shaking her frail body and digging deeper into her nearly translucent flesh, her once strong fire drowned in the sirine's grip.

The blade continued.

"It's always blood," Ghaelya whispered softly, remembering the previous night's dream and speaking the words that had been spoken to her. She swallowed hard, and the blade fell free, scraping on the rocks and shining brightly. It blurred her vision, and she blinked, releasing the tears that had collected there. "I'm sorry."

*There's nothing to be sorry for.*

Her arm struggled with the sword's weight, and she tried several times to lift it, to break it free of her every impulse to cast it away. Inexorably it rose and hovered over her shoulder, tapping lightly on the leather guard. Her arm obeyed her commands, though her heart had not yet joined in the necessity of the act.

"I want to believe that," she said, her voice breaking. "Forgive me."

*There is nothing to forgive.*

It seemed a gentle push, lifting the blade and letting it fall. The steel blurred at the end of her arm and buried itself deeply in weak flesh, breaking easily through brittle bones. Ghaelya couldn't breathe—she didn't want to. She cursed the pulse that pounded in her ears and the sudden inability to close her eyes, to not see the strange dark blood and the slowly withering expression of shock. Vines shook and twitched, ripples flowed through the sirine's mass, and the great dark eyes turned in their slumber.

Somewhere inside of her, ice-cold and overpowering, there was a scream, but she couldn't find it. The sword fell from her hand.

And the sirine screamed for her.

❖ ❖ ❖ ❖ ❖

Damps rocks cooled Uthalion's palms as he stared into the ethereal blue glow, the song's endless tide washing through his body. He pulled toward it, enthralled and unable to resist. At the bottom of the cavern entrance he found Ghaelya sitting with her back to him, a nightmarish mirror image slumped on the rocks in front of her. Dazed, his eyes wandered to the sword lodged in the lifeless body. Whispered words echoed over and over through the song, growing faster and faster as they blurred together, ripping through the air at a frantic pace until they were little more than a discordant keening.

"Forgive me."

*There is nothing to forgive.*

Gods have mercy, he thought, as the song was unleashed.

Whatever veil had kept him from the true force of the sirine's singing was lifted. He gasped at the exultant power and thought his heart would burst. A single wave of perfection flooded his senses, a thrall so deep he never wanted to be free. And he was ashamed at the meager, imperfect soul he brought to lay upon the glowing altar at her feet. Every muscle in his body flexed, and his back arched painfully, assaulted by what seemed an entire lifetime of memories in a long, rattling breath of transcendent joy and sorrow.

When it ended, and the taste of blood filled his mouth, a gaping pit of oblivion filled his mind, swallowing the heaven he had found hiding in Tohrepur.

The song withered to little more than a whisper, a faint longing that floundered weakly in his ears as it trickled through the cavern. He resisted it easily, as a man once caught in the open sea withstands even the strongest tides of the shore. He sat up, rested his head in his hands, and averted his eyes from the ethereal glow and the slumped silhouette before it.

Though the translucent form and haunting melody of the plaguechanged sirine filled the cave, it was Ghaelya's stilled silence that dominated the murmuring song.

"The flesh is strong," he whispered under his breath. "The flesh is strong."

Emerging from the cavern they found Vaasurri, awake and kneeling beside the prone form of Brindani. The dreamers had dragged away the carcass of Khault, fighting over it and tearing it apart among the forest of glittering spires, but they had not touched the half-elf. A few sat by watching curiously as Ghaelya knelt at Brindani's side and gently closed his eyes.

Mist-grass rippled around the pair, its deep green dulled by splotches of rust red.

Uthalion joined Vaasurri some distance away, sensing no threat from the beasts as they padded peacefully to the sirine's cavern. They settled into the mist-grass and formed a circle around the mouth of the cave as it whispered and sang to them. Several licked Khault's blood from their faces, and they growled if anyone came too near the cavern's circle, a behavior that assuaged Uthalion's concerns over the sleeping sirine. There was a cruel, possessive intelligence in the dreamers' expressions—he supposed they would not so easily lose their dreaming Lady again.

Darkness still reigned over Tohrepur as they exited the crystal forest, the other end of a night that had already begun its slow journey toward dawn and a new day for the restless ruins. There was no sign of the Choir, though Uthalion imagined he could hear pained moans from deep in the city streets. The sirine's vines still blanketed the stone walls and cobbled avenues, though the life in them seemed withered slightly— their flowers were less red, the scent not as sweet. At every corner they met the tortured gazes of the sirine's thralls, the Flock.

The pale citizens of the Choir's doomed cult stared strangely at one another, curious and dazed. Some made their way to the spires, frantically seeking for the song that had ended so abruptly, its river now a trickling stream. Others babbled incoherently, frustrated as they tried to form the words they had not used in so long, their minds shredded by restless nights and endless waking dreams. Still others sat and wept, rocking back and forth on street corners and inside the hollowed buildings, quietly mourning either the shattered thrall of the sirine or the slowly returning memories of lives lost.

Uthalion barely felt the weight of Brindani in his arms, carrying instead the heavy burden of the half-elf's memory as the hauntingly quiet stride of Ghaelya led the way out of Tohrepur. The journey home would be long and difficult, but he would sleep when he was tired, and he would dream of his wife and daughter.

Starlight glittered through the crystal forest long after the moon had set, and the dreamers could not yet smell the warming rise of the sun. They gathered, making their way through the shadows to sit and sprawl in the mist-grass around the cavern of the sirine. A few wandered to its edge and stared curiously at the blue glow upon the glistening rocks inside. Sleepless and tireless, it was long before they settled, troubled by thoughts that were new to them, an awareness that was both a comfort and a curse. Regret and pity and hate tugged at their minds, emotions at odds with the primal urges that pulsed in their hearts.

More than the mere wolves they'd been ages ago when a single pack had stumbled upon the slumbering sirine, they wondered at the new sense of fear they felt for the dreaming lady. Some paced restlessly, flexing their claws and baring fangs at each imagined enemy among the stone forest. They watched the spires, listened for the slightest noise, alert for any sign of the men that had come and stolen what had been theirs since, what they understood to be, the beginning of time.

At length they calmed, and as one they stared off beyond the spires, a low humming forming in their throats as the lady's true dream returned to them and them alone. Though they rested upon grass and dirt and were surrounded by towers of sparkling stone, the longing, endless song of the sirine carried them back to the shores and depths of another world and another time.

Their shining eyes glazed over and glowed fiercely as the song rose and fell like crashing waves. It sang in their blood and matched the bestial chant that droned throughout the forest of crystals.

White birds danced on the air in the sirine's dream, diving through warm winds and landing on soft sand. Distant wooden vessels of men grasped the wind in white sails, casting nets into the sea. Vast dark waters sparkled beneath a starlit sky as blue-black waves flashed and rolled restless to the shore.

# ONE DROW • TWO SWORDS • TWENTY YEARS

## A READER'S GUIDE TO

# R.A. SALVATORE'S
# THE LEGEND OF DRIZZT®

"There's a good reason
this saga is one of the most
popular—and beloved—
fantasy series of all time:
breakneck pacing, deeply
complex characters and
nonstop action. If you read
just one adventure fantasy saga
in your lifetime,
let it be this one."

—Paul Goat Allen,
B&N Explorations on
*Streams of Silver.*

Full color illustrations and maps
in a handsome keepsake edition.

# Ed Greenwood *Presents*

# Waterdeep

## Blackstaff Tower
### Steven Schend

## Mistshore
### Jaleigh Johnson

## Downshadow
### Erik Scott de Bie
#### April 2009

## City of the Dead
### Rosemary Jones
#### June 2009

## The God Catcher
### Erin M. Evans
#### February 2010

## Circle of Skulls
### James P. Davis
#### June 2010

Explore the City of Splendors through the eyes of authors
hand-picked by Forgotten Realms® world creator Ed Greenwood.

## FORGOTTEN REALMS

# THOMAS M. REID

## THE EMPYREAN ODYSSEY

What could bring a demon to the gates of heaven?

Book I
### The Gossamer Plain

Book II
### The Fractured Sky

Book III
### The Crystal Mountain
July 2009

What could bring heaven to the depths of hell?

"Reid is proving himself to be one of the best up and coming authors in the FORGOTTEN REALMS universe."
—fantasy-fan.org

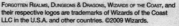

# TRACY HICKMAN
### Presents

# The Anvil of Time

## The Sellsword
Cam Banks

## The Survivors
Dan Willis

## Renegade Wizards
Lucien Soulban

## The Forest King
Paul B. Thompson
June 2009

## The lost stories of Krynn's history are coming to light.

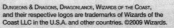

# DON BASSINGTHWAITE'S

## LEGACY OF DHAKAAN

From the ashes of a fallen empire,
a new kingdom rises.

The Doom of Kings

The Word of Traitors
September 2009

The Tyranny of Ghosts
June 2010

Everything you thought you knew
about MAGIC™ novels is changing…

From the mind of

# ARI MARMELL

comes a tour de force of imagination.

# AGENTS
## OF
## ARTIFICE

The ascendance of a new age in the planeswalker
mythology: be a part of the book that takes fans
deeper than ever into the lives of the Multiverse's most
powerful beings:

Jace Beleren
A powerful mind-mage whose choices now will forever
determine his path as a planeswalker.

Liliana Vess
A dangerous necromancer whose beauty belies a dark
secret and even darker associations.

Tezzeret
Leader of an inter-planar consortium whose quest for
knowledge may be undone by his lust for power.